RAVES FOR CHRISTOPHER BRAM AND HIS NOVELS

"A World War II story Hollywood never filmed and your father never told you. Christopher Bram's second novel is entertaining, sexy, and oddly touching."
—Stephen McCauley, author of *The Object of My Affection*

"Bram is a gifted writer, one who has a fine way with dialogue and can make any confrontation come to life. . . . Christopher Bram writes like an angel."
—*The Advocate*

"Christopher Bram's prose is clear and refreshing."
—New York *Newsday*

"Christopher Bram is well on his way to becoming a successful, self-assured writer."
—*New York Native*

CHRISTOPHER BRAM, a native of Virginia, is the author of *Surprising Myself* and "Aphrodisiac," the story that became the cornerstone piece in the classic short story collection of the same name. He is also a film and book critic whose reviews have been published in several national publications. He lives in New York City.

HOLD TIGHT

A NOVEL BY

Christopher Bram

A PLUME BOOK

NEW AMERICAN LIBRARY

A DIVISION OF PENGUIN BOOKS USA INC., NEW YORK
PUBLISHED IN CANADA BY
PENGUIN BOOKS CANADA LIMITED, MARKHAM, ONTARIO

PUBLISHER'S NOTE

This book is a work of fiction. Names, characters, places, and incidents either are the product of the author's imagination or are used fictitiously, and any resemblance to actual persons, living or dead, events, or locales is entirely coincidental.

NAL BOOKS ARE AVAILABLE AT QUANTITY DISCOUNTS WHEN USED TO PROMOTE PRODUCTS OR SERVICES. FOR INFORMATION PLEASE WRITE TO PREMIUM MARKETING DIVISION, NEW AMERICAN LIBRARY, 1633 BROADWAY, NEW YORK, NEW YORK 10019.

 PLUME TRADEMARK REG. U.S. PAT. OFF. AND FOREIGN COUNTRIES
REGISTERED TRADEMARK—MARCA REGISTRADA
HECHO EN DRESDEN, TN USA

SIGNET, SIGNET CLASSIC, MENTOR, ONYX, PLUME, MERIDIAN and NAL BOOKS are published *in the United States* by New American Library, a division of Penguin Books USA Inc., 1633 Broadway, New York, New York 10019, *in Canada* by Penguin Books Canada Limited, 2801 John Street, Markham, Ontario L3R 1B4

Library of Congress Cataloging-in-Publication Data

Bram, Christopher.
    Hold tight : a novel / by Christopher Bram.
      p.   cm.
    ISBN 0-452-26226-7
    I. Title.
PS3552.R2817H6   1989
813'.54—dc19
                                    88-38384
                                       CIP

First Plume Printing, June, 1989

1 2 3 4 5 6 7 8 9

PRINTED IN THE UNITED STATES OF AMERICA

To John,
Henri, Michael and Ed

1

AS FAMILIAR NOW as our own baby pictures, the images were still new and startling four months into the war.

The tree of black smoke towered over the broken battleship. A tiny launch specked with sailors bobbed alongside in the rolling gray water.

Then came the murky stairway packed with nude men, civilian clothes bundled in their arms, various hats perched on their heads. Their nakedness was vulnerably unbeautiful. But in daylight and khakis, with T-shirts and harsh haircuts, the acres of men jumped in perfect unison. Acres of tires, old tins and saucepans were displayed by proud schoolchildren; grid-windowed factories poured out miles of tanks and howitzers, while kerchiefed women in overalls took what looked like mounds of lipstick tubes and proved them to be machine gun cartridges. Suddenly, after so many years of dull confusion, there was purpose. Victory seemed only a matter of time. (The defeats in the Pacific—the surrender of Bataan, the siege of Corregidor—were not dwelt upon; there was no newsreel footage anyway.)

The black-and-white blizzard of news flashed outside the room where the projectionist's daughter listened to her father. This was the Lyric Theater in Manhattan and the projection booth was dark except for the gooseneck lamp bent over the workbench and the light that leaked from the casing around the running projector. The newsreel's narration and music swelled to a patriotic finish in the booth speakerbox. Simon Krull stood at attention by the little window and intently watched the screen. He touched the switches on either side of him. Another projector roared to life; the Looney Tunes theme came on. "So?" said Simon.

"I could, Papa, only . . ." Anna Krull sat on the high stool by the workbench. She clutched one cold hand with the other in the fold of wool skirt sunk between her knees. "I never know what to say to boys."

"Stuff and nonsense." Simon had lived in this country thirty years now, but still spoke with a grumbly trace of a German accent. People might mistake him for a Jew, but that sometimes came in handy. He bent down to adjust the lamp in the second projector. Streaks of light lit his long, gentle face from below. "What must you say to boys anyway? You are as beautiful as your mother was. All a girl must be is beautiful. That is her half of the conversation."

Anna thought her beauty was all in her father's eyes. In her eyes she was short and pudgy, and feared her large breasts only made her look fat.

Simon stepped around to the first projector, saw his daughter's frown, and stopped in front of her. "You *are* beautiful," he said.

"One day," Anna replied, although she was already twenty.

He petted her on the cheek, then brushed a blond curl behind her ear.

Anna smiled; she liked having him fuss over her.

"Maybe we get you a new hairstyle," he said. "And we can—whatever women are doing to their eyebrows. New clothes. A little rouge."

"But you don't like me wearing makeup," she reminded him. All he and Aunt Ilsa allowed was a touch of lipstick. "You don't want me to look like a floozie, remember?"

Simon withdrew his hand. He abruptly turned away and began to unload the first projector. "There is a war on," he said coldly. "We must all make sacrifices." He flipped back pinions and springs: he was angry. He carried the reel back to the bench and took a new reel down from the rack, without looking at her.

Anna bit her tongue. She hadn't intended to fight him. She said what she said only to play the good daughter. She wanted to wear makeup and new clothes, to go places she had never been, with her father's blessing.

She sat nervously on the stool and watched Simon work. He seemed so capable in the long, old-fashioned white coat that made him look like a butcher or surgeon. She trusted he was equally capable at this other thing he did. He had been doing it for six years. And today he was asking her to join him. She was overjoyed to have her father share his life with her like that, but beneath her joy she kept touching fear.

The harmlessly frantic cartoon played in the speakerbox and on the distant screen. Cartoons and features had not yet caught up with the newsreels. It was possible to forget there was a war, that everything had changed.

He stood with his back to her after the cartoon ended and he had started *Henry Aldrich for President.* He said to the little window, "I do not like having to make you part of this. I wish it weren't necessary."

"But I want to be part of this, Papa. I do. If I sound confused, it's only because . . . I don't know. Because I'm afraid I might fail you?"

He gazed at her from beneath his long, kind eyelids. "No. You will not fail me. You have kept my secret this long, I know I can trust you to be careful."

It had been their little secret for six years now, a special bond between father and daughter. Not even Aunt Ilsa knew what her brother-in-law did with his free time, or why he was so curious about so many different things.

"Which is why I ask you," Simon continued. "There is no woman I can trust the way I trust my own lamb. And it *is* necessary," he insisted, as much to himself as to her, "now that there is no longer that house in Brooklyn."

"What house?" They had an apartment on Riverside Drive and had never lived in Brooklyn.

Simon waved the question aside. "Nothing. Just a house. A place where sailors went."

Anna knew her father spent his Sundays walking along the waterfront, striking up conversations, noticing things. "A place you went to?"

The length of his face turned red, up into his thinning hair. "*No.*

It was not a nice place. Friends of a friend went there. Now they can't. I did not approve of these friends and am ashamed my friend depended on them. It is not fit that a young girl hear about it, understood?"

Anna respected her father's sense of propriety, but her interest was touched. A brothel? Even she knew such places existed. Her father would never go to such a place, but Anna wondered what it would be like.

Simon set up the film reel on the workbench hand winds. "*You* will not be doing anything to be ashamed of. I could not live with myself or your mother's memory if I thought that were possible." He began to rewind the film; the rhythm of turning and the whistle of film against the reels seemed to calm him. "You will go to dances and clubs. Proper places. You go to this U.S.O., where they always want nice girls to dance with the sailors. There are always many chaperones. You dance, you listen. Maybe you meet someone you like. Although, it could be dangerous if you meet someone you like too much."

"I won't," said Anna. But the possibility seemed to be already at the back of her thoughts when Simon mentioned it. She was surprised by how excited she felt at the prospect of going out into such a world.

"Maybe it is good you are shy with boys. If you were in any way wild, I would worry about you in such situations."

And she remembered her fear of men. That was where she would fail her father, and where the anxiety beneath her joy was strongest. She pictured herself at a dance, passed over again and again for thinner, more articulate girls. She never had been able to endure the thought of such humiliation for her own sake. She wondered if she could knowing it was for her father.

"I will increase your allowance, of course."

"The money's not important, Papa."

"It's only fair. And you will need something extra. For clothes and taxis. I won't want you coming home alone when it's late."

There was money involved, no great wealth, but extra funds that had enabled them to move from Yorkville to Riverside Drive, and that allowed Simon to support two women. He was very proud that neither his daughter nor sister-in-law had to work.

4

"Of course, your aunt is not to hear of this. Or suspect it either. We will talk only here. Maybe we will have you bringing me my supper every night. So people will not be getting suspicious."

Anna liked the idea. She felt far closer to her father here in his place that smelled of acetate and hot wiring than she ever did at home.

The last foot of film spun off one reel and slapped the table a few times before Simon braked the loaded reel between palm and fingers. He glanced at his daughter as he returned the reel to the rack. Then he reached down with both hands and lifted Anna's hands out of her lap. His fingers were soft except for the calluses like thimbles across the tips.

"I know it is a great deal I ask of you. But. Yes?"

Anna stared at him. He looked so tender and wistful, as if he feared she might refuse. That she could refuse had never occurred to Anna. "Of course."

"Good. Very good." He clasped her hands and lightly wagged them up and down. His blue eyes looked deeper into her blue eyes, until his long, speckled lids suddenly closed.

"Don't worry, Papa. It'll be all right."

"My own lamb," he sighed and lifted his eyelids, "is growing up."

The doorknob clicked, then rattled.

Simon jerked his hands back and stepped away, as if they had been doing something unseemly. Anna knew better, but the abrupt move hurt.

There was a knock outside and, "Hey, Mr. Krull! Who locked the doe?"

Simon went down the steps and let his assistant in. Alfred was a bony young man from the East Bronx, with bad posture and teeth of different colors.

"Here ya fags, Mr. Krull. They was out of Luckies. Out of everything, these gobs buying anything that's not nailed down. Hi, Miss Krull, ya still here?"

"She was just going." Simon took Anna's coat down from the peg and held it open for her. That was as close as he came to kissing her goodbye in the presence of others. "I will try not to be too late, dear."

"We'll have your dinner waiting for you in the oven, Papa." It was what she always said, but saying it today in front of Alfred, with so much else on her mind and her father's, was strangely exciting. She didn't want to go. She wanted to be given her first task, so that her excitement could be given purpose, shape. Her father held her coat until she was snugly inside it. "Goodbye, Papa. Bye, Alfred."

"See ya around," said Alfred, pretending to tinker with a projector while he stole a look at the inches of calf between her bobby socks and skirt. Anna thought Alfred repulsive.

She went down the five steps to the door, gave her father a last look and opened the door. A couple sat necking on the step outside. A sailor and girl. They turned around, startled by the light and Anna. The sailor saw Anna and proudly smirked, unaware of how silly he looked with his neckerchief twisted over his shoulder and his mouth smeared with lipstick. The girl was sleepy-eyed, young and unashamed; she seemed to challenge Anna with her eyes.

"Excuse me," Anna said sharply, pulling the door shut behind her, closing off the light and the whir of the projector. She gingerly stepped around the couple.

The town had filled up with servicemen this past month and one couldn't go anywhere without falling over groping couples. New York was one big barnyard. Anna went up the aisle toward the curtain hung over the exit, trying to forget about sex, wanting to feel important with her secret future. Away from her father, she didn't feel excited, only anxious.

Out in the balcony lobby stood two more sailors, talking and smoking cigarettes. Their uniforms made them look like black paper dolls. Anna noticed them notice her as she walked by. Could she do it, talk to male strangers? She had already walked past them and couldn't turn back without appearing brazen, but she wanted to test herself. She paused at the top of the stairs that went down to the glass doors, foyer and daylight. She looked back at the two sailors; neither noticed she was still there.

Then she saw another sailor down below, giving his ticket to Bobby at the door before he came up the stairs, two steps at a time. He was very tall and his black wool coat made him look huge, so huge he frightened Anna. But she stood her ground, waited for him to see her. He looked at the gold ceiling, brass handrail, balding carpet, at everything but Anna. He had a child's face and was grinning like an idiot.

His grin vanished when he saw her waiting for him.

Anna drew a deep breath and said, "Lovely day, sailor."

The sailor snatched his cap off his head. A sheaf of blond hair fell on his brow. "Yes ma'm. Beautiful day, thank you." He had a thick Southern accent.

"Yes. Well . . ." What next?

The sailor continued to walk past her, gawking, still clutching his cap in one hand. He was a hick, a complete innocent.

"Enjoy it!" said Anna.

"Ah will, ma'm. You enjoy it yourself." And he returned his cap to his head and kept right on walking.

Anna breathed a sigh of relief as she went down the stairs. She *could* talk to them. It wasn't her fault this sailor was too stupid to know how to take advantage of a friendly woman. Or, if he had rejected her because she wasn't pretty enough, that didn't hurt her the way it did when she had thought only of herself. The old anxieties were nothing but selfishness, and Anna had a higher purpose now.

She went out on Forty-second Street feeling pleased with the future. Things were happening; it was an exciting time. It was only right that things should happen with her.

2

HANK FAYETTE, Seaman Second Class, screwed his cap back on his head and loped across the balcony lobby. It was a nice surprise to have a stranger say hello. The North was supposed to be so unfriendly, yet that pudgy girl had greeted him just like any sane person on the streets of Beaumont, Texas.

Two sailors stood off to one side and watched Hank approach. One nudged the other; the other shook his head. Hank wondered what they were considering, but he didn't want to have anything to do with them either. This was his first day of liberty after two months at sea and Hank was tired of Navy. It was his first time in New York City and he wanted everything to be new. He had spent all morning and the better part of the afternoon riding the trolleys up and down this human beehive, getting a crick in his neck. There was something wonderfully unnatural about a place where buildings dwarfed the tallest elm tree. The city looked straight out of the planet Mongo in the funny papers.

The inside of the theater was as big as a circus tent, but the movie looked the same as movies in Beaumont, only taller. This was another one about the boy from the radio who talked through his nose. Hank almost turned around and went back out again, only he'd paid his four bits and there was no harm in staying long enough to see what happened. He stood at the back of the balcony, behind the partition, took off his bulky pea coat and draped it over the partition. There were plenty of empty seats up here for the matinee, but theater seats never gave Hank enough room for his lanky legs. He tugged at the scratchy dress blues that pulled too tight across his butt and wondered if the guys had been only ragging him about this place. It was just a big old movie theater.

There was a sudden smell of cologne, sweet and boozey. Then the smell faded. Hank looked left and right. He saw the back of a man sliding off to the right. The pointy crown of the man's half-lit hat was turning, as though he'd been looking at Hank.

Hank glanced back at the movie—Henry Aldrich was getting scolded by his mother—then looked around the sloping balcony. Someone got up, walked up the aisle, then sat down again. So many Yankees wore those funny shoulders that Hank wasn't certain which were men and which were women in this light. He looked up at the staggered windows of the projection booth and the beam of light that occasionally twitched inside itself.

The smell of cologne returned, and hung there. Hank waited a moment. When he turned around, he found himself looking down on the spotless brim of a hat. The man stood only a foot away. Like most people, he was shorter than Hank.

The man looked up, his face slowly appearing beneath his hat. He had a smooth, friendly face and a red bow tie. "You're standing improperly," he whispered.

"Beg pardon?" said Hank. "Sir?"

"If you want to meet people, you should stand with your hands behind you."

The man sounded so well-meaning and knowledgeable Hank automatically took his big hands off the partition and placed them at his back in parade rest.

"And you're quite tall. You should hold them a little lower."

"Like this?"

"Let me see." The man stepped up behind Hank and pressed his crotch into Hank's hands.

The wool was ribbed and baggy. Hank cupped his hands around a loose bundle inside before he realized what he was doing. His heart began to race.

The man lightly cleared his throat. "Uh, you interested?"

Hank let go and spun around. He looked, then snatched the man's hat off his head so he could see him better. Strands of light from the movie flickered in the brilliantined hair while the man anxiously reached for his hat. He wasn't so old, maybe thirty, and not at all effeminate. Hank let him take the hat back, then reached down to feel the man's crotch from the front.

"Oh? Oh." The man pulled his brim back over his eyes, glanced around, reached down and touched Hank, tweaked him through the cloth. "I see," he whispered. "I don't suppose you have a place where we can go?"

Hank closed his eyes and shook his head. It felt so damn good to touch and be touched again. The cologne wasn't so strong once you got used to it.

"I live with my mother, you understand. But I have some friends downtown with a room we can use." He removed his hand and used it to take Hank's hand, rubbing a smooth thumb across the wide, hard palm. "Do you mind going downtown?"

"Hell, no!" Hank cried and pulled loose to grab his coat.

"Shhh, please. Discretion." But the man was smiling to himself as he nervously glanced around and nodded at the curtain over the exit.

Hank followed him out to the balcony lobby, where the two sailors still waited. "What did I tell you?" said one. "Trade."

The man didn't look at Hank, walked quickly, trying to keep a step or two ahead of him. So even in the big city people were shy about this. Hank buttoned up his coat so he wouldn't show. He buried his eager hands in his coat pockets to stop himself from grabbing the man's arm or slapping him on the ass, he was so happy. His shipmates hadn't been teasing him when they joked about this movie house, laughing over why they wouldn't want to go there and why Hank might.

Out on the street it was almost spring, but a city kind of spring, just temperature. The other side of Forty-second Street was deeper in shadow now than it had been when Hank went inside, and the penny arcade there looked brighter. Gangs of sailors charged up and down the sidewalks, hooting and elbowing each other over every girl they saw, not understanding how much fun they could've had with themselves. Hank had understood since he was fourteen. Thumbing around the country or working at a C.C.C. camp, he had met plenty of others who understood, too. There had to be others on the *McCoy*, but living on a destroyer was worse than living in Beaumont. You had to live with them afterwards, which could get sticky if they started feeling guilty or, worse, all moony and calf-eyed. It should be as natural as eating, but people were funny and Hank did his best to get along with them. Most of his shipmates thought Hank was only joshing them or playing the dumb hick when he told them what he liked.

That Mongo skyscraper with the rounded corners stood at the far end of the street like a good idea. Hank's man stood at the curb, signaling for a taxi. The traffic was all trucks and taxicabs, with a lone streetcar nosing along like an old catfish. Finally, a square-roofed taxi pulled over and the man opened the door and signaled Hank to get in. "West Street and Gansevoort," he told the driver.

The man relaxed. He smiled at Hank, offered him a cigarette, then offered the driver one too. "I thought our homesick boy in blue deserved a home-cooked meal," he told the driver. The men smoked cigarettes and talked about all the changes the war had brought about. The driver asked Hank all the usual civilian questions about home and ship and girlfriend. The man smirked to himself when Hank mentioned Mary Ellen, but he didn't understand.

They drove along a waterfront, the low sun flashing gold on the dusty windshield between the high warehouses and higher ships. It looked just like the area around the Brooklyn Navy Yard, where the *McCoy* was in drydock. Suddenly, there was a long stretch of sun-light, and Hank saw the rounded metal ridge of a ship lying on its side in the river. "Poor *Normandie*," sighed the driver and said it was sabotage. The man said carelessness and stupidity; the two began to argue about how much they could trust the newspapers. The driver mentioned a house that had been raided in Brooklyn, where there were Nazi spies and all kinds of sick goings-on, but how the newspapers had to hush it up because they'd caught a Massachusetts sena-tor there. The man abruptly changed the subject by asking Hank if he had any brothers or sisters.

The driver let them out beneath a highway on stilts, in front of a yellow brick warehouse whose cranes were loading another zig-zag painted ship. The man watched the taxi pull away, took Hank by the arm and led him across the street, away from the river. "Almost there," said the man. "How long has it been? Two months? Oh, but this should be good."

"Hot damn," said Hank.

They walked up a cobblestone side street, a long shed roof on one side, a snub-nosed truck parked on the other. Whatever the place was, it was closed for the day. Hank thought he smelled chickens. There was a stack of poultry crates against one wall, a few feathers caught in the slats.

"Not the nicest neighborhood," the man admitted. "But what do we care, right?"

The street opened out on a square, a cobblestone bay where five or six streets met at odd angles. Two flatbed trucks were parked in the middle. The entire side of a tall warehouse across the way was painted with an advertisement for Coca Cola, the boy with the bottlecap hat wearing a small window in his eye. There were houses on their side of the square, three of them wedged together in the narrow corner. The man went up the steps of the white frame house that needed painting and rang the bell. Hank stood back and wondered what the man looked like without his overcoat, then without any clothes at all.

A little slot behind a tarnished grill opened in the door.

"Hello, Mrs. Bosch," said the man. "Remember me?"

The slot closed and the door was opened by a horsefaced woman with a nose like a pickax. "Uf course I ree-member you. Mr. Jones? Or was it Smith? But come een, come een." She spoke in a weird singsong as she ushered them inside and closed the door. She wore an apron over her flowered house dress and smelled of cooked cabbage. "And you breeng one uf our luflee service men. How happy for you."

Hank was shocked to find a woman here. The women back home knew nothing about such things, which was only right. But Yankees were strange and this woman was foreign. Hank had never seen an uglier woman. She and the man weren't friends, but she seemed to know what they were here for.

"And you are smart to come earleee." Her voice went up at the end of each sentence. "There is another couple before you, but I think they are looking for courage and will let you go in front of them."

She took their coats and hats and hung them on a rack. The man hiked his trousers and winked at Hank. He looked nice and slim.

The woman opened a door to the right of the narrow stairway and Hank heard a radio. The man stayed back but Hank leaned forward, so he could see what was in there. It looked like an old lady's parlor, with a red-faced, bald man and a pale boy sitting side by side on on a flowery sofa. They kept their hands to themselves, demurely folded in their laps.

"How are we doing, Father? I mean . . . *Mr. Jones,*" said the woman. "Will you mind if these two gentlemen go ahead and use the room?"

The bald man consented with a polite bow. He held up an empty glass. "Is it possible, Valeska . . . ?"

"Uf course. For such a constant friend as you, anything. I will tell Juke." Pulling the door closed, she mumbled, "Drink me out of house and home, the hypocrite. So it is all yours. Leaving us with only one thing."

"Quite so," said the man, taking a billfold from inside his jacket. He handed her a bill while he looked at Hank, as if the money proved something. Hank was used to money changing hands for this. Sometimes people paid him; now and then, Hank even paid them. Money made some people more comfortable with this, but it was of no matter to Hank.

"And it has gone up a dollar since the last time," said the woman. "The war, you know."

The man smiled, shook his head and gave her another dollar.

"Fine." She opened a door across the hall from the parlor and waved them inside. "I will be seeing you later. Enjoy."

The room was small, with scuffed linoleum patterned like a turkish carpet, and cabbage roses on the wallpaper. It looked like any room in any boarding house, except the bed had no blankets, only sheets. When Hank heard the door click shut, he spun around and grabbed the man.

His hands were all over the man, inside the beltless trousers, under the shirt tail, over soft cotton drawers and stiffening cock. The man kept his teeth together when Hank kissed him. He laughed when Hank got himself tangled up in the suspenders. The man unhooked the suspenders, stepped back, kicked off his shoes and shed his trousers, then insisted on undressing Hank himself. He was already familiar with the uniform's complicated fly and thirteen buttons. Hank couldn't keep still; he touched and grabbed, undid the man's bow tie and shirt, yanked the man's drawers down so he could get a good look at him. Hank often had sex with clothes just opened or rearranged, like when he was hitchhiking or making do in a storage locker or the bushes, but what he really liked was stark nakedness, the way it had been those first times, when an aunt's hired hand had shown him what they could do together after their swim in the pasture pond, squirreling around in the warm, wet grass while cows watched. Girls were for marriage and families, guys for getting your ashes hauled.

In heaven and naked, Hank lay back and grinned while the man loved him with his mouth. Because he was paying, the man still seemed to think it was up to him to do everything, but Hank didn't mind lying still for this, a cool mouth and tongue admiring his cock. He held the man's crisp, brilliantined head with both hands, then stroked the man's neck and shoulders. Hank's hands were callused, so the man's skin felt very smooth. Hank slipped a bare foot beneath the man's stomach and brushed his leathery toes against the wispy hair and hard cock. With his other foot he stroked the man's bottom.

Hank wrestled the man up to him so he could feel more of him. After Hank's cock, the man didn't mind Hank's tongue in his mouth. He still wore his socks and garters, which Hank pried off with his big toe. The man had a city body, spongey where it wasn't bony, but the patches of warm, cool and lukewarm skin felt good. Hank hummed and moaned and laughed without fear of who might hear them. They were safe here.

When Hank spit into his hand and reached between the man's legs, the man shook his head in a panic and said he didn't do that. So Hank got up on his knees, straddled the man, spit into his hand again and did his own ass. The man watched in blank bewilderment, said he didn't like that either, then laughed and said, "You'll do anything, won't you?"

They ended up on their sides, curled into each other, their cocks in each other's mouth. Sucking while getting sucked was like having two people talk to you at once, but Hank enjoyed the game of doing to the man what the man did to him and, even upside down, the guy knew how to suck cock. The man was cut, so there was a round head with eaves and a smooth stalk to tongue. Hank pressed his foot against the cold wall and rocked himself into the man's mouth, his own full mouth murmuring and moaning around the man. Hank still wore his dogtags and they were thrown over his shoulder, jingling and rattling while the bedsprings creaked. When it was time, Hank pulled his mouth back and let go with a string of yelps as it flew out of him. Before he finished, he was back on the man, twisting around to work his tongue against the best inch. The man was spitting and swallowing, trying to breathe again, but then he gave in to Hank, closed his eyes and lay very still. Until the weight in Hank's mouth became harder than ever and, simultaneously, seemed to turn to water. The man finished with a shudder, gritting his teeth and sighing through his nose.

Hank wiped his mouth, climbed around and stretched out beside the man. "Whew!" he said. "I needed that." He lay his leg over the man's legs and took a deep breath.

"Well," said the man. "You certainly seemed to enjoy it. How old are you?"

"Twenty." Hank gazed gratefully at his cock and the man's.

"I see. You've clearly been around. Uh, could you please let me up? We should be getting dressed."

"Naw. Let's stay like this. Wait a bit and have another go."

But the man was done for the day, maybe for the week. Beneath his politeness, he was slightly miserable. Still, better that than goo-goo eyes. Hank let him up and watched him wash off at the pitcher and basin on the dresser. His backside looked like dirty dough in the light of the bare bulb in the ceiling. Hank sprawled on the bed, hoping to change the man's mind, but the man didn't look at him until he was back in his suit.

"Is my bow straight?" he asked. There was no mirror in the room. He approached the bed and held out his hand. "That was thoroughly enjoyable," he said, shaking Hank's hand. "Good luck to you. Take care of yourself overseas." And he went out the door.

Hank smelled the brilliantine on the pillow one last time, then pitched himself out of the saggy bed. Yankees were no stranger than anyone else. The room was suddenly cold, the wash water colder. Hank quickly dressed, wet his hand and flattened his hair. He wondered if there was time to find someone else before midnight, when he reported back to the Navy Yard.

There was nobody out in the hall. Then Hank saw a colored boy sitting on the stairs with a bundle of sheets in his lap. The boy slowly stood up. His hair was as straight and shiney as patent leather.

"You took your sweet time, honey," said the boy, only he sounded like a girl. He batted his eyes at Hank like a girl, and curled one corner of his mouth. "Miz Bosch!" he hollered. "The seafood's out!" He went into the room muttering, "See what kind of mess you and your girlfriend left me."

The horsefaced woman came out from the parlor. The radio was louder and someone inside was laughing. The woman grabbed a handful of sleeve at Hank's elbow. "Your friend is gone but you are welcomed to stay. I have a visitor who is having a paaaardy." She pulled Hank down so she could whisper, "You do not have to do anything. Just stand around and act like you are having a good time. There is food and beer. Yes?"

Hank didn't want to leave. He let the woman drag him through the door and heard her announce, "Look what I have. A saaaylor."

The bald man and pale boy still sat on the sofa, but there were new faces here. A laughing fat man with a moustache arranged food on a table: piles of sliced meat and cheese on sheets of delicatessen paper, a loaf of machine-sliced bread still in its wrapper, a handful of Hershey bars. "Yes, welcome, welcome," the fat man boomed. "The more the merrier." Behind him stood a thin man with violet eyelids, hennaed hair and hands like spatulas. He eyed Hank and smiled.

A soldier in khakis sat with one leg over the arm of the armchair in the corner. He seemed quite at home, and bored. He glanced at Hank with the same cool arrogance soldiers always showed for sailors.

"Yes, sir, a good time is worth all the ration stamps in the world," said the fat man. "Hey, Valeska. Where's that beer you promised?"

The horsefaced woman closed the door behind her, then immediately opened it again to tell the bald man the room was ready. The man and boy walked out, one behind the other, without a word.

"Thank God!" said the thin man when the door closed. "Now we can let our hair down."

"Now, now," said the fat man. "It's not her fault she's a priest. Just another victim of life's dirty trick. Here, son. Help yourself to some of this fine salami. A growing boy like you must keep his strength up," he told Hank.

"He can help himself anytime to *my* salami," said the thin man.

Hank made himself two sandwiches while the men teased and flirted with him. Sex always left Hank hungry. He liked the men's friendly noise, but he didn't feel like touching them. The soldier, on the other hand, looked awfully good, even if he looked like the kind of guy who pretended to do it only for the money. Hank remembered how much money he had left and wondered how much the woman charged for use of the room. That would be a hoot, if he and the soldier went off together, leaving these two with their chocolate and salami. But the soldier only sat listlessly across his armchair, rocking his raised foot to the jingle that played on the radio.

The colored boy came in, carrying glasses and a pitcher of cloudy beer. Hank watched him more closely this time. He didn't mind the boy being colored—he liked that; it reminded him of home—but Hank had never seen a colored so womanly. The boy moved like a willow and swung his hips as he walked. Hank thought only whites, like the thin man, could be that way. The boy moved so gracefully he seemed boneless.

He set the pitcher on the table and caught Hank watching him. He did not look away but stared right back at Hank. He straightened up and perched the back of his hand on one hip. "What's the matter, Blondie? You a dinge queen?"

The fat man began to laugh.

"A what?" said Hank.

"If you ain't, don't go eyeballing me, Willy Cornbread," he sneered.

Uppity northern niggers: Hank couldn't make head or tail of them. He meant no harm by looking at the boy.

There was another program on the radio. New music came on, something click-clickety and South American. It snapped the soldier to life. He jumped up and began to jerk his knees and butt in time to the music. "Hey, Juke!" he called out to the colored boy. "Samba, Juke!"

The boy curled his lip at Hank and sashayed toward the soldier, already stepping with the guy as he approached him. They danced without touching at first, then the soldier actually took hold of the boy's hand and put his own hand on the boy's hip.

Hank couldn't believe it. The soldier looked Mexican or maybe Italian; he probably didn't know any better. But the fat man and thin man were amused, not shocked. And the two were good dancers, there was no denying that. The colored boy's baggy pants shimmied like a long skirt as he twitched inside them. The soldier's khakis tightened, went slack, then went tight again around his butt and front as he stepped to the music with all its extra beats.

"It must have been a sister who designed your uniforms," said the thin man as he passed Hank the glass of beer he poured for him.

Hank watched the soldier and drank. The beer was homemade and tasted like wet bread. The soldier's hair was black and curly.

The song ended and the dancers finished with a twirl. Hank applauded with the fat man and thin man. Colored or no, it had looked like fun. Hank wanted to be able to dance like that. He set his glass down, wiped his mouth and stepped in front of the soldier.

"Can you teach me that dance?"

The soldier was grinning over his samba. He grinned at Hank, then burst out laughing. "*You*, swab? I'd sooner dance with your cow, farmboy."

Hank was used to being taunted by Yankees, and there was nothing to gain by slugging the guy. "I can dance. Honest. Try me."

"No thanks, bub. I don't want my tootsies tromped on."

"You can dance with me."

It was the colored boy, looking up at Hank with a brazen smile.

He couldn't be serious. He was mocking Hank, sneering at the hick. His brown face was full of fight.

"This I gotta see," said the soldier, stepping back to the radio, tapping it as if that could hurry the program to the next song.

Hank just stood there.

"What's wrong, Blondie? You afraid you'll get soot on your hands?"

"No. Where I come from, whites don't dance with coloreds, that's all."

"Do tell. But do guys jazz with guys where you come from?"

"Sometimes." Hank didn't see what that had to do with it.

"But yeah. I know. You don't talk about it. While coons is something you talk about all the time. And that's all the diff. Come on, Blondie. Time you broke another golden rule."

More samba music was playing.

Juke did a box step to it, wiggled in a circle to it. "White dance. If this nigger can do it, you should too."

The boy was needling Hank, and Hank didn't like it, not in front of the others, especially the soldier. Maybe the soldier would like him if Hank showed he could dance with the boy. He moved his feet like Juke moved his.

"There you go, baby. Ain't so bad, is it?"

It wasn't, so long as Hank kept his eyes on Juke's two-toned shoes.

"Now move that tail of yours against the music. And step light. Shake that cowshit off your brogues. There you go, Blondie. Ain't you fine. Just like you and me was wiggling between the sheets."

Hank stopped dead.

Juke continued dancing. "What's the matter, baby?" No matter how sweetly he talked, his eyes had never lost their fight. "Oh, sorry. I forgot. You don't dig dinge. That's okay. I don't dig crackers."

"You're crapping me!"

"Am I ever, honey. And it feels so good."

Hank grabbed the front of Juke's shirt, but the boy was too small for Hank to hit. "Why you riding me like this? What did I do to you?"

Juke only pinched a smile at him, cool as ice.

The soldier rushed over. "Let the kid go," he said as he pushed his way between them. "Get your hands off him, you damn hillbilly."

"This is none of your damn business!" But Hank didn't want to hurt the boy; he only wanted to find out why the boy had it in for him. He released Juke, but Juke just stood there, not even bothering to step behind the soldier.

"You want to pick on somebody your own size?" The soldier threw his shoulders back, pulling his uniform taut across his chest.

He was shorter than Hank but looked tough and muscular. He stood so close Hank felt his breath when he spoke. Hank wanted to hit him and find what the body felt like. "Maybe I do. You want to step outside?"

"Maybe I do. Sucker!"

"Two big white boys," sang Juke. "Fighting over little old me."

"Shut up," said the soldier. "This is between me and him. Time you learned your lesson, hillbilly."

"I ain't no hillbilly, spick."

"I ain't no spick. I'm a wop, and proud of it."

"Oh boys," said the fat man. "I do love it when the trade gets rough, but . . . Let's not go flying off the handle." The man stood beside them, gingerly patting the soldier on the back. "We're here to have fun. Juke? Bring these boys some beer."

Juke rocked on his hips a moment, then stepped over to the table.

The soldier opened his fists and wiped his palms against his pants.

"And food? You haven't eaten a bite, Anthony. I know when I'm feeling ornery, there's nothing like a sandwich to calm me down." The man turned away to make the soldier a sandwich.

Hank and the soldier stood there, facing each other, catching their breath. Their bodies were still jumped into gear for a fight. Hank's muscles were humming; he ached to use them.

"You want to go off somewhere?" Hank whispered.

The soldier's jaw was still locked, but his eyes narrowed, surprised by the whisper. "To fight?" he asked.

"Nyaah. Not to fight." Once, it actually started in a fight, then, him and the other guy, drunk and bruised, went one step better. Tonight, Hank wanted to skip the fight.

The soldier stared, then glanced at the others.

The thin man whispered and giggled something to the fat man.

Juke brought them their beer. "You're not going to let that fat queen talk you out of a fight, are you?" he whispered.

"Juke, fuck off," said the soldier.

The electric bell out in the hall rang. "Juke! The door!" was shouted in the distance.

"Shit. Ain't no Joe Louis here," sneered Juke and he left to answer the door.

"Oh, God," said the thin man. "Will it be more possibilities or more competition? And just when I made up my mind, too."

The soldier drank his beer and looked at Hank. "You're nuts," he said, but kindly.

Hank grinned. "What's that lady charge for a room? I'll buy."

"Yeah? Sheesh." The soldier shook his head in disbelief. "Like I was *your* whore? Uh uh. I'd go halves with you. Only I don't think the witch'll let us do it. She doesn't want to piss off her repeat customers."

"Is there somewhere else?"

"Maybe."

The two looked at each other and thought it over.

There were voices out in the hall, then something fell.

The door had been left open. Suddenly Juke was standing there, mouth and eyes wide open. He had already screamed, "It's the Shore Patrol!"

Hank wheeled around, but the only door was the one where the boy stood, and an arm with an armband and club had grabbed the boy's collar.

"Dammit to hell. Dammit to hell," the thin man hollered at the ceiling. "I'm sick of this."

"Fucking mother of god," the soldier shouted, jumped on the sofa and tore down the heavy curtain. Hank jumped up beside him to help push up the window.

Someone grabbed Hank's ankles and yanked him off the sofa.

Hank jerked around and saw Juke gripping him while a Shore Patrol man pulled Juke backwards with a billy club across the boy's chest.

"Help me. Please," Juke pleaded. "I can't go back."

A woman screamed in the back of the house. The thin man stood there, cursing and spitting. The fat man stood with both hands raised over his head.

Hank swung his fist at the patrolman's face. The guy could not block the punch; his head jerked back and he let go of one end of his club. Juke scrambled over the sofa and jumped out the window the soldier had opened. The soldier had already jumped. Hank had his hands on the sill—a single light flared over a warehouse dock outside in the darkness—when someone grabbed the back flap of his jersey. Hank swung his fist and elbow behind him without looking.

Something hard banged his head. All at once, he was thinking every thought he had ever had: the excitement and burn of his first taste of liquor; his need to get through the window and back to his shipmates; his Baptist preacher's egg-smelling breath; his blinding anger during a fistfight with his father.

The thoughts slowed enough for Hank to notice he was on the floor now, sitting against the sofa. Everywhere were the canvas leggings of the Shore Patrol. Cold air poured through the open window behind him and there was scuffling outside. A man in a trenchcoat led the thin man, still cursing, out the door to the hall. And another man in a trenchcoat stood above Hank, a thin moustache across his upper lip, the hand at his crotch holding a square, blue pistol.

Hank reached up to touch the pain on one side of his head.

"Don't move!" said the man, pointing the pistol straight at Hank's face. "You stinking, Nazi fairy."

3

SO THE NEW WORLD was not as innocent as it claimed. A refugee from the Old World could not help feeling disappointed, but there was also a perverse sense of satisfaction.

It had begun with the first house, the one from the newspapers. The police noticed an uncommon number of sailors going to a house near the Brooklyn Navy Yard. Nothing worse than sex crimes had been suspected when the police and Navy raided the place on March 14. Then the arrested servicemen began to tell tales of overly curious civilians with foreign accents, and a very important gentleman who frequented the house. By the time the story reached the newspapers, the house had become a nest of German spies, the important gentleman a senator from Massachusetts. The FBI became involved. Two weeks after the raid on the house in Brooklyn, the FBI and Navy coordinated a series of raids all over New York: stretches of Fifth Avenue, the Columbus Circle entrance to Central Park, homosexual bars, brothels and houses of assignation, anywhere homosexuals congregated. It was never clear whether they hoped to catch the Nazi spies, the senator from Massachusetts, or simply put a stop to so much immorality. War was new and people were desperate to do something, anything. Whatever the intention, the raids had put them in touch with that immorality, and today made them part of it.

Erich Zeitlin was still startled whenever he found himself including himself with "them." He was an enlisted man and a foreigner. He stood between a filing cabinet and the window with closed venetian blinds, watched and listened and felt invisible. He knew "they" were wrong, but it wasn't his place to tell them, or his country.

The Bosch woman sat in their crowded cubbyhole at Navy Intelligence, horribly overdressed, wearing a hat like half a skullcap covered with cloth flowers and a wide-mesh veil. She was like a widow trying to look beautiful when she spoke to the director of a bank. She wasn't beautiful. She had a great, embarrassing blade of a nose, like the noses of Jews in German newspaper cartoons, only she said she wasn't Jewish.

"I am zo happy it has been approved," she sang. "I want zo much to do somethink for this country which has done zo much for me."

Her Czech-German accent embarrassed Erich. Why did corruption in America have to speak in a foreign accent? Erich himself had been in America only three years, but he had gone to university in England. People often mistook him for English.

"I luf this country like you wouldn't *beleeeeve.*" She lifted her veil to dab her painted eyes with the handkerchief she clutched. "We will do most wonderful work together, Doctor. I mean, Captain."

"*Commander,*" Commander Mason gently corrected her.

Erich himself often forgot his superior was an officer now and no longer a psychiatrist. It wasn't just the copy of Krafft-Ebing on the commander's cluttered desk. Mason's whole manner said civilian, professor, alienist. His khaki uniform needed pressing. He leaned back in his swivel chair, hands folded behind his head, gently smiling at the woman. Not even the presence of Sullivan, the man from the FBI, changed Mason's comfortable air of intellect and sloth.

Sullivan sat at the end of the desk between Mason and the woman. He was a cold, fish-eyed man with a bulky Irish face and a vain little moustache across the bottom half of his upper lip. "We do not condone what you do for a living, Mrs. Bosch. But there is a war going on," he announced, the phrase Americans forever repeated, as if needing to convince themselves. "And war makes strange bedfellows."

The woman laughed. "You don't have to tell me about strange bedfellows, meester. That is my business."

Sullivan pinched his mouth tight, the thin moustache curling into a ball.

Mason chuckled with the woman and nodded. "I prefer to think of this as a marriage of convenience."

Mrs. Valeska Bosch, late of Prague, late of Vienna, once a promising pantomime artist—Erich imagined her in a tawdry *tableau vivant* before he was born—ran a little house near the Hudson River docks. They had discovered her during their weekend of raids, and she had discovered them. After her arrest, while being questioned about suspicious characters among her clients, she had suddenly gushed love for Franklin Delano Roosevelt, and told them that a Panamanian ship at Pier 37 was bound for Lisbon with a disguised cargo of ball bearings. She knew her world situation, knew where the ball bearings would end up, and was blunt in telling how she got her information. The night before the raid, a Swedish second mate mentioned it while he dandled a boy on his knee, comparing balls and ball bearings. People felt very free and open at her place, she said. There was plenty of information that could be had there, if the Navy were interested. She didn't want money. She loved her country, hated Hitler and wanted to do her part in the war effort. Of course, if the Navy wanted a steady supply of information, they would have to protect her from the police, shore patrol and Lucky Luciano, who might be in prison but still had a hand in various doings along the waterfront. But she wanted to turn her little establishment, lock, stock and bed, over to Uncle Sam, so great was her patriotism.

Commander Mason was mad for strange, original schemes. As the commander's one-man staff, actually his secretary, Erich had sat through the first interviews, even helped to draft the proposal, confident nothing would come of it. This was innocent and righteous America, not Austria or Hungary. Someone in the rear admiral's office with less originality would kill the plan and denounce Mason for considering such a thing. Nevertheless, yesterday afternoon, word came down that the proposal had been approved.

The closed blinds were lined with daylight. Outside, men and women were enjoying the bosky air of a simple spring morning.

Mason brought his chair down and leaned both elbows on the desk. "Now, Valeska," he said, as if to a patient. "As to our line of action."

Mrs. Bosch lowered her handkerchief and proudly smiled with her long, red gash of a mouth. "I will come to you once a week and tell you everything I have been hearing."

"Oh, no. Much too slapdash. And we can't have you coming here regularly. You might be followed."

Mrs. Bosch laughed and waved her big bony hand at him. She was too old for such a girlish gesture. "Oh, Commander. Who would follow *meeee?*"

"German agents," said Sullivan.

"But agents do not come to my house. Only saay-lors."

"One never knows," said Mason. "But, for safety's sake, one of our people will come to you."

"Sounds goot."

"And, just to make things easier for you . . ." Mason made it sound as incidental as possible. "I'm sure you have your hands full as it is, running your . . . business. But we're asking you to take on a man or two of ours. As members of your staff."

This was the part Erich found hardest to believe. It was bad enough the Navy would be consorting with criminals, and that Mason wanted the Bosch woman to change her place from a house of assignation to an actual whorehouse, providing not just a room but the catamites too. But Mason intended to order several enlisted men to become sexual criminals. "They" had become no better than the Nazis.

Mrs. Bosch bugged her eyes in surprise. "Are you crazeee? You want to have your men living in my house? Nobody lives with me but my houseboy, and he fetches boys when I need them. You talk about safety and suspiciousness. My boys and customers will get suspicious when I have men always there, never doing anything."

"Oh, our boys will do anything your boys do. We have our nances, too, Mrs. Bosch."

"You don't need to tell me that. But my nances are different from your nances. Not every man can be a hooor."

"We'll choose carefully." The papers Mason fingered on his desk were dossiers on the dozen or so possibilities.

"I do not like it. What if I say no?"

"Then the deal is off," said Sullivan.

"What is wrong? You do not trust me?"

"Oh, no, Mrs. Bosch," said Mason. "We trust you. We trust you completely. We only want to hear *everything* that goes on there. A trivial remark, something you might not notice despite your acumen, might be a matter of life or death to us. So we need our own man on the inside. Do you agree? I promise whoever we choose will meet with your approval."

Erich stood in his corner and watched her. Part of the reason he was present today was so he could carefully watch Mrs. Bosch while the commander carelessly rambled, then give his reactions to Mason afterwards. Her long face looked very annoyed and sour. He hoped she'd say no. If she did, it might mean she wasn't sincere, or even that she was a double agent. There was always that possibility with foreigners. Whatever the reason, it would end the whole unsavory business. She thought about it a long time.

"What about the money?" she suddenly asked.

"What money?"

"When I provide the boys, I take half of what they make. Your men will be taking business away from boys who pay me half."

Mason broke into a grin that he shared first with the stony Sullivan, and then with Erich. "No need to worry there, Valeska. We won't take bread out of your mouth. Our fellows'll be on the government payroll. You can take a *hundred percent* of what they make, if you like."

And Mrs. Bosch did like. "And it will be only one or two? You do not want to be sending me more?" She sounded ready to ask that Uncle Sam provide her entire staff.

"One or two will suit our purposes," Mason said firmly. "Then you agree?"

She agreed, fervently. Her patriotism returned; she spoke of how proud she was to give of herself. She had nothing to hide at her house and would welcome Mason's boys with open arms, so long as they fit in and gave her a cut. It was left that, sometime next week, Mason would get back in touch with her, someone would be chosen to serve as liaison between her house and Mason, and they would send her the new men, whom she could inspect at her leisure. She stood up, swore her devotion one last time and departed.

"What a depraved woman," said Sullivan, closing the door behind her. "Opportunistic foreigner. Patriotism, my eye."

"Of course." Mason put a scuffed shoe on his desk and adjusted his sock and garter. "Erich? What time's the first interview with our . . . people?"

"Eleven o'—" Erich caught himself. "Eleven hundred, sir."

"Quite right. If you'll excuse us, Daniel," he told Sullivan, "there's some paperwork I have to take care of. Thank you for coming by. After all, this is your show too."

"It wouldn't be if I had any say in it," Sullivan snarled. "We're going to hell in a handbasket, if you ask me."

"An open mind, Daniel. We must keep an open mind. I'll keep you informed of all further developments. Goodbye."

Draping his trenchcoat over his arm, Sullivan muttered goodbye and went out the door.

"Irish Catholics," sighed Mason. "The most repressed blood bound up in the most repressive religion. What a redundant combination."

Erich adjusted the blinds and let a little more light into the room. He didn't like the FBI man either—Sullivan was vulgarly moral—but right now such bullishness seemed more human than Mason's cheerful insouciance.

"Let's just hope he doesn't foul up this gift from heaven." Mason leaned back in his chair again, folded his arms across his chest and gloriously sighed. "The beauty of it. A bordello for inverts and spies. Release the sexual desires a man has to keep hidden, and all his other secrets tumble out after."

The first interview was in fifteen minutes, but Mason had wanted to get rid of Sullivan only so he could think aloud, toss thoughts at his subordinate. Erich was used to this. Mason had asked that Erich be assigned to him ostensibly because he needed someone who knew German. The real reason was that Erich was from Vienna and Mason assumed he knew all about Freud. Mason thought Freud was a charlatan, but it was no fun mocking the man in the presence of people who didn't know what you were talking about. Erich regretted the assignment. He had gone to the trouble of getting waivers and permissions to enlist because he hoped to forget himself in the Navy and learn to stop thinking.

"We're on to something," Mason gloated. "There's no telling what might come of this. Clandestine sexuality as a conduit for clandestine intelligence? Once again, my hat is off to the Germans. We never would've thought of it on our own."

Erich pretended to look at the folders he'd picked off Mason's desk. "I doubt they did it as deliberately as we're doing it," he said softly.

"No. I suspect these German spies, whoever they are, only stumbled upon this homo whorehouse and found it so useful. But that's the way it's always been: the German proposes, the American disposes. Good old American know-how." He suddenly glanced up at Erich. "Am I only projecting unconscious doubts of my own, as your Dr. Freud would say—or do you have reservations about our scheme, Erich?"

Erich tapped and tamped the folders together before he laid them back on Mason's desk. "I do, sir. Now that it's been approved."

"Really? I never would've guessed," said Mason admiringly. "You're certainly adept at hiding your feelings, Erich. So. Do you object on practical grounds or moral grounds?" The commander sounded only curious and playful.

"Practical. You're involving your—*our* government in something corrupt. Prostitution and criminal sexuality. Sir."

"Sex. Of course," said Mason. "You people of Leviticus," he chuckled. "You're positively Bostonian."

Erich refused to be baited. "My reservations have nothing to do with prudery. I'd feel the same way if we were consorting with gangsters."

"Mrs. Bosch is hardly a gangster."

"She's hardly my maiden aunt, either." Actually, she reminded Erich of a maiden aunt, the one now safely interned in England. "All I mean to say, sir, is that we're involving ourselves in something dangerous. We could harm the men we send to this woman."

"The ends justify the means, Mr. Zeitlin?"

"Sometimes," Erich admitted. "But here the ends are so nebulous."

"You think so? You don't think our elusive Mr. E. and Mr. K. are going to rise to our bait? It takes a thief to catch a thief? Or, in our case, it takes a sui generistic 'H' overt to catch a sui generistic 'H' overt."

This was an important part of the scheme, one they hadn't revealed to Mrs. Bosch. They hoped to catch the homosexual spies who had frequented the house in Brooklyn.

"I don't know, sir," Erich answered after a long pause.

"Well, I don't know either," said Mason. "And, quite frankly, I don't really care. Because there's no telling what else we might stumble on. The coming and goings of an underworld we know nothing about. The secret lives of family men and politicians. A peephole on the rich, sexual underside of everyday life. Along with the necessary tidbits about neutral cargoes. No, Erich, our search for these spies is only our jumping off point for a venture into the unknown. And a bone to throw to the unimaginatively literal minds in the rear admiral's office, and our colleague, the G-man."

The commander's ulterior motives were worse than Erich had imagined. "What we're doing is only an excuse for voyeurism?"

He hadn't meant to be so blunt, but his superior only smiled.

"Voyeurism? But that's what we've been doing all along. Intelligence is only voyeurism with a higher purpose. What makes this project different from the others is that our higher purpose has not yet declared itself. But that's science for you. You cannot predict in advance what will or will not prove useful. You must keep an open mind." Mason looked up at Erich and narrowed his eyebrows at him. "Is that what disturbs you about our project, Erich? It's awakened the voyeur in you?"

"Not at all, sir." He was suddenly angry and knew he couldn't show it. "I have no interest in these people, prurient or otherwise."

"No trace of curiosity? Not even a hint of 'Peeping Tom' you're reacting against?"

"If I'm reacting, it's against something I fear is pointless and compromising." Why couldn't he work for a superior who expected him to obey orders, nothing else, instead of a bloody psychiatrist?

"I believe you," said Mason. "Yes. You're a good man, Erich. Principled, objective, incorruptible. Sit down, please. Just for a moment."

Erich warily sat in the chair opposite the commander. It still smelled of Mrs. Bosch's lilac and talcum. Mason's flattery worried him.

Mason brought his chair level and folded his hands together on the desk. "It is, as you said, a most corrupting situation. We need someone incorruptible. To serve as liaison between myself and this place."

Erich stared. "Me?"

"You're perfect. Intelligent. Incorruptible. You speak German and French. You have that smooth, jaded, European worldliness: too proud of your sophistication to open yourself to new experiences. No fear of *you* developing undue interest in any dirty doings, is there?"

Was Mason only mocking him? Erich had assumed they would use Sullivan or a junior officer for this.

"Yes. I think I'm right. I *will* make you our go-between."

"Sir. I don't feel qualified. I know nothing about that life. And I have doubts about the whole project."

"Your lack of sympathy guarantees your disinterest. And your ignorance—well, this war is going to be an education for us all."

"But Doctor, I mean, *Commander*—"

"I can't imagine why you'd refuse, Erich. Unless you have fears about yourself 'going native.' "

Erich froze.

Mason was smiling to himself. It was the perfect, psychological argument. He had Erich cornered.

"No, sir. I like women." He didn't know what else to say.

"I never suspected otherwise. Then you'll accept the assignment?"

Erich sighed. "If that's your order, Commander Mason."

"Don't worry. We'll come up with a good cover for your visits. You won't have to pose as a customer. *That* could get sticky," he laughed. "Maybe we could say you were Mrs. Bosch's bookkeeper. You do look like a bookkeeper, Mr. Zeitlin."

Erich knew that. There was nothing naval about his stubby body, his round, baby-fat face and round-rimmed glasses. He filled his uniform no better than Commander Mason filled his. Middle class Viennese Jews had no military tradition for Erich to draw from. His Navy whites only made him feel the distance between who he was and who he was supposed to be. He suddenly wanted to close the distance by sounding like a good subordinate.

"Yes, sir. How often will I go to this place, sir?"

"Once or twice a week. It depends on what kind of information starts turning up. You won't have to live there, Erich. We'll have our plants for that."

Maybe he could go in the mornings, when nothing was happening, and not see anything but Mrs. Bosch and their men. Only what kind of men would they be dealing with? Maybe they wouldn't be able to find men suitable for this house. There was still that possibility. Erich turned hopeful.

"Eleven hundred, Commander Mason." He pointed at his wristwatch. "Our first men should be waiting outside."

"Quite right. Yes. This should be interesting, for both of us. The first lesson in your education, Erich."

"Yes, sir," Erich replied, turned sharply and stepped outside.

The corridor felt reassuringly sane and proper. Teletype machines were heard through open transoms, firing out good, conventional war-related reports. Navy Intelligence had temporary quarters in an old office building near Wall Street. Large, oak-paneled rooms were divided up by drab, beige, plywood walls. Brass light fixtures from the twenties remained, and an occasional portrait of a man fat with money. A beautiful Wave swiveled her hips down the corridor and two ensigns nudged each other as they watched her glide past. Erich noticed how attractive she was—the tight skirt gave her a fanny that stretched down the backs of her legs—then shuddered to think he felt *obligated* to find her attractive.

But he liked women. He genuinely did. He wasn't comfortable with American women yet—you could never be sure which class they were from and what liberties you might take—but that would come in time. His discomfort with this business had nothing to do with fears about himself. He loved women as much as he loved music, and concentrated on music now only because that was what was most familiar in this alien world. He should know better than to let Commander Mason's nonsense intimidate him.

A moment passed before Erich noticed the six sailors scattered over the wooden pews in the front office. Mason had scheduled them in batches, which Erich thought unsafe. But the men didn't fraternize with each other. Most of them shouldn't know each other, but they still sat apart, as if they knew why they were here and didn't want to be seen together. They looked awfully young. Erich took the sheaf of orders they had left with the yeoman at the reception desk and called the first man. He looked like any other sailor, not at all effeminate. A little guilty, but no more guilty than any enlisted man on his way to see an officer.

The interviews went quickly. Erich began to think his hope might be fulfilled. None of them were good potential prostitutes.

Their names had been chosen from lists of men charged with homosexual activity. Some were up for court-martials; others had spent time in the brig and were back on active duty. Navy regulations were not clear on the subject; it was left to the discretion of each commanding officer whether a man should be discharged, imprisoned, or scolded and forgotten. The Navy was too busy with the war to concern itself with combing out sexual undesirables.

Nobody admitted to being homosexual. Mason invited confessions by claiming he saw nothing immoral about it—which was true; he thought it a form of mental illness—but there were no takers. Some admitted to homosexual acts, but always under extenuating circumstances. One was drunk; another needed five bucks to take his girl to dinner; a third was homesick and Father O'Connor had been so kind and he didn't want to hurt the chaplin's feelings. Others wouldn't admit to having done anything. How could they know it was a pansy bar, said the three who'd been picked up in a raid on the New Amsterdam. "I thought it was U.S.O.," said a sailor who'd been arrested at the house outside the Brooklyn Navy Yard.

There were several men from the house in Brooklyn, all still in their dress blues. They had been transferred off their ships and kept in New York to testify at the trial of Gustave Beekman, the man who ran the house. Now that the trial was over, the Navy didn't know what to do with them. Mason hoped he'd be able to use at least one of these men. They might be able to recognize Mr. E. and Mr. K. and, better yet, they'd be familiar with whorehouses. But these men were as denying and evasive as the rest.

"What a bunch," grumbled Mason after the short, feisty sailor who said he went to the house in Brooklyn only because his buddy dragged him there. Earlier, they'd spoken to the buddy, who said it was the short sailor who dragged *him*. "Either they're compulsive liars or just plain stupid. Either way, we can't use them."

"What are we hoping to find?" asked Erich.

"First off, real homosexuals who are trustworthy. I thought we could start with the homosexuals who said, 'Yes, I'm a homosexual.'"

"What if they don't exist, sir?"

"They exist. The Navy tries to screen them out, but I'd assumed a *few* would've slipped in."

Erich went out and called the next sailor. It was another man still in his blues, who'd been in the brig until last week and missed the seasonal issue of whites. But he wasn't from the house in Brooklyn. His papers said his name was Henry Fayette and he was charged with resisting arrest during the raid on the Bosch house. Erich looked at him, watching for signs of depravity, but the man only looked like a big, blond, dumb peasant. When he stepped into their office, he stood there for a moment and looked around, before he eased his back and shoulders into "Attention" and saluted Commander Mason.

"Seaman Fayette, sir." His Southern accent reduced his name to one syllable, a cross between "fat" and "fate."

Mason told him to sit down, make himself comfortable. Erich returned to his observation post between the window and filing cabinet.

"Henry," began the commander. "May I call you Henry?"

"Whatever you want, sir. Although my friends call me Hank." He sat there stiffly, forearms resting on the tops of his thighs, big hands hanging between his knees. He glanced at Erich, the blinds, the bookcase to his right, needing to see where he was before he could give his full attention to the officer in front of him. Most men noticed only the officer.

"Then Hank it'll be. No need to be formal here. And everything you say is strictly confidential, Hank. Do you have any idea why you're here?"

"Something to do with that house I was at? And my slugging the Shore Patrol. People keep asking me about that house, but I've told what little I know. I was only there that once." He glanced at Erich again.

Erich tried to make himself look stony and unresponsive.

"I'll tell you about it, too, sir, if that's what you want. But I really wish everyone would finish with me, so I could get back to my ship. I feel funny sitting out the war like this."

The man seemed unaware that he'd done anything wrong, but Erich was skeptical about such ignorance. American enlisted men could be as cunning as servants, disguising their cunning as obstinate stupidity.

Mason began to ask his questions. His confidence was unshakable; he didn't seem to notice that this was another one from whom he'd get nothing. Fayette kept mulishly coming back to his desire to return to his ship and shipmates, until Mason said he'd see what he could do for him, just to get on with the questioning. He offered Fayette a cigarette.

"Thank you, sir. Don't mind if I do."

Mason lit it for him with his gold lighter. "How do you like girls, Hank?"

Fayette drew on the cigarette and exhaled. "They're okay. I suppose I'll marry one someday."

"Then you're not a homosexual?"

Fayette looked at the slim cigarette in his thick fingers. Then he glanced back at Erich, curiously, almost amused, one enlisted man sharing with another his distrust of an officer. The glance annoyed Erich, as though it suggested a conspiracy more personal than rank.

Mason, too, glanced at Erich, but only to share his new interest in this man: he was the first not to deny immediately that he was a homosexual. "You do understand the word, don't you, Hank?"

Fayette sighed impatiently. "Yeah, well, lots of people have been asking me that lately."

"We can forget about them. This is something completely different. Nothing you say goes outside this room, Hank. I promise you. It won't be used against you. In fact, the sooner we learn all there is to know about such a unique fellow as yourself, the sooner we can get you back with your shipmates, Hank."

"Yeah? Really?"

"Yes. So, Hank. You've had sexual relations with men?"

"Yeah." As if it were a matter of no importance and he was expecting more dangerous questions.

Mason sat up, slowly, so as not to betray his excitement. He picked at Fayette's sheaf of papers. "Uh, you've had sexual relations with *more* than one man?"

"Yes, sir."

"Then you enjoy it?"

Fayette looked blank for a moment, then broke into a grin, a big, imbecilic grin. "If I didn't enjoy it, I wouldn't do it. Sir."

The answer shocked Erich. And the grin. Maybe the man really was as ignorant as he seemed.

Mason was smiling now, to keep Fayette talking. "You talk about it, Hank, as though you think there's nothing wrong or strange about it."

"Well, *I* find nothing wrong with it. But I know other people do."

"That doesn't bother you? That other people think it's wrong?"

"No. Some people think it's wrong to drink liquor, but that doesn't stop others from drinking it."

Erich decided the boy must be feebleminded, an idiot. Nobody with normal intelligence could be this innocent. And the commander had lied to the poor creature and was leading him on. It seemed unfair.

"Hank? Have you ever wanted to dress up in women's clothes?"

"No, sir. Can't say that I have."

"Hmmm. And your family? What do they say about this?"

"I never had a reason to talk to them about it. Not something I had to talk about with anybody, until this stuff."

"Your officers never said anything?"

"No. Why should they? I never wanted to do anything with *them.*" He laughed, glanced at Erich, then stopped laughing.

Erich tried to relax, tried to hide what he was feeling. He was only a fly on the wall here. He should not let his presence affect what was happening.

"But you did things with your fellow enlisted men?"

"No, sir. Or nobody on my ship."

"Ah. Then with them you felt you had to keep your desires to yourself?"

"No. Not really. They knew what I liked, my friends anyway. They just thought it was funny. I never did anything with them, so why should they care? I did it at boot camp a few times and can't

36

tell you what a mess that made. Some guys got upset, a couple got jealous, one guy got into a fight with me because I wouldn't promise myself to him and nobody else. That taught me to keep my hands to myself, until I was off by my lonesome."

"Your shipmates only found it funny? Nobody ever taunted you or picked on you because of your desires?"

"No, sir. They like me and I like them. They make jokes about it, but we all find each other funny. I mean, in my section we have me, a dago, a Jew-boy, and a mick. Also, I'm bigger than they are. They know I could flatten them, so they take me as I am."

The boy was definitely feebleminded. Erich cringed when he heard homosexualism put on the same level as being Italian or Jewish. More shocking was that the Navy had accepted such an obvious imbecile, regardless of his sexual misconduct. It wouldn't matter to an imbecile whether he had sex with a woman, a man or an animal.

Mason asked more questions about Fayette's sex life. It was as though he too had recognized the man was a mental defective and unqualified for this project, but was mining him for pathological data. Fayette had his first sexual experience at fourteen, with a farmhand, outside Beaumont, Texas. Since then he'd had sex with truck drivers, hobos, a Bible salesman, assorted roughnecks, a school teacher and most of the people at a Civilian Conservation Corps camp. He reported his sexual history without shame or pride, only surprise that an officer wanted to hear about it. He hesitated when Mason asked for technical details—Erich began to think of excuses for leaving the room—but went ahead and gave them, saying in effect that he was willing to do anything the other guy wanted; it was of no matter to him.

"Uh, Commander." Erich tapped his watch. "Sixteen hundred. You have four more people to see today, sir." If Mason wanted to study this case, he could do it on his own time, without Erich having to be present.

"What? Oh, yes. I was forgetting. This has been fascinating, Hank. 'More worlds than are dreamt of in your . . .' But, there is the matter at hand." Mason cleared his throat and sat up straight. "You want to get back to your shipmates, Hank. I presume you feel a great duty to them, and to your country."

37

"Yes, sir. I enlisted to serve my country, not to sit locked up in New York City."

"What if I told you that you could serve your country, and your friends at sea, by staying in New York a little longer and doing what you like to do?"

"Pardon?"

What was Mason doing? Erich had mentioned the time so they could finish with this poor soul and see the others. Surely he didn't intend to use *this* man.

But that was what Mason intended. First, he told Fayette not to mention this to anyone, that many lives depended on his keeping this a secret. Then he told him that the Navy wanted him to live for a couple of months in a homosexual brothel. He gave him the more practical version of why: the search for two possible Nazi spies. "Only for two, maybe three months. Until we catch these two men. Afterwards, we'll get you back on your ship. Are you willing to do that for us?"

A normal man would respond to the proposal with shocked disbelief or outright laughter, but Fayette only sat there, thinking it over. "I don't know, sir. It's like nothing I ever expected. Me serving my country by having my jollies? And I've never done it as a whore, not regularly. That might feel funny." He looked down at the floor and dug at one ear with a finger while he thought it over.

"I shouldn't need to tell you that by working for us you'll also be working for your shipmates, Hank. We believe one of these spies is the mastermind of a spy network providing U-boats with information that's enabled them to wreak havoc on our convoys. We nab him and we save lives, possibly your friends' lives."

Erich had grown accustomed to lying, but it seemed criminal to lie like this to an idiot.

"No. I can see that," said Fayette. "I want to help, only . . . a whorehouse? Kind of like that place where I was arrested?"

Mason glanced at Erich, realizing that Fayette already knew the Bosch house. Maybe that would change the commander's mind.

But Mason said, "Kind of. Only that was more a house of assignation, wasn't it? This one should be more organized, and you'll be living there. Be just like living in a barracks, I imagine. I think we can arrange that you're paid a bonus while you're there. Not combat pay, of course, but something commensurable."

Fayette didn't notice he was being bribed. "That's no mind," he mumbled, frowning at something happening inside his head.

"And we'll transfer you back to your ship as soon as possible. Otherwise, there's no telling what the navy might do with you. There's been talk of making an example of the people picked up in the sex crime raids."

Fayette didn't recognize he was being blackmailed. "I'm sorry I'm so slow in getting used to this. If you just order me to do it, I'll get used to it soon enough."

"Well, we can't just order you, Hank. We have to have your permission." The rear admiral's office had at least insisted on that much. "But it's not a decision that has to be reached today. All we need to know is that you're interested. We might find someone better qualified and not even use you."

"I'm interested. I'm definitely interested," Fayette muttered. "I want to help you, only . . . No, I'll get used to the idea."

"Good," said Mason, thanked him, said they'd be in touch with him and told Erich to show the man the door. Then Mason took on a look of boredom and began to write.

Fayette stood; Erich had forgotten how large the man was. But Fayette didn't seem dangerous. He appeared unsteady, confused. Only at the door did he remember to salute. He looked at Erich before he stepped out to the hall; he had the ghostly blue eyes of an infant. It was unnerving, like finding a child's eyes in the face of a dog. Erich quickly closed the door and turned around.

And Mason let himself go. "Hot dog!" he cried, slapping his desk with both hands. "We found one!"

"Yes, sir." Erich went back to the filing cabinet, although there was nothing for him to do there. With his back to the commander, he said, "But isn't the man an idiot? An imbecile or moron or whatever the medical term is? Feebleminded."

"Yes, yes, he does show imbecilic tendencies. But I was looking at this." He held up Fayette's papers. "Semiliterate, but he scored high on oral tests. He has the moral awareness of a donkey, but that's not important to us. An idiot savant. Thank God. I was beginning to think we were going to have to turn to the prisons."

"Then he *is* mentally deficient?" Erich was shocked to hear he was right, as though he'd been hoping he had misunderstood the American sailor.

"He has to be. No other way someone could be so unaware of how sexually sick they are. But it's a godsend. I realize now that this was exactly what we were looking for: a sick man who didn't know he was sick."

"But . . . a man like that has no business in the Navy. Shouldn't he be in a mental hospital?"

"Which is exactly where I intend to send Hank. Once we're done with him."

I am only an enlisted man, thought Erich. I am a foreigner, I have no right to judge what is right or wrong here. But the dishonesty of this business, and his own helplessness, disturbed him. They were exploiting a child.

"That's the way it is," said Mason. "Nice, personable fellow like Hank, no telling who might hear about our escapade if we sent him back to his ship. No, we'll send him to a good hospital, where he'll be happy and they can treat his homosexuality. Psychosurgery, electroshock treatment: science has made incredible advances in helping people like Hank. And there, nobody will believe the stories he tells."

Erich stood up straight. "Yes, sir. Very good, sir." He almost clicked his heels, he was so intent on losing himself in rank, protocol, the larger purpose of the war. He owed nothing to that American stranger. His one loyalty was to the war.

4

ANNA LOOKED UP again and saw the person she never dreamed she could be: a beautiful woman with a mouth like a red diamond, penciled crescents for eyebrows, hair perfectly scrolled along the sides, a shiney dress, a plunging neckline and skin like cream. Behind that beautiful woman was the perfect setting: a night club with night-blue walls, white satin palm trees, tiny colored lights in the ceiling and seats upholstered in zebra stripes. The room in the mirror was full of elegant men and women who rubbed elbows here just as they did in the columns of the society pages. A velvety orchestra played in the dining room upstairs.

Unfortunately, also reflected in the mirror over the bar was Teddy, Anna's date for the evening, flopping on the next stool.

"Decadent brats, all of them. I got this friend who says his girl-friend knows someone who says Bitsy Rockefeller's a hophead. Errol Flynn, too."

Teddy was drunk. He had lied to her when he said they knew him at El Morocco and he and she would be mingling with café society. The best the bribed *maitre d'* could offer were two stools at the bar, by the entrance to the famous room. Teddy's noise managed to spoil even the pleasure of that. When Anna turned away, embarrassed, he began to harangue the bartender with his gossip and hearsay.

Anna had met worse in the past two months. Enlisted men were especially bad, feeding you lines about how they were giving their lives for their country, and the least you could give in return was one last, happy memory. Anna had learned how to evade their paws while pumping them for rumors and stray details. Teddy was a civilian who said he worked with the Foreign Information Service. Drunk tonight, he let slip that he didn't work there yet, that he only knew someone who knew someone who might get him a job there. Anna should have expected as much from a "writer" met at Sammy's on the Bowery.

In her two months as a spy, Anna had learned much about the world. She had learned to like cocktails and how to talk to men without seeming like a tart. She had discovered she was attractive. She had also found that, while her father might be the center of her world, he was not the center of their spy ring. Before Pearl Harbor, Simon had worked alone, which had protected him when the FBI swept up agents associated with the German bunds in Yorkville. Simon mailed his findings directly overseas, using the packets he received from the American Ordnance Association. Anna, when younger, often helped Papa steam open the packets in the kitchen after Aunt Ilsa went to bed. Simon slipped his additional information inside with the association's latest news about weapons, resealed the envelopes and forwarded them to an address in Lisbon. The packets looked so official they were never opened by inspectors in peacetime. But America's entry into the war closed that route and Simon had to tie himself in with other agents if he wanted his material to reach Germany.

He never sat down with his daughter and explained who their bosses were. "The less you know, the better," was Simon's constant answer to questions. Anna was used as a messenger a few times, giving skittish strangers folded squares of rice paper or frames clipped from newsreels that were wrapped in foil to look like sticks of gum. Simon hated using her for that; there was always the chance the contact wasn't really one of them. He did not trust the competence of his colleagues. Once, walking in Riverside Park with his daughter, they had run into a Mr. Eisman, who Simon introduced as a friend of his. Simon had no friends and Anna immediately sensed that this smiling man with a vandyke and dachshund was someone important, that this encounter was no accident. Simon looked uncomfortable; Mr. Eisman put his homburg over his heart and said he was most pleased to meet "the little lady." After they parted, Anna knew better than to ask if Eisman was their boss or even one of them. The newspapers suggested New York was riddled with spies, but there was no way of telling who was and who wasn't.

Teddy wasn't, of course, and he had revealed himself as useless to her. Anna wished she could forget Teddy and her father tonight and just enjoy her glimpses of sophisticated people. There was no romance in her work, only bums who talked and bums who didn't know anything.

Various couples and parties were escorted to the bar and asked to wait until their tables were ready. They chatted among themselves and paid no attention to the two nobodys, no matter how loud Teddy became. A handsome young man with perfect hair and a perfect chin waited alone next to Teddy, languidly leaning against the bar, as at home here as in his own livingroom. He had the world-weary eyes of someone whose photograph had been taken many times for the newspaper.

"The usual, Mr. Rice?"

Mr. Rice made a slight hum and a tall glass full of ice and amber immediately appeared at his elbow. He cut his eyes at Teddy for a split second—Teddy was ranting about what was wrong with Hollywood—then looked out at the room, coolly, beautifully bored.

The fellow was so suave he made Anna's stomach hurt. He wore his tailored black clothes like a second skin and sipped his drink as lightly as he would a cigarette. The double corners of his display handkerchief were pure geometry.

"Eleanor Powell's another!" Teddy crowed. "Eleanor Powell's a goddamn dancing horse! No wonder she's Adolf Hitler's favorite movie star."

Mr. Rice turned and glared at Teddy.

"It's true," Teddy insisted. "Old Schickelgruber never misses an Eleanor Powell movie. The Gestapo smuggles 'em in now through Switzerland."

"And what does that prove?" Mr. Rice said angrily, surprisingly passionate.

"What's the matter, buddy? You pals with horsey Eleanor or something?"

Anna sighed and looked away. This was too embarrassing.

Mr. Rice leaned forward. "Miss? Is this man annoying you?"

Anna's heart leaped into her mouth. The man had noticed her? "Yes, but I . . ."

"You don't need to protect him. Gus!" he called out, snapping his fingers for the *maitre d'*. "What's happened to this place? There's a drunk making a nuisance of himself and you let him sit here?"

"Sorry, Mr. Rice. I'll take care of it immediately. Sir?" The *maitre d'* took Teddy's arm and helped him off the stool. "If you'll come with me, please."

"What are you? . . . Hey!" Teddy was so drunk it took him a moment to understand what was happening. "Let go of me! My money's as good as his!"

"This place is getting as common as Grand Central Station!" said Mr. Rice. "I wonder if you want to keep my patronage, Gus."

"I don't know how he got in, sir." The *maitre d'* called for a waiter to help him hustle Teddy to the door.

"Let go, you apes. I'm a writer. Ask my girl there. Tell 'em I'm a famous writer, Annie."

Mr. Rice stared at Anna.

Anna wanted Mr. Rice's respect. And Teddy deserved this for leading her on. "I never saw this man in my life. Until he started annoying me."

"You lying bitch!" Teddy cried as he was hauled away. "See if I ever go out with you again!"

Anna watched Teddy disappear around the corner and breathed a sigh of relief, already hoping that thanking the manly Mr. Rice might give her a chance to meet him. "How can I ever repay you, Mr. . . .?"

"Rice. Blair Rice. Pleased to have been of service." He shook her hand like a gentleman. His fingers were smooth and manicured.

"I was waiting for a friend, and that drunk started talking to me. But one dislikes making a fuss. Oh, my name's Anna. Anna Cromwell."

"Pleased to meet you. With so many men away, one finds it necessary to step in now and then. Damn riffraff. Uh, beg your

44

pardon." He looked at her, as if noticing she was beautiful. He nodded goodbye and faced forward again.

Anna hoped he was only being polite. She was determined to continue this. "Do you know Eleanor Powell?"

"What? Oh. Not at all. She's in musical comedies, right?"

"Why did you come to *her* defense?"

Mr. Rice studied Anna. "I simply don't like hearing riffraff run down anyone at the expense of, uh, the Germans. The Hitler and Schickelgruber jokes. Despite what's happened, I still have a special fondness for things German."

Anna was overjoyed. *She* was German. She was immediately curious about how deep this fondness went. "I don't know much about politics," she ventured, "but sometimes I almost feel we're fighting the wrong people."

Mr. Rice's blue eyes widened slightly. He promptly sat on the stool vacated by Teddy. "Yes. You're right to feel that way. So few people do. It's the right war, but we're fighting on the wrong side. The Communists are our real enemy. We should be helping Hitler crush the Communists, instead of the other way around."

Anna noticed the bartender frowning while he dried a glass, only Mr. Rice was clearly much too important a personage for anyone to contradict. She never thought about politics and her father never discussed Nazism, but she wanted to explore Mr. Rice's admiration of Hitler, wondering if she could parlay it into an interest in her. She had to be very careful. "The newspapers tell us things, but I never know what to believe. The Jews and all."

"Oh, that," said Mr. Rice. "Grossly exaggerated. And it's not as though we don't have anti-semitism here, too. Just look at our country clubs and resorts. Anti-semitism is so *declassé*, but it's being used to discredit the National Socialists' good work."

She let Mr. Rice do all the talking, staring into his stern blue eyes without incriminating herself. He spoke at length on the question of whether Roosevelt was a fool or a knave, betraying his class the way he had. He then compared the leveling effects of Bolshevism and democracy.

The *maitre d'* reappeared. "Your table's ready, Mr. Rice. I apologize for the disturbance earlier, sir." He did not look at Anna, who he knew had arrived with the "disturbance."

Mr. Rice merely nodded and turned back to Anna. "It's so rare one gets to meet someone so intelligent, I hate to end this. You said you're waiting for someone?"

"Yes, but they're already a half hour late. I wonder if I've been stood up."

"Would you care to join me? For another drink maybe? Until your party arrives."

"Your wife or girlfriend won't be joining you?"

Mr. Rice laughed. "Hardly. I'm unmarried and quite unattached."

Anna hid her joy by resisting his kind invitation a moment longer, then accepted his arm; she left the bar with Mr. Rice.

The room seemed finer than ever when she actually entered it, and on the arm of such an important, elegant man. He nodded at a table they passed, grudgingly. The *maitre d'* led them to a banquette on a dais in the corner, zebra-striped seats around a white tablecloth. Anna asked Blair—she thought of him as Blair now—if there were anyone here tonight she should know about.

"Not really," he said, looking over the tables. "Whom do you see here?"

Anna explained she rarely went out, what with being away at Bryn Mawr.

"It was much nicer last year. So many men from good families have caught war fever and enlisted. The idiots. In their place you get these social climbers in uniform." He angrily nodded at an Army officer laughing at the next table.

Anna suddenly wondered if Blair was one of them. They were everywhere, so why not this wealthy young man who admired Hitler and hated the war? But an agent would not be as outspoken about his beliefs as Blair was. That was a pity, because it would be wonderful working with such a man, the two of you bound together in your shared secret. Which gave Anna an idea. It was a dangerous idea, but it would not go away.

After they ordered their drinks, Blair talked more about himself—Yale and Park Avenue, his doddering father and once wonderful mother, his misery during the Nazi-Soviet pact, his elation the day Hitler invaded Russia.

A man with a bloodshot nose came up to their table, accompanied by a pretty girl with bare shoulders and a pale, half-familiar face. They were selling raffle tickets to benefit the Red Cross. Blair politely refused, saying he had already donated his mother to that organization.

"Oh, please, Blair. Pretty please with ice cream on it," whined the girl.

And Anna recognized who she was.

"You old fud," said the girl when Blair remained adamant. She then sailed off to the next table, dutifully followed by the little man.

"Wasn't that Brenda Frazier?" Anna whispered. "The debutante?"

Blair made an apologetic hum. "I once took her out when I was in college."

Such connections took Anna's breath away. She assumed all famous people knew each other—Brenda Frazier, movie stars, congressmen and presidents. She wished her father were here to hear this, but Anna was on her own. "You must know scads of important people," she began.

"Not really. Well, I suppose some might think the people I know are important."

"Have you ever thought about, oh, using your position to do good?"

"What can I do?" said Blair. "That's my tragedy. Knowing what's right and not being able to do anything about it."

"I'm sure there's something you could do."

Blair narrowed his eyes at her. "What a funny girl you are." He lightly laughed. "Anyway, blowing up bridges and things is hardly my line."

"But you probably hear things that would help the men who blow up bridges." Anna knew of no saboteurs, but that seemed to be the language Blair understood.

"Perhaps. I do hear things." He smiled, sheepishly. "It *has* crossed my mind. Once or twice, when I read about such goings-on in the newspaper. But how does one make himself available? There's no listing in the phone book for Nazi spy rings. Unlike the Communist Party."

Anna hesitated. She glanced around the room, then reached beneath the table and found Blair's hand.

It was her usual act to keep a sailor or merchant marine talking, to lead them on. But when Blair's hand slowly turned over and his fingers lightly pressed her fingers into his cool palm, she was the one who felt changed. She had to do this; it was the right thing to do.

Blair gently smiled, then stared at their clasped hands. When he looked up at her, his cool, handsome face was tense with understanding, doubt and hope.

"Blair?" she whispered. "Can you keep a secret?"

Two weeks later, Thomas Blair Rice, III, of El Morocco, the Stork Club and 21, sat in a saloon off the boardwalk at Coney Island. The sidings were down, but the breeze that blew in from the darkening beach and ocean was not enough to clear away the saloon's stink of beer, cigars and b.o. He wished Anna had chosen a nicer place for him to meet her father. He had certainly taken her to enough nice places since the night they met. Even their bench in Central Park would have been better. They were late and Blair was nervous enough already. If they didn't come before the blackout, they would never find him.

Out in the twilight, people clattered in herds along the wide, bare boardwalk. In the smokey light inside the saloon, they drank, yammered and laughed, as if they didn't know there was a war, not even the handful of men in uniform. The only sign of the war was the jukebox, raspberrying the room again with "In Der Fuhrer's Face." Cattle, Blair thought. Luckily for them, he was coming down from his tower of intellect and class to save them from their leaders.

"Nine o'clock! Lights out!" Wardens shouted up and down the boardwalk. The saloon went black. Even that was a lark for the masses. They giggled and hooted; someone made ghost noises. To the right of his table, a man and woman shamelessly moaned together. Blair was disgusted by his picture of what they might be doing. He was infuriated over wasting an hour here without meeting Anna or her father. His eyes adjusted to the darkness. The ocean and sky were two dark shades of blue beyond the partially blackened globes of the streetlamps outside. Cigarette ends winked around the room. Someone struck a match, held it high and called for more beer. Blair thought about getting up and feeling his way out.

"You're Anna's young man?"

Blair jumped an inch off his chair. He had not heard anyone sit at his table.

"Yes. Of course. Is that you, Mr. Krull?" Anna had told him her real name at their second meeting.

"Speak softly. I can hear you." The man's voice came from the side of the table toward the wall, so there was no silhouette, only a low, softly accented voice. There was a whiff of sen-sen when the man leaned closer. "Anna's told me much about you. You want to help us?"

"Yes. Where is Anna?"

"She's here. She pointed you out to me. She will join you, after I leave." A sigh. "Sad when a father and daughter cannot be seen together too frequently."

"Anna speaks very highly of you. I respect that in a woman."

The man ignored the compliment. "I want to discover what you can do for us. You were at Yale?"

"Class of Forty," said Blair.

"And you were in— What club? Skull and Crossbones?"

"Skull and *Bones,*" Blair corrected him. "And not a club, a society."

"Then you are close friends with some very prestigious people?"

"Close, no. I haven't stayed in touch with anyone from school. They were too naive, too ignorant." So ignorant they never accepted him in Skull and Bones, but Anna and her father didn't need to know that.

"Surely you kept one friend from then?"

"No. Everyone I knew were Popular Front dupes or worse. None of them understood how Hitler had saved Germany from Bolshevism, or how—"

"Admirable principles," the voice said sharply. "But we must keep them to ourselves. People get ideas."

Blair was sorry. He had looked forward to talking politics with a real Nazi.

Anna's father wanted to talk about Blair. "Friends? Family? Surely you know someone highly placed in the government."

"No. My family, God bless them, has never dirtied its hands in politics. Cousin John's in the Navy, but we stopped speaking to each other a year ago."

"Hmmm. And what line of work are you in?"

"None at present. I was in advertising briefly, but I couldn't bear the dishonesty."

"What a difficult young man you are."

Blair laughed. "Not difficult. Just principled."

"You're not what I expected."

"Thank you."

"Nevertheless, I think you can help us. People above suspicion are rare, and a man of your class? I understand you belong to several exclusive clubs?"

Blair proudly listed them.

"You are attracted to my daughter?"

The question took Blair by surprise. "Yes. Yes, I admit I find Anna attractive, sir."

"Would you say you are in love with her?"

Blair opened his mouth, but couldn't say anything. He cleared his throat. "I *like* your daughter, yes. Uh, isn't this awfully personal?"

"I want only to understand your feelings for her. But you do care about her?"

"Yes. Of course."

"Then you must be very careful in your talk. Not just for your sake, but for Anna's. We do not want anything happening to her. A little loose talk and—"

"You can trust me with Anna," Blair said. "I'm very careful about what I say. And my feelings for her are of the highest—"

Before Blair could finish, the chatter around them broke into shouts of "Look!" "Out there!"

Out on the horizon, faint sparks of color flashed, red and yellow scratches of light at the line where the sky met the ocean. A ship had been torpedoed outside the Narrows.

Silence passed over the room as everyone looked out in wonder. There was only a trumpet solo on the jukebox, then a faint rumble like thunder. All at once, people started talking again, questioning, guessing, laughing nervously.

Blair turned back to Anna's father. "Uh, some of your work?"
No answer.

Blair realized he no longer smelled sen-sen. He cautiously reached into the darkness and—felt the ribs of an empty chair.

"A light, my love?"

A woman's voice on his left! Anna's?

Blair fumbled with his matches and finally struck one. Anna's face flared up beside him, black-lashed blue eyes and white skin. She was comfortingly beautiful.

"Thank God," he said. "You startled me."

She smiled as she steered his hand over and lit her cigarette on his match. "Thank you." She blew the match out, but her small hand held on to his in the dark. "Did you have a good talk with Papa?"

"Very much. I wish we could've spoken longer. But he never gave me an assignment."

"There'll be plenty of time for that. I hope."

"Oh, yes. I think the three of us will get along beautifully."

Anna's hand clutched tighter. Each time she drew on her cigarette, a soft red face glowed beside him. Without the colors of her makeup, Blair could see the young girl she really was. She never smoked in front of her father, she said. She was still her father's girl, which pleased Blair. The war had loosened the morals of so many women, but not Anna's. He occasionally thought. about sleeping with her and was relieved to know she could never sink to that.

She was unlike any woman he had ever met, neither a giggly tease nor an obsequious tramp, and Blair thought he was in love with her. Or maybe it was the cause and world behind her that he loved. When she first told him what she was, he feared she was making fun of him, or that she was another screwball trying to make herself interesting. But she was real, it was real. After being alone with his wisdom for so long the wisdom had turned sour, Blair found Anna, who brought love and political action into his life, in a single glorious explosion. He already thought about marrying her, only he did not know enough about her background.

"Let's get away from here," he said. "Catch a cab back to Manhattan. Go someplace where I can be myself again." He missed the shell of composure the right kind of nightclub gave him.

"Can we wait a little first? We shouldn't leave too soon after Papa."

"Of course."

There was a new thudding out over the ocean, deep and steady.

Destroyers hunted for a U-boat, their depth charges detonating below the horizon.

Anna sighed and squeezed his hand again. "Poor guys," she said. "All of them."

Blair admired her pity and decided he felt pity too. It was as sad as it was shameful that men who should be fighting side by side were killing each other. If it took defeat to shake his country awake, Blair was willing to do all he could to bring about that defeat. But one did not have to be vicious.

They held hands in the dark and listened to explosions deep beneath the ocean. It was wonderful. They had each other and the great task before them.

5

"NEW GUINEA," said the voice, and there was a gray hillside, a palm tree like a great burnt match and the blackened bodies of midgets in a ditch. "Fried Jap," the voice called them. An American with sooty face, white eyes and teeth grinned at the camera. "All in a day's work for this happy GI."

Hank wanted to meet the GI, have a beer with him, kill Japs with him and feel like brothers. Hank felt funny having the GI out there while he sat safe and cool in the Lyric Theater, sock feet propped on the balcony railing. His half-empty seabag filled the seat beside him. This might be his last trip to the movies for weeks, but Hank fidgeted with the impatience and embarrassment that always came over him during the newsreel. Funny. On the *McCoy* all he ever thought about was getting into port and getting laid. Now that he was getting laid regularly, and starting a duty where he would do nothing but get laid, all he thought about was getting back to the tin can. He was homesick for familiar faces, crowded quarters and a routine so solid you felt free to grouse about it, like a family, without that grousing leading to distrust or doubt. Hank disliked doubt; it was too much like thinking. And it seemed unclean right now, what with the war and all.

Even one of the cartoons today included the war: a frantic black

duck with a Hitler moustache. There was nothing about the war in
the feature, but it was about a suffering woman, a secret marriage
to a man who soon dies, a baby put up for adoption, and Hank
quickly lost interest. Down below and up here in the balcony, the
usual men began to move around.

Hank had been coming here regularly since his release from the
brig a month ago, while he lived at the Y and waited for the Navy
to make up its mind. Hurry up and wait, as they said, and it was
already June. Coming to this theater was what had gotten him into
trouble in the first place, but Hank liked to stick to places he knew.
He needed at least one familiar landmark in his life now that everything else was confusion. And he was lonely, a little nervous—about
what, he wasn't sure— and bored. Sex was a fine way of forgetting
yourself for an hour or so. He was more watchful now, more careful
where he went and with whom. This city wasn't as free and easy
as he had thought that first day, but a little caution was all Hank
needed to have a good time. There had been a couple of guys who
were so much fun naked that Hank saw them more than once before
they left town or simply disappeared. The city was a giant railroad
depot that people passed through on their way to the war. Only
Hank remained behind.

A young man suddenly sat in the aisle seat beside him. The young
man squirmed, tapped his fingers on his knees, then promptly got
up again. Hank turned to watch the slender silhouette climb the
aisle toward the smokey projector beam that fanned overhead.
There wasn't enough time before he met Commander Mason. Hank
had come here today only because he had nowhere else to go after
checking out of the Y. And maybe as a way of saying goodbye to
the place. When he couldn't follow the young man, Hank suddenly
resented what the Navy was doing with him, but only for a moment.

They had chosen Hank and nobody else for their special assignment. He wanted to be proud of that, but it still felt peculiar. What
he did with whom had always been as private as what he dreamed
when he was asleep—and usually as impossible to keep track of. But
people were suddenly treating his sex life as something that made
Hank odd and useful. He wasn't accustomed to so much attention,
especially from people who had no intention of going to bed with

him. Over the past month, Mason had met twice with Hank, privately. They met in the bar at the Hotel Astor, which was around the corner and seemed to have its share of men like Hank. The first time, Hank couldn't help wondering if the commander, who came dressed in civvies, wanted to get laid himself. But no, the officer was all cold curiosity beneath his oily smiles, as impersonal as a Navy doctor sticking his finger up your ass. He met Hank in secret because agents might be watching the building and would notice the comings and goings of someone as distinctive as Hank, or so he said. Hank preferred to believe him. He disliked Mason, disliked his way of repeating over and over what was expected of Hank, as if Hank were too stupid to remember.

But none of that should matter. There was a war on and Hank wanted to help them catch their spies as quickly as possible, so he could get back to the *McCoy*. His only real crime, Hank thought, was slugging that Shore Patrol—this sex business was only a sideline, an accident. Working at this house should square away his trouble with the Shore Patrol. That should be more important to him now than any uneasiness over the Navy's interest in his sex life. And the war took all kinds of unimportant, personal things and made them important. Kitchen fats, old tin cans, newspapers—why not sex?

The movie was not quite over when Hank put his shoes back on and left. There were the usual pairs of men talking in the balcony lobby. Goodbye, thought Hank, and wondered what it was going to be like going to bed with guys he might not like. Downstairs, he passed a buxom young woman chatting with the brass-buttoned usher who took tickets. Hank had seen her before, usually in the lobby, although she didn't seem to work here. She looked ladylike enough, despite her thick mascara and lipstick, but Hank wondered if she was one of those girls who preyed on sailors. Well, he was going to prey on sailors himself, wasn't he? She glanced up as he went out the door, stared for an instant, then quickly averted her eyes, as if ashamed.

It was already night. Half the little lights beneath the marquee were out and the streetlights were dimmed, but there was still enough illumination along the sidewalks for Forty-second Street to look like a state fair. Hank had forgotten how warm it was outside. Civilians in their shirtsleeves jostled with packs of servicemen.

Doors and windows were wide open. A bouncy song on the radio faded in, then out as Hank walked past a smoke shop. Bells fired away inside a penny arcade where kids in white T-shirts crowded with servicemen around the pinball machines. There was the smell of french fries, then chop suey, then, when Hank passed a group of women filing their nails outside a bar, perfume. A checkered man in a doorway tried to shout Hank into his store to sell him a suit. "Easy credit! Wide lapels! The babes will hoot when they see your zoot!" Seabag on his shoulder, Hank only shook his head and headed toward the Hotel Astor. He had learned you didn't have to stop and explain to these people why you weren't buying.

Broadway was just as crowded but not nearly as bright. The Astor bar was off-limits to servicemen unless they were accompanied by an officer or civilian. Hank was in his whites, so he stood outside and waited for Commander Mason. Two or three stories above the street, Times Square faded into darkness. The enormous signs that had been a blaze of light a month ago, before the brownout, now loomed black and sinister above the shuttling streetcars and taxis. The Planter's Peanut sign was just a few black lines against the night sky. So much darkness made Hank think of home. You could even make out a few stars overhead.

People stopped along the curb to read the news bulletins that flickered across the electric sign around the *Times* Building. Nothing new: Germans in Russia, Germans in T O B R U K, whatever that was, Japs on islands whose names sounded just as made-up. Hank leaned against the hotel, reading what he could. He didn't see Commander Mason anywhere. Then a short civilian with a big head and thinning hair stopped in front of him and frowned.

"Fayette," the man finally said.

Hank dropped his bag and saluted. "Sorry, sir. I was expecting Commander Mason, sir." But he didn't recognize this man.

The man didn't return his salute. "Do not salute me. I am not an officer. And don't call me 'sir.'" He wore a shiny black raincoat, even though it didn't look like rain. Light flashed on a pair of eyeglasses when he glanced left and right. "Commander Mason cannot be seen going to this place. So he sent me to take you there."

Hank recognized him. It was the enlisted man who had been in Mason's office that day. Mason's secretary or assistant, or whatever the Navy might call him. Hank was relieved. He felt more comfort-able with other enlisted men. "Yeah? Okey-dokey. I guess you're gonna be the one who visits me at this house?" Mason had mentioned someone coming to see Hank.

"Yes," the man said curtly. "Are you ready? Let's get done with this." He stepped away and raised one arm to hail a cab.

The man sounded angry about something, and foreign. Not quite foreign-foreign, but Yankee-foreign, educated-foreign. He was as wooden as a new ensign. He didn't look at Hank when they got into a taxi, and didn't speak to him as they drove away from Times Square. All the windows were rolled down and the cool night air eddied in the back of the cab. The roof was so high Hank's cap didn't scrub the ceiling.

"Oh, I'm Hank. Since we're going to be working together," Hank told the man.

The man placed a finger to his lips and nodded at the driver's cropped neck.

But Hank saw no need for silence and, anyway, this guy was no officer. "So what should I call you, mister? I got to call you something."

The man sighed irritably. "Oh. Jones."

Hank began to giggle. The man was so solemn it was funny. "But they're *all* called Jones! I'll get you mixed up with all the others."

The man glanced at Hank, then faced forward again. He sat straighter than ever. "Erich, then." It must have been his real name, because he hurriedly added, "Or whatever you like, it's of no importance."

Hank got the feeling that the man was afraid of him. If it was because Hank liked men, the man had nothing to worry about there. Erich's face was soft like a boy's, but he looked kind of doughy. And Hank never wasted his time on guys who weren't openly interested; it was too much work. Still, feeling the man's fear made Hank more comfortable with Erich, amused and almost protective towards him. Nervousness was warmer than Mason's cool, insulting cheerfulness.

The taxi turned down a narrow side street where the streetlights were out and the only light came from tenement windows and doors and the taxi's headlights. People sat on stoops and hung out windows, all of them turning their heads to see a taxicab go down their street. After another block, there were no people, only lettered warehouse walls and shed roofs like long porches. The taxi bounced and flew out of the street into an open space as dark and dead as Hades. Erich told the driver to stop.

"Middle of nowhere," said the driver, but he pulled to a halt and flicked on the light. Everything outside the cab went black. "Mind if I ask what ya fellas are lookin' for?"

"Yes, I do mind," said Erich. "How much do we owe you?"

The driver told him, then wearily added, "Nope, none of my beeswax, bub. Just thought this place might be handy to know if I got more fellas who asked where they could go with their boy-friends."

Dimes and nickels fell from Erich's hand. He rapidly swept them off the floor, then jingled them into the driver's palm and stepped out, blushing.

Hank stepped out, pulling his seabag after him and smiling over Erich's embarrassment. You might have thought they were going to have a party and this was the guy's first time.

The taxi's taillights swung out and away, floated in the darkness and vanished.

Hank and Erich stood beside the hulk of a flatbed truck and a horse-drawn wagon without a horse. The first light Hank saw was a single bulb burning over a loading dock in the distance. The pattern of cobblestones toward the dock gleamed like fishscales.

"Don't be alarmed," said Erich nervously. "The house is over here." He took a step toward the far side of the square, and tripped. The man had no night vision.

Hank followed, hearing their footsteps and the whistle of Erich's raincoat. There was starlight, once Hank's eyes had time to adjust. Except for the hard, lopsided pavement, Hank felt as if he was walking the back streets of Beaumont again. He could smell the river, then—chickens? He inhaled a feathered, limey stink of chick-ens. "Hey. I think I've been here before."

"Yes." Erich sounded ashamed. "You have."

Hank stopped and looked at the horizon of roofs against the stars, turned and saw a high, black warehouse that was big enough for the

Coca Cola sign he had seen when there was light. "Yeah, we came from a different direction, so I didn't—" He suddenly turned on Erich. *"Jesus peezus!* It's gonna be the place where I got arrested!"

Erich stood ten feet away. His raincoat rustled. "They could not tell you before, in case plans were changed. They could not have you coming here before it was time." Erich coughed into his hand. "I don't see why any of this should matter to you. A brothel is a brothel."

"Yeah? No. I guess." It shouldn't matter, but the secrecy of it bothered Hank. He was to work for them, find them secrets, and they kept secrets from him? Hank didn't know what to make of that.

They were walking again and a bundle of narrow houses climbed up against the starry sky in front of them. Hank recognized the house, although all three stories of windows were blacked out, as if the place had been abandoned since his arrest. As they stepped to the right, a red light appeared just inside the doorway, glowing on a closed door and two signs: "Rooms To Let" and "No Vacancies." There was a faint hum of machinery coming over the roofs, from the direction of the river.

"Please wait here," said Erich. "Or you might walk once around the block. We shouldn't be seen arriving together."

"How come? Is there something else I'm not supposed to know about?"

Erich looked up at Hank, narrowed his eyes at Hank, startled by his question. "Uh, what makes you think that, Hank?" It was the first time he'd spoken his name, and he said it as if he was talking to a child.

"Nobody ever told me it was gonna be *this* place. A fella can't help wondering what else you're not telling him."

"Oh? Of course," said Erich. "If it had been up to me, I would have told you. But you know the brass. Who can understand why they do half of what they do?" He glanced at the house, then behind them, then continued to glance around while he spoke. "We cannot discuss this here, Hank. But they have their reasons. And they're looking after your well-being, as well as the well-being of their—*our* country. I know no more than you do. But we owe it to our country to trust them."

Hank had expected a simple, straightforward answer. He couldn't understand why Erich had dragged their country into this. Of course he trusted his country.

"If it will put you at ease, we can enter together. Is that satisfactory?"

"I guess," said Hank, although that wasn't exactly what bothered him.

Erich drew a deep breath and went up the stairs to the door. He looked as if he was still blushing. It was only the red light on his smooth face, but Hank wondered if that was what suddenly made everything seem secret and fishy: Erich's nervousness at being mistaken for one of "them." Erich's small hand reached out from his raincoat and rang the bell.

High heels clicked up to the door. The window behind the brass grill opened.

"Mrs. Bosch? We are the friends of Mr. Mason?" said Erich.

"Mr. Mason? I am not knowning any Mr. Mason," said the voice behind the grill.

Erich cleared his throat. "Mason, Mason?" he repeated. He went up on his toes and furiously whispered at the grill, "*Commander* Mason?"

"Oh, *Commander* Mason," the voice loudly sang. "Of course. Come eeen, come eeen." And the door was opened by the long, ugly woman Hank remembered from his first visit. She wore a fancy silk party dress tonight, and had a gardenia in her hair. "Why didn't you say you were from the commander?"

"Because we don't want the whole world knowing." Erich peered into the hallway before he stepped inside. He angrily waved Hank in and pulled the door shut. He stood there for a moment and listened. There was music upstairs.

Hank recognized the hallway, although he didn't remember the new brass lamp that sat on a table against the wall, or the framed prints of dogs playing poker. He suddenly remembered sex, and the black-haired soldier who had danced the samba. Hank wondered if the soldier would find his way back here, too. That would be nice.

"You are the one?" the woman said to Hank.

"Uh, yes'm."

"Ah! You are a nice big one."

"You don't remember him?" said Erich. "From the night you were raided?"

She squinted at Hank and looked him up and down, frowning with her big, painted mouth. She shrugged. "All these sayloors look alike to me. But you were here?" she asked Hank. "You poor boy. What a scare they give us. But that will never happen again. Will it, Officer?"

"I am your bookkeeper," hissed Erich. "Mr. Zeitlin? Anyway, I'm not an officer."

"Whatever. We will be as safe as we are in church."

"Where is everybody?" Hank asked. He noticed no noise coming from behind the closed door to what he remembered was the parlor.

"Oh, things have changed since your visit," the woman announced proudly. "I have expanded my business. It is all upstairs now, both floors. I use this floor for my offices and home. So people who drop by will not be seeing too much. Here, come into my offices and we will do what needs to be done."

She opened the parlor door and bowed them inside. It wasn't a parlor anymore. A green-shaded lamp cast its light on an opened rolltop desk, a green blotter, and an abacus. And a fat, moonfaced man in a white suit.

Erich froze and the woman had to push her way around him.

"Carlo!" she snapped at the fat man. "I told you to get out. I have no time for you now. I have business with my . . . bookkeeper."

"But *cara*. Please." The man was hoisting himself out of the chair beside the desk. "Two hundred dollars. If I don't pay them tonight, they say they'll break my legs."

"Your gambling debts are no concern of mine."

"You can't loan me a little two hundred dollars? After all I've done for you?"

"You think I am made of money?"

"Valeska. Angel-blossom." He stepped up to her, stroked her shoulders and kissed her neck. "For old time's sake?"

The woman remained as hard as an axe, her thick red mouth pursed.

"Mrs. Bosch," said Erich, "can't this wait until we finish going over your accounts?"

"I will be with you shortly," she told him and let Carlo kiss and stroke her a moment more. "Very well," she told Carlo. "I will loan you money."

"Oh, thank you, dearest, sweetest, kindest . . ." He kissed the hand and arm she held out to him while she turned her back to the others and fished out keys from somewhere on her person. He released her only when she went to the desk and unlocked a little door there.

"But two hundred is much too dear for me," she said, pulling out a cash box and unlocking it. "I give you one hundred."

"But, Valeska! I need *two*. If they don't get the full amount, they'll make me a cripple!"

"Nonsense." She licked her fingers and counted out bills. "This will make them happy. What can they do?" She began to laugh. "Break just *one* of your legs?"

"It's not funny, Val. You don't know these people."

"Then you are not wanting my little hundred?"

He grabbed her hand before she could return the money to the box. "I didn't say that. I am grateful for this much. I am *so* grateful." He kissed the hand that held the money until she let him take the bills. "I don't know how I'll ever repay you, my dearest rosebud."

"You'll repay me as you always do. At fifty percent. Now run along to your gambler friends. I have business with my bookkeeper."

"Of course, my lamb. Certainly." He bowed and backed away from her—and bumped into Hank. "I beg your pardon. I . . . Valeska? Should I take this young man upstairs before I go? Introduce him to the others?"

"No, Carlo. Run along. I will take care of him."

Carlo nodded and left, delicately closing the door. They heard the front door immediately open and slam behind him.

"I thought," said Erich through his teeth, "that nobody else would know about this."

"That Carlo," Mrs. Bosch sighed. "Not to worry about him. He doesn't suspect a thing. He only hangs about and finds me customers sometimes. I help him out only because he was my second husband." She locked her cashbox, returned it to its slot in the desk, then locked the little door. "Poor Carlo. I hope they don't hurt him too much."

Erich righteously cleared his throat. "Do you have any questions, Mrs. Bosch? If not, I'll be on my way."

"Not so fast. There are things I have to clear up, before I accept this bill of goods." She faced Hank. "So. You are a cocksucker?"

Hank lightly nodded. It had been strange enough with Mason, who had fancy words for it, but to hear the real words from a woman? He had felt funny around her the first time, and was just as uncomfortable with her now.

"You're forgetting he was here before," said Erich. "He might not look like a homosexual, but you shouldn't be fooled by his appearance."

"You do not have to tell me that. They come in all shapes and sizes." She poked Hank's arms and stomach. "Hmmm. He is beefy. Turn, please. Yes. Very All American."

"Are you going to check his teeth, too?"

"His teeth? His teeth are not my concern." But she pinched the corners of his mouth to take a quick look.

Hank glanced at Erich. Erich had made a joke, which was a surprise, and the joke suggested Erich was on Hank's side after all. But when Hank looked at him, Erich still avoided his eyes. Erich looked straight at Mrs. Bosch, although it was obvious he didn't like her at all.

"And you *are* a cocksucker? This is not something they are ordering you to do? Because it must be sincere. It is not something a man can fake, when push comes to shove. And do the customers *complain?*" she sang. "You have fucked with many men?"

"Yes ma'm."

"Are you clean?"

"Madam!" said Erich. "This is unnecessary. Do you think they would choose a man who was infected, or who wasn't a deviate?"

Mrs. Bosch shrugged. "What does the Navy know from whorehouses? Have you ever had the clap, young man?"

"Once," Hank admitted. "But they fixed me up with something and I'm fine now."

"Show me." She gestured at his crotch.

"Please," said Erich. "Can't this wait until after I leave?"

"No. Because if your man is diseased, I'm sending him back with you. One man, and my house will be clapped out of business in a month. Come on, mister. Open up."

Hank was grimacing but he began to unbutton his fly. He shifted around so his back was to Erich. He didn't want this to be any more embarrassing for the two of them than it already was.

"What a nice one. Does that hurt?" She squeezed. "Now pull the skin back. Hmmm. Looks plenty healthy. You can put him away."

"Satisfied?" said Erich.

"For now." She looked for a place to wipe her hand and rubbed it against Hank's blouse. "But we will have to see him at work before we can be certain."

"What are you suggesting? That you bring one of your boys in here and have them perform for you?"

Mrs. Bosch laughed. "What an idea, Mr. Zeitlin. Oh, no. All I need is a week or two to see how he gets on with my customers. If he doesn't, I can send him back, right?"

"Yes. Only he'll do fine here. Won't you, Fayette?"

"I'll do my damnedest," said Hank, and tried to get the man to look into his eyes, without success.

Erich quickly went over the instructions again, for Mrs. Bosch's benefit as well as Hank's. With customers, Hank was to say he was still in the Navy. With the others who worked at the house, he was to say he had been kicked out. Nobody, absolutely nobody, was to know his real purpose in being there. Erich would visit the house every Monday afternoon, but Hank was to telephone a special number if anything important came up between meetings—meaning encounters with suspected German agents, which could not be mentioned in front of Mrs. Bosch. Erich asked if Hank had any last questions, took another promise of secrecy from Mrs. Bosch and said he was going.

"Aren't you forgetting something, Erich?" asked Hank.

"What?"

"Aren't you going to wish me luck?"

The request startled Erich. He stared into Hank's eyes, hard, as if he was trying to see through his eyes to his thoughts. "Of course," he mumbled and held out his hand. His gaze slid from Hank's, but the grip of his small hand was tight, desperate, like the grip of a civilian who thought that, just because you were in the service, you were going to die and he had to say goodbye to you in the name of the whole world.

"Goodbye," said Erich and hurried out of the room. The front door was slammed very hard.

Such nerves and shyness and coolness, ending in a painful goodbye when they'd be seeing each other in less than a week? Hank could come up with only one explanation: the boyish little man was falling in love with him. Which was a bother, but kind of touching, too. It was a relief to realize all the man's strangeness was caused by something so simple. It would pass.

"Now, we talk. Just you and me," said Mrs. Bosch. She stood in front of Hank, clasped her hands together and told Hank he was to call her "Valeska" and look upon her as a big sister. "We are all a family here." She explained that seventy-five percent of anything paid Hank was to be given to her. In exchange, she would provide him with bed and board. He was to be her "special boy," the only one who actually lived in the house, and she trusted he would provide services that would justify his special standing. All her other boys lived outside, dropped in on their own or were sent for when business was heavy. Boys being boys, they had only so many performances in them per night. "Sometimes I wish I am dealing in girls instead. All a girl has to do is lie there, no matter how tired she is. But that line is all full up. And those girls can be so catty. I luf my 'gay' boys."

She told him the house rules, duty hours, times for meals—he was to eat in the kitchen with her houseboy. He would have his own room, which he was to keep clean. "My houseboy can't do everything, what with cooking and laundry. I get him now and he will take you to your room. Afterwards, I will introduce you to my boys." She pressed a button on the wall and an electric bell rang in the hall. "One more thing. What you do for Uncle Sam is no concern of mine. My lips are sealed. But while you are living here, I am boss. Understood?"

"Yes, ma'm."

She nodded, then abruptly pitched forward, threw her arms around Hank and whispered, "You will never tell them anything that might hurt our poor Valeska?"

Her embrace was all bone and sinew. Hank stood there, stunned, looking into the wiry hair and white gardenia just inside his focus. "No'm," he said.

"You want something, Miz Bosch?"

The woman released Hank and they both turned. The door had been opened by a colored boy with straight, shiny hair. It looked like the boy from the night of the raid.

"We have a new member. This is . . . What is your name?"

Hank told her, while he watched the boy, pleased to find a familiar face here, even a black one.

"Hank will be living here. I want you to take him up to Leo's old room, show him where everything is and bring him to the sitting room."

Juke sneered and nodded. "This way, honey. And take your own bag, I ain't no—" He had seen only a white uniform. Now he saw Hank's face. "Blondie? You?"

"You were here the night we all got arrested," said Hank.

"Uh huh. Wahl hush mah mouth," said Juke, mocking Hank's accent. "What're you doing back at this toilet?"

"You know my houseboy?" asked Valeska.

"Well, kinda." Hank didn't know why he should be pleased to see the boy again. He had only gotten Hank deeper into grief that night, when Hank slugged the Shore Patrol. But he was a face from the past, which was something.

"Then I am not needing to tell you not to be taking any lip from him. If he gives you trouble, you tell me. He works here only because I am protecting him from reform school and the police."

"And 'cause I'm cheap," Juke muttered.

Valeska pretended not to hear. "Go. I will come up shortly."

Hank lifted his seabag and followed the boy out into the hall. It was funny, using a colored to make yourself feel at home when life turns strange on you. But Hank knew he had to be careful. Seeing a casual acquaintance again, in the right circumstances, could turn you into old friends, which Hank couldn't afford right now. It was a good thing the boy was colored.

"So you found me again, Blondie. You must have hunted high and low, but you finally sniffed me out. You can't guess what it means to a girl to be loved like that."

"Shit. I forgot you even existed." Hank wondered if this would complicate things. Nobody was supposed to know who he was, or who he had been.

"Doll face. You still can't tell when somebody's pulling your leg? Not to be confused with pulling something else. Up the stairs here. Just follow my twitchy behind."

Hank followed Juke, ducking where the ceiling lowered. "How come you're still here? Getting arrested didn't cure you of whorehouses, boy?"

"Me and fancy houses suit each other fine. You're one to talk, Blondie. The Navy know you've turned professional?"

"No. I . . ." But Hank realized he could use the fact that Juke had been here that night. "They kicked me out. After the raid. I'm wearing these because they're the only clothes I have to my name." Juke would gossip; word would get around. Lying didn't come naturally to Hank, but he would have to learn to lie here, just as he had to learn how to be alone and not trust anyone.

"Save those whites, baby. Johns go ape over sailors. But they gave you your walking papers? My, my. We queens are safe nowhere, are we, honey?"

They passed the music Hank had heard downstairs, coming from behind a closed door on the second floor. They started up another flight of stairs.

"So what happened to you after the raid?" said Hank. He had never talked so much to a colored, but he needed to talk to someone and better a colored than someone you might take seriously.

"They put my sweet ass on ice. Jail. For a month. Nothing they could charge me with but public nuisance. That's their word for queen. Then they give me to a parole officer and he gives me back to the Witch-woman. For a fee. Mrs. Simon LeGreedy. So she's got that to hold over me, but there's ways of tricking around her. She's twice as smart as the bimbos here think she is, but only half as smart as she thinks she is. You make friends with old Juke here and he can make it worth your while." They were on the third floor now, in a hallway where the wallpaper was faded and peeling. Juke reached inside an open door and turned on a light. "Here we are, Blondie. The honeymoon suite."

The room wasn't much. A hospital bed and a deal cupboard, a bare lightbulb hanging on a cord, a chipped bedpan on the painted floor. There was a curled picture of Tarzan, clipped from a magazine and tacked to the wall. A canvas shade was pulled over the window.

"You're lucky you're in the back. Windows up front are painted over for the blackouts and farmers start pulling up at five every morning to set up their market out front. Hard for a girl to get much beauty sleep before noon. But all that racket should make you feel right at home, farmboy."

Hank tossed his seabag in the corner and opened the top drawer of the cupboard. The bottom was lined with old newspaper—a black and yellow debutante ate cake—and was empty except for the blade of a safety razor and a racing form.

"Leo, the guy whose room this was," said Juke, "was caught trying to break into the Witch-woman's money box. He got arrested for dodging the draft a week later. The Witch-woman's got friends in high places somewhere. I don't know who, but some big deal's got his finger in this pie."

"Uh huh." Hank didn't look at Juke, afraid the answer showed in his eyes. He wished the boy would leave him in peace, so he could have time to tuck away his thoughts before he faced the others.

But Juke continued to stand in the doorway, arms crossed over his chest, hands on his shoulders. "Hey, Blondie," he suddenly said. "Don't think I forgot you decked that Shore Patrol for me. Didn't do me much good. But don't think I forgot."

Hank looked up. The boy sounded sincere. "Nothing to remember. I would've done it for anyone."

"Yeah? Yeah, I think you would've. Anyway, I remember."

They looked at one another, neither of them wanting to say aloud that one might have cause to be grateful to the other.

Then Juke undid himself from his arms and put one hand on his hip. "So shake your ass, honey. We haven't got all night. The Witch-woman wants you in her sitting room, pronto. Save your douche for later."

Hank couldn't help smiling. This boy was so funny, so strange.

His girlishness made him seem perfectly harmless. It might be good having him here for company. The boy seemed faithful enough, even trustworthy. It would be good for Hank's soul having him around. Like having a dog.

6

ALPHEUS COOPER, known downtown as Juke, took Hank downstairs, trying to think of ways he could use this cracker. It would be handy having someone so large and dim as your friend around here. Juke had tried it with others, but they all thought they were too slick to take favors from a crazy little nigger, much less return them. This homeboy was anything but slick. He was in obvious need of good management and Juke was the one to give it to him. Juke might feel stupidly fond of the guy, or maybe it was only pity for someone so ignorant they might risk their neck for yours. But Juke knew how to keep feelings like pity or affection under control. At seventeen, he'd learned the hard way that a smart queen's one concern in this world was looking after her own ass.

He went down the stairs, which creaked under the weight of the sailor thudding behind him. "Don't let these girls fool you with their airs, Blondie. Nothing but dicks and smiles and the brains of chickens." Of course, he thought Hank was nothing but a dick and a smile. How else could anybody think there was easy money in peddling your ass? But every boy thinks he's the one exception to the stupidity around him. It didn't hurt to play up to this hillbilly's pride, so long as Juke didn't make a fool of himself.

He opened the door to the sitting room. One of those lousy songs that was all voices and no orchestra played in the new phonograph cabinet Mrs. Bosch had bought as bait.

"Oh, boy? There you are. Yes," said the cockney steward sitting in an armchair with Bunny in his lap. Bunny was pale and fish-eyed, smiling dreamily. The beet-faced steward held up an empty, suds-laced glass. "Me and my pal here need more of that horse piss you people call beer."

"Yes, suh. Right away, suh." But Juke only ushered Hank inside and closed the door. The cracker was looking over the room as if he'd never seen furniture before.

It was early and the steward was the only customer. The half dozen others, sitting on the long, black camelback sofa beneath the black window shade or on the love seat or around the card table, were whores. The music was turned up loud enough for a party, but it didn't look like a party here. Everybody was waiting for something. The guys playing acey-deucy at the table looked up when Juke brought Hank in, then went back to their cards when they saw it was only more competition. The steward went back to trying to coax a response out of the unresponsive Bunny. Things never picked up until more money came into the room.

"Bigger than when it was downstairs," said Hank.

"Uptown, we do up a place like this with *style*," Juke scoffed. "Fancy drapes and colored lights. That overhead light makes everybody look like they're at the morgue. But Mrs. Bosch's too cheap for any of that. She could get herself a classier line of whore, too," Juke whispered. "Instead of trash."

A sharper man would wonder if Juke were calling *him* trash, but the cracker only nodded and looked at Mick and Smitty on the sofa, thumbing through Mick's copy of *Strength and Health* magazine. Mick was older than the others and worked out at a gymnasium. Smitty worshipped him, which was a laugh. Everyone was taken by Mick the first time they saw him, or at least by the biceps stretching his rolledup sleeves. It hurt Juke to find his cracker eyeing him.

"Watch out for Mick," Juke whispered. "The muscles? He's cuckoo in the head."

"Uh huh," went Hank. "Do you remember that soldier from the night we got arrested? A wop? Or spick, maybe."

"Soldiers are soldiers, honey. I see so many."

"This one danced with you. He seemed to know you pretty good. You two did one of those Mexican dances."

"Oh him. I kinda remember. Why?" Juke didn't remember, but he wanted to hear what the cracker was driving at.

"Does he still come around?"

Juke laughed. "Baby! This place is Grand Central Station. You almost never see the same dick twice!" What a Willy Cornbread this boy was. And romantic? He had come to a whorehouse pining after an old trick. "You poor dear. Whoever he was, he's out getting his cookies off in Japland or somewhere. Take it from me—you *can't* fall in love with trade."

Hank dug in his ear, then shook his head and laughed. He was so slow he had to *decide* if something was funny. "Get out of here. I was just asking. Anyway, I don't fall in love with guys."

"You're one of those?" cried Juke in mock horror. "You just do it for the green?"

"Well, no. I do it cause it's fun. If that's what you mean."

"Well, thank God." Juke pressed one hand to his chest. "Then you *are* queer. I was afraid you were one of those poor dears going against nature just to make a dollar. Times are rough, and a man's got to do what a man's got to do. Even if it means a little cocksucking."

The cardplayers glanced over, looking uncomfortable.

"It's a good time," said Hank. "That's all."

Juke felt he was wasting his spiel on the cracker. The boy had no irony, but he didn't take offense, either. "Then count yourself one lucky girl, Blondie. Because everybody else here thinks it's work." The cracker didn't even nettle at being called a girl. But Juke felt the others in the room listening. He could always play to them. "Nasty and unmanly. Nothing but real men here. Real men who have to make money. That's what I admire about white people. Their discipline. No colored man could go down on a dick unless he really enjoyed doing it. Shiftless. But these tough white boys?" Juke swept his hand at the room. "They just close their eyes and suck. Give them some jack and they'll swallow their pride. Swallow just about anything."

"Hey, coon!" shouted one of the cardplayers. "Put a sock in it!"

"Ignore him," said Smitty. "Just nelly crap from a nelly nigger. We got to put up with it all the time."

The angry cardplayer was a sailor who had never been here until last night. He seemed tough. Juke had to see how deep that toughness went. "Put a sock in it? *You* put a cock in it. Darling."

The sailor hunched over the table and clutched his cards. "Somebody ought to knock that fairy on his ugly black ass."

"Fairy, huh? Fairy!" Juke struck an indignant pose, perching the back of one hand on a tilted hip. "I may be more ki-ki than some of you trade. But today's trade is tomorrow's queen. And I know for a fact that that big old stevedore you took upstairs last night settles for nothing less than the deep, brown eye."

The sailor jumped up, cards flying. He grabbed Juke by the front of his shirt and shouted, "Shut up, nigger, or I'm punching your headlights out!"

Juke was up on his toes, thinking of the new shirt he didn't want ripped. "Oh, but I love being touched by a real man."

"You think I'm kidding? You think you're funny?" The guy wasn't twenty yet. He had more pimples than hairs on his chin.

But before Juke could needle him about his skin, the cracker elbowed his way between them. "Come on. The kid didn't do anything to you."

"The hell he didn't. I didn't come here to be called fairy by no nigger."

"You just come here to *be* a fairy," said Juke.

The sailor's grip on Juke's shirt tightened and the big Southerner tried to elbow them apart.

"Back off, squid. This is between him and me."

"Yeah, swab," called out another cardplayer. "Let the shine get what he deserves. He's been asking for it."

Smitty chimed in with, "One good bop. Put that nigger back in his place."

The cracker glanced around him, surprised by everybody's reaction.

Juke wasn't surprised. They couldn't live with who they were. And he could. They hated him for that, and Juke basked in their hatred, like envy. It was worth it, even if it sometimes cost him a punch in the nose.

What did surprise Juke was the cracker. Majority rules, but the cracker didn't back down, even when he saw which way the wind blew here. He stood between them, his face all screwed up in disgust. Juke remembered another time this had happened, only then it was the cracker that wanted to slug him. Maybe the man was so itchy for a fight, to prove he was still a man, he didn't care whose side he was on. Maybe he was defending Juke only because he didn't know any better. It was exactly what Juke had hoped to get out of the man, but he didn't know what to make of it when it happened without him having to trick it into happening.

Juke took his feelings and made a joke of them: "My hero."

"Shut up," said Blondie, and he turned back to the sailor. "I said let the kid go. He's smaller than you." Even angry, the cracker still looked slow and stolid. "What kind of man are you he can't take a few names?"

"And what kind of man are you he wants to stand up for a coon? You think you're Mrs. Roosevelt or something? A nigger lover?"

The arm that blocked Juke suddenly knocked Juke back and swung forward. The cracker hit the sailor in the stomach. The sailor let out an abrupt, loud groan and doubled over.

"Oh, yes!" cried the steward. "Just like the movies. Go to it, boys!"

Others jumped up and hollered, eager to see the sailors fight it out.

But the slugged man remained bent over, arms clutched around his stomach.

And Hank just stood there, fists at his side, looking almost embarrassed. "I ain't no nigger lover," he said.

The door flew open and Mrs. Bosch charged in. "What is the hubbub? Juke! Are you making trouble?" She looked around, saw the doubled-over sailor and the guilty Hank, then settled her fury on Juke. "What are you doing up here? You loll about and we get nothing but trouble. Shoo! There are things in the kitchen that must be done."

Her hand shot out to cuff him on the head, but Juke knew how to duck Mrs. Bosch's blows. He gave her a put-upon sigh, to show he wasn't intimidated, then stepped toward the door. He watched Hank, wanting to see if he could tell by looking at him why he'd done what he'd done.

"Calm down, everybody. We are all family, remember. There is a war on and we must not fight with each other," Mrs. Bosch told the room.

Hank only glanced at Juke, angrily narrowing his eyes at him. Then he looked away, folded his arms across his chest and made a face at the floor.

"Everybody. Sit down and listen up. You—there is a problem with your tummy?" Mrs. Bosch asked the sailor.

Juke pulled the door closed, took a few steps down the stairs, stopped and listened.

"Boys," began the Witch-woman. "We have a new member to our establishment tonight. I know you will make him feel at home. His name is—"

"Hank," went the cracker's voice.

He was definitely a cracker, even if he had forgotten himself for a moment and stood up for a nigger. Juke was from Alabama and although he had run away to the North and Harlem when he was thirteen, he remembered how unpredictable poor whites were with coloreds: treat you like cousins one minute, like dirt the next. It was worse than with whites with money or Yankee whites, who never let you forget they thought you were dirt. Juke went down the stairs, telling himself he wasn't going to get mixed up with any cracker, especially one so ignorant he didn't know it was bad to be queer. That only made the cracker more unpredictable than ever.

Back in the kitchen, there was bread and meat to be sliced for the fools upstairs. Instead, Juke sat down at the oilcloth-covered table and flipped through an old issue of *Life,* his revenge on the Witch-woman for blaming everything on him. He was to blame, of course, and he was proud of that, but it didn't lessen his anger at Mrs. Bosch. If she was going to treat him like a no-account nigger, he was going to act like one. He turned the pages and looked at the pictures. It was the usual lies. There were no colored faces, of course, except for two bare-assed cannibals on a desert island where the Americans were building an airstrip. Everybody looked so clean and whole-some and apple-pie good. Seeing through the lies made Juke feel very smart. For some reason, he badly needed to feel smart again.

The doorbell rang. Juke stood up and sauntered out to the hall to answer it. He recognized the two men through the peephole, so he didn't have to clear them with Mrs. Bosch. The way he felt tonight, he could have let anybody in, plainclothesmen, G-men, whatever, although the Witch-woman really did seem to know someone im-portant in a high place.

The two men were dressed in tailored suits, although Juke had figured out long ago that they were Army officers of some sort. You'd think they could have any enlisted man they wanted, instead of having to come here for it.

"Hello, boy. Valeska's expecting us. What's tonight's selection look like?" One of the men handed Juke their hats and a dollar bill.

"Very good, suh. Just up the stairs, suh."

And they went up the stairs, as bland and normal as two prosperous businessmen in *Life*, to suck and fuck with white boys. They looked so damn smug. They thought their secret didn't show.

Juke saw nothing for them to be proud of. His nature announced itself in every wave of his hand and he liked it that way. He could at least be honest about that, even as he samboed the white money. Men of color were just as bad, strutting about like preachers, puffed up with the notion that their high-toned neighbors never dreamed they had so much in common with nelly queens and street trash. If Juke was going to watch people make fools of themselves, he preferred to do it downtown, where the fools were white. The condescension of "real men" felt less personal when it came mixed with white condescension. Juke had been kept for three months by a Harlem deacon when he first came north, and the man had treated him as no better than a slut, a piece of ass, a woman. The people downtown might not appreciate his conk or his "collegiate" clothes, but their indifference beat a colored man's possessive contempt any day. There were even customers who asked for Juke—Dutchmen and limeys, mostly—and there was one man who slipped Juke a fiver, just to sit in a chair on the other side of the room and watch while the man was cornholed by Mick or anyone else who didn't mind an audience. That was another reason why he preferred to work downtown: the spectacle of white people acting like donkeys. He wasn't here because he found white men attractive. He wasn't, he often told himself.

He was back in the kitchen, the magazine turned to a picture of Joel McCrea, when the doorbell rang again. When he came out to the hall, Mrs. Bosch was clomping down the stairs, like a horse.

"I am taking care of this, Juke. You take the beer and sandwiches up to the boys."

"Right away, Miz Bosch. *When* I make the sandwiches."

"*Juuuk!* What have you been doing all this time? You lazy. . . No, you take up the beer and glasses. *I* will do the sandwiches." She was exasperated, but the Witch-woman spoke more kindly to Juke when there were no witnesses.

Juke went back to the kitchen while Mrs. Bosch answered the door. He took several milk bottles full of her homemade beer from the icebox—the woman was too cheap to buy a good refrigerator—and poured them into the big glass pitcher. Even cold, it was cloudy, dreary stuff. Resentful once over a humiliation upstairs, Juke had added his piss to the pitcher, and nobody noticed a thing. He set the pitcher and badly assorted glasses on a tray and carried them out.

"Mr. Johnson sent you?" Mrs. Bosch was asking a rat-whiskered man in the hall. Two other men were already climbing the stairs. "But *which* Mr. Johnson? That's right, Juke. Upstairs, and tell them that the sandwiches are shortly coming."

"Yes'm." Juke went up the stairs, beer splashing out of the pitcher into the tray. One of the two newcomers stood shyly in the open door and Juke called out to his back, "Gangway, darling. Coming through." He steered around the man into the room.

"About frigging time!" shouted the steward. "I only asked an hour ago, you lazy black bastard." Bunny still sat in the steward's lap, his shirttail out and fly undone, blinking over something that had nothing to do with the steward.

Juke set the heavy tray on the table and looked around the room. The card game had broken up now that more customers had arrived. The sailor Juke had baited was now flirting belligerently with one of the disguised Army officers. But Juke didn't see Hank, his cracker, anywhere. Then he noticed that the other Army officer was gone.

Jealousy, like a hard bubble, swelled in his chest. And Juke instantly knew that despite all his care and sidestepping and smarts he had fallen in love with the cracker, and was going to pursue the man until he won him or broke a heart.

7

LOVE WAS ENTWINED with a good cause, and the cause looked stronger than ever. Rommel was smashing across North Africa. The Japs had been routed at Midway, but the Japanese only confused the issue. If Japan sued for peace, maybe Americans would see the situation in Europe more clearly. After all, it wasn't Hitler who bombed Pearl Harbor. The early summer evening was beautiful.

Blair Rice boarded the Fifth Avenue bus at Seventy-Second Street, went up to the upper level and took a seat toward the back, as he had been instructed. He wore a straw boater this evening, as instructed. He disliked the unfashionable hat—it made him feel like his father—but it was the last week of June and his family and their acquaintances had left New York for the summer, war or no war. The city was his. The bus floated Blair through the city, past the enormous, blue-shadowed chateau of the Plaza where he had danced with debutantes. Past the sun-bronzed Savoy where he met his mother for tea, Bergdorf's where his mother bought her prettiest clothes, Scribner's where his father bought books on Egyptology. This was Blair's city and today he felt more important than ever, full of love, charged with secrecy, entrusted with a mission. There was an opened pack of Luckies in his inside coat pocket. A piece of paper, rolled tight as a toothpick, had been slipped inside one of the cigarettes. What a cunning man Anna's father was. Blair would show he could be as cunning. Part of him felt he was only play-acting, but that was just the old observer in him, the Olympian intellectual, the connoisseur of action. Well, today he was not just appreciating an act, he was committing one.

Bands of gold, dusty sunlight crossed the avenue at each cross street. Except for a soldier and girl who cuddled at the front of the open deck, Blair floated alone above the shop windows and thin, dinner-hour traffic. His contact was to get on the bus somewhere in the Forties. It would be a woman. Anna hadn't told him who the woman was or how they knew her or what she would do with the information in the cigarette. He wasn't even told what the information was and only guessed it might be more cargo lists and shipping schedules, bits gathered by Anna in her conversations with sailors. Blair still disliked the easy way Anna had with other men, even if it were for a good cause. Blair loved the cause as much as he loved Anna, but it hurt his pride and propriety to see her so friendly with the *hoi polloi*.

He reached Forty-Second Street without anyone new climbing to the upper deck. The bus idled at a stoplight and Blair watched the river of hats in the crosswalk below. Footsteps clocked their way up the metal stairs just as the bus lunged forward. A woman stood at the top step and gripped the railing while she looked at the empty seats. Thirtyish, she wore a floral print dress and white gloves. It had to be her. She took the seat in front of Blair's.

Blair waited for her to turn around and ask about his hat. That was the password. Instead, she twisted sideways in her seat and pretended to watch the buildings glide past, while she took in Blair from the corner of her eye.

Blair stared at her, waiting for the woman to face him.

She slipped a hand into the wide neck of her dress and mopped her sticky back and shoulder. There was a gray handprint of sweat and dirt on her glove. Then she looked straight at Blair and smiled. "Was so hot in my apartment, had to get out. Get some air," she said. "Nice and cool up here." A few strands of hair blew loose from her bun.

"Yes," Blair announced. Why didn't she mention his hat? Had she forgotten? He adjusted the brim, to remind her. The waffled straw felt like a thick, stale cracker.

"Such awful weather we're having. Not the heat so much as the humidity. But you certainly look cool as a cucumber."

A subtle reference to his hat?

"We used to get out of the city in the summer, my husband and I. But now that Bill's off in the Army . . ." She sighed and gazed at Blair, patiently, as if expecting something from him.

It had to be her. Blair couldn't imagine any other woman talking to a complete stranger like this, except a floozie. This woman looked and sounded like a dull, proper housewife.

"When we first met, my husband had a hat just like that. You don't see many men wearing them anymore."

"May I offer you a cigarette?" Blair said.

"Don't mind if I do. Why, thank you."

Blair reached into his pocket, found the pack, then found the cigarette. He turned it over in his fingers, saw the faint pencil mark and passed the cigarette to the woman.

Her red nails brushed his fingers when she took it. But instead of dropping the cigarette into her purse, *she stuck it in her mouth.*

Was she only faking for the benefit of anyone watching? But there was nobody up here to see them.

She looked at him, waiting. Then she said, "That's okay," opened her purse, took out a lighter and flicked the lighter with her thumb.

Blair watched in horror as the tip of the cigarette caught fire. She wasn't the woman. He should snatch the cigarette from her lips before she smoked its secrets, but Blair was too stunned to move.

"Perfect," sighed the woman, smoke pouring from her mouth and vanishing in the airstream. "A little breeze, a cigarette and a handsome young stranger."

How could he have been so stupid? He wanted to get off immediately, but what if the cigarette didn't draw right or went out and the woman noticed paper ash inside? He had to sit there and watch while this harlot smoked it down to nothing.

"Something the matter? You don't look too good."

"The atmosphere," Blair mumbled.

"They have the right idea," said the woman, pointing the cigarette at the couple towards the front. "That's the only way to feel comfortable on hot, lonely evenings."

She had almost smoked the cigarette down to her red fingernails, when she suddenly flicked the butt into the air. The bus was wheeling around the Washington Square Arch, turning in the traffic circle in the center of the park. Blair leaped up and grabbed the railing by the steps.

"You're not going?" said the woman. "One more trip up the Avenue? Keep me company?"

Blair raced down the curved steps and jumped to the pavement as the bus slowed for the next stop. He didn't look back to see if the woman got off to follow him. He crossed the circle to the curb where the butt would have landed.

He snatched up one butt, then another, then a third, then saw that the stone gutter was sprinkled with cigarette butts, tattered cigar ends, waxy candy wrappers. Where the hell were the street sweepers? He leaned over to grab up a cluster of butts and the hat dropped neatly from his head. It landed upside-down on its flat crown. He grabbed up the hat with both hands. Then he crushed it together between his hands, tried pulling it apart, then crushed it again. He stood at the curb, mangling and cursing the hat, trying to rip it in two, while Jewish couples and solitary bohemians glanced at him and continued their evening strolls. Finally, he took the hat, broken but whole, flung it into the bottom of a trash barrel and stepped angrily up the street, cursing the city, the war, himself.

It took him forever to find a taxi. The war spoiled even that, and the driver who finally picked him up was an unshaven clod who had to be told where the Yale Club was. Blair was meeting Anna there. He rode uptown dreading her. She was going to think him an idiot, a fool.

Looking perfectly sweet with her white purse and white polka-dotted blue dress, Anna sat in a leather chair in the wainscotted bar of the club, smiling and sniffing at a sloe gin fizz. An army officer sat in the next chair, chatting with her. Blair winced when he recognized the officer as a classmate.

"Darling. Hello." Anna stood up and went up on her toes to kiss Blair on the cheek. "I was wondering what was keeping you. Luckily, I had Captain Jervis here to keep me company."

Blair nodded at the captain. "Evening, Jervis."

"If it isn't old Puffed Rice. This delightful lady is yours? I never would've guessed. And why are you still here?"

"I decided to summer in the city this year." Blair checked out Anna's shoes and stockings, assuring himself she hadn't worn anything that might embarrass him with a classmate.

"What I mean is, why aren't you in uniform? Everybody else we know is. Except for Donald, of course. And we *know* about Donald. Uncle Sam reject your hide?" He was gloating over the possibility, Jervis, who had been too busy chasing waitresses in New Haven to know Abyssinia from Czechoslovakia.

Blair's asthma, which had saved him from having to compromise himself, shamed him at moments like these. So he lied. "The Government couldn't spare me for active duty. They felt I was more important where I was."

"Which is . . .?"

"I'm not at liberty to say."

"Hush-hush, huh?" Jervis hid his awe with a light laugh. "Well, if they can find uses for scrap metal, Puffey, I guess they can find a use for you."

Blair produced a pained smile. At times like these, there was a terrible urge to tell smug fools what he was really doing. But tonight the urge only reminded him of his failure. He noticed Anna lightly frowning at him as she sat down again.

The waiter came over, silver tray under his white-jacketed arm. "What can I get you, Mr. Rice? We've been requested to push the rum, on account of the war, but the bar is still fully stocked."

"Nothing for me, Ben. Thank you." The waiter left and Blair turned to Anna. "Time for us to go, darling."

"Can't I finish my drink first?" Anna sweetly asked. "Captain Jervis was just telling me about his assignment to England. I'd love to see England. You *did* say England, didn't you?" She picked up her drink and leaned toward Jervis.

"Did I?" Jervis lightly laughed again. "I should watch what I say in front of our government man here. Loose lips, right? But 'over there,' yes."

Blair sat in the chair across from Anna, whose jaw was now set against him while she coldly looked at him.

Jervis remained carefully coy about his orders and Anna had to content herself with chitchat while she sipped half of her drink. She eventually bid the captain good night and said she hoped their paths crossed again before he shipped out.

"Without my old college chum, I trust," said Jervis with a wink. "I think the two of us could have a high old time together."

Blair bid Jervis good night and hurried Anna down to the street and the warm darkness.

"Oh, darling," she murmured. "Why did you tell him you were with the Government? He was a real chatterbox until you got there."

"He's a silk-tie wolf, a Don Juan. I don't think you should see him again."

Anna sighed and took Blair's arm. She held on to him affectionately as they walked, but also so they could speak to each other as softly as possible. "Don't be jealous, dear. He's no different from the others. I thought we'd cured you of being jealous."

"I'm not jealous. I went to school with him and don't trust him."

"If you could be a little friendlier with your classmates, dear, I wouldn't have to flirt with them."

They were walking west, along another blacked-out cross street, the only light coming in patches from shop windows, the shadows of closed gates fanning over the sidewalk.

"Dim-out," scoffed Blair. "Brownout, ration cards, war bonds, rum. None of it's necessary. Nothing but a ruse by the Government to involve people in the war. If New York were bombed, *that* would wake people up."

"How did it go?" asked Anna. "The meeting."

Blair swallowed to clear the dryness in his throat, only there was nothing to swallow. "The woman never showed up."

"Oh, God. You're sure you were on the right bus?"

"Yes, it was the right damn bus! The woman just never got on it!"

"Don't get angry, dear. I believe you." She patted his shoulder with her free hand. "Papa's been having a terrible time with those people. Luckily, he has better ways of getting his information out. We'll just give the cigarette back to him and he'll take care of it. Give it to me and I'll put it in my purse, so we don't forget."

"I don't have the cigarette. I destroyed it."

"You . . .?"

"The woman never showed." But he couldn't tell her what really happened. "There was a man on the bus. Who kept watching me. He might have been a plainclothesman. So when the woman didn't show, I decided better safe than sorry. I smoked the cigarette."

"Blair," she whined. "Who would follow *you?* Nobody's going to—"

They had come to Fifth Avenue and could not continue talking. There was more light. Handfuls of pedestrians strolled past the clinging couple that stood on the corner, waiting for the traffic light to change. Blair looked down at Anna. She was scowling at the gutter. They crossed and were alone again in the shadows.

"The man kept looking at me," Blair repeated. "Maybe it was nothing. But we can't be too careful."

"Papa spent so much time making up that cigarette," said Anna sadly. "You sure you didn't get nervous, want a cigarette and smoke that one by mistake?"

"No! Do you think I'm an idiot? I smoked it deliberately. I don't smoke otherwise." He preferred she think he did the wrong thing deliberately, not by accident or out of helplessness.

"I know you're not an idiot. I love you," Anna whispered. "I do. It just worries me what Papa's going to say. He doesn't trust you, sweetheart. He thinks you're arrogant and have no common sense. He wonders if you'll be any use at all to us."

He tried to be angry with Anna's father, a voice in the darkness, but it was like trying to be angry with Anna. Blair's anger turned against himself and he felt ashamed. "I get you into the Yale Club," he meekly reminded her.

"You do. But you shouldn't be so arrogant with your friends. Or jealous," she added, as kindly as possible.

"Jervis is a braggart. You can't believe half of what he tells you."

"Half is good enough for Papa. He mentioned 'Sledgehammer'

tonight. If you hadn't come in when you did, he might've dropped more clues about exactly what that is."

"Sorry," Blair murmured.

"Oh, dearest. What are we going to do with you? You have to learn to forget your pride. We're involved in something much bigger than either of us."

Yes, there was that. Blair's pride was all tangled up in a need to prove himself to Anna and her father. He proudly wanted to be humble.

"Where are we going now?" he asked.

"*I'm* going to the Canteen. See what I can pick up there tonight."

"Take me with you."

"Why? You don't like that 'element,' remember?"

He didn't. Blair had been to the Stage Door Canteen once with Anna and hated it. But he burned to do something tonight, even if it meant being friendly to enlisted men.

"Please, Anna. Give me another chance. Let me try to make up for some of the mistakes I made tonight."

He pleaded with her until she finally said, "Okay. On the condition that you don't tag after me like a puppy. Or big brother."

"I promise. I won't let you down, Anna. I'll be humble and charming and . . ."

"Once we're inside, we have to work alone. Okay? But good. Yes. It'll be good for me too. Knowing that the man I love is somewhere in the room."

They worked their way through the crowds and traffic of Times Square to the Stage Door Canteen. There was a line of soldiers and sailors beneath the awning out front, but Anna and Blair went straight to the door. A woman there knew Anna as a weeknight volunteer and let the two in, warning them it wasn't a very good show tonight.

Anna became very quiet and breathy in the rose-colored front lobby. She seemed to be willing herself into becoming the kind of girl who could flirt with strangers. She drew one final breath, smiled wanly at Blair and told him to run along, she'd be fine. She hurried past the cloakroom into the big room and disappeared into the crowd that lined the dance floor.

Blair stood in the doorway and looked the place over. A full orchestra with voluminous Latin American sleeves packed the tiny stage. The dance floor was packed with dancing couples, most of them doing the samba, but a few ignoring the beat and merely stepping about with their arms around each other. The air was warm and full of smells—harsh, rusty sweat and sickly sweet perfumes. A few large fans on floorstands buzzed near the windows, barely keeping the streamers tied to their grills aloft. Soldiers and sailors of all heights were wedged between the pillars along the dance floor, watching the orchestra or looking for unattached girls. Every girl there was dancing. Anna reappeared, already dancing with a skinny, baby-faced marine. The two moved badly together, the marine because he concentrated on getting as close as possible to his partner, Anna because she wanted to keep some distance between them, and because her thoughts were somewhere else.

Blair was in love with her. He was certain of that. But it was like being in love with a whore. No, he refused to think of Anna like that. And he did not feel as jealous seeing her with servicemen as he had been earlier tonight, seeing her with Jervis. Jervis was of his class and these people were so far beneath Blair he refused to be threatened by them. What threatened him was Anna's success here. She was a sweet little college girl who loved her father, and yet she ran circles around these people, learning what she needed to know. She had to think Blair was an idiot, a fool. He was in love with her, but he was also in competition with her. He was determined to prove to Anna that he could be as good a spy as she was.

"Nice band tonight," he said to the sailor who stood beside him.

The sailor chewed gum in time to the music. "They stink," he said. "Xavier Cugat and his Waldorf Has-Beens. I came here to see some stars."

"You just get into port, sailor?"

"Nyaah."

"You on a ship?"

"Yup."

Blair summoned up a little patience. "But you've been in port a while then?"

"Uh huh. Drydock."

"What's the matter with your ship?"

The sailor looked over at Blair for the first time. "Look, buddy.

I'm tryin' to listen to the music, see? Ya want to cheer me up, cheer me up by scrammin'.'"

"Yes. Of course. Sorry." Blair edged away from the sailor, thinking, "Plebeians." He tried to look at ease, but he was self-conscious anyway, surrounded by so many men in uniform. Even the singer stepping up to the microphone on stage was in uniform, a boyish, black-haired soldier with his overseas cap tucked under the tunic's shoulder strap.

"And now," announced the bandleader, "welcome one of your own. Private Frank Nashe of Brooklyn, New York."

The soldier leaned into the microphone. "This one's for Helen," he said. In a clear tenor voice, he crooned "White Cliffs of Dover," the Latin band accompanying him with maracas and muted horns.

Blair noticed only a handful of male civilians, mostly volunteer workers. There was a fat man in a white suit who obviously didn't work here—he was on crutches and had one leg in a bulbous plaster cast—but such company did not make Blair feel any better. Blair worked his way back from the dance floor, looking for men who weren't interested in the music.

"You just get into port, sailor?"

A sad-eyed, freckled boy sat on a windowsill near the refreshment table. He was more polite than the first sailor, although his eyes kept darting away to check out the room. He was from Missouri, was a machinist on a troop transport and thought Rita Hayworth was one classy dame. His ship was to be in New York another week before they made their next trip.

The fat man on crutches slowly vaulted past them, looking Blair up and down as he went by. His look made Blair nervous. Was the man FBI? Blair waited until the man was gone before he asked his next question.

"Is your next trip with Sledgehammer?"

"Naw. The *Fort Snelling*. Same ship I've always been on."

If they had never heard the name, there was nothing else Blair could ask without making them suspicious.

"Y'know, it's nice having someone to talk to, mister. But it's only fair I warn you—I like girls."

"Of course," said Blair. "Who doesn't?" What an odd non-sequitur.

"Okay. So long as you know I won't go off with you. No matter how much money you might offer."

"Certainly." What was the fellow talking about?

"Just out of curiosity, do the people at the door know what you are? Or do they just look the other way?"

Blair froze. The sailor knew he was a spy. How?

"Just wondering. I'm hep." The sailor sounded anything but threatening. "But they frown on that kind of stuff back where I come from. I was curious how they treated it up here."

"Treated what, sailor?"

"You being a homo. Beg your pardon."

Blair relaxed. He was so relieved the sailor didn't think he was a spy that a moment passed before he recognized what the sailor did think he was. "A homo? I'm not a homo." He suddenly felt nauseous.

"I thought you were. But okay." It didn't seem to faze the sailor.

Blair told the boy good-night and hurried off along the wall. They thought he was a pansy? He looked down at his light-gray suit, then at all the white or khaki uniforms and instantly felt everyone thought he was a nance. Idiots. If they only knew. Let them laugh. Torpedoes guided by what he learned tonight would kill them all. And thinking that suddenly made the idea bearable. Better than bearable, because there was something to be gained from being seen as a pansy. A harmless, limp-wristed pansy. No sailor would think twice about what he told a fairy. He saw Anna out on the dance floor, faking a naughty laugh. Yes, he told himself, I can be as cunning as she is. His nausea vanished. He stood in a corner with his back to the room, practiced flipping his wrists, then looked for another potential talker.

"Hello, sailor. Enjoying the music?" But it didn't sound as queer to Blair's ear as it had sounded in his head. There had been a pansy or two at Yale—theater types like Donald—but Blair had always avoided them.

"Something the matter with your hands, mister?"

"My hands? No, they're this way naturally."

"I got an uncle with palsy. His hands sometimes get like that."

"No, my hands are fine, thank you." Blair wasn't doing something right.

88

"He soaks his in hot water and epsom salts. That relaxes them."

"Let's not discuss my hands. Let's discuss you."

But the sailor was too concerned about Blair's hands to talk about anything else, even after Blair tucked his hands into his coat pockets. Blair thanked him for his concern, wished him a pleasant evening and walked away. It wasn't going to work. Maybe he was too manly to pose successfully as a pansy.

He was resentfully eyeing Anna—she danced with *two* soldiers now—when he heard something thud and skid up beside him. He turned. It was the fat man on crutches.

"Good evening," said the man. He looked and sounded Italian. His round, sweaty face and oiled, black hair reflected spots of light from the bulbs overhead.

Blair only nodded at him. Was the man some kind of detective?

"Nice night, no? Good to see our boys enjoying themselves."

Blair muttered an assent. The man's white suit was soiled. There were enormous stains under his arms where he hung on his crutches. The left leg of his trousers was slit up to the knee to make room for the gray, swollen cast. It was awfully elaborate for a disguise.

"I have watched you," said the man. "I see you like sailors."

"Yes, well . . ." Blair decided to appear banal. "They're serving their country. The least we can do is come down here and make them feel appreciated."

"Good, clean boys," the man said admiringly. "If you like, I could introduce you to a few."

"That won't be necessary." But a detective wouldn't talk like this.

"Maybe. But I have seen you strike out many times with the boys here. The boys I know *want* to be appreciated."

"Where?" Maybe the man was some kind of Canteen host, spotting lonely sailors and searching out people to talk to them.

"Not here. The boys I know are in a place where you will have the privacy to appreciate them to their fullest."

And the light finally went on in Blair's head. "You think I'm a pansy."

"We don't have names for what some men like. Manly men who prefer the company of manly men." The fat man shrugged.

"You're talking about a brothel," Blair said distastefully. "For pansies?" He had never heard of such a thing.

"Shhhhh," went the man. "Not really. More a hotel, really. A little hotel. Where men meet each other, for drinks and conversation. And there are rooms available. For those who *need* to spend the night."

The existence of such a place disgusted Blair. And this man was its pimp! "No thank you. Not interested. I'm only here to talk to sailors."

"We have nothing but sailors," the man insisted. "Good, clean boys, away from home. Homesick boys. Manly boys with nothing to do while they are in port. If you only want conversation, no problem. The friendliest sailors in all the city come to this place."

Blair's disgust remained, but his feelings of revulsion only challenged him. A place full of talkative sailors? "I would only want to chat with them."

"No problem. We are as much a social club as we are . . . the other thing."

It made sense. By going to such a place he could prove to Anna, and her father, that he could rise above personal feelings to serve the cause. And he would be going to a place where *she* could never go.

"Okay," said Blair. "Is it near here?"

"Very near. We can go by taxi. I trust you have money."

"Of course!" Blair looked around the room for Anna. "If you'll just wait a minute, I'll be right back. I have to tell someone where I'm going."

The fat man smiled and shook his head. "Uh, I prefer you not do that. We cannot trust everyone, you understand."

"I guess not. No." Blair saw Anna chatting with a thin sergeant. He had wanted to see the look on her face when he told her where he was going, but that could wait until tomorrow—when he had tons of valuable secrets to share with her.

The fat man told Blair to go first and he would meet him outside. "It is better we not be seen leaving together. And besides, this damn leg." He tapped the plaster with his crutch. "Badly lit stairs."

Blair watched Anna as he walked toward the door, wanting her to see him leave. She finally saw him. He gave her an okay sign with his thumb and index finger, signaling her that he was doing something good. She looked puzzled, then reluctantly nodded and waved goodbye with just her fingers, as if she thought he was leaving out of boredom, nothing more.

He would show her. Anna would never think the same of him after tonight.

8

BEHIND DRAWN CURTAINS, in the hot, airless sitting room at Valeska Bosch's, Lily Pons sang a perfect high note.

"Put on some swing! That dame hurts my ears!" cried Smitty, sitting barechested on the love seat with a rich, affectionate Cuban.

Sash stood by the phonograph cabinet, protecting his new recording. Sash was new, a salesclerk who lived at the Men's Residence Club, where Smitty lived. Smitty had noticed him in the showers there. Sash was short for "Sashweight" and it was visible down his trouser leg, hanging halfway to his knee. He had already been meeting men on Fifth Avenue when Smitty told him about Valeska's. Sash was a ridiculously proper hustler—despite the heat, he wore a necktie tonight—and very ambitious. "I listen to this so I won't spend my life in the gutter with the rest of you," he sniffed.

"Jack-off in your hat," said Smitty. "You ain't any better than we are."

The Cuban, who knew no English, chuckled at Smitty's anger and continued to stroke the boy's muscles.

"Ow!" went Smitty when the man touched the blue eagle tattooed on his arm. "Don't. That's new. Still sore." He snapped the Cuban's suspenders.

The tattoo was identical to the one on Mick's arm. Mick sat on the end of the sofa in nothing but skivvy shorts, the cotton hiked up to his hips, his torso looking like a stack of shiny white boulders. He solemnly turned the pages of a Mickey Mouse comic book.

An Englishman and a young American studied Mick from the other end of the sofa. The two had arrived together and introduced themselves as Prospero and Ariel. It was a private joke they expected nobody else to understand.

"So who shall it be? What about the sallow youth in the corner?" Prospero nodded at the boy sitting by the oscillating fan, Bunny.

The fan lifted the sweep of hair off Bunny's damp forehead each time it passed. Bunny's eyes were closed. He occasionally twitched or scratched himself, as if bitten. His sleeves were buttoned around his wrists tonight so nobody would see the needle marks. It had been two days since his last fix and Bunny desperately needed to make some money. Now that he was here, he felt too sick to do anything.

"Too runt-of-the-litter," said Ariel. "Pity doesn't excite me."

"Then it's going to be our Bohunkus Americanus?" Prospero meant Mick.

"Will you let me make my own damn choice?"

"Since it's my birthday present to you, you can at least let me share in the choosing. How about the foul-mouthed urchin? Like a real-life Dead End Kid."

Lou, a fifteen-year-old who lived in the neighborhood, stood by the food and ate a baloney sandwich, hurriedly, in case Mrs. Bosch walked in. Lou came here only when his mother worked the night shift at a defense plant in Queens.

The Englishman turned nasal and American to imitate the voice of a street kid: "Look at me, fellas, I'm fuckin', I'm fuckin'."

"The Dead End Kids are *your* fantasy," said Ariel. "I want something more adult."

Two very adult, thick-necked petty officers sat stiffly on the chairs against the wall, looking like nervous schoolgirls at a dance. Carlo had met them the night before at Mary's, on Eighth Street, and given them Valeska's card. Nobody knew if they were customers or trade.

The door opened and Mrs. Bosch entered, escorting a handsome young man in a tailored light gray suit and no hat. Already nervous, the man froze when he saw half-clad men in the room. He apparently had been expecting something else.

"This is our leetle club, Mr. Jones." Valeska waved her account book at the room. "Just like Carlo tell you. If you like the Stage Door Canteen, you will luf us. Make yourself at home. If you do not see what you want, you need only ask. Would you like a cold refreshment?" She suddenly noticed Lou, holding half a sandwich behind his back. "You are still here? It is getting late. I will not have your mother coming here again, looking for you."

"Aw, Mrs. Bosch. Can't I stay for just one blowjob?"

"Boy! Not to talk like that here! Scat!" But she turned to the new Mr. Jones. "Unless *you* be wanting him."

Jones pinched his mouth shut and shook his head.

"Only a child," Valeska agreed. "We let him hang about because he amuses us." She hurried Lou out the door with a slap to the back of his head. "Everybody having a goot time? Anyone needs anything, you just ask. Have a sit, Mr. Jones. Enjoy." She closed the door behind her.

Jones stared at the door, then drew a deep breath and tried to stand very tall and arrogant. He stepped toward the sofa and carefully sat down between Mick and Ariel. He sat there like a stone, noticed Mick's legs, looked away, heard the opera aria and looked around the room until he saw Sash and the phonograph. He smiled contemptuously at the music, then turned to Mick. "You just get into port, sailor? Uh, you are a sailor, aren't you?"

"Like hell I am," Mick growled, not looking up from his comic book.

Jones instantly lost the confidence he had mustered. He quickly moved to the edge of the sofa, so he wouldn't see Mick.

Ariel leaned backwards and forwards, annoyed at having his view of Mick blocked. That forced him to make up his mind. He leaned behind Jones and said, "Hey fella? You want to go upstairs?"

Jones bent over and gripped his knees, trying to get out of the way.

Mick looked up and shrugged. "Sure. Why not?" He stood up and tossed the comic book behind him. He slowly turned around, letting the room see he had been chosen once again.

"I knew it," Prospero whispered. "I knew you'd pick him."

"Oh, be quiet," said Ariel, placing his hand on Mick's back to guide him out.

Mick corrected him, putting *his* hand on Ariel's back, then opened the door for Ariel, like a gentleman with a lady.

On their way up the dimly lit stairs, Mick and Ariel passed Hank coming down the steps behind a man with a moustache and wedding ring. Mick and Hank nodded to each other, indifferently.

The man with the moustache left Hank at the sitting room door without so much as a good-night. Hank was used to that by now. The house was full of guys who thought money took the place of manners. It took the fun out of sex. Hank watched his customer go down the stairs, then entered the sitting room.

Lily Pons was soaring again and Smitty, cuddled under the Cuban's arm, howled like a dog with her.

Hank glanced around to see if anyone new had come in. His two weeks here had made him familiar with the regulars, both paying and paid. His fellow whores were an odd bunch. He couldn't say he especially liked them. Each had a peculiar fear or pride that was always getting pinched by someone. It was like that on board ship, too, but there, beneath the nerves and tempers, people shared a trust in each other that held things together. Here, people were afraid to trust.

Hank spotted Jones on the sofa, staring at him. Hank was barefoot, had taken off his top and wore a sleeveless T-shirt, but his white bellbottoms were enough to announce he was Navy. Juke was right—some guys went nuts over uniforms. Or maybe this guy just liked them big and blond. After the man with the moustache—just Hank's mouth, but it had taken forever and Hank's lips were still numb and red—he was in no hurry to go back upstairs with someone else. And this fellow looked like just another useless civilian. Hank tried to save one go each night for a foreigner who might say something handy. Or, barring that, someone Hank actually wanted to lay. But after two weeks here, Hank had forgotten what it was like to be so horny a glance from the right kind of guy could give you a hard-on. Sex was a chore when you didn't need it.

The beer pitcher was empty and Hank was thirsty. He went back out and down the stairs to the kitchen.

"Hey there, Blondie. Was it top or bottom this time?" Juke stood at the sink, breaking up a block of ice with a hammer.

"None of your beeswax." Hank took a milk bottle full of cold water from the icebox and drank straight from the bottle.

"You see the man you're looking for?"

Hank lowered the bottle. "What man? What're you talking about?"

Juke laughed, high and sharp. "You seem to be looking for somebody. Somebody in particular."

And Hank understood. The boy still didn't know what Hank was doing here. "Hogwash. I'm just looking to make a little money."

"I hear you. And you don't fall in love with guys. Love is for women and making babies. You say. But here you are, hanging around like you're waiting for somebody in particular. Lena wonders if it's that dago from the night we was arrested."

"Lena?" said Hank. "Who's Lena?"

"Personal friend of mine. But you'll never meet her. Not while you sit pining around for a wop with skinny legs."

Hank smiled and sat at the table. "You're just jealous, boy. You wish I was chasing you."

"Ha! You wish, farmboy. I know you're dying to get your hands in *my* pants."

"I'd sooner stick my hands in a meat grinder."

"I hear you. But I'd brown a dead mule before I let you lay one cracker hand on my black butt."

"Dead mule be a step up for you."

Hank had learned how to deal with Juke. You played along. Juke's sexual teasing was as much a game as the joshing Hank knew from Texas or the blunt insults he remembered from city boys on his ship. Hank could play Juke's game once he decided there was no malice in it. Or real sexual feeling. They mocked and teased each other like two randy straights who could say it all to each other, because they knew they had no intention of ever jumping into bed together. Or that was how Hank saw it. He trusted Juke knew that Hank was white and Juke wasn't and nothing could happen between them. Hank had seen Juke go upstairs with the rare white man who went in for that sort of thing, but those men were crazy. Juke said so himself.

The boy was forever telling Hank things, drawing him aside to share a nasty comment or dirty secret about one of the whores or regulars. Hank went to Juke now and then when he wanted a little conversation—or not conversation, really, but the shared noise that passed for company with Hank when he was lonely. He had learned to like the boy's noise. Funny thing, but maybe because of the color line between them, like a good safe wall, Hank found Juke to be the one soul here he felt like trusting.

"That hammer's too much for your bitty hands," said Hank. "Want me to do that?"

Juke stopped banging at the ice. He looked at Hank, square in the eye. Then his gaze slipped from Hank's eyes, the way it often did, the way coloreds back home never quite looked at whites. It was funny to see that with Juke, who was usually so northern and uppity. It made Hank uncomfortable, as if he liked Juke being uppity.

Juke suddenly turned away and smashed the hammer into the ice. Fresh chunks bounced around in the sink and two smaller pieces flew out. "You think I'm too nelly for ice?" he sneered over his shoulder. "Uh uh, doll-face. You just sit there, rest your peter and dream about your mysterious stranger." And he resumed smashing the ice, more furiously than before.

There were moments when Hank wanted to tell Juke why he seemed to be looking for someone, why he was here. Hank was lonely with his secret.

"And you may gaze at my butt," said Juke, "and wish."

Something crashed upstairs, then thudded, and there was shouting.

"Whooey!" cried Juke, grinning. "Miss Muscles again?"

Hank jumped up from his chair and ran out to the front hall, Juke right behind him. They looked up the stairwell.

The door to the room on the second floor opened and people crowded into the doorway to look up to listen to the noise on the third floor. Hank and Juke ran up the stairs, past the listeners, towards the shouting.

They were coming up the last flight of stairs when a door flew open, throwing light on the brown wallpaper up there. A naked body tumbled backwards from the door and fell against the wall.

97

"You little son of a bitch!" Mick shouted. "I ain't no cunt!"

Hank raced up the last steps, Juke right behind him. Juke was laughing. He seemed to love seeing whites go at each other.

Ariel stood naked against the wall, hands covering his mouth and nose, his eyes wide open, his bony legs shaking. Mick, naked, stepped toward him, stepped back, his hard cock wagging like a blackjack while he shook his fists at the man.

"You think I'm a punk? You think you can stick your prick in me like I was some damn pansy? I oughta break your pansy neck."

Hank rushed up to Mick to keep him from getting to Ariel.

"You see this?" Mick flexed one arm. "You see this?" He grabbed at his cock and balls as he hollered over Hank. "You think I'm a woman?"

"Take it easy, Mick. The guy didn't know your drift, that's all." Hank laid his hands on Mick's rock shoulders and lightly pushed him back toward his room. Hank wouldn't mind getting off with Mick, if the man weren't crazy.

"That pansy expected me to roll over for him!"

"I pay you good money!" Ariel blubbered. "Why shouldn't you do what I want!"

Juke giggled and patted Ariel's chest. "Hush, baby. You're getting blood on me."

Ariel's nose was bleeding over his mouth and chin. He sprayed bits of blood at Juke when he sputtered. His pale skinny frame shivered and Juke supported him by one arm.

"I'm a man!" Mick shouted. "Don't anybody forget it!"

A door down the hall opened and Smitty and the Cuban looked out. They had just started and the Cuban still had his trousers on, which he held up with both hands, Smitty his boxer shorts. Smitty came down the hall. "Mick! What happened, Mick? What'd the little bastard do to you?"

"Keep out of this," said Hank. "We're just cooling him off."

"Keep out! This is my buddy! Nobody pulls anything on my buddy when I'm around!" Smitty was almost as muscular as Mick, but a head shorter.

"Get the fuck away," said Mick. "All of you. This is between me and him."

"You can forget me," said Ariel. "Because I'm leaving. You people are nuts. When somebody pays for a whore, they expect—"

"Who you calling a whore?" Mick shouted.

"Yeah, who's a whore?" cried Smitty.

Hank had to press all his weight against Mick to keep him from lunging at Ariel.

Juke drew the man away from the wall. "Time we cleaned you up and got you out of here. While you're still in one piece."

"Madam! Madam!" the Englishman hollered from below. He ventured up the stairs while he called down for Mrs. Bosch. The others were still crowded in the door to the sitting room, hearing more than they saw. The Englishman called up. "Chester? Are you all right?"

"I refuse to stay here another minute," said Ariel. "I demand my clothes."

"Mick, darling. The gentleman needs his clothes." said Juke, suggesting Mick get out of the door to the room.

"Come on, Mick. Screw 'em. Just a bunch of fairies." Smitty took Mick from Hank and started him down the hall. "Josie? You mind if my buddy joins us?" he called down to the Cuban. "He's sort of upset."

"I'm a man, a man," Mick muttered as he stepped heavily down the hall, making and unmaking fists while the sides of his squared buttocks flexed and unflexed. He walked with his legs far apart, as if he had to step around his genitals. The Cuban looked pleased as he closed the door behind Smitty and his friend.

Prospero, the Englishman, had come to the top of the stairs. "You couldn't be satisfied with a sweet, harmless boy," he scolded. "You had to feast with a panther."

"Oh shut up. You and your lower classes."

They took Ariel into the room, returned the bed to its place against the wall and sat him on it. Juke poured water from a pitcher into a bedpan and brought it over. "You're a mess, baby. Couldn't you tell that queen treats her cherry like it was a diamond?"

Prospero took over, wiping his friend's face with a cold washcloth and chiding him for choosing "the thug." His wiping grew gentler, his grip on his friend's back firmer. Hank intended to leave, but it was so strange seeing one man treat another like they were husband and wife, or parent and child. Then the man began to kiss the blood off Ariel's chin.

"That'll be all," he told Juke and Hank. "You can go. And please close the door behind you."

Hank pulled the door shut and Juke said, "What do you bet Mrs. Bosch charges them for each other?"

Nothing surprised Hank anymore. Mick was crazy about his asshole. Men married other men, then came here together to get a taste of a real man. As if a man were more of a man if you had to pay for him. The Englishman had gotten worked up seeing his boyfriend beat up, and Hank had been with customers who wanted him to beat them, whip them with a belt or even spit on them, things Hank couldn't do because his heart wasn't in that. Were they sick or was he stupid?

Mrs. Bosch was on the second floor, herding everyone back into the sitting room. "Things are fine. Nothing is wrong. Enjoy yourselves." She turned to Juke as he came down the stairs. "And what have you done now?"

"I didn't do nothin'," said Juke. "A john got too friendly with Miss Muscle and she tried ripping the man's head off. But Blondie and I sewed him back together."

Mrs. Bosch looked to Hank, who confirmed the story with a nod. She shook her head and sighed. "That Mick. He is all boy. Still, I would throw him out on the street if he was not so popular. So what is happening now?"

Juke told her who was doing who and where.

"Always with the horseplay, you boys. Do you not realize we are running a business? Okay, Juke. Back to the kitchen. You have had your fun for tonight. And you, Hank Fayette, make with the customers. I am losing money talking to you."

"I just finished with a customer," Hank said. He was annoyed with the woman for the way she spoke to Juke, for the way she never thanked him or Juke for keeping the peace, for her way of conveniently forgetting Hank's real purpose in being here.

"Yes. And he tells me you showed no enthusiasm."

"I got him off!" Hank said indignantly.

"Yes? Well, some people are never satisfied. You must work

harder. The customer is always right. We must all work twice as hard, now that Mick is indisposed."

Hank and Juke shared a quick look over the woman—Hank disgusted, Juke coldly amused—as Juke started down the stairs and Hank was hauled into the room by Mrs. Bosch, who looked around for unattached men. Hank wished she were a man. Then, when this assignment was over, he could slug her.

"Ah," she said. "Mr. Jones." She took Hank by one arm to the man in the light gray suit who still sat in the same spot on the sofa. Not even the commotion upstairs had caused him to move.

"Mr. Jones? I find someone who is wanting to meet you. He is a sailor. You did say you liked sailors?" She pushed Hank forward. Hank had no choice but to sit on the sofa beside the man. Mrs. Bosch hurried off to force a few other matches.

Jones sat stiffly. He moistened his dry lips, took a deep breath and said, "Hello, sailor. What ship are you on?" His eyes blinked constantly. His small talk was very dry and nervous, like a list of questions he'd written out in advance.

Hank answered him. Everything he told him was three months out of date, so Hank had no worries about divulging secrets. Hank had never been particularly conscious of what he told people until he started working with Mason and Erich. People often asked about boring details, just to make conversation. This man asked so many questions Hank began to wonder. No, there was nothing suspicious about the man. His accent wasn't foreign and he looked clean-cut, even handsome. He was nervous about something, but the prospect of sex sometimes made these clean-cut types nervous. Hank wouldn't mind seeing the man naked. He looked close to Hank's age.

Mrs. Bosch took Bunny from his post beside the fan and brought him across the room to the two shy petty officers. She thought the boy was only being demure tonight. She introduced him to the petty officers, who immediately seemed interested in him. She rubbed her hands together and looked around the room again. She went back to Hank and the man on the sofa. "You two are getting along famous?"

"Yes, thank you," Jones said brusquely, and nodded at her to leave them alone.

"Then you should be going upstairs. While the night is still young."

Jones blanched. "That won't be necessary."

Hank wished Mrs. Bosch would stay downstairs, listening to classical music on the radio the way she usually did. She didn't understand that different men had different needs. They weren't machines.

"You do not like this sailor? Who *do* you want?" she demanded.

"I find our friend perfectly suitable. I just don't think it will be necessary for us to go upstairs."

"We do not allow window-shopping here! Okay. You have had your fun. If you do not choose someone right this minute, I must ask you to leave. I do not run a public museum."

Jones stammered, "But the man who brought me here said—"

"I do not care what Carlo told you. You can leave or you can go upstairs. But you cannot stay in my sitting room one minute longer."

"Mrs. Bosch," said Hank, "we'll go upstairs when we're ready, all right?" Hank felt sorry for the guy. This was obviously his first time in such a place and Mrs. Bosch's pressure was only making it worse.

"If it's the money that concerns you," said Jones, "I'm willing to pay you for the privilege of sitting here and talking to this man."

"Ha!" Mrs. Bosch folded her arms across her chest. "Pay for gab?" she said incredulously. "What are you? A spy?"

Already pale, Jones turned white.

"If you are a police dick, forget it. I have friends in very high places."

"N-n-n-not a spy," said Jones. "For anyone. I like to talk. That's all."

"Then you can talk upstairs, where the fee is the same whether you talk with your mouth or your willy."

"Let's go," said Hank. "We can talk up in my room." Mrs. Bosch wasn't going to leave the poor guy alone as long as he stayed in the sitting room. She had latched on to this man as an occasion to prove she was the boss here. "We don't have to do anything you don't want to do."

"No? I want to continue our conversation," Jones admitted. "I'm not a spy," he repeated. "For the police or anybody."

"Of course not. I was only making with a joke." Mrs. Bosch softened now that she saw she was having her way and would be getting her money. "You go upstairs with our sailor friend. Where you can talk or whatever. In private. Enjoy." She motioned them up from the sofa and escorted them out to the stairs. "Juke!" she hollered down. "Where is that ice, you lazy boy?"

Jones followed Hank up the stairs. "Hag," he muttered. "She'll get hers at the day of reckoning. Just you wait."

The man's anger surprised Hank. He had seemed so meek downstairs.

"You were telling me about why you prefer the southern route. How far south do you go when . . ."

They were passing the door to Mick's room. Prospero and Ariel cooed and moaned in there.

"The South Atlantic?" began Jones again. "Bermuda? Don't U-boats ever . . ."

This time, his voice caught as they passed Smitty's door. He heard deep sighs and Smitty's directions, "Deeper, Mick. His forehead's sweating. He's almost—"

"Here we go," said Hank, opening the door to his room and turning on the light. The wall was thick and they couldn't hear voices from next door, only the bump of the bed against the wall.

Jones immediately sat on Hank's bed, as if faint. He didn't look to see if he sat in anything. The sheets hadn't been changed since the man with the moustache.

Hank closed the door. It didn't have a lock. He pulled his undershirt up over his head. "Hot up here. We're right under the roof. You want to get more comfortable?"

Sometimes that was all it took. Privacy, a bed, the pulling off of clothes: these shy ones turned into wildcats.

But Jones looked up in a panic. "You don't have to do that."

Hank had begun to unbutton his fly. "No? You'd rather do it for me?"

"No! I don't want to do anything. We're only here to talk! Remember?" The man was absolutely terrified.

"Okay." Hank hesitated, then finished unbuttoning himself. "But I'm shucking my pants, if it's all the same to you. I want to be comfortable." Hank did it for the man's sake. The guy wanted sex, or else he wouldn't be here. However, the guy's fear was stronger than his need now. Hank wanted to bring back the guy's need. He stamped his pants to the floor—he had gone back to his old habit of not wearing drawers. "Feel better already," he said, running a hand over his fuzzy blond front. "What were we saying?"

Jones looked at the floor. Hank walked in front of him to sit on the bed and Jones twisted his head around to avoid seeing Hank. "We were talking about . . ." He stood up the instant Hank sat down beside him, went to the lone chair with the missing slat, turned the chair to one side and sat there. "Talking about how you avoid submarines."

"Why you so interested in subs?" Hank couldn't help smiling.

"Just curious. I know someone in the navy. A brother. I worry about him."

The brother sounded fake but Hank told the man what little he knew about convoys and U-boats, just to keep them occupied while Jones became accustomed to the situation. The situation began to excite Hank. He stretched out on his back and lightly shifted his nakedness against the rough sheets and the mattress that seemed to be filled with sand. He was touching himself with one hand, jiggling his balls, flipping his cock back and forth. He stopped watching Jones to watch himself thicken and stand. He pulled back the skin.

"Stop that!" Jones turned away again before Hank saw him watching.

"Stop what?" Hank slowly stroked his cock, as if it were a cat, and smiled at Jones.

The man clenched his teeth and stared at the wall. His hands were in a ball between his lap and knees. The crotch of his trousers was half tented.

"Your behavior's disgusting," he told the wall. "Get dressed and we can continue this conversation like civilized men."

"You don't want me to do this to you?" Hank continued stroking. "Your bone's gonna tear a hole in your pants."

The man threw one leg over the other and gripped his knee. "Trash! Don't think you can poison me with your disease!"

Hank almost laughed, he was so surprised by the man's anger. "Hey, friend. You got a bone. You should enjoy it."

The man glared at Hank, legs and body twisted around his sex, his face full of anger. "You're nothing but an animal!"

"I like being an animal." And Hank gripped his cock harder and jerked the skin back and forth, to defy the man.

"Go ahead," the man spat. "Like an ape at the zoo. A navy full of your kind doesn't stand a chance against Hitler."

Was this the man's kink? To abuse you while he watched you jerk off? He was getting Hank angry and Hank wanted to jizz on the expensive gray suit. Pounding furiously, he rolled to one side and aimed his cock at the man.

The man jumped from his chair and backed toward the door. "Your days are numbered, mister! When real men have finished with degenerates like you . . . ! When Hitler has finished with you apes and Bolsheviks . . ."

Hank had one foot on the floor and was ready to get up and chase the man with his cock, when he heard what the man was saying. Hank almost stopped pounding, but to stop would show the man Hank understood. He lay back and closed his eyes to buttonholes, to watch the man through the slits.

"Then your indecency will be wiped from our country! We will do what Hitler did for Berlin." The man stood still now that he thought Hank was completely involved with his cock. His fear was gone. He stared at Hank, only Hank couldn't quite read the man's face through his blurred eyelashes. "When our leaders finally come to their senses, when they understand what some of us knew long ago—"

"Huh?" Hank breathed hard and made faces. "Some of who?"

"A handful of men and women. Who are working for the real America. While the rest of you wallow in depravity."

The man supported the Nazis. He seemed to be talking about other Nazis. But would a Nazi spy be as blunt about his beliefs as this man was? The man was upset and not thinking clearly, but no spy could afford to lose control like this. Still, there had been all those questions about convoys, and the man certainly wasn't here for sex. He was here for something or someone else.

Hank could feel his cock soften a little while he thought, and he wondered if he should roll away from the man and fake a finish, so the man wouldn't guess that he could think. But the second Hank decided the man was a spy, his cock stiffened like a flexed muscle. He groaned, arched his back and writhed, all for effect, but when he began to shoot, it took his breath away. It had been so long since he had done this to himself it was like a new act, and his doing it in front of an enemy, against an enemy, gave it new power. Good as it was, Hank never forgot the presence of an enemy.

When he opened his eyes, he found the man standing over him, a few feet away, coldly looking down at him like a doctor or coroner. Hank took a deep breath and gave his body a shake. "Wow. You missed a good one, buddy. But if you get your jollies talking about the war, no skin off my nose."

The man shuddered and looked away. "Disgusting. Covered with your own scum." He felt something in his coat, then reached inside to get it. "Yes. This is what I like to see. Our servicemen enjoying themselves. Cigarette?"

Now that it was over, the man abruptly wanted Hank to think he had enjoyed this, that there had been no fear or hatred involved. He winced at the sight of his own pack of cigarettes, then sneered proudly and passed the pack to Hank.

Hank lit a cigarette and pretended its smoke was the most wonderful thing in the world. Pay close attention after sex, Mason had told him, when people are apt to drop their guard. Jones hadn't had sex, but there was a forced calm in his voice as if he expected Hank to drop *his* guard.

Jones sat down in his chair again. "Uh, could you please cover yourself?"

Hank drew the sheet over his crotch and one leg.

"Yes, it's good to see you enjoying yourselves. Because I fear for your futures. I do. When this Sledgehammer thing comes off and you land in . . . where? France? I fear you boys won't be any match for the Germans."

"Sledgehammer? What's Sledgehammer?"

"You *never* heard of Sledgehammer?" The man's contempt returned. "This thing the whole East Coast is preparing for?"

"Oh *that*." Hank knew nothing about it, but he was instructed to play along with suspects. And he'd been given items to pass on to them, bits of information that had no truth to them. At least Mason *hoped* there was no truth to them. Nobody knew anything and there was no telling what was being planned. "That's not for France," said Hank. "That's for Dakar." He pronounced it "Duh Car."

"The car? Oh, *Dakar!*"

"You know. Over in Africa."

The man's eyes focused sharply on the air, seeing something before him. He touched his upper lip with his tongue. "But how do you know? Did they tell you?"

"Hell no. They don't tell us nothin'. Scuttlebutt. And I work in the chartroom and we all of a sudden got all these Africa charts. Gonna be hot as granny's stove down there. Right next to the Equator, you know."

"Dakar," the man repeated. He almost laughed, he was so pleased. "Yes, hot," he said. "Hotter than you could imagine. I will worry for you, sailor. I really will." He was smiling as he reached into his pocket and brought out his billfold. "If the Germans don't get you, the tsetse flies will." Fingering the bills inside, he stood up, pulled out a halved bill and flicked it at Hank. The green bill came open, fluttered about and landed on the floor beside the bed.

Hank leaned down to snatch it up, as if that was what was important to him. "Jeez, mister. A ten-spot?"

"Keep the change," Jones announced. "It was most enjoyable. Watching one of our servicemen enjoy himself." He made no effort to disguise the contempt in his voice. He treated Hank as someone too stupid to recognize a lie.

Hank wanted to wad the bill in his fist and shove it down the man's throat. "Hey, buddy. Anytime you want to watch me . . ." Hank had to get the man to return. Only if the man became a regular could they follow him and find out who he was. What was the next step? Nobody had gone into that with Hank. "And if you want to talk about the war, I'm the fella to see. Working in the chartroom, I get the real skinny. Stuff you never hear about in the newspaper."

"I'll keep you in mind," Jones said coolly. "This has been most entertaining." He looked straight at Hank as he reached for the door. His fear was gone but he wasn't as cool as he pretended. He hated Hank and there was a vengeful cut to his gaze, as if he wanted to see this naked body a corpse. Then he pulled the door shut and was gone.

Bastard. Hank wanted to use the ten to wipe himself off, but ten dollars was ten dollars. Hank stood up and angrily washed himself at the basin on the dresser. The man was a spy. He had to be a spy, but it was the man's contempt that angered Hank now that he was alone, the man's arrogance. The man had talked admiringly of Hitler, asked about secrets, shown disgust for what Hank and the other men here loved to do, all the while thinking Hank was too dumb to guess what was happening. Hank had just had sex in front of a man who didn't think he was human. He was going to do all he could to see the bastard identified, tracked down and caught. But Hank wanted to pay the man back directly. He burned to punch the man's teeth in and fuck his bloody broken mouth.

The image startled Hank. He had thought of sex as pleasure, relief, even here where it was also a duty. Only nuts like Mick saw sex as a weapon. But the house, the war, that bastard who had treated sex as vile—all were confusing Hank about something that once had been as simple as eating.

9

ERICH ZEITLIN RETURNED to the Sloane House from a Sunday concert at Town Hall, full of Brahms and memories of Brahms, to find a message at the front desk: "Mr. Fate called and says he must see you immediately."

Erich brusquely thanked the desk clerk and rode the elevator upstairs to change out of his uniform. He doubted it was anything important, assumed Fayette had only come up with more questions or, at best, misunderstood someone. They had uncovered nothing of interest in two weeks, not even a contraband cargo. But, putting on civilian clothes in his cell-like room, Erich found he was glad to have somewhere to go that afternoon. Sunday, the one day he had to himself, could be interminable.

The subway ride downtown was slow and miserable. Portions of families sat in stupors in the glaring electric light, burnt air pouring through the open windows when the train was moving, stale air sighing from the small caged fans when the train was stalled. Up and down the car a few hand fans paddled away. Collars were unbuttoned and stockings were down. These people had no notion of public decorum. One might as well be sitting with them in their kitchens. Erich felt guiltily alone among them.

At least when he was in uniform, he looked as though he belonged here. His foreignness was especially painful after the concert this afternoon, when, for two hours, he had belonged to *something*. Town Hall was full of refugee profiles and accents, people older and even more lost than Erich. Sitting among them in his uniform, he was both one of them and an American, too. And there had been the homeland of the music. All that overstuffed orchestral furniture had grown dowdy to Erich's ear by the time he had gone to England, but now, with that dowdy, bourgeois life gone, he found Brahms, Bruckner and Mahler beautiful again. History had hurled him so abruptly into the future, he grasped at the past, even his father's past.

Erich loved his father, E. I. Zeitlin, the chemist. He loved him so much he had spent years trying to make a life independent of the respected man, studying philosophy in Vienna, mathematics in Zurich, economics at Cambridge, his failure in each only prolonging his dependence. Erich was in America only because of his father, hired by the University of Chicago and allowed to bring his family from Austria despite the quotas and restrictions that kept most Jews out. If Erich had suffered in some way, he might feel he deserved to be here.

In the station at Fourteenth Street, where Erich got off, a tall young man with a banjo and a runty skull-faced man with a guitar sang hillbilly war songs. There was no open guitar case or upturned hat set out out for contributions. The two seemed to believe their songs did good and sang them for free. "This machine kills Fascists," was painted in blue on the short man's guitar.

Up on the street, it was peacetime and Sunday.

The farmers' market in front of the Bosch house was breaking up when Erich crossed the square. Tarpaulins came down and broken crates were hurled into a garbage truck. Mixed with the trucks and wagons were a few automobiles owned by victory-gardeners, trunks piled with vegetables. Beneath the shed roof to the right of the house, poultry butchers hosed off the pavement. Sunday was ignored for the duration. "Victory Chicken," declared the sign painted on the poulterer's wall, with a picture of a giant chicken chasing Hitler.

Two men in paper caps and bloody aprons nudged each other and laughed when they saw Erich go up the steps to the house. Erich rang the doorbell and wished it were answered more quickly. He hated standing out here in broad daylight.

The door was opened by Mrs. Bosch herself. She wore a brown hat with white netting and was pulling a white glove on. "Meester Zeitlin? What are you doing here?"

He explained he had come to see Fayette, of course.

"He is here, but he is sleeping, I think. We not to keep bankers' hours, you know. *Juuuk!*" she hollered into the hallway. "I would get him myself, but I must get to six o'clock mass. My houseboy will take care of you."

Before he could remind her Fayette was *their* secret, Mrs. Bosch clomped down the steps and set off across the square, quick and serene, piously indifferent to the whistles and catcalls from the chicken butchers.

Erich stepped inside and cautiously pulled the door shut. The sudden silence was unnerving. The house seemed abandoned and dead.

Then the houseboy strolled out of the kitchen. "Mrs . . . ? Oh, you again, Mr. Bookkeeper. Mrs. Bosch ain't here and I'm only the lady of the house."

The boy had a polka dot kerchief tied around his head and his sleeves were rolled over his shoulders. His brown arms were leanly, startlingly muscular. Noticing him on earlier visits, Erich assumed the boy was as frail as a girl, sexless and harmless. Those arms seemed like the ultimate stroke of perversity. The boy smelled of harsh soap and bleach.

"Yes. I passed Mrs. Bosch on her way out. I'm here to, uh, see Mr. Fayette."

The boy looked blankly at him, then sneered and said, "So you're taking your fees out in trade."

Only a Negro, Erich told himself, and it was of no importance what a Negro thought. Erich cleared his throat and said, "Get him for me, boy. I need to speak to him."

"You get him yourself," Juke snapped back. "I got things soaking."

Erich knew he was being fought, but he wanted to get this over with as quickly as possible. "All right then. Where is he?"

"He's somewhere. I forget."

"Please."

The boy smiled. "Up these steps. Third floor. Third door on the left. But I should warn you, honey, he gets mighty ripe when he's been sleeping in his funk all day. Or maybe you like 'em cheesy."

Erich pinched his lips bloodless, then immediately climbed the steps to get away from the boy. He could feel the boy's obscene eyes following him until he was past the second floor.

The hallway on the third floor was hot and dusty. The doors to all the rooms were open and there was plenty of light, but no air. Bare mattresses lay in each room. Erich knocked on the doorjamb of the third door on the left, careful not to look inside. No answer. He peered around the open door. Not only was the bed empty, the mattress was gone. Someone clearly lived here, however. Clothes lay neatly folded on a chair. There were no books, no knickknacks or framed photographs to suggest what kind of person lived here, only the stamped metal wafers of the dog tags that lay with their chain on the dresser. A half-wit had no other identity he could impart to a room.

"Who's down there? That you, Juke?"

The voice came from down the hall. Erich looked and saw a man's shadow stretched along the end wall in the sunlight that came from around the corner.

"Fayette? It's me . . . Erich." First names were the closest American equivalent to *du*, but Erich had no alternative. He was afraid his last name, divulged by Fayette, might tie both of them back to Navy Intelligence.

"Thought it was you. Had to be sure. Come on up, Erich. Cooler on the roof."

Around the corner was a rickety staircase. Fayette stood in the door at the top of the stairs, the sunlight at his back glowing in the nimbus of hair on his arms and legs. He wore an undershirt and boxer shorts—the silhouette inside the white shorts was edged with orange—and his sailor's cap was upside down on his head, to keep the sun out of his eyes. He took the cap off as Erich came up.

"Sorry I wasn't downstairs waiting for you," he said. "You'd gone out already when I rang you this morning, and I needed some shut-eye."

Seeing him so large and blond and out of uniform, Erich told himself this man would be a storm trooper, if they were in Germany. The idea didn't make him feel any better about what they were doing with Fayette.

Fayette stepped back when Erich reached the door and stood in front of a view of warehouses, zig-zag painted ships and bright river. The view opposite was curtained off by rows of patchy sheets tugging and floating on clotheslines. Erich felt unbalanced when he stepped through the door, until he realized the flat roof slanted away from the street. A mattress and sheet lay on the tar paper where Fayette had been sleeping.

"I came when I received your message," Erich said coldly. "Why did you need to see me?"

"You want to sit? This might take some telling."

"I'll stand, thank you." He remembered to take a quick look back inside the door.

"We're fine up here," Fayette assured him. "Just the colored boy down there and the stairs in this joint are like walking on a squeeze-box."

Erich was doubtful, but it sounded reasonable. "All right. I'm listening."

Fayette went down in a crouch, laid his arms across his thighs and balanced his whole body on the balls of his·feet. He took a deep breath and announced, "I think I met a Nazi spy last night."

Then he told a story.

He addressed the tar paper and air while he told the story, as though he were telling it just to himself or making it up as he went along. He even raised his eyebrows over some of the details or worriedly smiled over others, as if he had never heard any of this himself. He gave a yarn instead of a report. Erich impatiently waited for him to get to the point, already doubting that there had been a spy.

There had been a well-dressed man who asked too many questions. When Fayette undressed and abused himself in front of the man—"I know you don't like hearing that stuff, but if I start skipping I might leave out something important"—the man went crazy, cursing America and praising Hitler.

Who wouldn't go crazy, Erich told himself. Cursing America was nothing new. Praising Hitler sounded suspicious, but people unleash their nastiest secrets when they're upset; homosexuals probably adored Nazi men.

Erich knew he was overly skeptical toward Fayette. Part of it was prudence, but there was more. Afraid of the pity he felt for the man, worried that sympathy might cloud his judgment, Erich distanced himself by distrusting Fayette, doubting his every word. Not that he thought Fayette was lying. Lying required cunning and Fayette was incapable of that. Wasn't he? Doubt was a slippery slope and, once begun, Erich found himself doubting that Fayette was what they thought he was.

But the spy didn't sound very plausible, especially when the man finished his tirade, sat down again and resumed asking questions. No spy could be that stupid. Fayette himself admitted it was odd. The man sounded too arrogant and well-off to be an agent. Maybe Fayette accused him of being a spy to get even with the man for his insults, only Erich didn't believe the sailor capable of anger or vengence. Half-wits were naturally gentle.

Erich forgot about keeping his coat clean and settled his back against the black wall beside the door.

"The guy just sat there, smug as a preacher's cat, and started in on asking about something called Operation Sledgehammer."

"Sledgehammer?" The name broke into Erich's thoughts.

"You ever hear of that?"

Erich had heard the name last week from Mason, in the presence of a lieutenant commander who sharply reprimanded both of them. Whatever it was, it was too important to mention. "No. Never," he told Fayette. "But this man asked about it?"

"Yup. Talked like it was some big attack somewhere, so I told him that's exactly what it was. Told him it was Dakar, over in Africa, just to lead the guy on. Like Mason told me to do. And the guy bought it, repeated it to himself like it was some magic password. He was so happy he gave me a ten-spot. Rich little bastard."

"You had never heard the word before? Commander Mason never mentioned it?"

"Sledgehammer? Nope. But this guy seemed to think I should already know it."

Erich tried to keep his skepticism, but too much skepticism could be dangerous. "The man never gave you his name? Again, what did he look like?"

Fayette described him once more. Brown hair, gray suit, smooth pale skin, a face like the faces in advertisements for expensive shirts. The details seemed more than just storytelling embellishments this time, but the man had no distinguishing marks or characteristics. Fayette said he spoke and looked a little like Robert Taylor in the movies, only Erich didn't know who that was. If Fayette had invented a spy, or imagined one, he would give him something special or sinister, at least a foreign accent. This man sounded like a less likely suspect than Erich himself. He was so implausible he must be real.

Never shifting from his crouch, large hands dangling between his knees, Fayette looked up and said, "So what's our next move?"

"That's nothing for you to think about," said Erich. "It's up to us." But what was the next move? No clear routine had been developed for a case such as this, as if Mason had never taken seriously the possibility of stumbling upon a spy. "This was the first time the man ever came here? You're certain of that?"

Fayette nodded. "But I think he'll be back."

"Why? You said yourself he definitely wasn't here for . . . sex."

"No. But he sure got all hot and bothered by the skinny I fed him. I told him there was more where that came from. And he didn't seem too bright."

"No." But could you trust an idiot to recognize stupidity?

"You gonna have somebody outside, watching the house? Have me give a signal or something when he shows, so you can follow him afterwards and find out who he is?"

"Commander Mason will decide our next course of action." Maybe the sailor had only seen too many movies, but he had thought things out and that made Erich uneasy.

Fayette cocked his head to one side, thought again and said, "What is it you're not telling me, Erich?"

The question startled him. "What do you mean?"

Fayette rocked slightly on the balls of his feet, then shook his head. "I don't know. Something. Like you don't believe I really found a spy. Or something."

"I believe you experienced everything you told me."

"But you don't think the guy's really a Nazi spy?"

"It's too soon to leap to any conclusion." Erich's voice had become even colder, more distant. Fayette might not suspect they were lying to him, but he suspected something. Suspicion and doubt made Fayette seem less simple, more normal.

"Well. What if you're here next time he comes by? So you can hear him with your own ears and judge for yourself."

"What're you talking about? No!"

Fayette laughed. "I didn't mean for you to watch him and me. That'd be nuts. But what if there was a telephone in the room and it was left off the hook? Then you could listen in on how this guy talks and see if I'm crazy or not."

"Nobody thinks you're crazy, Fayette." Actually, it was a good idea, unnervingly clever and clear. This man was not an idiot. "But it will be up to Commander Mason what we do next. I'm only a petty officer, Fayette. An enlisted man like yourself. I have little say in any of this."

"Yeah?" It was Fayette who sounded skeptical now. "But tell him my idea, will you? Although I guess you people already have all kinds of machines and inside dope you can use to find this guy. Maybe they already know who he is and don't need either of us to point him out."

Erich said nothing. Fayette's faith in their superiors was childlike, but Erich himself had once assumed the people in command knew exactly what they were doing.

"Whatever. I'll do anything Mason or anybody else wants me to do. I want to see that silver-spoon shit behind bars. And the sooner you guys catch him, the sooner I get back into the war, right?"

"In all likelihood."

Erich heard himself be ambiguous. But before he could backtrack and produce a complete lie, there was a creak of stairs below and a high voice singing deep inside the house.

"Juke," said Fayette. "The colored boy."

"Ah. Then we should finish this," Erich whispered. "I have what I need to know. For now. You'll probably see me again tomorrow, at the usual time. I'll have spoken to Commander Mason by then."

"And you'll tell Mason my ideas? For what they're worth. I want him to know I'm in this with you people a hundred percent."

"Of course."

The creaking drew closer, the song clearer. They heard a bruised falsetto voice singing "The Man I Love." The boy stepped through the door to the roof, an empty wicker basket in his arms. He cut his eyes at the two men, smiled with half of his mouth and continued singing. He went to the clothesline and began to take down sheets, standing sideways so he could watch the men from the corner of his eye. He seemed to sing the song at them.

Fayette slowly stood up. "Appreciate you laying down that bet for me, mister," he told Erich. "Tough for me to get to the track and I'm new in town. I don't know any bookies."

"Quite all right. It's a pleasure doing business with you, sailor," Erich answered. But Fayette's cleverness, the womanly song, the image of the boy's feminine headgear and his muscular arms? If Fayette wasn't an imbecile, that meant he was genuinely depraved.

"I know the way out," Erich called to the boy and hurried down the stairs. He tried telling himself that it was better this way, that the man they were using was a criminal and not a guileless innocent. But he couldn't work up the contempt necessary to feel relieved by the discovery. The sailor proudly believed he was doing good for his country.

Juke continued to sing his second-favorite singer's best song—he believed he sounded just like Billie—while he folded a fresh-baked sheet and watched the bookkeeper depart. He waited for Hank to explain the visitor or mock the cold little man now that he was gone. Hank just stood there, frowning at a thought, looking like a man trying to pick up something too small for his fingers. Without ever acknowledging Juke, he padded over to his mattress and lay down again.

Fool cracker, thought Juke. He yanked down and folded up one row of sheets without looking at Hank, then the next, unveiling the view of rooftops way to the east, miles of flat roofs speckled with white people who had come up to catch the first coolness of the day. The sun had settled into a low bank of clouds and there was an orangish glow, like candlelight.

Hank looked whiter than ever in this light, smooth and edible. His hands and face had more color than the rest of him, but in a good way, like he was two colors of ice cream.

Juke stood beside the door with the basket full of sheets, staring at Hank, reluctant to go without saying something. "So what horse did you bet on, Blondie?"

Hank looked up, startled, as if he had forgotten Juke was still here.

Juke walked over to him and looked down at Hank. Standing so close to him, he suddenly wanted to smash the basket into Hank's face. "Liar. You ain't sanding me. That man your lover?"

"What're you jawing about? Lemme alone." He squinted up at Juke. "Maybe he is my lover. What's it to you?"

"Shit. That man ain't nobody's lover. Gimme your underwear." Juke held out one hand.

"Something eating you, Juke? Come on. I got things on my mind."

"Your underwear stinks. Gimme it. I'll wash it." He snapped his fingers at Hank. "Whoever heard of a bashful whore?"

"I wash 'em out myself. But, if it's so damn important to you . . ." Only looking annoyed, he peeled off his shirt and, lifting his ass, the shorts. He sat there with his legs apart and thrust the wad of clothes into Juke's hand.

It didn't mean a thing to him to show himself to Juke. Juke had glimpsed him before, when he was asleep or drying off after a bath, but this was different, because it was deliberate. Hank showed no shame, no awareness of what seeing his nakedness might mean to the person standing over him. Feeling that, it pained Juke to see the groin curve inward to a clump of damp hair, the sagging purse of balls, the big indifferent cock.

Juke held the bouquet of dirty cloth in his hand. "Then wash 'em yourself!" he shouted and flipped the clothes into Hank's face. "Dumbass cracker!" He wheeled around with the basket of sheets and charged down the stairs, before he said anything that might make the man think he was jealous or something.

Hank picked up his underwear, put it back on and wondered what he had said wrong. As if he didn't have enough to worry about—a spy, a secret, Erich's secret which he thought was love but now thought might be something else—without the colored boy going nuts on him.

10

"OH, DARLING. I knew you'd come through. Papa will be so pleased." Anna held Blair's hand between her hands and stroked his manicured nails with her thumb. "And Africa," she said. "We never dreamed it would be anywhere but—" She remembered where they were, lowered her voice and leaned closer. "Where is Dakar exactly?"

They sat on a bench by a narrow path in the southwest corner of Central Park. It was late afternoon and the sunlight through the trees fell in tatters on the smooth trunks and untrimmed grass. The quiet of the woods was underlined by a distant rumble and honk of city traffic and, up in the bushes on the hill behind them, the thin, whistley music of a portable phonograph. Blair assumed there was a couple back there, kissing and petting to the cheap songs.

After last night, everything suggested sex to Blair. His mind had been poisoned. Even the Brahms concert at Town Hall that afternoon, marred anyway by so many jabbering Jews, degenerated into background music to the images Blair could not shake from his head. He kept seeing the sailor flopping on the bed like a landed trout, and wished those writhings had been the man's death throes. He could not notice anyone, male or female, without wondering what they did in private and with whom. It was disgusting. But now, compensating Blair for his plague of dirty thoughts, was Anna's admiration of him.

"You are so clever. A man who works in the *chartroom*? This will convince Papa how wrong he was about you."

"I'm only too happy to be able to help out," Blair said gallantly.

"I love you for being so clever."

Footsteps crunched gravel as another couple came around the bend in the path, a soldier and an older woman who embraced and kissed as they walked. It was a miracle they could see where they were going.

Anna took hold of Blair's arm as the couple came closer. The front of her white blouse was all ruffles, pushed out like the petals of a flower by her breasts. She watched the couple and moistened her lower lip, leaving a gleam of light there.

Blair began to see Anna writhing on a bed.

She laid her head on his shoulder and waited for the couple to pass before she whispered, "And where's this social club?"

Blair frowned. "Greenwich Village. Near the waterfront." He had not told her everything, of course. He was too ashamed of where he had been, especially now, when he was with someone as virtuous as Anna. Remembering who she was, he was ashamed of the way he had been thinking of her, but he felt better picturing Anna than he had picturing the sailor.

"You weren't too arrogant with them, I hope."

"I can control my feelings when I have to." He pressed his legs together to hold himself down, but the warmth of his own thighs only made it worse. Her breast lay against his arm like a cool pillow.

"Can women go to this place?"

"No. Only men. Sailors. It's very quiet. A place where they can read, relax, write letters home. That sort of thing."

"This sailor. He never said anything about *when* it was going to be?"

"No."

"Hmmm. I'll tell Papa about where and all. Right away. But it'd be even better if we could find out when." She drew away and looked into Blair's eyes. "Could you go back there and feel this man out on that?"

"No!" He had not intended to answer with such feeling.

Anna looked puzzled. "But why? You said you made good friends with the man."

He pictured the sailor again, obscenely gripping himself and leering at Blair. The stiffness in his own trousers sickened him. Blair shook his head. "I don't know if he'll still be there. And it's not a nice place. Full of riffraff and . . . cheap cigars."

Anna laughed. "But it'd be worth another visit, wouldn't it? Maybe you'd make some more friends there. Oh, darling. We've come this far. Can't we go a little—" Her eyes focused on something beyond Blair.

He glanced over his shoulder and saw a policeman strolling down the path. The cop was busy with the billyclub he held by its leather strap, flipping the club like a baton, twirling it like a yo-yo.

Anna swung herself in front of Blair so they would be only another amorous couple. She placed her hands on his back and laid her chin on his shoulder.

Blair lightly put his arms around her. The weight of a woman always surprised him, like the surprise he experienced the few times he rode a horse and found the animals were not as airy as they looked. He breathed her perfume and hair.

The policeman crunched past without a word. There was a repeated click each time he caught his club, when it knocked against his wedding ring.

Anna began to pull back. Blair grabbed her head with both hands, turned her face toward him and kissed her mouth.

All of her eyes—up this close, his eyes could not bring the double images together—were open and surprised. Then she closed her eyes and gripped his shoulders.

Her lipstick tasted like raisins. Her hair felt crisp and lacquered. He moved his hands down so he would not spoil her hair. Her blouse slid against the skin of her back and the seams of her bra. His hand followed the seam around, under her arm, to the breast squashed against his chest. She had nothing in common with what he had witnessed last night.

Remembering that, he kissed her harder, wedged his thumb between his chest and her breast and felt the spot where the squared seams met.

She moaned through her nose, reached down and pulled his hand away, but continued kissing. Her moan faintly echoed the sailor's groaning.

He placed the hand on her hip, then abruptly brought it over her lap, as if to assure himself for good that this was different.

She stopped kissing. "No, don't, please . . . Blair."

His hand was pushed away, but not before he felt a comforting absence beneath her skirt.

"But I love you," he said gratefully. He could enjoy being sprung up like a broken toy now that he trusted its purpose.

"And *I* love you. Only—" She looked around. There wasn't a soul in sight. Even the phonograph in the bushes played nothing, suggesting its owners were too occupied to turn the record over.

"We could go to my apartment," he suggested. "You've never seen where I live."

"Oh, Blair." She drew a deep breath and attempted to smile. The penciled skin of her eyebrows was crimped in worry. "I don't want to do anything I'll feel bad about afterwards. I'm not that kind of girl."

"I know. And I'm not that kind of man. But I love you. It's only right we should want to . . ."

"Part of me wants to," she whispered. "But . . . It feels wrong wanting to now, what with the war and Papa and all." Her hands slowly wrestled with each other in her lap. "It feels selfish."

He did not know what to say to that. She was right, of course.

A few birds had begun singing in the first coolness of the evening. The yellow scraps of sunlight faded in the trees. They sat together in silence, waiting, as if desire were something that would pass by, like a policeman.

"Getting back to what we were talking about," Anna announced. "This club. I know it's asking a lot of you, darling, but won't you please be brave and go back there? One more time?"

The idea of the house still repelled Blair, although he felt safer with his dirty thoughts now that they had a suitable object. If he and Anna were lovers, in the fullest sense of the word, then he could face the men there. But he didn't know how to explain that to Anna without abusing her innocence, or making her wonder about him. He leaped over the explanations and said only, "I can be brave if you can, darling."

She looked blank, until he lightly laid his hand on her arm.

"You mean, you won't go back unless I give myself to you?" she said calmly.

It sounded awfully caddish phrased that way. Blair swallowed his guilt. "We should give each other little rewards for doing the things we don't want to do."

But Anna didn't appear insulted or threatened. The suggestion seemed to tempt her. "Then I wouldn't be doing it for myself. I'd be doing it for Papa, wouldn't I?"

"And the cause," Blair added. "Only I don't want you to think I won't do *that* unless you do *this*. It would just make it easier for me to face such riffraff, knowing I had your love, Anna. Completely."

"No. I don't think that." But she sat there thinking something. "If I do this to help you, then it isn't selfish, is it?"

"It's selfless. Admirable." That approach made it seem like a horrible sacrifice, but Blair didn't care so long as the woman he loved went home with him.

"No," said Anna. "There's selfishness there. But it's being put to good use." She lowered her eyes and smiled. "Okay then. I will."

"Oh, Anna." He held her shoulders and kissed her smooth, moist forehead. "Yes. We should. We love each other. The cook and maid are off tonight and we can—"

She stopped his mouth with hers, kissed him with her arms around his neck. This time she parted her teeth a little and let his tongue touch hers. Then she drew away, looked down and smoothed out his necktie over his chest and stomach. "Yes. We will," she whispered excitedly. "When you get back from that place."

"What? Not tonight?"

"Don't you see, dear? It'll be even better when we won't have anything else on our minds. Our reward to each other for a job well done."

"Maybe." But Anna didn't talk like a tease. She seemed as confused and eager as he was. "You promise?"

"Of course. Because I want to, Blair. I love you."

They were lovers, and yet they bargained with each other like shopkeepers.

But Blair believed her. He could pass again through that den of perversion, knowing he had this waiting for him afterwards. "All right, then. I will."

"Oh, goody." And she embraced him again and kissed him deeper than before.

The bushes rustled behind her and, his mouth joined to Anna's, Blair saw a fat woman stumble onto the path, followed by a stocky, strutting sailor carrying a portable phonograph. The sailor's back and seat were covered with dirt and leaf mold.

11

MRS. BOSCH'S BOOKKEEPER came over Monday afternoon, as always, and spoke to her for a long time in her office. She called for her houseboy and sent him out to buy a Czech newspaper, which meant he had to go over to Union Square. Shortly afterwards, two electricians arrived at her door—Sullivan and another younger FBI man. They exiled Fayette to the kitchen and spent a long time up in his room. They hung a microphone on the ceiling up there—an enormous perforated metal sausage they disguised with a Chinese lantern—and ran a line that looked like the lantern's electric cord down to the floor, along the baseboard and out the window. The line hung loose and uncovered down the outside of the house, then passed through the cellar door. There was only the furnace in the cellar, and no reason for anyone to come down here at this time of year. The ceiling was low. Sullivan's partner, tall and gloomy, kept banging his head on the joists, but without so much as a curse or groan in response. The paw prints of a small dog or large rat ran across the uneven dirt floor. The place smelled like something had died down there.

When everything was set up, Erich was called down to listen in. "After all," said Sullivan, "you're the one who's going to be using it."

"*Me?* I thought that was your job."

"You're nuts if you think the FBI's going to sit around listening to queers go at it." He patted the shoulder holster beneath his overalls, his gun proof of who he was. "It's not decent. No, we'll set things up and tail anybody you want tailed. But we're leaving the ear-to-the-keyhole business to you and your superior, thank you. We're G-men, not peeping toms."

Erich had hoped he'd be able to keep his distance during this phase. Maybe Mason would do all the listening. The commander had jumped so quickly at Fayette's suggestion that Erich again suspected he was more interested in monitoring pathology than in catching spies.

He accepted the earphone and wire headband Sullivan handed him, placed it to one ear. There was only electric air, like the roar inside a seashell. Then, beneath the roar, as if deeper inside the shell, Erich heard Sullivan's partner, who'd been sent back upstairs. The glum young man stood three floors above them and sang, "I Know an Old Lady Who Swallowed a Fly." The thing actually worked, dammit.

Afterwards, Sullivan and his partner explored the backs and alleys behind the house, finding a route between the slaughterhouse and high wooden fences that would get them from the cellar to the street without going through the house. Then, by going around the block, they could reach a spot opposite the front door in time to see the man after he left Fayette's room. Sullivan replaced the red light over the front steps with a white one, so they could see what the man looked like before they followed him into the darkness.

Erich and Sullivan returned after dinner, accompanied by Commander Mason. Sullivan's partner remained in the government-issue black Ford parked around the corner. Mason, out of uniform, dressed like a man who was going to putter around in his garden, was more full of himself than ever. He brought a folding canvas chair with him. With the others standing around him in the glare of a work light hung on a nail, Mason sat there wearing the headset, happily grinning at his ability to hear everything in an empty room upstairs. Nobody entered the room. After an hour, the mere idea of the thing was no longer enough for Mason. He began to get bored. He passed the headset to Erich and tried to talk to Sullivan about the mother Sullivan still lived with. Sullivan sat on a crate and played solitaire, laying the cards on the dirt floor at his feet. Each time the ceiling beneath the front hall creaked, Mason snatched the headset from Erich, but nobody ever entered the room. They heard doors and, once, they heard a bed collapse, but nothing in the room itself.

Shortly after ten, there was thunder in the distance, then a rattle of rain on the cellar door. The air crackled loudly in the earphone, turned into violent static and began to flick on and off, until the earphone went dead.

"Drat," said Mason. "What if one of us poses as a customer, goes up there with Fayette and fixes it?"

"Sir," said Erich. "The houseboy has seen me twice in two days. If he sees me tonight, he'll get suspicious." The thought of going inside made his stomach cramp up.

"Naturally," said Mason. "I was thinking maybe I should go up." The man was dying to see what went on in this house.

Sullivan bent over the open suitcase, fiddling with the batteries and vacuum tubes inside. "Outside line's shorted out," he announced. "The rain. Nothing we can do until we replace the connectors with ones that're waterproof. You can go in there if you like, Commander. But won't be a thing you can do tonight, unless you want to stake out the room from under that pervert's bed."

Mason seemed to consider that, briefly. Then he lost his temper. "Why in blazes didn't you use the right thingamabobs to begin with?"

Sullivan remained aloof and remorseless. "It did not seem necessary."

Mason glared at him, glanced at Erich, then the ceiling. They were trapped down here by the rain, with only their ideas of what might be going on upstairs.

"So," said Mason, admitting defeat. "Let's hope this spy, imaginary or otherwise, stays home tonight because of the storm." Failure had brought out a little skepticism in the commander about the enterprise.

The rain let up around midnight and they stumbled out through the alleys with their equipment to the car—the blind leading the blind, thought Erich.

Erich returned the next afternoon, the houseboy was sent on another errand, Sullivan fixed the line and Erich learned from Fayette that the man had not been there. When he reported back to Mason, the commander said he had a previous engagement that night and was leaving Erich in charge.

Tuesday night, Hank sat in the kitchen with Juke, eating Juke's chicken stew. Mrs. Bosch took her dinner in her office, with a single glass of wine "for the stomack," so Hank and Juke usually ate alone. Hank used to enjoy eating with Juke, his taunts and teases, even his calling Hank "po white trash" for covering everything with catsup and stirring it together into one pink mass. But Juke had been acting strange lately, pestering Hank when Hank wanted to give his full attention to the web of secrets thickening around him, or, when Hank wanted to talk, responding to his remarks with cold shrugs and sulky silence. It was as though, whatever Hank wanted, Juke would do the opposite.

Tonight, like last night, Hank was conscious of the men in the cellar, what they might hear, what they might think. It was like when he was a kid and felt God, or someone out there, watching and judging his every move. It made him worry he might be wrong about the swell being a spy. The wire getting fouled up the night before only gave him something else to worry about. Hank wanted to distract himself by swapping insults with Juke—"This chicken or some poor pigeon you snagged?"—but the boy refused to respond to the baiting.

Juke sat there, drawing figures on the oilcloth with his fork when he wasn't picking at his food. From where Hank sat, the indented marks looked like valentine hearts. The boy rubbed each one out as soon as he drew it.

The back door was open and there were the usual smells of stewed garbage, river and chicken lime. It was dark now. Erich and the others should be arriving soon, or maybe they were already down there. They had no signals to let Hank know what was happening. He wouldn't know if the wire worked or even if there was anyone down below listening until tomorrow, if Erich came by. It was like not knowing for sure if Jesus was real until you died and went to heaven.

Out in the alley, the steady hum of machinery coming from the docks was broken by a nearby clatter and bang. A garbage can had fallen over.

Hank listened. He watched Juke so hard that Juke looked up and paid attention to what he had heard.

"Just a cat," said Hank, trying to undo the suspicion he had aroused. But he thought he heard a heavy suitcase knocking against a leg. The men were returning. "Or dog or something," he added.

Then, on the raised railroad track toward the river, a train started up, couplings banging taut up and down the line, like a slow string of firecrackers. There was a rumble of empty boxcars and every other sound outside was buried.

"Dumb hick," sneered Juke. "The city. Things are always bumping in the dark."

Hank breathed again, then realized Juke had just insulted him, like his old self. "We can't all be city slicking queens," he joshed back.

"Least you know where you stand with a queen." Juke jabbed at his food. "I saw your friend the bookkeeper sniffin' around here today. Again."

"Him? He's no friend of mine. He was here talking to Bosch again."

"You two looked close as thieves Sunday."

Hank laughed, badly. "Hell, boy. That man doesn't know me from Adam's housecat. He was just being nosey about what goes on around here."

"Then how come you go tight as a drum when I mention him? And I get sent out of the house every time he comes by?" Juke looked at him, squinting one eye as if he were trying to see around a corner. "You and him and Mrs. Bosch are up to something. Don't tell me you're not."

"We're not. You're nuts, boy." But Hank couldn't look at Juke. He was uncomfortable having to lie to the boy, having to turn his friendliness on and off. He tried to turn it on with an old joke. "You're just jealous of me and the four-eyes."

"Shit." Juke curled his lip over his yellow teeth and sat back in his chair. "Pig-fucking cracker. Dumbass asshole."

Hank grinned, relieved to have Juke taunting him again.

"Dirt-eating Willy Cornbread. Look at you. Just sitting there, smiling like a fool. Nothing I say means shit to you. Cause I'm just a nigger, ain't I?"

Hank lost his grin. This talk was different. "You're no nigger, Juke."

"No? Then what do you call this?" He pinched the tea-colored skin on his arm. "Greasepaint?"

"I mean, I don't think of you as a nigger."

"Then what do you do think of me then? You sure don't think of me as a man."

"I do." An effeminate man but— "A young man. Colored."

"Colored. Yeah. You can't never forget that, can you?"

"I forget it. Sometimes." Which was true, only Hank didn't know if that was good or bad. Juke could be so screwy he became nothing but Juke; his being colored seemed only incidental.

"Prove it."

"How?"

"Fuck me."

Hank's mind stopped and he saw the boy—flat nose insolently raised, pink lower lip curled out like a dare—looking at him.

"Or suck me. Or let me suck you. Or even kiss with me, cracker."

"You're razzing me again, aren't you?"

"You suck and fuck anybody and his brother here. But you never dream of laying a lily-white hand on me."

"No. Cause they're customers. You're a friend. And we're . . ."

"*Different.* Yeah. See, you can't forget I'm just a nigger. You ain't no friend of mine. I'm just something you kill time with between white dicks."

"You *are* feeding me a line," Hank insisted. "You said yourself you don't like white men."

Juke's furious look suddenly turned cold and stony. His fork tapped the table. He hissed at Hank through his teeth. "Dumb whore," he said. "You think I want to sport with you? You think that's what I'm talking about? Shit." He exasperatedly rolled his head around his shoulders, as if squirming loose from the idea. "No, baby. I'm just testing you, proving to you what you think of me. Which is shit. We ain't friends. We ain't nothing. You're just using me and I won't be used anymore. I don't even want to eat with you anymore." Juke jerked his chair back and stood up. "Dumbass whore," he said. He marched into the pantry where his cot was and slammed the door behind him.

The boy was going crazy, Hank told himself again. But he really felt he had been behaving badly around Juke, running hot and cold with the boy. If only he could explain himself to the boy, tell him why he was here and why he had secrets, then Juke should understand. But that was too dangerous. It was safer to consider bedding with a darky to reassure the boy, although Hank couldn't picture Juke naked and the boy himself said he wasn't interested.

The doorbell out front rang and Juke didn't stir from his room. Before Mrs. Bosch could holler for Juke, Hank went out and answered the door. It was only Smitty and Sash, Sash carrying two new records in their paper sleeves.

"Hey, look at the new houseboy," said Smitty. "You gonna start wiggling your fanny and sucking watermelon, sailor boy?"

Hank kept his fist at his side and said, "Shut the fuck up."

Out in the alley, on the way in, Erich saw the open kitchen door above the fence and Fayette chatting with someone at the table, probably the houseboy. Erich watched, wondering how much Fayette had told the Negro, and walked into a garbage can.

The empty can banged over, clattering like the bass end of a piano. Erich and Sullivan froze.

A train began to bell its way out of the yard by the river. Nobody had come to the kitchen door. Erich breathed again and resumed walking.

"Clumsy kike," Sullivan whispered.

Of course, thought Erich. He had presumed Sullivan hated him for being a Jew, and now he knew.

They carefully lifted the cellar door, tiptoed down the steps into the damp darkness, closed the door, struck a match and found the worklight. The cellar was suddenly bright and grim. The bricks in the foundation were old and uneven, arranged into long, wiggly lines by cement as thick as daub. The wall looked almost medieval in this country where everything was usually so slick and new. Erich stood there, wondering what kind of family had lived here a hundred years ago when the house was built, while Sullivan knelt at his suitcase and set things up. Even without Commander Mason present tonight with his psychology, Erich felt they were posting themselves inside somebody's Unconscious.

"Wild goose chase," Sullivan muttered, passing Erich the headset. "I bet you a week's salary this fella isn't going to show tonight. If there is such a fella."

"Maybe." Erich disliked Sullivan enough to want the man to be wrong. He believed Fayette's well-dressed Fascist existed, but wondered if the man was actually a spy, or if he would return to the house tonight or this week. Erich wore the headset like a collar around his neck. The hard plastic earpiece became uncomfortable when pinched against his ear too long and he could hear the faint room noise well enough without having to drown himself in it.

Erich sat in the canvas chair Mason had left behind, and waited. He had brought a book with him tonight—*Jews Without Money*, purchased to acquaint himself with American Jews—but he was reluctant to pull it out in the presence of someone who had called him a kike.

Sullivan sat on a crate, took off his jacket and took a yellowed roll of chamois cloth out of the inside pocket. He unrolled the square of cloth at his feet. There was a toothbrush, a tiny screwdriver and a can of lighter fluid inside. He unsnapped the shoulder holster and brought out his blunt revolver. He lovingly turned it in his hands a few times before he popped it open and emptied the bullets into his palm. "Wild queer chase," he mumbled, taking the toothbrush and stroking the bared drum with the bristles. "Consorting with criminals, when what we should be doing is locking those people up for good. Or castrating them. If they're not going to use their reproductive organs the way God intended, they have no business using them at all. Never wrestle with pigs, you only get dirty."

"Your gun," said Erich. "Have you ever had call to use it?"

"Affirmative. There's been times when this little sweetheart was all that stood between life and death for me." Broken open, the revolver looked like only another gadget, such as a can opener.

"Then you've actually shot people?"

"No. It's never been necessary to fire it at anyone," Sullivan said, without a trace of embarrassment. "But I could, if the situation required it. It's a vile, nasty world out there. I'm surprised you don't carry a gat."

The ostentatious expertise, the slang from the movies—Erich recognized it was all a show for his benefit. He was glad he didn't carry a side arm. Not only did the responsibility frighten him, the associations repelled him. In Europe only brownshirts and other thugs carried firearms. Over here, guns were an emblem of manhood. Erich could not understand this American language of masculinity, where isolation, silence and guns were more important than family, money or education.

"How far did you get in school?" Erich asked. "Just out of curiosity."

"I have a college education," said Sullivan, gazing at Erich, suspecting an insult. "Mr. Hoover insists we have a degree in law or a certificate in accounting."

"You studied law?" This dense anti-Semite who tried to talk like a tough?

"Accounting," Sullivan announced. "But just so I could get into the Bureau. Don't think I'm some pencil-pushing milquetoast, because I'm not."

"Of course not." Erich suppressed a smile. It was almost funny. By American standards, the uneducated sailor upstairs, idiot or not, was more of a man than either Erich or this armed accountant who lived with his mother.

The thin line of moustache along Sullivan's upper lip suddenly looked strange to Erich, as if it had been painted there with mascara. Erich winced. Just being in this house was addling reality. He hoped the suspect would come soon, while reality was still salvageable.

The taxi prowled the side streets behind Pier 59, Blair in the back taking nips from a silvered flask of Scotch and looking for the house. There was one house in roughly the same position to a square as the house from Saturday night, but Blair remembered the house having a red porchlight and this house had a white one. But it had to be the house. Blair knew he was procrastinating.

He should have come Sunday night, when his desire for Anna was so strong and clear it would have carried him through his doubts. He had meant to come last night, but had delayed leaving his apartment for so long that when it began to rain, he could tell himself nobody would be there. Tonight he was using a little Scotch to fortify his memory of Anna. He took another nip and told the driver to return to the first house, the one with the white light.

When the cab coasted to a stop, Blair knew it was the place. He paid the driver and stood on the dark sidewalk after the taxi had driven off. The flask was still in his hand, so he raised it to his mouth one last time. It was empty. Was he drunk? If he was drunk, he should come back another night when his mind was sharper. But Blair knew how small the flask was. His lightheadedness was more fear than alcohol, although there was nothing for him to be afraid of. He was going to watch a man masturbate, nothing more.

He slipped the flask over his heart and rang the bell. The door was answered by a colored boy without respect or manners. He listened coldly to Blair's introduction, then directed him up the stairs with an insolent twist of his head. Indignation replaced Blair's nervousness. Under different circumstances, he would see to it that the boy was fired.

The room upstairs was smaller and meaner than Blair remembered, more shabby-genteel than sordid. He had nothing to fear from something so far beneath him. A few young men lounged about like stray cats. A few older men leaned over them, as if examining the upholstery on the furniture. Toscanini's Beethoven played preposterously on the phonograph. Poor Beethoven.

Then Blair saw his sailor. Even he was more common-looking than Blair remembered. The image of the naked man thrashing on a bed had grown so large in Blair's mind that he was expecting a marble giant. Uniformed and vertical, the sailor was a bit taller than the others, but hardly demonic. He stood in the corner, listening to a short man with florid hand gestures and an eyepatch, sleepily nodding at the man, until he saw Blair. The short man turned to see what the sailor was seeing. Painted on the man's black eyepatch was a startling blue eye.

Blair coolly nodded at the sailor, then pretended to look around the room. He did not want to see the sailor naked again.

Hank hurried across the room. "Hey. If it isn't my old buddy. Good to see you again." And he slapped his spy on the back.

The blow was so hard it took Blair a moment to realize he had been touched by the sailor, and he didn't want to be touched. "Yes. Good evening," he said, looking past the sailor to the two boys squabbling over the phonograph.

"I was hoping you'd be back," said the sailor. "Fine time we had us the other night." His confident friendliness was almost insulting.

"Yes," said Blair. "I enjoyed talking with you. I wanted to talk some—"

The painted eye was suddenly beside them.

"Excuse me, suh," the man with the eyepatch told Blair, "but Ah saw this fahn speciman fust." He reached up to clasp the sailor's shoulder. "Ah don't want to sound greedy, but Ah was under the impression Ah was next on his dance card."

"Sorry, bub. But this here's an old friend of mine. We haven't seen each other in a coon's age. Have we, friend?"

The sound of two Southern accents and the smell of liquor on the short man's breath made Blair feel all three of them were drunk. He couldn't take his eye off the painted eye, blue brushstrokes on black and larger than the man's real eye.

"In that case," said the man, "would you care to make it a pahty?" He smiled and raised his eyebrows at Blair. "The three of us, Ah mean. You're a rather fahn speciman of manhood yourself. Be an honor for me just to watch, even."

Blair's stomach almost turned itself inside out.

The sailor burst out laughing and threw an arm around Blair. "Thanks, but no thanks, old buddy. My friend here's a mite on the shy side. Three's a crowd. You understand?"

"Pity," said the man. "Wahl, no use making a fool of mahself chasing after this boy. Maybe you'll leave some for me when you're through." He politely nodded to Blair and departed, looking for unattached men.

The sailor withdrew his insultingly intimate arm. "Got rid of him, didn't we? Yup, want to have you all by my lonesome."

It was humiliating enough to be treated by these people as though he were one of them, but it was worse having this pervert condescend to him. Even the sailor's friendliness sounded condescending and fake. There was a calculating look in his eyes—he was already thinking of the money—that turned his overdone smiles and words into mockery. How could anyone who had done what this man had done in Blair's presence think he was better than Blair?

"So," said the sailor. "You want to go on up?"

"Shortly. I want something to drink first."

He expected the sailor to get it for him, to recognize who was master and who was servant here. But the sailor only said, "Nothing but beer. If you want something stronger, you'll have to talk with Mrs. Bosch."

"Beer will do," said Blair, not making a move toward the table with the pitcher and glasses.

The sailor stood where he was, grinning and calculating at Blair.

Then the door opened and the colored boy entered with a bowl of chipped ice that he slammed on the table. "Suck on this," he told the room, then wheeled around, and was almost out the door when he saw Hank with a customer.

The sailor was watching the boy. His smug confidence disappeared and he looked worried, uneasy.

The boy hung in the door. "Taking it slow tonight, aren't you, Blondie? All this white dick's getting mighty old."

But the sailor didn't tell the boy off or even laugh. He nervously turned his back on the boy.

"Lickorish!" hissed the boy, and he pulled the door shut.

"Crazy coon," the sailor mumbled. "Pay him no mind."

Blair thought Southerners hated coloreds, but the sailor seemed distressed by the boy, even frightened of him. Or maybe it was the mere suggestion of sex with a colored that disgusted the sailor. It disgusted Blair too, but to a Southerner it must be a fate worse than death. It would be as humiliating to a Southerner as sodomy is to a man. Blair wanted to humiliate the sailor.

"So. You said you wanted a beer?" The sailor seemed ready to get it for him.

"Not anymore. Let's go up." Blair knew he could not make his proposal in the presence of others.

"Fine by me. Time's a' wastin'." He hurried to the door and opened it for Blair.

They started up the dark, creaking stairs and Blair waited until he reached the landing before he turned around and stopped the sailor. "This time, I prefer something different."

"No skin off my nose." The sailor stood a few steps down, so his face was level with Blair's chest. "We can just sit up there and talk tonight. You don't have to watch me do anything."

"I want to watch you," Blair said, smiling. "With someone else."

The sailor looked at him, then looked up toward the top floor and over the bannister to the floors below, only there was nobody in sight. "Yeah?"

"Yes. You and the colored boy."

It had all the effect Blair had hoped for. The smirky, blockish face looked confused, then blank, then horrified, then blank again. "Shoot." The sailor tried to grin. "You serious, mister?"

"There's fifty dollars in it for you."

The sailor hesitated. "Nyaah. Let's just talk tonight. You like talking, remember?"

"No. I don't feel like talking tonight. It's you and the colored boy. Or nothing." Blair was so bent on humiliating the man, he didn't care if he learned what he had come here for tonight. Or perhaps he could shake up the sailor so badly he could learn everything. Blair was amazed at what he was doing. He must be drunk.

There was still a look of watchful calculation in the sailor's eyes, but his face was slack and numb. His tongue rolled around the inside of his mouth, as if there was a terrible taste there. "Fifty dollars?" he muttered.

"To be split with the boy as you see fit. Although I expect a colored would jump at the privilege of doing things with a white man *for free.*"

"I don't know. What if *he* says no?"

"Why don't you ask him?" It would be wonderfully cruel to hear the sailor ask a nigger to go to bed with him.

"You're serious? This is really what you want?"

"We all have our odd peculiarities. Maybe this is one of mine."

The sailor stood very still, wheels turning inside his head. He suddenly leaned over the bannister and hollered, "Juke! Hey, Juke! We need you!" He turned back to Blair. "He mighta gone out."

"Call again."

The sailor did. There were footsteps down below and the boy's black hair and white eyes appeared in the narrow slit of the telescoped stairwell. Blair thought the boy's straight hair made him look like a monkey wearing a toupee.

"Oh. It's you," the boy answered.

"Can you come up a minute, Juke? There's something we have to ask you. Please?"

"Oh, yeah? What could you want from me?" But the boy started up the stairs.

"We'll go to your room," said Blair. "This kind of business should be transacted in private, don't you think?" The humiliation that had already begun with "please" would be even sharper when observed in close quarters.

The sailor resumed his walk up the stairs, then stopped and said, "No. We can ask him here."

"Oh, no. People might hear us. I have my reputation to think of." As if he cared what these lowlife degenerates thought of him. "Come along. You don't want to make me cross and lose your fifty dollars, do you?"

That fifty dollars actually seemed to give Blair complete power over the sailor, because, disgusted as the man was, he nodded and trudged on up the stairs.

"Come along, boy," Blair called down. "Time is money."

The sailor opened the door to his room and nodded Blair inside. He hesitated a moment, then entered, whistling as soon as he stepped into the room, walking into a corner and out again, whistling to himself as if terrified.

Downstairs, Erich was thinking about the celibacy of Brahms when he heard the tuneless whistling just below his ear. He pulled the headset on, adjusted the hard earphone and listened.

Sullivan looked up from his gun, now laid out in pieces on the cloth at his feet. "Our good fairy's got a customer?"

"No. I mean, yes," said Erich. "But not just any customer. He gave the signal."

"Damn." Sullivan stared at the pieces of his gun. He began to screw things back together. "Well?"

"Nobody's talking." Erich heard footsteps, then a straining chair, then another string of whistled notes.

"Maybe there isn't anybody," said Sullivan. "What if your fairy's up there alone and he does different voices. Maybe he's up there with Charlie McCarthy."

Erich raised his hand to silence Sullivan. Someone else had come into the room. Someone began to speak.

"Uh, close the door, will ya. Juke? I told him what you were gonna say, but this man here wants to ask you anyway."

Erich recognized Fayette's voice, edged with static like a news broadcast from across the ocean. What was the houseboy doing up there?

"Yeah? What didja want to ask me?"

The boy sounded as sassy as ever, but, without seeing his face, Erich didn't think he sounded especially Negro, at least not like Negroes on the radio.

"It's not my responsibility to ask. That's your prerogative, sailor."

The third voice was cool and measured, as precise as an Englishman's, but with the faintly nasal flatness of Americans. It did not sound like the voice of a spy. All Erich could picture was the kind of overaged young man you saw portraying youths on the New York stage.

Nobody spoke for a moment, then the houseboy said, "Been getting piss-elegant, Blondie? Oh, but darling, that paper lantern doesn't do a thing for this room. You have to turn off the light and turn on the one in the lantern."

Erich went pale.

"They're queering off already?" said Sullivan. "You're gonna make yourself sick if you listen to everything. It's gonna make *me* sick watching you listen."

Erich pressed the cup of the earphone hard over his ear, as if listening could stop the boy from giving them away.

12

JUKE STOOD under the Chinese lantern, fingering the cord and looking for a switch. He seemed to have gone to it only to prove his indifference to the tension in the room.

Hank had to blurt out the proposition, just to get the boy away from the microphone: "This man wants to watch. Us."

There. As soon as Hank said it, humiliating himself and Juke, he wanted to kill the man. Ever since he saw him tonight and remembered the man's contempt, Hank had been hating him, disguising his hatred with all the friendliness he could fake. Now he wanted to break the man's neck. But there were the men in the cellar to think of, listening to every word, and his country. The man should die for being a traitor, and not because of something personal.

Juke stood as still as an eight-ball, eyeing Hank. He had to be insulted. He was already angry with Hank and the idea that Hank and the man wanted to use him should make Juke furious, Hank thought.

The boy slowly turned to the well-dressed man already sitting in the chair. "Did I hear right? Not me watching you and him, but you watching him and me?"

"That is correct," said the man, narrowing his eyes and smiling at Hank, holding the seat of his chair with both hands.

"I told him you'd say no," said Hank.

"Yeah? You told him that?"

The boy's surprise sounded sarcastic. Hank hoped Juke would spit spiders at both of them, even if it meant driving the spy away.

Instead, the boy said, "How much you paying?"

"I'm paying your *friend* enough to make it worth his while," said the man. "It's up to him what kind of arrangement he wants to make with you."

"So, Blondie. What's a man have to pay to make you lay with me?"

"You don't have to do it, Juke. We don't need his money," Hank insisted.

"Fifty dollars," the man announced, relishing his ability to make trouble. "And if you don't do it, I'm leaving and neither of you will see a cent." He lowered his voice and snidely added, "Offer the boy a dollar. That should be enough."

And Juke began to grin at Hank, first with the right side of his mouth, then the left, the grin growing more shark-like as it stretched to its limit. "Okay. I'll give you a dollar. *Boy.*"

"That ain't what he meant," said Hank.

"I know what he meant. And I'm offering you a buck. Or are you worth that?"

"Beautiful," said the man. "Perfect."

Juke and Hank stared into each other's eyes, Juke viciously grinning, Hank stunned by the boy's craziness. Juke flared his nostrils as he took a deep breath.

"I don't want to put you through this," Hank whispered.

"Baby, I want to," Juke whispered back. "I'm gonna flush you down the toilet and out the sewer. And you're gonna be the cheapest piece of ass I ever had."

"No whispering," said the man. "I pay to hear everything. What're you saying?"

"Nothing," said Hank, staring differently at the boy.

Juke answered the look by thrusting his chin up and yanking his yellow necktie open. Then he stepped back and began to unbutton his fancy red shirt.

"You, too, sailor. Off with your clothes."

Hank glanced at the man—he sat there smiling bitterly, his jaw clenched—then at the paper lantern. The men downstairs were going to think him an idiot for letting this happen, and sick for doing it, but Hank didn't know what else could keep the man here long enough to start talking. He drew his blouse up over his head, wondering what he had done to make Juke hate him so much.

Juke was quickly undressing, coolly at first, with a steely look at Hank as he shook his shirt off his shoulders. But he stopped looking when he jerked his two-tone shoes off and threw them at the floor, then pulled at his belt as if he wanted to cinch himself in two. Undressing angered him and his anger confused Hank. If Juke wanted sex, if he was horny for Hank, Hank could understand that, queer as it was having a colored hot for you. Coloreds preferred coloreds, and found whites lousy lays. Juke said so himself. But Juke seemed to be doing this out of hatred.

Juke dropped his striped cotton trousers and kicked his feet out of them. He wore white boxer shorts that made him look blacker than ever. Then he bent over, yanked the shorts down and stepped out of them. When he stood straight again, he was a dark skinny kid with slicked hair, squashed nose and a prick that stuck out like a spike.

"Ah," went the man. "They're right about coloreds being . . . born ready."

Juke looked at Hank, but with less fight in his eyes. He looked almost resentful, or hurt, lips parted as if to tell Hank this was his fault.

Hank turned away to take off his pants. It embarrassed him to see Juke like this. Juke naked and hard wasn't quite Juke anymore. But seeing any hard cock was enough to work Hank up. Looking down at himself, he turned back to Juke, his cock becoming more like Juke's. Neither of them were cut. Two country boys, they stood there looking at their own and each other's bones.

"But it must be a myth about size."

The man's voice broke the trance. Juke glared at him, turned and shook his hips at the man, wagging his stick at him as if it were up for his benefit. And shook his black bottom at Hank.

"No! Get that thing away from me, nigger! Get on the bed. I don't want either of you closer to me than the bed." The man shooed Juke away with the back of one hand, his other hand still gripping the seat of the chair.

"I sure the hell don't want to touch *you*," said Juke, backing up to the bed, then stretching out on it.

"Now you. Get on the bed," the man ordered Hank. "Touch him. Touch the nigger."

If they were alone, Hank could forget who and what Juke was, forget everything but the sex, just as he always did, no matter how old or fat or ugly they were. But with the man insisting how vile this was, with Juke watching Hank and waiting to see what he could do, with the men somewhere inside the paper lantern, like God looking over your shoulder, Hank remained painfully conscious of everything.

He sat on the bed. He was naked but he still felt dressed, he was of so many minds. Touching another cock usually erased everything. He took hold of the cock in front of him. It felt like any boy's bone, a roundness with something square about it, like an end splice in a piece of half-inch rope, more slender and tense than a man's bone, as springy as a jew's harp. It was the best thing about sex with boys, although Hank preferred men. He drew the skin back and there was a sweet moan.

Juke was watching him. His pinched smile looked like a sneer, but there was still a pinch of hurt or something personal to his eyes. Then he reached out and grabbed Hank's cock.

Eyes and fingers—it was suddenly too intimate. Hank lowered his head so he wouldn't see Juke. His reflex to what was happening in his cock and hand brought his head down further and he took the boy's cock in his mouth.

"Yes. That's what I wanted to see you do. You're not so manly after all."

"What're they doing? You're not writing anything down," said Sullivan.

The pad lay on Erich's lap. His pencil was tapping a page that was blank except for the date and time of the suspect's arrival.

"He seems . . . I think . . . He's ordering Fayette to have sex with the houseboy."

"The nigger? And he's doing it?"

"Apparently." But why should that be any worse than a man doing it with a man? "Maybe he has no choice."

"Or he's doing it to make us sick. Stop listening. I'm turning this off until they finish. We didn't come here to listen to that."

"No. Something might get said. We have to listen." And afraid of what Sullivan might think of him, Erich added, "I can hardly hear anything, anyway." Which was true. Only when the suspect spoke was there any suggestion of what might be happening. The rest of it was sighs and static and Erich's imagination. All he could picture were their faces, Fayette's sharper than the houseboy's. Their bodies were abstract, the action imprecise, a covertly sexual dream where nothing was specific. Erich found himself falling into what he heard. It was all so disturbingly vague, general and sexless. Then the man spoke again—"You look like you're eating tar, sailor"—and it became obscene again. It was the presence of the spy that made the act upstairs specific and obscene. Consciousness was obscene. And Erich realized his listening made him part of the obscenity. He was a Jew of consciousness here.

Hank was aware of the room in his mouth. He had room to move his tongue up and down the skinny bone, feel it and taste it, brush his lips against the skin and kinked hair at its base. The fingers on his cock seemed to open his mouth and mind to anything. Then the fingers let go of him, joined the other hand in his hair, and Hank's mind closed up with thoughts. Such as the bad thing about boys being that they finished so quickly. Remembering that, Hank remembered Juke and thought about having a nigger come in his mouth. Then a voice said something about tar. Hank's tongue worked harder, against the voice, while his mind told him he was only finishing the boy as quickly as possible so he could get the man to talk and prove he was a spy.

"Kiss him. I want to see you kiss him."

Hands yanking his hair pulled Hank off the prick, pulled him up to Juke.

It was like Juke and the spy had done it together. But the spy sat five feet away, looking on in proud disgust, his hands still gripping the chair. Juke's hands held Hank's face over his face for a moment, as if he were afraid to kiss.

The boy's eyes were yellowish brown and his brown lips were rimmed inside with pink. But the body beneath Hank's was smooth and warm. Hank's mouth suddenly felt terribly empty. All right, he thought, I'll go to hell, and he was kissing Juke.

Full of tongues, Juke covered Hank with his hands. What he had intended wasn't happening. Juke had expected it to be quick and thoughtless, a hurried fuck by Blondie that would get the cracker out of his head for good. A fuck like a dump. The only pleasure was going to be the bit of humiliation. But it felt painfully good to be with Hank like this for a few minutes, even if it was for someone else. Juke could finish anytime he wanted, but not yet, not even when Hank went down on him and it was like a mouthful of angels. He wanted another minute. He wasn't going to give two whites the satisfaction of seeing him come first. He wanted to feel contemptuous of Hank for being such a mouth artist.

Hank kissed good, too, like he didn't know kissing wasn't manly. Touching the bulky shoulders, the broad back and tight white ass, Juke wondered if looks were deceiving and the man was just another queen. Proving that might cure him. Juke preferred men, for all their hypocrisy. He reached around from below and laid his hand behind Hank's balls. The man's legs parted, as if he wanted it. The circus queen watching them wanted to see a white man shame himself with dinge, and Juke was loath to give her an added thrill. But he wanted this for himself, and the muscular weight on top of him grew disturbingly attractive. His dick was good and slippery from the sucking. It bent like a spring when he pressed it against the hole, then popped right in, and Juke forgot his planned contempt.

The kissing went straight to Hank's cock and anus. He had to use one of them. When he felt a hand and then a cock between his legs, his body responded. He let the cock in. He settled into it. It felt like only a thick, deep finger, until it began to move and touched all the right places. He dug his fingers into the pomaded hair and kissed the boy deeper. The conked hair beneath the pomade felt coarse and Hank knew again the boy was colored. There were the men downstairs, but they wouldn't know *this* was happening. There was the spy five feet away, but Hank hated him and didn't care what he thought. None of it mattered now, because the boy sure knew how to fuck.

It's only making it worse, thought Juke, closing his eyes, moving with the body that now moved with his. But the man sure knew how to fuck.

It was remarkable what fifty dollars could do. The sailor lay on a picaninny and kissed him. Blair sat and watched, gloriously uninvolved and powerful. It was as satisfying as ordering an enemy to eat garbage. His mind was racing and he decided he was drunk after all, with strength if not with alcohol. Not even his proximity to the bed bothered him now. The sailor's twisted masculinity did not intimidate him tonight as it had when Blair was alone with him. Tonight the sailor was fully involved with someone else, a nigger at that, proving that his sexuality had absolutely nothing in common with Blair's. Blair disdainfully watched, as if at a barnyard.

Sitting this close, he did not have to see them whole. He hadn't liked it when the sailor and houseboy stood on the other side of the room and undressed. There was nothing uglier than a naked male with an erection, like a statue with a nail driven into it, and a colored male was almost as grotesque. But sitting close and seeing them in parts made them less male, less human. When the sailor fellated the boy, it was like the unsettling gibberish that passed for modern painting: a cross-section of a machine covered with hair. But Blair knew what it meant and was satisfied by the idea. Kissing was familiar enough for him to enjoy seeing it: the white face profaned itself with a black one, a man with a man. He imagined colored spit to have the consistency of dog saliva.

The sailor grimaced, broke the kiss and gripped the boy's skull. Blair thought he was going to kill the boy. Then the sailor regained control and resumed kissing, almost angrily it seemed. He had to be disgusted with himself for what he was doing. Blair felt it was only his money and watching that kept the sailor at it.

"Yes. Is that so bad? No worse than kissing your dog."

From the corner of his eye, he caught a new movement to their bodies. The sailor's bare buttocks still disturbed Blair. He thought about ordering the houseboy on top. Pictures of natives were so common there'd be nothing suggestive about *him*. Then Blair noticed the way the black hips and white buttocks rolled against each other, as if linked. He had to lean to the left to see if what he thought was happening was actually happening. The houseboy seemed to have his penis in the sailor's rectum. Perfect. Disgusting, but perfect. And yet the sailor continued to kiss the boy, oblivious to this new humiliation.

"He has his dick in your asshole, sailor." It was only Blair's contempt that enabled him to use such words. "Did you know that? Did you know this nigger is fucking you like a woman?"

Erich heard the man through the headset and shifted in his seat, flexing his buttocks together.

"What's happened now?" said Sullivan.

"Uh, an act of sodomy."

"What! Isn't that what they've been doing all along? What else is there for queers to do?"

Erich nervously shook his head. He wouldn't tell Sullivan who was doing it to whom. Sullivan might renounce the whole enterprise if he knew their man was the pedicant. Without knowing why, Erich was disturbed to learn that himself, as if he expected something better from Fayette. As if he thought a man's honor was in his ass. He didn't like remembering that part of his body.

Their bodies were sweating and as slippery as tongues. Hank's balls and cock rode against the warm, wet stomach like they were part of the cock that rode inside him. He was so deep into fucking that a moment passed before he realized the spy had said something. It was of no matter. The men in the cellar would catch it if it were anything important. And remembering the men, Hank had to choke back his urge to start moaning.

Juke kept going. It was a long, slow fuck, the kind he liked but rarely got. If only Hank could admit his pleasure with a little noise, then Juke could admit his. Their heavy breathing made it sound like work, but Juke wasn't going to be the one to break the silence. Whores, they were both experts, he told himself. That's all this was, and he raised his knees so he could use his legs to push deeper.

"Just like a woman," Blair repeated, annoyed the insult was getting no response. "Is the Navy full of women? There are no women in Hitler's navy."

The blond queer—he was no longer a sailor or even a man—lifted his mouth from the houseboy's mouth and looked at Blair. His eyes were half closed, his lips thick and dark. And he just looked at Blair while his body continued its slow, obscene squirm. The houseboy rolled his head over and looked at Blair through his heavy eyelids, shining black body rocking away.

It was suddenly disgusting, all of it. If one of them were hating it, if there were the suggestion one was violating the other, then Blair might be able to watch. But to have both of them shamelessly look out at him from their shared pleasure was sickening. They made *him* feel like the pervert.

"All right," he said. "That's enough. You can stop now."

Erich drew a deep breath, relieved.

Juke went at it harder, to stop Hank from listening to the man. Hank closed his eyes and shook his head.

"Stop it! I told you to stop!"

But Hank gritted his teeth and kept going. It wasn't just the sex. It was his anger with the spy, with the men listening, even with Juke for being part of this that made Hank hold tight to the fucking. To hell with the others. This was his body, his pleasure. And he let loose with a deep, loud groan.

Juke responded with his own high, sweet sounds.

Erich heard two people killing each other.

Blair jumped up from his chair. "Stop or you won't see that fifty bucks!" They made vile noises at him and he stepped forward, burning to slap the white's face and bring him to his senses. Then he saw the white ass with black testicles. "You're being fucked by a nigger! Good white hillbilly. What would your pappy say?"

Hank threw his hand out and grabbed the man's necktie. With a flip of his arm, he whipped the tie twice around his hand and yanked the man's face in. Gripping the tie, he turned back to Juke and violently kissed the boy.

Blair tried to pull back and his tie choked him. He tried to use both hands to undo the sailor's grip, but the fingers were like a knot. The sailor's other hand gripped the back of the boy's neck. Blair was so close to their faces he felt their humid breaths and smelled their hot skin, saw the black tongue and was horrified the sailor would force Blair to kiss the boy.

Juke saw the red face straining at its necktie and was afraid Hank would kiss the man, pull him on the bed and make him part of this. Juke fucked harder, so they could finish alone. But Hank went at it harder, too, kissing, then biting, holding the man's face a foot from theirs.

"Okay, mister." Hank broke the kiss and spoke in gasps. "You wanna sneer? Sneer at this!" And he threw his head back and came, yanking at the tie and thrusting into Juke. He crowed like he was raping the spy, or raping Hitler and ending the war. It felt so strong it had to accomplish something.

Seeing Hank go, feeling the squeeze around his cock, Juke let go, loudly, closing his eyes and giving in, like it was a busted artery that could bleed him white of Hank.

They heaved and groaned like epileptics, faces clenched around their open mouths. Blair panicked. "Let go, you damn—" He pulled back so hard his necktie choked him and he couldn't speak. He thought he would pass out. He squeezed his eyes shut and heard the accelerating breaths and moans of two animals being tortured to death. He wanted them to die.

Erich closed his eyes. He opened his mouth a little, as if that could help him picture what was happening. He knew they weren't killing each other. The women in brothels in Vienna groaned like that. So did the barmaid he saw for a time in Cambridge. But one voice dropped out, then the other, and Erich remembered these were two men. Women went on much longer, although Erich had suspected they were pretending sometimes. He wondered if Fayette and the houseboy had been pretending. He hoped so, because it was difficult to condemn such passionate pleasure, no matter how unseemly or unnatural it was.

"They've finished," he calmly announced.

"About time," said Sullivan. "I hope for your sake the creep says something. Or you would've had to hear all that for nothing."

Erich remembered the spy and wondered what Fayette had been doing to the man to upset him. He thought he should feel sorry for the spy—the two of them had something in common here—but, spy or not, he despised the man.

Blair opened his eyes. It had seemed to go on forever, like an instant when you think you're drowning. The hand suddenly dropped from his tie. Blair stumbled back. The sailor lay on the boy like a corpse. The boy lay very still, breathing through his bared teeth. There was a harsh smell in the room like the stink of the ailanthus trees that were budding all over the city.

He could kill them both, if he had a gun or knife in his hand. He was humiliated. He had been a fool for thinking he could humiliate a degenerate, when such people were beneath shame or human feeling. He refused to let them know how ashamed he was of his helplessness. And there was his purpose in being here to consider. Blair had not forgotten that. He backed into the chair and sat down again.

"Yes. Very good. *That's* what I wanted to see," he claimed.

The sailor slowly lifted his head and looked at him.

"Quite a show. You can get dressed now."

The sailor rolled off the boy, but lay on the bed, facing Blair. His penis was a vile shade of red, the hairs on his stomach matted and gluey.

"You can get dressed, I said. Please."

"You don't want to talk? About the war and stuff."

"Of course. You know I enjoy talking with our servicemen, getting 'the real skinny,' as you call it." He was pleased to have the sailor suggest it, despite their battle of wills. This was going to be easier than he thought. "But wouldn't you feel more comfortable if you had some clothes on?"

"No. I feel comfortable like this." He propped his head up with his arm and elbow. There was a look of defiance in his eyes.

Blair refused to acknowledge the look. "Very well. But what about your . . . colored friend. I can't imagine he'd have much of interest to contribute."

"Juke?" The sailor whispered to the boy and lightly jostled him, without taking his eyes off Blair.

The boy seemed to have fallen asleep. He murmured something, then rolled against the sailor, covering the white nakedness with a black one.

"Never mind. Let him sleep," said Blair. He wanted to get this over with as quickly as possible, while his cleverness was still intact. "So. Any new scuttlebutt?"

The sailor's eyes roamed the room. "What do you want to know?"

"Nothing in particular. Just some more inside information with which I can impress my drinking companions. Such as, oh, something more about Sledgehammer."

"That Africa thing? Wahl," he drawled, "I know about that only because of the charts they sent us. They tell us nothing, you know."

Erich's pencil raced over the pad, getting as much of it down as possible. He knew no shorthand. The man's questions were certainly dangerous, but he didn't talk like a spy. His conversation was so transparent, even direct, that Erich thought he might be what he said he was, a prying civilian who wanted to be let inside. The man wasn't even suspicious when Fayette suggested they talk, despite all that had happened before. If the man were a spy, he must think Fayette a complete idiot. But Erich had once thought that himself.

"Oh, before I forget," said Blair, reaching into his pocket and extracting his money clip. A book of matches fell to the floor. Blair noticed them, then forgot about them while he concentrated on keeping the sailor talking. "Your fifty dollars." He peeled off two twenties and a ten and returned the clip to his pocket. "But you said it was going to be Dakar. French West Africa. I presume they'll drive north and attack Rommel from the rear, after they beat the French."

The sailor reached across the sleeping boy and accepted the money. He just held it in his hand, as if fifty dollars didn't interest him. Blair wondered if he'd made a mistake flashing the rest of his money.

"There hasn't been any word about *when* this invasion might be?"

"Hell, no. That's the last thing they tell us. But there've been rumors," said the sailor. "Like January."

"Next year?" Blair couldn't believe that.

"Or August."

"That's only next month." Blair felt the sailor was toying with him, teasing him with something he really knew. Or mocking him for watching them copulate. "What makes people think it'll be so soon?"

"War's been going on for six months now. Time we invaded somebody."

"But has there been anything to substantiate the rumors? Back them up?"

"Wahl, we been doing landing drills every day now, like it was gonna be sometime soon. That's why *I* think it's gonna be August. And the ack-ack guys just got an issue of those big-brimmed helmets like you see in Tarzan movies."

"Hmmm."

"Also, and this is why I don't think it's gonna be any earlier, everybody in my section who had leave scheduled for August or after has had their leave cancelled. But not the July guys."

"Really?" Now *that* suggested something.

"And, best of all, the officers' wives and families are starting to trickle into town for visits, no matter what part of the country they live in. Like they know they're not going to see their honeys for a long time."

When the sailor started, he sounded almost as though he was making it up as he went along. But that was only the hillbilly's slow-witted way of speaking, Blair decided. Because it certainly sounded convincing. "Can you think of anything else that points to August? What makes people say January?"

"Nothing really. Except that they don't want to think they're going overseas anytime soon."

"I see. But if you were a betting man, you'd bet your money on August?"

"At two-to-one odds, mister."

There. He was finished with the degenerate. He did not have to pretend to be friendly anymore. "So. Africa in August. You should love Africa, sailor." Blair smirked and nodded at the sleeping boy. "If you live to set foot on it."

But neither the insult nor threat disturbed the sailor. He coolly looked straight at Blair and said, "You're real smart, mister. And tough. But I scared the shit out of you a minute ago, just by fucking."

"Nonsense. I was worried you were going to get my suit dirty." But there was no need now for Blair to defend himself politely. "Anyway, you weren't *fucking.*" He spat the word out. "You were the one being fucked. By a nigger."

"Better him than you up my ass, mister."

"I'm no pervert, you degenerate." He kept his voice as low as the sailor's, manfully refusing to lose his temper.

"Yeah? I hear your buddy Hitler's got a streak of pansy in him too."

"Hitler—!" He was sick of hearing that about Hitler, and to hear it now from a pervert? "Adolf Hitler knew how to deal with sickness like yours. When he found Roehm in bed with a catamite, he pulled out his pistol and shot both of them himself. Which is what you deserve. Only this country is soft on perversion. I'd go to prison if I killed you and your friend, and you're not worth it!"

The colored boy just lay there, but he couldn't be sleeping through this. Sex probably blew away the little intelligence coloreds had.

The sailor just smiled, as cool as ice. "So why do you come here, mister? Why did you pay to watch us? You envious?" And he began to whistle, then sing:

> Goering has two, but they're both small.
> Himmler has something similar.
> And Goebbels has no balls at all.

Blair despised that low song, which reduced everything to sex. "I come here just to see how bad things are in this country. Your kind of behavior wasn't tolerated before Roosevelt. And it wouldn't happen under Hitler."

"So you and your friends'll take care of me."

"My friends and I will see to it that your kind is wiped from this country. Look at this city. It's worse than Weimar Berlin. You'd think war would put an end to such filth, but no, it's made it worse than ever. Girls sleeping with servicemen. Pansies picking up sailors. Sailors sleeping with *niggers*. War has proved how depraved this country really is. We deserve to lose!"

"I don't see you doing anything, mister. You just like to watch, huh? That's all you're good for."

"What do you know?" Blair sneered. "For all you know, I could be a Nazi spy." He finally said it. He'd been dying to say it, just to put the fear of God into the pervert, to shake his arrogance. "What if I am? What if everything you told me tonight will go straight to Berlin, and a fleet of U-boats will be waiting for you at Dakar? Won't you feel like a fool, causing hundreds of thousands of deaths because you were so busy satisfying your animal lusts?"

That startled the sailor. He glanced at the ceiling, then shook his head and said, "Naw. You're not a spy. Right?"

"Maybe. Maybe not." But Blair would only go so far. This fool might believe him. "Of course not. I'm an American. A better American than you. But a city as rotten as this one is full of spies. The way you talk, you've probably already cut your throat." Blair stood up. "For all you know, I'm with the FBI. Maybe I came here just to test you, to see if you knew how to keep your mouth shut. But you'll never know that for certain, until they come to arrest you."

"You leaving, mister?" The vague threat must have unnerved the sailor, because he spoke much louder than before.

"He's leaving," said Erich, although Sullivan had been reading all of it over his shoulder and was already putting his coat back on. "You ready?"

Sullivan patted his pockets and holster. "Dumbest spy I ever heard of. Or the craziest. I bet I trail this clown right back to a ward at Bellevue." But he hurried up the steps and out the cellar door.

Blair fixed the knot against his throat and smoothed the crumpled necktie flat against his shirt. "Yes. This has been most interesting. Most entertaining. The depths we've sunk to." He opened the door.

"Good riddance," said the sailor. "See you in hell."

For that, Blair left the door wide open. Let anyone who walked by get a glimpse of them in there. He wanted to be able to tell someone, "I just watched a nigger screw a sailor. Most amusing." But there was nobody in the hall or on the stairs. What Blair really wanted to do was kill both of them. Going down the stairs, he felt ashamed again for seeing such indecency and not being able to punish it.

The front hall was empty. He opened the front door and stepped outside. His feelings of shame and helplessness suddenly lifted. He never had to come here again. He breathed the thick night air and wondered where he could catch a taxi. He wanted to get home and telephone Anna. She had promised to come see him the very night he learned what he had learned. He couldn't wait to tell her what he knew, in his apartment, among his things, in his bed.

The street was dark and wide open. Stars were visible overhead. The silence was wonderful, freeing him to think about Anna, love and his success as a spy. His footsteps lightly echoed in the bay of blacked-out buildings, like a second pair of shoes.

Juke heard the man leave, then felt Hank's warm weight get up from the bed when Hank went to shut the door.

"It's over. He's gone," Hank said loudly, as if to wake Juke. But he looked down at the bed and said, "I knew you was playing possum."

Juke rolled over and faced Hank, smirking. "Oh, but I wasn't," he sang. "You loved me silly, Blondie." He watched for Hank's response to his taunting, not wanting to show any real feelings until he had some idea what Hank felt.

Hank only bent down and picked a book of matches off the floor.

"And I fucked the bejeezus outa you," Juke announced. "You ain't telling me that's the first time you got fucked."

"That's for sure," Hank muttered, opening and closing the matches, reading what was printed on them. "What's an El Morocco?"

"Huh? Just a place. A clip joint for whites with too much money. That circus queen forget her matches?" He knew Hank was stalling, ashamed to admit he'd been fucked and enjoyed it. But a guy who was truly ashamed would have pulled his clothes on fast, and Hank just stood there, bulky and naked, like they'd done nothing more than had a nice swim together.

"I guess it's where that creep hangs out." Hank carefully set the matchbook and the folded money on his dresser. "You want some of this?" he asked, tapping the money. It was as if he wanted to hide what had happened with a few bills.

"Ain't you forgetting?" said Juke. "I was paying you. One dollar. You want it now? You think I might stiff you? Again?"

Hank looked at him, turned away and said, "Screw you." But he said it without anger. He stood at the dresser, then gingerly picked up the pitcher there, poured some water into the knicked bedpan, wetted the stiff washcloth that hung from a nail on the wall and began to dab at his front.

Juke hesitated. He knew he had gotten himself where he wanted to be: under Hank's skin. But it was a dangerous place to be. There was no telling what the man might do to shake him out. Juke had to be very careful, or he was going to get hurt. And, despite all his wishful thinking, the sex had only gotten Hank deeper under Juke's skin.

"You might not like admitting it," said Juke, "but your body sure had one hell of a party here."

"Yeah," said Hank. "I'd be lying if I didn't say part of me enjoyed that." He mopped himself with the washcloth, as if to get rid of the evidence.

"And I'd be lying if I didn't say part of me enjoyed it, too. You sure know how to have a good time, Blondie." Juke didn't want to go too far, so he went at it from another angle. "That circus queen was sure one sick woman. What was all that shit about spies and FBI? Sounded to me like she was out to screw your head up."

Hank slowly, absently nodded. Then he shyly turned around, holding the washcloth over his genitals. "I'm sorry I did that to you, Juke."

"Did what? I did it to you," Juke said with a laugh.

But Hank stayed serious. "Did it with you. For that creep."

"Would you have done it without the creep?"

"No." But Hank said it softly, as if he was sorry. "Only I don't know what I'm doing anymore. Everything's so topsy-turvy right now." He looked down at himself while he rubbed himself clean, then stopped rubbing. "I just never thought of you that way, Juke."

"What way?" Did he know? Had Juke given himself away during the sex? If Hank knew Juke was in love with him, then that would give Hank the upper hand. The possibility frightened Juke, and yet he found he was hoping Hank knew.

"For sex. As someone good for a lay."

"Whadja think I was? Potatoes and gravy?"

"No. Just that you people have your sex with each other, and we have ours. I'm sure dogs never think about sex when they think about cats."

Meow, thought Juke, but kept it to himself. No, it was better this way. The cracker was confused enough by lust. Talking to him about love would be like talking about Santa Claus. "Well, you know what they say," said Juke. "It's all pink on the inside."

"Yeah. I guess."

"But you do know how to enjoy yourself. For a white boy."

"Yeah. Well . . ." Hank hung up the washcloth and quickly rubbed his front with the hand towel. He walked around the foot of the bed to where his clothes lay on the floor. He wouldn't look at Juke while he pulled things on.

"You know," said Juke. "I wouldn't mind doing that again some-day. Next time that john comes back wanting another show."

"No. I don't think we'll see him again."

"Some other creep then. The woodwork's full of them."

Hank buttoned up his white bellbottoms and could then look back at the bed. "Juke. I plain don't know. That was real good, only . . . I don't know if we should do it again."

Juke sat up with his knees against his chest, so Hank wouldn't see he was getting hard again. The man hadn't said no. And after sex, even good sex, many people talked like they were never going to need sex again. Hank's confusion was as good as a yes.

"No sweat, Blondie. It's not like you're the best I've ever had. But it's good keeping in practice while we're waiting for the real thing."

Hank wiggled into his blouse. He was dressed again, but Juke would always see him naked whenever he looked at him now, for better or for worse.

"Hey," said Juke. "You wanna go to a party? Night after tomor-row night."

"You mean . . . a party party?"

Juke laughed. "You think I plan the other kind of party that far in advance? Just some of the girls. And boys. Be fun. Get you out of this hole for a night. You never go anywhere, Blondie. No wonder you feel crazy all the time."

"Yeah. Maybe. I should do something to celebrate."

"Celebrate what?"

"Nothing. Not celebrate. Just have a good time." Hank looked like he'd said too much. About them? "Uh, this party all your people?"

"All *our* people, honey. And all flavors. Neapolitan. But mostly vanilla, if that's what's worrying you."

"All right. Let me think about it." He nodded, tried to smile, then said, almost apologetically, "I better get down the hall now. To the head."

"Sure thing, baby. You have a good douche. But think about that party."

Hank opened the door, checked the hallway and stepped out.

Juke waited a moment, listening. Then he threw his back against the mattress and groaned, "Alpheus! You stupid little queen!"

Erich flicked off the amplifier. He peeled the headset from his head. He had no business listening to any of that. It had nothing to do with spies. Fayette and the houseboy seemed to be in love with each other, although neither wanted to admit it. At least that's what it meant when a man and a woman danced around each other in that manner. Maybe it meant something different when it was two men. Erich no longer attempted to argue with himself that these were degenerates, creatures with utterly foreign emotions and thoughts. They were men and human. Distressingly human.

He packed everything into the suitcase with the amplifier. Someone would have to come back tomorrow for the microphone upstairs and the outside line. Erich carried the heavy suitcase out to the street. The Ford was gone. Sullivan's assistant would be following Sullivan in the car, moving in to pick up his boss only if their prey caught a taxi or had his own automobile parked nearby. Erich felt very alone walking through the dark streets to the subway.

In his narrow room at the Sloane House, he slid the suitcase under the bed, changed his clothes and combed his hair. He immediately went out again, walking uptown towards Times Square. He wanted to meet a woman tonight, a soft body with long hair, breasts and a womb. He needed to direct all his raw turbulence at someone who could give him back his moorings.

13

IT WAS ALMOST NOON the next day when Anna left her lover's apartment. She floated down to the street in the lovely oak-paneled elevator, enjoying the respectful smile in the elderly attendant's eyes. She knew she was glowing; the man had to see her happiness. Down in the lobby, a young man in a rumpled suit and cream fedora looked up from the newspaper he read on the sofa when she walked past. He uncrossed his legs, as though he had to have both feet on the floor when he saw someone so happy and beautiful. Anna enjoyed having men see her like this. When she glanced back from the revolving door out front, the young man quickly looked away, embarrassed to be caught admiring her.

Park Avenue looked richer and less forbidding this morning, now that she had been inside its austere stone walls. The morning was beautiful and Anna decided to cross the city through Central Park. There was still a trace of coolness in the shadows beneath the trees. Her cotton dress felt light and airy against her skin. She had never been so conscious of the naked wholeness beneath her clothes.

It had been wonderful. The late night taxi ride across town, the doorman paying the driver, the enormous rooms upstairs, the new furniture, the wide fragrant bed. Blair had his own apartment. His mother and father lived on another floor in the same building, but they were away for the summer and there had been no fear of unexpected visitors. The help had been given the evening off. There had been strangeness at first, kissing and touching in complete privacy, knowing there was no one around to stop Blair, or Anna, from doing anything. Blair became uncomfortable when she did too much, and he was horrified when she impulsively gave his thing a quick kiss. So she let him lead, and that was fine. He had loved her breasts, gratefully kissing and handling them, and was fascinated by her privates, his fingers constantly combing the hair between her legs even when they were done. She was sorry it had not lasted longer, but it was the doing that was important, not the feeling. Blair looked distressed this morning when he saw the dark-edged spot of blood on the sheet, which surprised Anna. She thought men were supposed to be proud of being the first.

Anna slowly walked through the park among the children, nannies and great black perambulators. She stopped by Bethesda Fountain, set her hands and white purse on the stone balustrade and looked down at the plaza and fountain. She wanted Blair to ask her to be his wife, but she wasn't going to spoil today's happiness by thinking too much on that. Out beyond the rainbowed spray of the fountain, a weekday scattering of rowboats milled about on the lake. In one, a young man in shirtsleeves pulled on the oars while an elderly woman sat in the stern holding a white parasol with ruffles. The couples in the three or four other boats were all male, sailors, or a sailor and civilian in one. Anna felt sorry for them. Every man deserved a woman. Without women, they looked like little boys out there and Anna felt sorrier than ever about what their Government was doing to them. She was sorry there had not been time for Blair to take her for a ride on the lake today, but she needed to get to the Lyric soon and tell her father what Blair had learned.

Walking away from the fountain, back into the shade and toward the bandshell, Anna noticed a man in a cream fedora talking to a peanut vendor. It looked like the young man with a similar hat from Blair's lobby. He had a newspaper under his arm. He turned away slightly when she saw him, tugging down the brim of his hat so she couldn't see where he was looking.

Anna continued walking, straight toward the wide promenade tented with elms. She stayed calm. She adjusted her own hat as she drew level with him—he was ten feet away—and saw that it was the same man, the same rumpled suit. During the first month of helping her father, Anna had learned not to be upset by coincidences or wolves. But a wolf would have attempted to cross her path, even tried to speak to her and this man simply let her pass.

The promenade was long and lined with benches. Anna could not leave it without drawing attention to herself. She walked its full length, without once looking behind her. She stopped by the statue of a poet at the foot of the promenade and took a cigarette from her purse. She turned around while she lit it, as if shielding the flame from a draught: the cream fedora was gone. Of course. What detective or agent would follow her from Blair's building? Blair was above suspicion with the police. Nobody knew either of them. Still, one couldn't be too careful. The cigarette lit, she went ahead and smoked it. Anna frequently felt she had an audience out there, somewhere, although the spectator in her mind's eye was always her father.

There were few horse-drawn carriages on the park drive this summer, as if even horses had been drafted. Anna followed the path away from the drive toward the playground, its squeaking swings and squealing children. Her father used to take her here when she was little. After last night, she wasn't little anymore. Anna felt a brief tug of sadness over that. The benches around the playground were lined with black and white: all nannies and sailors. There was a solitary whistle as she walked by, but any sailor who came to watch children was going to be on his best behavior. She circled the playground and climbed the path up the hill, stopping to take one last look at the children down below. Then she saw him again, bent over a water fountain a hundred yards away, his cream fedora pushed to the back of his head.

She resumed walking, more quickly now. She set off for Columbus Circle, thinking she might lose him in the crowd there. As she approached the street, the park grew thicker with men and women on their lunch break. The white monument and green newsstand at the entrance were mobbed. Anna was short. The man following her—if he were following her—would not be able to see her in this sea of heads and hats. She went down the stairs to the subway but, through the bars, saw that the platform was empty. A train had just come and the man might see her if she stood on the platform alone, waiting for the next train. She went back up the stairs and passed the man in the cream fedora, racing down the steps. He did not lower his head fast enough to hide the startled look on his face.

The jolt of seeing him up close panicked Anna. She ran up the last steps and pushed her way through the crowd until she reached the curb, then stepped into the street and raised her arm to hail a taxi, until she realized no cab could stop here. She stepped back into the crowd. She told herself to stay calm. Her heart was racing. She would not run. If the man saw she knew he was following her, he would follow more closely and be impossible to lose. She firmly clutched her purse and started to walk up Broadway.

Three blocks up, she abruptly stepped into a drugstore. She went past the crowded lunch counter to the pack of people waiting to use the bank of telephone booths in the back. An emergency, she told them and asked to use the next available phone. The men promptly agreed; the women required a little story. Finally, she sealed herself behind the folding glass doors of a booth, sat on the wooden seat and dialed the Lyric Theater. She asked for the projectionist and said she was his daughter.

Outside the fingerprinted glass, beneath the rotating fans, there was no sign of the man. But he wouldn't stand where she could see him once she was in the booth.

Simon's voice came on. "Yes? Anna?"

"Papa?" Her thoughts instantly cleared. "I wouldn't be calling you, except—Papa, I think I'm being followed."

"Where were you last night?"

Her mouth went dry. "With Blair," she said. "At his apartment."

Simon was silent a moment. "And you were followed from there?"

"Yes, Papa." And she told him about the man and each place she had seen him.

"You are certain it is the same man and not just the same hat? It is not an uncommon hat."

"No. I'm sure, Papa. I've seen him up close. I'm sorry I messed things up, Papa. I really am sorry." She was close to tears.

"Stay calm, dear. You must stay calm. Nobody is blaming you. What did you learn from your *boyfriend* last night?"

There was his usual contempt in his mention of Blair, and Anna had to think twice before she realized what Simon meant. "August. He spoke to his sailor friend and the friend has good reason to think it'll be in August. He did well, didn't he?"

"August. That is good to know. *If* our friend isn't working for the police."

"You think Blair . . .?" All through her panic, Anna had never considered the possibility. "No! That's impossible."

"Then why were you followed from his apartment?"

"I don't know. But Blair's one of us. I'm sure of that. I know him too well. I couldn't be in love with him if I didn't know him through and through." She hadn't meant to confess her love. She waited for her father to react to that.

"How much money do you have?" Simon asked.

She told him.

"Very good. Listen to me. You must go to a hotel for women, a clean hotel, and take a room. You are to stay there tonight. You cannot come to the theater. You must not come home."

"Papa! *Please!* I was wrong. It's all my fault. But don't punish me like this. I need to see you."

"I am not punishing you. If you are being followed, it's too dangerous for you to see me. Not to worry. Maybe the man is only a masher. If so, it will only be for tonight. This hurts me as much as it hurts you, dear."

"Yes. You're right." But Anna still felt he was punishing her. She felt she deserved to be punished.

"Find a clean room in a nice place. Do not, under any circumstances, go back to your Blair's apartment. You are not to see him again. *Ever.*"

"But Blair's not with the police, Papa. I know he's not."

"Even so. He is arrogant and inept. Somebody must suspect him of something, or that man would not have followed you from his apartment. We have learned what we needed from him. We must now wash our hands of him. He is a danger to both you *and* me." Simon paused. "I am sorry you feel so strongly about him, Anna. But there is your family to think of. This boy endangers all of us."

"Yes, Papa."

Simon closed by telling her not to telephone home, but to call him at the theater at noon the next day. He would explain her absence to Aunt Ilsa. "Everything will be fine again. I promise. Do not fret, dearest. Goodbye."

Anna hung up, her stomach tensing. Talking to her father, she felt she could put aside her love for Blair. Alone, she was painfully in love with him again.

She pushed the booth door open and stumbled out, remembering to glance back at the other booths, looking for the pale hat. She didn't see the man anywhere in the drugstore. Out on the sidewalk, she burrowed into the crowd and let the current of people carry her uptown. He was sure to be somewhere behind her. It was his fault she was now cut off from her father, his fault and Blair's.

The crowd began to thin out up toward Sixty-sixth Street, where rows of mud-colored tenements pressed against the grimy hotels and pawnshops along Broadway. Aware of where she was, Anna was suddenly aware of something else she should do. There was a bar with a pink-gray neon palm tree in its sunlit window. Anna went inside. The place was quiet, with a handful of men her father's age picking at the free lunch that came with their beer. She went into the ladies room and splashed water on her face and neck. She came out and went straight to the lone phone booth wedged in the corner. She closed the door, thought a moment, then slipped a nickel in and dialed Blair.

Blair was still in his robe, sitting in a wing-backed chair, slippers on the oriental carpet, cup of coffee at his elbow, pretending to read the good, gray *Times* while he floated in his dream of success and love—love was so much clearer now that he was alone with it— when the telephone rang.

"Anna? Darling, hello. I was just thinking about you. How did it go with your father? Was he impressed with my discovery?"

From where he sat, he could see his and Anna's city through the enormous curtained windows. He sat at the top of the world. Last night had been wonderful, laying to rest all his foolish fears about being powerless. He was so buoyed up with love and strength and confidence it took him a moment to hear Anna's flat, breathless tone, then to understand that she hadn't seen her father. Then that a man had been following her. From Blair's lobby.

"Oh, my God." But he said it automatically, only in response to Anna's tone. "You're certain of that? I don't understand. Why would anyone care about you seeing me? This is awfully unreal over the telephone, darling. Why don't you meet me at Morocco in an hour or so? We can discuss this face to face, have an eye-opener and—"

"Blair! Can't you see? They're watching both of us! You most of all. If they see us together again, they'll know for sure. And if they know about me, they'll know about Papa, and that'd be the end of everything. We can't risk seeing each other."

That hit first. He was losing Anna almost as soon as he had had her? It was too cruel, too ironic. Then he understood why. "They're watching *me?*" He was blank before the possibility, until he remembered the house last night. "Damn. Damn them."

"What is it, Blair? You know why they're watching you?"

There was nobody else who could have accused him, even falsely. The homo sailor had done it out of spite; he couldn't know for certain Blair was a spy. The homo sailor had gone to the police with a lie inspired by Blair's taunts. It was a queer's revenge on a real man.

"You blabbed to some stranger, Blair!" said Anna, reading that into his silence.

"No. I didn't blab to anyone," he said angrily. "What kind of idiot do you think I am?" But he felt like an idiot, reduced to helplessness by a pervert. His feeling of power collapsed and he was left with a numbing hatred. It was as if the hatred had been there all along, left over from last night but temporarily blocked by love for Anna and confidence in himself. "You can't see me? You couldn't do something to lose this man and come over? You could stay here, Anna, until this was over and done with. We could lay low together."

She was silent for a long time. "No. I only saw the one man, but there's sure to be others. I might lose him, but I'll never know who else is following me. And . . . I promised my father I wouldn't see you again."

"Who are you in love with, Anna? Me or your father?"

"I . . . You have no right to talk to me like that. I feel angry with you already, for letting my feelings for you get us into this."

It hurt that she blamed love. The queer had poisoned everything. "I'm sorry. I didn't mean that, Anna. But I love you. I'll do something to fix this. I will."

"How? What's there you can do?"

"I don't know." he admitted. "There has to be something. I won't just sit by helplessly and let us end like this."

"It's not just us, Blair. If the police suspect you of anything, there's a chance you'll be arrested.

"That's not important to me." He wanted to be heroic and selfless, but the truth was that Blair couldn't really believe *he* was in danger. It was too impossible. "You're going to take a room somewhere, you said. Call me when you know where you'll be, Anna. So I can reach you when I've cleared this mess up."

"Blair. Don't do anything rash. Please." Concern surfaced in the voice that had had all emotion frightened out of it. "Don't do anything that might hurt me and my father."

"Of course not. Don't talk foolish. I love you." He waited for her to say she loved him, but she said nothing. "Goodbye, Anna. We'll see each other in a day or so. I promise."

"Yes? Maybe. Okay then. Goodbye, Blair." And she hung up.

Blair quickly returned the receiver to its white cradle, as if he had things to do. But he only sat there, very still, for a long time. It was only right that she loved her father more than she loved him. With his stupidity and helplessness, it was right that she not love him at all. He had to do something to prove himself to her. He had to clear away the danger he had created by consorting with degenerates. If he went to the police and explained to them who he was, then told them their informer was a homosexual prostitute . . . But that solution was as distasteful as it was impractical. Even if he found the people responsible—police or FBI or whatever—and even if they believed him and he was cleared and the queer put in prison, he would be turning over to the authorities a task that should be his. His own failure would remain with him for the rest of his life. What then?

There was an annoying tickle across his ankles, a sickening caress of something silky. Blair looked down and saw Ming, his mother's Siamese cat, rubbing herself on his leg. He picked her up just as he always did, held her in his lap and stroked her. He suddenly disgusted himself. Here he was, a grown man in wartime, lounging in his robe and caressing a pussycat. He lifted Ming beneath her forelegs and looked into her glassy, mascaraed eyes. She returned his look with perfect calm, coolly acknowledging his harmlessness. It was unnerving to find such human eyes gazing back at him from the face of a cat.

Blair stood up and went to the window that looked out on Park Avenue, carrying Ming in the crook of one arm. He pushed open a panel of the window with his free hand. Ming hung on his arm, boneless and unthreatened. Only when he held her with both hands and lifted her toward the window did she snap to life, twisting and scratching, her pink mouth wide open.

"Stupid pussy," he said, thrust his arms out and released her.

She seemed to hang in midair for an instant, flipping herself about as if she could save herself by landing on her feet. The further she fell, the more anonymous she became. The sharp slap reached Blair's ear a split second after the end of the fall, it was that far away.

Blair looked down at the small gray patch on the sidewalk. A woman under a big hat with feathers approached, her poodle straining at its leash to sniff the dead cat. She jerked her dog back, walked more quickly, then called the uniformed doorman out from under the canopy over the building's entrance. The man saw the cat and looked up. Blair jerked his head back inside. He was pleased with himself, satisfied he could be cold-blooded.

14

"HIS NAME IS Thomas Blair Rice III, born in 1918, the son of independently wealthy parents. The family's money is in real estate, all of it managed by a Mr. Karl Lowenstein. The father's an antiquarian and is a member of several archeological societies. The mother used to be an avid America Firster. Now she does a little volunteer work with the Red Cross.

"Rice attended both Choate and Yale, distinguishing himself in no way at either place. A classmate at Yale told us, 'He was known to the drinking set as an intellectual, and to the intellectuals as a drunk.'"

"Typical spoiled rich kid. He doesn't sound like a likely foreign agent, Mason, no matter what your contact thinks."

"No, Admiral Whyte. But let Sullivan finish his report. There's more."

"While at Yale, Rice joined several America First-type organizations, but never stayed a member for long, apparently put off by their pacificism. He was arrested in May 1938 for taking part in an attempt to break up a Young Communist League rally in New Haven. No charges, although he was placed on probation at school. On his police record, there's only that and two counts of drunk driving. His drinking seems to have tapered off since college. None of the five people we talked to from his class at Yale admit that they've stayed in touch with him. They remember him as a harmless, silly snob who admired Hitler and Mussolini, hated Communists, and dated several well-known debutantes.

"After he was graduated from Yale in 1940, he worked briefly at J. Walter Thompson, an advertising agency, in some sort of vague, managerial capacity. He is frequently seen at the Stork Club, 21 and El Morocco. Rice was exempted from the draft. No strings were pulled. He has asthma."

"Thank you, Sullivan. As you said, Admiral, not the most likely suspect. But you've read the transcript of our contact's conversation with the suspect, all heard and duly recorded by Mr. Zeitlin here. And there's the fact that the suspect did go to a male bordello but didn't do anything."

"I'd think his not doing anything is a fact in his favor, Mason."

"Maybe. Although his mere presence there suggests latent homosexual tendencies. More important, he seemed to be there primarily to gather information. For whom? Anything is possible. As you can see by the biographical material, we're dealing with a very unstable personality. Which is why I feel we should continue to monitor the man's activities."

"I don't know, Mason. There're too many maybes here and not enough facts. The transcript does sound fishy, but it might be just some drunk, rich 4F shooting off his mouth. What about you, Sullivan? What's the FBI's take on this matter?"

"The FBI agrees it's terribly iffy, Admiral. But nothing a spoiled brat like that did would surprise me. He might be a foreign agent. A bad one and perfectly harmless on his own. But there's the possibility he could lead us to others more important and dangerous."

"Hmmm. All right then. You have my permission to continue surveillance of the man. But only for a week. One week from today, we'll review the additional evidence. If there's been nothing else to suggest the man's a spy, we'll terminate the operation. This war's too important for the Navy or FBI to squander valuable personnel on the doings of some poor little rich boy."

"What about the girl? The one seen leaving Rice's apartment yesterday."

"What did you find on her, Sullivan?"

"Not much. She registered at the Martha Washington under 'Mary Austin of Kansas City, Kansas,' but we have no records on such a person. She might be nothing more than a prostitute or party girl, but she could also be Rice's contact."

"No. I don't like the idea of our men chasing after dollies. Call your men off her, Sullivan."

"Yes, sir."

"That'll be all for now, gentleman. I thank you for your efforts, but I'll be damn glad when this unsavory business is over."

Mason and Zeitlin stood up and saluted. Sullivan and the other FBI man stood and nodded. They filed out of the rear admiral's carpeted office and past the two whispering WAVEs in the front office, none of them speaking until they were out in the hall.

"I wish you'd put up a fight over the girl, Sullivan. She could prove important." said Mason, undercutting his criticism with a smile.

Sullivan frowned and stood up straight. "We're shorthanded as it is. In point of fact, I have to spell one of my men myself now. Goodbye." He and the new man turned and walked away, as identical and business-like in their padded gray suits as a pair of adding machines.

Erich followed the commander back to their office on the floor above. The presence of others in the hallway or on the stairs didn't deter Mason from talking about Rice or criticizing Rear Admiral Whyte's inability to appreciate sexual warfare. Erich waited until they were in the office and the door was closed to mention the sailor.

"So what do we tell Fayette, sir? It's been two days since his encounter with Rice. He probably feels very confused over being left in the dark."

"Tell him he did well." Mason made himself comfortable behind his desk. "Tell him we're working on his lead and'll let him know what we turn up, if anything."

"Yes, sir. And what do I tell him when he asks how much longer he has to stay?"

"Meaning . . .?"

"He's going to think he found our spy and it's time we return him to his ship."

"Is that still so important to him? If I were Hank, I'd want to enjoy that brothel for as long as possible. Considering where he's going when he's finished."

"But Fayette doesn't know that."

"No. And ignorance is bliss. Why spoil it for him?"

Mason frequently changed plans without telling his subordinate, but clearly he had not changed his plans for Fayette. Erich felt uncomfortable. He wanted to get away from his superior.

"It's after four, Commander. I need to go back to the house, retrieve the microphone and perhaps speak to Fayette. If it's acceptable to you, sir, I'd like to go now. Before their business hours."

"Perfectly acceptable. We've done all the mischief we can do here for today." Mason flipped through a new manual on his desk. "If you don't mind me asking, Erich, what makes you so concerned about Fayette all of a sudden?"

"Concerned, sir? Not at all. I only want to keep the machine in working order."

"As a doctor with patients, I've learned to be very careful not to identify too strongly with them. Not to become too involved. One must stay detached."

"I am quite detached, Commander Mason."

"It's especially tricky with mental incompetents, because we can't help seeing them as children. And children are eminently lovable. No, when we're finished with Hank, he'll be sent to a place where he'll be happy, cared for and protected."

Mason had heard Erich's reports over the past two weeks, had read the transcript of Fayette's clumsy but effective fencing with Rice, and yet he still assumed the sailor was mentally deficient. Hadn't he noticed the cunning, even the distrust, becoming more apparent behind the man's slow innocence? Fayette was not eminently lovable. Erich wanted to point that out to Mason, insist on it. But if Fayette weren't an imbecile, he was a criminal. A life in a mental asylum was preferable to life imprisonment in Portsmouth.

"Was there something else, Mr. Zeitlin?"

"No, sir. Nothing. I'll be going now."

Erich rode uptown to the Sloane House, to change into civilian clothes, then rode the subway down to Fourteenth Street. The additional trip and the act of changing clothes made this visit feel strangely important to him, as if he intended to accomplish something different from earlier visits. Keeping Fayette's mental capability a secret, Erich had realized he was protecting Fayette. Walking up the stairs to the street, Erich realized he wanted to tell Fayette more than was safe. He wanted to warn him.

Erich did not know where the urge had come from. As soon as he acknowledged it, he felt it had been at the back of his thoughts for the past two days, ever since he heard Fayette and the houseboy make love. He wasn't sure why the sex act should seem crucial. Making love with the streetwalker he met the same night—a green Midwestern girl who found Jews exotic—Erich felt a peculiar kinship with Fayette, as if sex were sex, and hearing a man fornicate made you his brother. No, hearing that should repel you, even when it was with a woman, especially if you disliked the man. But Erich did not dislike Fayette. Listening in on him and the houseboy, he had not been repelled or morally sickened, only embarrassed by his own superfluity. For so long Erich had tried to detach himself from this wrong by thinking of the man as an idiot or a pervert. But he had discovered Fayette's intelligence, and the man's "perversion" had not sounded nearly as disgusting as its reputation. No longer protected from him by the names, Erich saw Fayette plain. His conscience would not shut up. Like Erich, Fayette was a foreigner in any country, only he didn't know it, yet.

Approaching the square, Erich noticed the black Ford pulled up on the curb, the low sun reflected in a bronze oval stretched over the fender. There was a man slumped behind the wheel, as if taking a nap, and Erich saw the open eyes in the sideview mirror—Sullivan's partner from the other night. Erich walked past without either of them acknowledging the other. He was surprised they were still watching the house. They had their hands full following Rice. Crossing the square littered with slats and cabbage leaves from the day's market, Erich could feel the FBI watching him. He stepped into the shadow of the house, walked up the steps and rang the bell. His complicity sickened him, but warning Fayette did not feel quite right either. It might only cause the sailor to desert, which would send him to prison for certain. He had to be careful not to sacrifice Fayette just to soothe his own conscience. At the same time, he had to take care not to let carefulness cause him to do nothing. Erich knew he was so accustomed to guilt that inaction came much too easily to him. An American would behave differently.

The door was opened. It was Fayette.

He was dressed in freshly laundered whites and wore his cap, as if all set to report back to his ship. But he looked surprised to see Erich, unpleasantly so.

"You," he whispered. "Yes?"

He stepped back when Erich quickly stepped inside and closed the door. He was looking sideways at Erich, one blue eye half-hidden behind his nose. He seemed mistrustful. Or maybe he was ashamed of what Erich had heard the other night. The idea of shame disturbed Erich. It made Fayette more human than ever.

"I came to pick up the things from the other night. Is it safe to go up to your room?"

Fayette rocked on his heels, like a guilty child. "Yeah, sure," he said, then turned and started up the stairs.

Erich followed, knowing he should be deliberating over what to tell Fayette, but unable to think of anything except that the seat of the pants creasing and uncreasing in front of him covered an anatomy he had heard sodomized.

Up in the room, they closed the door. Erich moved the chair to the corner and stood on it. He was too short to reach the paper lantern, so he had to ask Fayette to take it down.

"Oh, you'll be pleased to know we're acting on your discovery. Commander Mason said to say you did well."

"Yeah?" Fayette passed him the lantern and microphone and stepped down. "Good. Does that mean I'll be getting out of here anytime soon?"

"They want you to remain here a little longer, Hank. Until they verify that this man is a spy." Erich used Fayette's first name deliberately, to suggest trust, but it sounded as condescending and phony as Mason's constant use of it. "I'm sorry they've left you in the dark these past two days, Fayette." He began to wrap the cord around the mike.

Fayette stood at the door and folded his arms. "So who was listening to me Tuesday night? You or the G-man?" He spoke angrily.

"Uh, I was."

"Guess I gave you quite an earful. Me and the *nigger.*"

"Not at all." Erich felt himself blushing. "You sounded as if you were enjoying yourself. As best you could. Under the circumstances." When he looked up, he found Fayette staring at him curiously, the anger put aside.

"You don't think I'm some kind of animal? For doing it with a colored?"

"No. You had no choice. You had to do it for us. Besides, I'm not American. Race doesn't mean the same to me as it does to you." Or rather, the *Negro* race, which apparently was what Fayette's shame was about. He could still say "nigger," although it rang false after what Erich had heard through the microphone he now packed into his briefcase. Feeling the sailor relax, Erich decided they needed to continue this conversation so he could gain Fayette's trust before he decided exactly what to tell him. "Can I buy you a drink somewhere? What you did the other night calls for a celebration, don't you think?"

"Maybe. I'd like that. I should get away from this stuff, even if it's just for an hour. But I promised to go to a party tonight. With Juke. The colored boy." He lowered his eyes. "Kind of to pay him back for the other night. That's all. That's why I'm done up in my dress whites like this."

"Another time then." But Erich wanted to do it tonight, before his nerve and good intentions changed.

"Sure. Only I really do need it tonight," he admitted. It was as if they read each other's thoughts. "Hey. All I got to do is show my face at this party. Then you and I could go somewhere for a beer. You mind coming along and cooling your heels for a half hour?"

"What about Juke?"

"Aw, Juke's just Juke. He has no right to squawk. I don't owe him anything. I don't."

Erich wondered what had happened since Tuesday, if anything. Whatever was going on between Fayette and the houseboy could hold for another night. This was more important. "Where's this party being held?"

"Somewhere on the waterfront not too far from here. Starts before sunset, so it can't be anything too wild. You mind, Erich?"

"Not at all. Let me take care of this first." He went to the window and shook the cord loose, then reeled it in, wrapping it around his arm. All he was going to do was share a few facts disguised as suspicions with Fayette, just enough to put Fayette on his guard. It would be up to the sailor to choose his own course of action. Erich could alleviate his conscience without making himself fully responsible for any harm that came to the man. Besides, he did not know exactly what Fayette *could* do. "I'm finished here," he said when the line was packed up with the mike.

"Before I forget, I got something I wanted to give you." Fayette opened the top drawer of his dresser and passed Erich something. It was a book of matches, covered with blue zebra stripes and bearing the name "El Morocco" in tall, skinny letters. "Fell out of the spy's pocket the other night. Maybe it'll help find him."

"Yes. This could prove helpful. Thanks," said Erich and pocketed the matches, although they already knew Rice frequented this particular night club.

"I hope you people nail that bastard. What's his name, anyway?"

"They want to keep that private, Hank. For legal reasons."

"No skin off my nose. I never want to see the sonovabitch again in my life."

"Hank!" The name was hollered from downstairs.

"That'll be Juke. Must be time to go. I'll tell him you're coming with us."

They went down the stairs, Erich wondering what he was getting himself into, not just with the party, but with his decision to unlock some of the secrets without unlocking all of them. It would be like plucking one apple from the base of a pyramid of apples, without causing an avalanche of apples.

The houseboy wasn't waiting for them in the front hall, only the Bosch woman who was talking to a young colored girl in a white dress. Erich wondered what a girl was doing here.

"Where'd Juke go, Mrs. Bosch?"

The colored girl turned around, looked demure, then burst out laughing.

"Juke?"

"Aren't I divine?" said the girl. She was the boy. His lips were painted bright red and he wore a wig in a snood. He turned once, flaring the dress. He lifted his knee and presented a white high heel. There was a glimpse of red toenail in the open-toe. "And you're going to be Lena's beautiful white sailor accompanying her to the ball," he said, delicately slipping a brown hand with red fingernails inside Fayette's arm.

Erich stared at Juke, trying to see the houseboy hidden inside the girl. He remembered the boy's arm muscles and shoulders, but it was a long sleeve dress and the shoulders were padded, although there was probably less padding and more shoulder here than in most women's dresses. The white gardenia pinned to his shoulder did not look inappropriate. And yet this was the boy who had been the man with Fayette. It was too confusing, like contemplating the sex life of a hydra.

Then the boy noticed Erich.

"Meester Zeitlin?" said Mrs. Bosch. "What're you doing here?" But when Erich didn't answer, only continued to stare at Juke's eyelashes, she said, "Yes. Doesn't he make the prettiest gurrl? I let him fix up one of my old dresses, but everything else is his." She plumped up his snood, smoothed out his shoulders. "He has worked so long for me he now has my good taste."

Juke's made-up eyes shifted from Erich to Fayette.

"Juke. Are those earrings of mine you are wearing? Who told you to wear my good mother-of-pearl? I gif you an inch and you take a mile!"

Fayette, too, stared at the boy, his tongue poking the inside of his cheek. "What kind of party is this, anyway?"

"A drag ball, darling. Isn't the dress a big enough hint?" Juke sneered at Fayette, angrily. He pointed an unladylike thumb at Erich. "Why's *he* with you?"

"Yes, Meester Zeitlin. Why today? We don't see you except on Mondays," said Mrs. Bosch with a wink so quick it looked like a twitch.

"Haven't you noticed?" said Juke. "He comes by all the time now. To see his boyfriend."

"Not my boyfriend," said Fayette. "Just a friend. He's coming with us to this party, Juke. If it's okay with you."

"What if I say he's not invited?"

"Then *I'm* not coming."

Fayette and the houseboy stared at each other.

"He thinks you are Hank's boyfriend?" The Bosch woman was giggling. "That is very funny, Meester Zeitlin."

"It's all right, Fayette. I have other things to take care of." Erich did not want to involve himself in a lovers' quarrel, if that's what this was, and he did not want to attend a transvestite ball. "We can talk some other time."

Juke turned on him. "What's the matter, bookkeeper? Not man enough for a few drag queens?" The boy was crazy. He insulted Erich for giving in.

"Not at all. Mr. Fayette gave me the impression this was a casual gathering. If it's a fancy dress affair, I'm not suitably dressed."

"Mrs. Bosch be happy to let you wear one of hers," said the boy.

The Bosch woman howled, laughing so hard she had to pull her handkerchief out of the front of her blouse and cover her mouth. "Eef only your boss could see. . . . !' "

"Pay no attention, Erich. Come along. There's gonna be regular guys there. Like me." Fayette turned away from the others and whispered, "Ten minutes won't kill us."

Erich felt Fayette wanted him there for protection against Juke. "Thank you, but I don't want to be a fifth wheel."

"You won't be. It's not like me and Juke are a couple or anything, just because he's dressed up as a girl. We're just some guys going to a party."

Juke looked at Fayette. He nervously tapped the spike of one high heel against the floor. He chewed on his lip, before he remembered the lipstick.

A car horn honked out front.

"Oh, shit. That's the taxi I phoned for. Okay, you want to bring the bookkeeper, bring the bookkeeper. Bring the garbage man and a full-piece orchestra for all I care. Let's get going."

"See? I told you Juke'd come around."

Erich still didn't want to go, but with everyone heading for the door he did not know how to get out of this.

"You be careful with those earrings!" Mrs. Bosch shouted behind them. "You lose one, Juke, and I strengle you!"

There was a yellow taxicab with red fenders waiting out front. Juke hobbled down the steps and across the cobblestones, gradually gaining enough momentum to walk gracefully in heels. By then, he had reached the cab. He stood at the door without opening it.

Erich understood first and opened it for him.

"Thank you, Erich, darling," said Juke, sounding like a lady. "You *did* say your name is Erich?"

Seeing the black Ford still parked across the square, Erich wondered what Sullivan would think when he heard Mason's assistant had gone off with the sailor and a Negro transvestite. Luckily, Juke looked like a real woman, at least to white eyes.

"We won't stay long, I promise," Fayette whispered as he stepped in.

Erich climbed in beside him, pulled the door shut and they were off.

"Pier 44, darling," Juke told the driver. "I am so pleased you thought to bring your friend, Hank. For a girl to arrive with a man on each arm suggests she's very much in demand."

The driver said nothing, but studied them in his rearview mirror, unaware that this trio were even more peculiar than they seemed. Erich felt as if there were actually four of them in the backseat: himself, Fayette, Juke in drag, and the real Juke.

They had gone less than a mile when the taxi pulled to the curb.

"Here we are. Do pay the nice man, Erich. That's a dear."

Erich paid and stepped out after them. They stood at the foot of a short open pier flanked by enormous green warehouses. A gate in the chain link fence was wide open and a row of empty boxcars was parked on the track that ran out to the end of the pier. There was a smell of creosote and dead fish. The sun was an orange disk hovering in the murky air across the river.

Juke opened his purse and brought out a pair of white gloves, which he wiggled over his hands. "Valeska's," he explained. "You can't wear gloves in taxis, though. Door handles just aren't as clean as they used to be." He noticed Erich and Fayette looking around in bewilderment. "Don't be frightened, darlings. We're exactly where we should be."

He led them through the gate and down the pier. More of the river came into view, plumed with columns of black smoke from the tugboats, ferries and lighters swarming over the wide, smokey-orange water. Up ahead walked the silhouette of a couple in evening clothes. Then, just beyond the last boxcar, was a double-deckered gazebo, docked to the side of the pier. It was actually a boat, turned into some kind of restaurant or night club. Chinese paper lanterns swung in the breeze beneath the canopy over the upper deck—innocent paper lanterns. The deck below was dark with murmuring people. As they came closer, Erich heard a piano against the noise of cranes and boat whistles outside. People like Juke could not afford to congregate in more conspicuous places, he decided.

"Hank, dear." Juke took hold of Fayette's arm as they approached the party. "You're forgetting I'm a lady."

Beneath the awning over the red-carpeted entrance stood a handsome young man in a cut-away and a roundly plump figure in a tiara and strapless red dress. The slant of sunlight showed the blue shadow of a shave beneath the hostess's face powder. He had just finished welcoming the couple in evening clothes. The handsome boy stood beside him like a mannequin chewing gum.

"Alpheus! Lena, I mean." The hostess embraced Juke and made kissing sounds on either side of his snood. "What ever happened to you? We never see you at Chick's."

"Didn't you hear, Kate? I moved downtown. Uptown life had simply grown too, too."

"Frederick's here," the hostess said meaningfully.

"Oh?" Juke hesitated. "Oh, Kate, dear. I'd like you to meet Hank. Hank is in the service."

"So I see," said the hostess, his eyes eating Fayette. "Where did you ever find such a delectable piece of seafood?" He reached out for a quick touch, his bracelets jingling.

"Pleased to meet you, ma'm, uh, sir," Fayette said with a stiff nod, glancing at Erich, more concerned for him than with being touched by a transvestite. He was probably touched by transvestites every day.

"And this is Erich. Erich's a bookkeeper."

The hostess gave him a quick, disappointed look. Erich knew he should not feel judged by someone so absurd, but he was abruptly conscious of being short, pudgy and balding. He adjusted his glasses, as if that could make a difference.

"I realize, of course, that Erich's not dressed for the occasion," Juke said blithely. "You couldn't make an exception just this once, could you?" He *expected* Erich to be turned away, which was why he had given in so easily to Fayette.

"Well . . . One can't be as picky as one was in days of old," said the hostess. "And since you also brought this beautiful sailor—Welcome to our little soiree, Erich." He held out a hand for Erich to squeeze, a hand the size of a football. He waved Erich inside and stage whispered to Juke, "But I declare, Lena. What ever do you see in such a drab little Jew? I hope he's loaded."

"Fabulously loaded," Juke purred. "Thank you ever so much. Ta-ta for now." He turned to join Erich and Fayette inside, dropping his honeyed smile the instant his back was to the hostess. His ruse had failed. "Piss elegant fake," he grumbled. "Since you're in, go get yourself a drink and try not to embarrass me," he told Erich. "I'm introducing my date to a few old friends. Nobody you'd want to meet."

"This won't take long," said Fayette as Juke led him off.

Erich watched them go, then looked around, feeling more numbed than shocked. He noticed the evening clothes of various cuts and ages, a few uniforms—all enlisted men—and many elaborate dresses and hairdos. The different aromas of perfume were so strong you couldn't smell the river anymore. He was so accustomed to the presence of women at such gatherings that he assumed there were real women here, until he looked for them. A blonde with puffed shoulders had an adam's apple like a rock. A pale Negress with a hat like a saucer did not quite know what to do with her purse. And someone who looked like Rita Hayworth—too much like her—had startlingly big feet. But everyone seemed well-behaved and civilized, despite an occasionally loud, uncivilized laugh. A baby grand piano at the end of the deck scattered lazy chords over the scene. The sunset behind the piano looked like a wall mural. They might all be in a midtown night club, except for the presence of enlisted men and Negroes. Erich decided he could live with this until Fayette was able to get away.

He found the bar beside the bulkhead of the stairs, asked the long-haired bartender for wine and had to take brandy instead. Looking around for Fayette, he took a deep sip of the drink. The floor suddenly seemed to sway. He lowered his glass and stared at it. Bottles and glasses behind the bar were ringing together.

There were delighted shrieks from people along the rail. Erich looked up and saw the mural of the warehouse sliding by. When he turned to look for the pier, it was ten feet away, getting further away as he watched. The floor was trembling.

"We're free! We're free!" someone screamed, and the piano broke into a bangy boogie-woogie. Men began to dance, some with men, some with men dressed as women. Others rushed to the stern and hooted at the golden skyline pulling away behind them. "Screw you, cops! Screw you, Mob!" screamed Rita Hayworth, then pulled up her dress, pulled off her BVDs and waved them like a big hanky at the city before she tossed them into the boat's wake.

People rushed the bar and Erich was surrounded by crackling crinoline. He pushed his way through the surprisingly hard bodies to the railing, although it was too late now to jump. A hand on his shoulder suddenly turned him around. It was Fayette, red-faced and grimacing.

"Damn that Juke! He never told me this boat was going any-where!"

"Did he say when we'd get back?" Hearing himself, Erich realized he wasn't nearly as upset as Fayette. There was nothing either of them could do.

"No. Damn little so-and-so. I could wring his scrawny black neck. Shit. We're stuck here until it's over. I got you into this shitty mess, Erich, and I'm sorry."

"No harm done. No. Nothing we can do but enjoy the ride," Erich offered, wondering why he wasn't more upset. The disguises and noises around them made him think of Carnival in Vienna and Zurich. Maybe it would be no worse than that. "Maybe we can find a quiet corner and talk, Fayette. This is as good a place as any to have that drink." Trapped with Fayette for several hours, Erich could force himself to say everything that had to be said.

"Yeah," Fayette answered, without enthusiasm. "If I can get five minutes peace from that pesky picaninny." He looked out over the crowd. "Where is he? I better find the fool or he's gonna be riled I gave him the brush." And Fayette shouldered his way through the party, looking for the person he said he wanted to avoid.

There was such screaming they left the pier that one hoped the boat was capsizing. So many deaths by drowning would be splendid, cleansing the city of degenerates, ridding Blair of the fairy who had brought him misery.

He stood in the shadow of a boxcar, making fists with his black gloves while he watched the boat carry his enemy out toward the channel. The gloves made him feel capable, ruthless. He had leased a car that morning and driven out to Flushing and back to shake anyone who might be following him—it couldn't be as difficult as Anna claimed to lose a tail. He had watched the house behind the docks all afternoon, parked in an alley, waiting to catch the sailor alone. He had followed the sailor, who was with a man with glasses and a colored girl, to this place. He had seen enough of the other people arriving—trash mocking good society through imitation—to understand what kind of party it was. Blair had invested too much time and cleverness in following the sailor this far to give up now.

The sun sank rapidly on the other side of the river. Blair waited until the boat was a distant shadow in the blue haze. He came out from behind the boxcar and approached the dockworker returning to his shed. He asked the man when the boat was expected back.

"Sometime after one, thweetie. Your boyfriend leave you behind?"

Blair did not deign to answer. He turned and walked back toward the gate, where his car was parked. He had a pint in the glove compartment and his first gun, purchased only a few hours ago.

15

KATE SMITH'S Pre-Fourth of July Aquacades and Garden Party, which was what the hostess called his floating ball, made its way up the Hudson, music and giggles pealing over the water. The lights on the lower deck and in the paper lanterns were turned on: the boat became a vision of fairyland floating through a world at war. The Narrows to the south was fretted with ships massing for a convoy to Britain; a black blimp rode the smoke-streaked sky above them. Liberty ships in war paint lined the waterfront, loading up with munitions, tanks and folded airplanes. Behind the spotlit piers, the browned-out city unrolled as a handful of lamps, like a dim, earthbound constellation. There was only the bubble of light of the Hotel Astor's rooftop dance floor to suggest that people on shore still enjoyed themselves.

The boat passed beneath the stern of a troopship moored in the old berth of the French Line, coasting into a smell of fresh laundry that blew down from the ship's fantail. Soldiers in underwear and dog tags began to appear along the railings overhead, whistling and hooting. "Look at those babes, will ya?" "How's about a kiss, sister!" "I love ya, ladies!"

Guests packed the starboard side, hooting back and throwing kisses. "Yoo hoo!" "Oh boooys!" "Jump down and join us if ya ain't got nothin' better to do!"

One soldier climbed on the railing and pretended he was going to dive overboard. Then someone shouted, "Those aren't dames! That's a boatload of fairies!"

"Like we can be choosey?" cried someone else. The soldiers continued their hollering and pleas for love until the vision vanished behind the next pier.

Juke looked for Hank, then decided to use his time to prepare Lena for their moment of truth. He lightly stepped over to the bar and ordered a cold rum daisy. The white bartender asked if he were Lady Day, and a bitch from Chick's said he looked like Bessie Smith, but Juke was Lena, sleek and beautiful and resiliently vulnerable. Wearing Lena's cool sexiness, Juke felt freed from his usual need to be tough and knowing. He turned himself inside out with drag, so that his toughness was hidden and his softness public. He would not have to hold his cards so close to his heart when he was feeling so feminine and elegant.

> Hold tight, hold tight.
> I bite all night
> An' 'jaculate my jack
> Into some seafood mama.
> I browned him twice.
> Was very nice.

They sang camp versions of popular songs around the piano while couples shook shirtfronts and earrings out on the dance floor. Juke recognized sisters and customers from Chick's, the Harlem fancy house where he had lived and worked for a year, before Freddie. He recognized Sash, the snob from Valeska's who thought he could fuck his way up in the world if he listened to the right music. Sash was in drag tonight, preposterous and tacky: dotted swiss, too little makeup, a goldilocks wig and men's black tie shoes. His sugardaddy was a long, cadaverous man with tailored evening clothes and banana-yellow hair. Juke looked forward to humiliating Sash back at the house for being a woman, and a tasteless one to boot.

There was Freddie, just as Kate had warned. Juke noticed him standing off to the side, sternly watching everything like some deacon from an important uptown church, which was what Freddie was. Short and black and built like a child's coffin, Freddie escorted a timid colored boy wearing a flat little hat. Juke recognized the boy's blue Sunday dress and pearl necklace. Freddie kept a wardrobe for his "wives" and chose partners based on whether they could wear what he already owned. Only Juke's shoes had been new the three months he lived with Freddie. Juke wasn't cut out to be a deacon's wife, but at least it had gotten him out of Chick's.

Freddie saw Juke, and coldly turned his square black back to him. The snub meant nothing to Juke. Insisting Juke be a woman and nothing but a woman, Freddie had used a strap on him if he so much as peed standing up. There had been no love left when Juke finally got his black and blue butt out of there. And Juke, or Lena rather, was in love with somebody else tonight.

He had finished his daisy and ordered another when he spotted Hank again. The sailor must have been on the other side of the stairway bulkhead before. Taller than the others, blond and fresh, he stood out like a stiff pecker. He glanced around as he wandered through the crowd, as if looking for Juke.

"So sorry, darling. But I won't be needing that second daisy," Juke told the bartender. Faintly goofy with alcohol and fear, he adjusted his gay decievers and reshaped his snood, then drew a deep breath and walked his coolest, most killing walk toward Hank. He was making a fool of himself, but it was Lena's doing, and Lena was hopeless. The slight tilt of the deck almost pitched her off her high heels. "Darling! Wherever have you been?"

"Oh, there you are," said Hank, halting. "Wondered where you'd gone to." But he stood there looking like a dog who had chased a car and caught it.

"You've been neglecting me, you naughty boy." She took Hank's arm but the arm remained stiff, held away from Hank's side. The reluctance hurt. Juke wanted to kick Hank in the seat of his pants, but Lena remained a lady. "Shall we take a little night air on the upper deck?"

"Any different from the air down here?" Hank uncomfortably looked around, as if to avoid looking at Juke. "Now that I found you, I'm thinking we should go find Erich. He's not used to this stuff."

Juke noticed the little bookkeeper up toward the bow, clutching his fat briefcase under one arm while he tried not to watch two men kiss. Hank could not be in love with such a pursey four-eyes. He must have dragged him along tonight for another reason. Screw the hymie, thought Juke. "Don't be silly," said Lena, pulling Hank toward the stairs. "Anyone who didn't know you might think you were afraid of being alone with me."

Hank took one step up the stairs, then another, then said, "I am."

The honest answer threw Juke. He said nothing as they climbed into the shadows of the upper deck. Fear confessed seemed like intimacy.

The only light was the glow of the red paper lanterns. The breeze was cool and brackish. There were couples up here, but it was early and they were only talking. For a moment, walking arm in arm toward an unoccupied stretch of railing over the bow, Juke felt he and Hank were a couple. Then Hank pried his arm loose so he could grip the railing with both hands, and the feeling was broken.

Juke stood with one hip against the rail, leaning out a little so he could see Hank's red-lit face. "What're you afraid of, darling? You afraid bad man-eating Lena's gonna throw herself at you?"

He did not look at Juke, only at the terraced darkness of Washington Heights now chugging beside them. "Not that," he muttered. "But the other stuff."

"What other stuff?"

"You know."

"What, darling?" But they could talk like that all night, each trying to get the other to say it. "Do you mean if Lena's in love with you and wants to know if you're in love with her? She is, darling. And she knows you must feel something for her, or you wouldn't be so scared of hearing it."

What Juke could not say in his own voice, even to himself, was said by Lena's lipsticked mouth as easily as a remark about the weather. He waited for Hank to respond. The sailor rocked himself on the locked arms that held him back from the rail. He suddenly turned and looked at Juke.

"Could you lay off with this Lena crap? Could you just go back to being you?"

"Me? But I am Lena, darling. I've always been Lena."

"Horseshit. You're Juke in a dress saying 'darling' all the time. That's all. It's getting on my nerves. Give it a rest."

Juke's pride was hurt to hear Lena dismissed as a bad job. "What's the matter, *darling?* Don't you like girls?"

"I don't feel easy around them, no. Especially when I know they're men. And when I've been to bed with them." He was looking ahead again, at the George Washington Bridge approaching them like an enormous airborne cage. "I don't love you, Juke. I don't fall in love with men and I'm not in love with you."

"But maybe you're in love with Lena. Or you wouldn't be such a mind reader."

"Juke! What the hell do you want from me?" he pleaded. "Look. You wanna fuck again, we'll fuck again. But you're putting me off with all this love and Lena crap!"

"You want to do it again?"

"Yeah. Why not?" He lowered his head. "Wanted to do it last night. Almost came downstairs to see if you were still awake. Wanted to see what it'd be like for me to fuck you. Alone." He nodded to himself. "Was a slow night last night."

"Oh, darling!" Juke cried, grabbing Hank's shoulders and going up on tiptoes to kiss him. But before his lips touched, Hank's hand covered Juke's mouth and shoved him back. It was like an elbow in the heart.

"Why're you doing that? We're not gonna fuck here. And you got crap on your face." He wiped his hand against the rail. "If I wanted someone soft and smeary, I'd go after real women. Wait till we're back at the house if you want to do it tonight. When you can clean up and there won't be these people."

And Lena angrily understood: Hank was granting him nothing. Fucking without money changing hands didn't mean a thing to a faggot too dumb to feel guilty. It was a way of passing time, like drinking or cards. Hank hadn't been hiding any feelings when he said last night had been slow. It would have meant more if Hank were *afraid* to go to bed again with Juke.

"You want to fuck me?" said Lena. "To even things up for me fucking you?"

"Kind of. I want to see if I can give as good as I got."

"You really loved it the other night, didn't you?" Juke sneered.

"I liked it, yeah. Who wouldn't?"

"Real men, baby. Don't you know? Only queens take it up the ass."

"That's horseshit. Who cares who puts it where so long as you enjoy it?"

"And what if it's a nigger dick?" said Juke. "Or is that rule horseshit, too?"

There were rules, and they were never stronger than when you broke them. Juke loved to break rules. Hank knew few rules and seemed dumb and unchangeable because he never broke any, except one.

Hank was looking down at his hands, as red as Juke's hands in this light. "Yeah. Well. I sometimes forget you're colored. Least when you're in civvies," he argued to himself. "And you see white men with colored girls sometimes, even in Texas. It's for pussy, not love, but nothing wrong with that. Only bad thing is babies sometimes happen, which ain't gonna happen with us." He had dug a finger into his ear, as if to hear his own thoughts better. He suddenly flipped the hand at the air. "Hell, Juke! It's tough enough me admitting I want us to fuck some more while I'm still at the house. What else do you want me to say?"

"While you're still there?" said Juke. "Where you going?"

"Wherever they ship me out."

"Navy kicked you out for cocksucking. You ain't going anywhere," Juke insisted.

"Yeah. Yeah, they did," Hank admitted.

"Right. Just because you're in sailor drag, don't forget Uncle Sam spit you out for good." But that brief moment of panic made Juke feel very vulnerable. Hurt and angry, he had let Lena slip away. He gathered her up again and took refuge in her attitude. *"Darling.* If it's just pussy you want, forget it. You can't have Juke without loving Lena. Lena is nobody's whore. Juke may turn a trick now and then when Lena's away, but not while she's around. And Lena is always around when her fool boy's in love."

Hank had his hands on his hips. He was frowning at Juke. "Why you got to muddy it with mush? Okay. You've laid your cards down and I've laid mine. I'm not gonna play your game and say I love you, Juke, because I don't. There. Nothing else for us to say. See you later." Hank turned and walked toward the steps, hands still parked on his hips.

Juke refused to run after him. Watching the white, butt-snug uniform undulate through the red darkness was like seeing Hank naked again, and Juke turned back to the river. He propped one elbow on the rail and rested his chin in his hand, reaching back with the other hand to unbunch the garter snaps digging beneath his dress. Juke knew he'd end up back in bed with the cracker, despite love and pride and Lena. Maybe he'd hate himself so much after the next time he could cure himself. Then when Hank came sniffing around for nookie, Juke would refuse to give it to him. There was still time to turn the tables on the oh-so-butch clod. Juke just hoped, for pride's sake, he wouldn't get in bed with Hank tonight.

Wishing hard that Juke wouldn't be following him, Hank hurried down the steps into the light. The party was going off in all directions. Some guests were loud and hysterical. Others were passed out in the corners. The fat man who called himself Kate stood on the piano, flipped his skirt above his knees and sang "Most Gentlemen Don't Like Love."

Hank walked once around the stairway bulkhead. He stepped over a row of shoeless legs in real or painted nylons. He found Erich on the other side, somberly listening to a hawk-nosed man in feathers. Hank grabbed Erich's arm and turned him around. "When the hell do I get out of that damn house?" he demanded.

Erich looked blank. "Toscanini proves the shallowness of the American music scene," he told the man in feathers. "Uh, excuse us." He stepped away with Hank. "Not so loud," he whispered. They stepped around the corner to the side of the bulkhead that faced the bow. "You've finished with your friend?"

"Damn straight I finished. Crazy little bughouse coon. Everything's gone bughouse. This boat's a floating bughouse. If I don't get somewhere normal soon, I'll be ready for the bughouse myself."

Erich knocked his head on the life ring behind him. He stepped over an inch and leaned back. "There are worse places to be than that house, Fayette."

"Yeah. Like here."

"Other places. Prisons and mental hospitals—the bughouse,"

Erich said gently. "Which is where the authorities frequently send men with your inclinations."

Hank only half listened to him. Looking around the deck, he blamed the party for his confusion and Juke's craziness. All this frou-frou crap. Sex usually cut the crap, but these people seemed as sexless as women to Hank. It had been sexier back on his destroyer, where everyone pretended they never thought about each other's cock. Even Juke seemed sexless here. But Hank remembered otherwise.

"You shouldn't take your good fortune for granted." Erich seemed to be telling him to quit complaining and enjoy it while it lasted.

Hank had told Juke the truth. He felt terrible about it. It was one thing to lay with a colored—skin was skin in bed and accidents do happen—but perverse to *want* to. Saying it out loud was downright obscene. But Hank had said it, had humbled himself to the boy, only to have it thrown back in his face. He wanted to strangle the kid, but when he thought about grabbing Juke's neck, he thought about kissing his face. Sex in the head was less innocent than sex in bed. Hank usually got it out of his head when he got into bed with the next person, but the wrongness of it made Juke stick. He wasn't in love with Juke. Love meant more than thinking about the same person every time you thought about sex. He had to get out of that damn house before he forgot the difference.

Erich took forever to say whatever he was saying.

"I need a beer," said Hank. "You want something?"

"Thank you, no. Do you understand what I'm suggesting, Fayette?"

"Yeah. I'm not getting back to my ship anytime soon."

"That, yes. But also . . . You can't believe everything people tell you."

"I'll buy that. Hard to believe half of what I tell myself nowadays."

"Fayette! Have I been so oblique? What I'm trying to tell you is you should consider the possibility they won't send you back to your ship. You should consider the possibility they might send you to the bughouse or even to prison."

Hank looked at the startling idea from a long way off. "Why?"

"For being a sexual deviant, of course."

"But so's everybody else here," said Hank. "Except you."

"Yes. But you're the one the Navy knows about and is using. They're not comfortable with that. One way they could assuage their consciences would be to place you in an institution when they're finished with you."

"Who told you this? Did Mason tell you this?"

Erich was rigidly silent. Then, "No. Nobody's come right out and said this. If they had, I would have told you sooner. But no, Hank. I've worked with Commander Mason long enough to understand he thinks deviance is an illness and should be treated. Other superiors think it should be punished. I shouldn't be going behind their backs like this, but I had to share my suspicions with you. I like you, Hank."

Hank thought a moment, studied Erich and said, "You're a Jew, right?"

Erich was taken aback. "Yes. Why?"

"Jews are naturally suspicious. They don't trust anybody. I'm not judging you or anything, but that's the way you people are."

"Perhaps," Erich admitted. "With good cause. But everybody on this boat has good cause to be suspicious, you included. You're a criminal in the eyes of most people, Fayette. You cannot afford to be so trusting."

"It's different over here than where you come from, Erich. People in important positions don't ask you to do something, then punish you for doing it. That's lousy. Not even Mason could do something like that. This is America. It's the people you think are your friends you have to watch out for." Hank laughed at his joke, although he knew it was about Juke. "You sure you don't want a beer?" he asked, stepping away.

"Go ahead and laugh, Fayette. I've told you what I thought you should hear. I don't know what else to say that would make your situation clearer."

"And I appreciate you telling me, Erich. But I don't think it's something for us to worry about." He walked around to the bar and asked for a beer without the funny glass. He did not want to go back to Erich. He had gone to him in the first place to talk to somebody normal after his conversation with Juke. Worrying about the Government was easier than worrying about Juke, but Hank was sick of worrying. He took his bottle of beer up to the bow, leaned over the spume curling against the prow and pretended he was alone. He took off his cap, and the night air felt good in his hair. Time passed quickly when Hank was by himself, when he could stare out and think about nothing. Neither Juke nor Erich reappeared at his elbow.

The boat continued up the Hudson, past towns whose peacetime lights glimmered among black woods and ghostly cliffs. The lights of a passenger train raced along the opposite shore in a long dotted line. Hills and stars slowly swung around as the boat turned to make the trip back.

The party began to lose its frantic edge, seemed to burn down as more miles passed. The hostess and his friends continued singing around the piano, but their songs grew softer, more sincere. A few couples slow-danced in the stern, barely moving, just embracing and swaying. The boat seemed full of dreams and melancholy. Some men stood alone and brooded. Others necked, or better, in the shadows. Conversations were carried on in whispers. Hank heard two voices whispering in the darkness above his head, from the upper deck rail where he had stood with Juke. One voice resisted, the other coaxed, "Come live with me. I'll make you happy."

The air grew smokey again as warehouses and shipping reappeared along the shore. Hank wished he were back on the *McCoy* and he could keep going, down the river and through the Narrows, out into a nothingness as black and open as the night sky.

Instead, the pitch and rhythm of the engine changed and the boat drew in toward the city. Hank recognized the green-black warehouse jutting up from the river. Behind him, partygoers sighed and a few queens roused themselves for a final round of camping before they returned to life ashore. There was a flickering of light behind the warehouse, like an electrical storm. The boat swung around the warehouse and the pier came into view. A cherry light blinked brightly on the roof of a police car.

More white and blue cars were parked up and down the pier, with paddy wagons and a dozen cops, the cops all getting to their feet and unbuckling nightsticks.

All talking stopped, then the piano. There was only the drum of the engine bringing them into the slip. The trance lasted a second, and broke. All at once, everyone on board was cursing, screaming advice, running in circles. The boat sounded like a burning house full of tropical birds.

"This is the police!" shouted a voice in a megaphone. "You are ordered to dock your vessel immediately. All occupants are under arrest."

Men who had brought other clothes grabbed their bags, pulled off their dresses, pulled shirts and trousers over brassieres and garter belts. The deck was scattered with dresses and lone high heels. "I work for the city!" cried Rita Hayworth. "I can't get arrested!" He pulled up his dress only to remember he had no underwear, and no other clothes. He stood there, laughing hysterically.

Hank walked through the chaos, looking for Juke or Erich. Juke ran right past him, looked over the rail on the side away from the pier, then ran back to Hank. Hank expected him to squeal for help, like a girl. He ran like a girl. Juke ripped off his wig and thrust it at Hank.

"Take this. And these." He took off his shoes and stuck them into the wig. "Oh, shit. Take these back with you, too. They're Bosch's." He unclipped the earrings and put them inside one shoe.

Hank held the wig like a sack. "Where you going?"

"Jail if I don't get my ass outa here! I'm on parole and the law just loves sticking it to drag queens." Juke looked stranger than ever, his own hair flat and bobby-pinned, his mouth still slashed with lipstick. "I'm gonna swim for it. Don't look at me like that. You don't have to marry me, just hold my shit."

"Lay off. I'll hold your stuff," said Hank. "You think that's smart?"

Juke hiked his skirt up to climb over the railing. "Anything beats getting traded around for chewing gum on Riker's." He stood on the ledge, looked down, then out. The warehouse was fifty yards away on the other side of the slip. The boat was still moving.

Toward the stern, beneath the noise, the piano began to play again, accompanying a loud falsetto voice. Perfectly calm, the hostess stood in his red dress with one hand on his heart and sang "God Bless America." Others began to join him.

"Good luck," said Hank.

"Screw you," said Juke. "You don't care if I'm living or dead." He held his nose and jumped back, white dress fluttering up his legs as he dropped feet first. There was a loud splash and he was gone.

A spoke of light flashed across the clouded green water as a police boat beyond the stern swung its searchlight. Then the water was black again, bubbling along the moving hull. Hank saw nothing, until he made out a pale shape twenty yards off, bobbing in a dog-paddle toward the pilings under the warehouse. He had done something wrong, like there was something he should have done to protect the boy. He was relieved Juke could take care of himself.

The engine was cut off and the boat coasted in towards the pier with the chorus of "God Bless America" rising above everything else. The song was punctuated by the percussive splashes of three more men jumping overboard.

The hull ground against the bumper pilings. A wall of blue summer uniforms, with peaked caps and steel badges swarmed onto the boat.

"Shut up and get moving."

"Get moving, sweetheart."

"No lip, you. If I want lip, I'll drop my pants."

"Shut up with the yammering! No singing!"

Cops grabbed a few arms or necks, but most only poked with their nightsticks. The men were herded together and moved off the boat. Two deckhands came up from the engine room and sheepishly went about the business of tying the boat up.

"You there! Can the song! You think you're Kate Smith or something?"

The last voice stopped singing. "But I am, officer."

"You making fun of America's favorite singer?"

"It's more in the nature of homage," the hostess declared.

There was a gasp and a dull crack, followed by the sound of a man choking. Everyone who saw what happened froze. When the hostess was led off and Hank could see him, the man's face was covered with blood. It startled at first like blood, then looked like an entire tube of dark lipstick smashed over a face. It took time to accept it was blood. The short tuxedoed piano player and a well-dressed colored man had to hold up the hostess so he could walk.

"You see that? Now stop gawking. Get moving. Like good little girls."

A few cops went at it with happy hatred. Others refused to look at you. They muttered at you but glanced at each other, shared their contempt or smirks only with each other. If they looked at you, they looked right through you. Hank was glad Juke had gotten away. The boy was sure to have done or said something that would get his head knocked in. Or Hank's head. Hank had been knocked cold once for Juke; nothing was gained by resisting. Still, he couldn't help looking for the cop who clubbed the hostess, in case he met the cop again someday, alone. But the cops all looked alike, Hank hated them so much.

Herded onto the pier, the guests were divided into two groups. Anyone still in drag was immediately led off to the pie wagons. The others were muttered and prodded over to a place between a boxcar and the water. The men accustomed to the protection of male clothes were more frightened than the drag queens. A single word from a cop was like a pistol fired beside the ear. Hank was protected from fear by his experience and bottled rage. He found Erich in the group beside the boxcar, standing very still and pale, looking not so much afraid as like a man lost deep inside his thoughts. His briefcase hung on his arm.

"You'll be okay," Hank whispered. "Tell them you're with Navy Intelligence. You got some kind of card or papers, don't you?"

Erich nodded, not caring. He saw the wig and shoes in Hank's hand.

"Juke's. So he could swim for it."

They both looked out at the water but saw no one in the dark slip or the thick grove of pilings beneath the warehouse.

Men milled through the crowd, searching for people they knew. Assurances and fears were whispered about. A pair of cops stood in front of them, between the boxcar and water's edge, idly slapping nightsticks into their palms. Another pair stood behind the men, so nobody could step around to see what was happening on the other side of the boxcar. People bent down to look under the boxcar and saw stockings and heels climbing into the paddy wagons. Once the drag queens were hauled off, somebody whispered, the rest of them would be beaten up by the cops.

"Do they do that here?" Erich whispered.

Hank found himself hoping they would. If the cops came in swinging, he'd swing back, even if it meant getting beaten to a pulp. Anything was better than this furious helplessness. He felt paralyzed by good sense and the fear around him. "Maybe you better show them your papers," he told Erich. "Before things go crazy."

"No." Erich spoke firmly. "I can't do that. Not in good conscience."

"You there! Shut up! All of youse shut up! You think this a tea party?"

Motors started up on the other side of the boxcar. Yoohoos and insults were shouted from the backs of the paddy wagons that reappeared down the pier, driving toward the gate. Four paddy wagons were followed by two police cars. They passed through the gate and disappeared beneath the elevated highway.

A plainclothes cop came out from behind the boxcar and approached the pair of cops watching the men. They spoke, glanced at the men, laughed, then walked off, all three of them. The pair of cops at the other end walked away too.

The men stood where they were, looking at each other in bewilderment.

"Hey! What about us?" Erich shouted.

The plainclothes cop stopped and turned around. "You? What about you?"

The others stared at Erich, furious with him for speaking up.

"You're free. What else ya want, sweetheart? A kiss?" sneered the plainclothes cop. "There ain't enough pie wagons in the city to take all you fruits. So we're taking only the pretty ones. Count your lucky stars you're ugly."

"Then you're not really enforcing the law," said Erich indignantly. "This entire operation was only intended to give you and your men a bit of fun tonight. Which makes you no better than the gangs of Nazis who—"

Hank jumped in front of him and turned Erich away from the cops. "Shut up. Just shut up." A mass beating was one thing, but Erich's goading would only get *him* singled out by the cops.

"You feel left out, Nelly Belle? You want us to haul you in? Maybe we can slap you with something stiffer than a disorderly charge while we're at it."

"He don't know what he's saying," Hank shouted over his shoulder. "He's all upset right now. What the hell you think you're doing?" he whispered to Erich. "This ain't your fight."

Erich pinched his mouth shut, as if he realized that, too. But his eyes were full of fight. Hank was surprised to find anger behind those sober eyeglasses.

"This is your lucky day, Nelly Belle. I'd rather go get a drink than go back to the station and book you. See ya in the funny papers, ladies." And the cops walked off, laughing. Doors were slammed and the rest of the baboon-snouted cars drove down the pier.

"You all right?" Hank released Erich's shoulders. "It doesn't pay to speak your mind to those bastards."

"Yes. I just . . ." Erich looked around.

The others were walking away, relieved, embarrassed, unable to look at each other. Free, they could feel strange they weren't arrested while friends were. Even Hank felt strange. There were exaggerated sighs of relief and attempted jokes as people wandered toward the gate.

"It was just too familiar," said Erich. "It's not the same thing, but it felt the same. If they actually enforced the law, then it wouldn't feel like brute malice. But they use the law for a bit of sport! They just use it to tell you you're a thing and not a person. It's appalling! Aren't you appalled?" But when he stared at Hank, the righteousness went out of Erich's eyes. He stared like a man suddenly looking into a mirror. "You still think you have no business being suspicious?" Erich said softly. "You still think I'm just a nervous Jew?"

"Cops are bastards. They always have been. But the Navy looks after its own." Hank felt uncomfortable with Erich's look and indignation. The indignation sounded fake, like he was hiding something with it. "The Nazis go at Jews like this?"

"Or worse. Much worse if the rumors out of Poland are true." He seemed to explain something to himself. "Although it's bad enough being expelled from your own country. So it's not the same thing after all." He gave the briefcase full of cord and microphone a nervous shake. "Let's get out of here. This place disgusts me."

"You go ahead. I better look around and see if Juke's still here. He's gonna need his shoes." Hank assumed Juke was already walking home barefoot. He just didn't want to spend anymore time with Erich.

"Yes. You do that. Good night, Fayette."

They parted without shaking hands or mentioning when they'd meet again. They turned their backs on each other. Hank walked out to the end of the pier, calling out Juke's name once or twice. When he started for the gate, Erich was nowhere in sight. Hank walked alone, distrusting Erich, distrusting the Navy, distrusting his distrust, knocking shoes packed in a wig against his leg.

16

BLAIR WAS SITTING in his car when the police first arrived. He heard tires thud over the railroad crossing, looked out and almost urinated on himself when he saw a patrol car at the gate. But the police drove onto the pier without noticing the chromeless, war-model automobile parked with two older autos against the chain link fence. Blair slouched down, swallowed his fear with the help of his pint of Scotch and waited for the police to go away. More patrol cars began to arrive, then paddy wagons, and Blair understood what was happening. He cursed his luck and the police. He loved the police, admired their uniforms and ability to act, but they spoiled everything tonight. They'd give a boatload of degenerates a proper punishment, and throw Blair's prey into a place where he couldn't get him. There was nothing for him to do but sit there and watch the show.

The boat finally reappeared, all lit up like a birthday cake. Some absurd singing was replaced by satisfying shrieks and yelps when the police went into action, but Blair's view was blocked by boxcars once the boat was docked. He was sorry he couldn't go out on the pier for a better look. Under different circumstances, he might even have offered a police sergeant money to let him join in. A phase of murmuring and occasional barked commands followed, rather boring. Then the paddy wagons began to roll through the gate and Blair decided it was over. He started up his car and backed out to the street, careful not to turn on his headlights until he was halfway down the block.

Blair was bitterly disappointed. He had so much fire tonight and nothing to do with it. He could hire a lawyer to bail out the sailor, anonymously, so he could get him back out in the open again. A lawyer would have to wait until morning. In the meantime, he couldn't go home. They were watching his apartment and Blair would have to lose them all over again. He decided to drive out to Long Island where he could find a nice inn for the night.

The West Side Highway hung above the street like a long, trestled roof, hiding the street from the city. Blair did not know this part of town, so he drove back the way he came, toward the farmers' market and that vile house. He turned down a side street and the automobile pounded over cobblestones. The headlight beams wagged up and down the length of a dark, curbless street, bouncing around a small figure walking up ahead. The figure hobbled down the middle of the street, its back to the car. A sopping white dress stuck in brown splotches to its skinny body. Her wet, black hair was short and she walked in an angry, jerky ungirlish manner, barefoot. Blair slowed down, touched his horn and she glared at him over her shoulder. It was the boy. Blair couldn't believe his luck. A wash of make-up reddened the mouth and bruised the eyes, but it was definitely his colored houseboy. The boy continued walking, drifting to the lefthand side of the street to let the car pass.

Blair drew alongside him. "You want to get in the car, boy?"

Without looking at him, the boy kept walking. "Ain't you got eyes, mister? This little girl ain't blowing nobody tonight."

Blair kept his temper. He used the clutch to stay level with the boy. "You don't recognize me, do you?"

The boy resentfully turned his head. "Oh. Yeah, you're the circus queen."

"We have some business to discuss."

"You want to talk business, come by during business hours. All I want right now is some dry threads and reefer."

The car pulled ahead twenty feet while Blair reached into his coat pocket. He stopped the car beside the shed roof of a poultry butcher.

The street in the rearview mirror was pitch black, but an electric light burned dimly over the loading dock outside the passenger window. Blair twisted the revolver out of his pocket and pointed it at his own window. The boy continued walking, until he was beside the car again.

"This might change your mind."

The boy looked, and stopped.

Blair lifted the gun higher into the light. Its sculptured weight had seemed almost magic when he first held it in the pawnshop in Flushing that morning. The magic became very real when the gun was pointed at someone.

The boy's hands began to rise. "You want a blowjob that bad?"

"Shut up. And put your hands down. I just want to talk." He had to use his left hand to shift the auto into neutral while he kept the gun aimed at the boy. "Don't run off. I'm not going to hurt you." He opened the door and stepped out. "I think you know why I'm here."

The boy glanced up and down the street, then stared calmly at the gun. He screwed his mouth into a smirk, as if he found this merely ridiculous.

"Back there in the corner. We're not going to converse in the middle of the street." The boy would be too close to him inside the car—he might grab for Blair's gun. "You heard me. Move."

The boy rubbed one bare foot over the other, then obeyed. His feet slapped insolently on the packed clay floor beneath the roof. Locks hung on the closed sliding doors. Empty chicken crates were stacked between the posts supporting the roof, screening off a corner from the street. The place stank of chicken ordure and offal. A faint band of light slanted through the space between the roof and stacked crates. Everything else was darkness. Blair's shoe struck something movable and hard. He rolled it with his foot and decided it was a pipe. He stood with his weight on it, in case the boy saw it and tried to use it to defend himself. Coloreds probably saw better in the dark than whites.

"Romantic enough for you, mister?" The boy stood with his face half-visible, a spark of light in each eye. The pale dress hung in the darkness.

"Shut up. I still have a gun pointed at you. You might be more respectful when you hear there's money in this for you."

"Yeah? How much?"

"Two hundred, three hundred dollars. Maybe more."

The boy bared his teeth and shook his head. "Shit, mister. You ain't got dough like that or you wouldn't go pointing that puppy peter at me."

Blair reached into his left coat pocket and pulled out the hard roll of bills. "You see that?" He held the bills up to the light. "That's three hundred dollars."

"I can't see. Let me feel it." Even then the boy sounded as if he was sneering.

Blair slipped the roll back inside his pocket. "Stand back. Stand closer to the wall. I need to see where your hands are."

The boy's face backed into darkness. A pair of hands appeared, fingers lightly drumming the pale dress. The fingernails were painted, like Anna's.

"They arrested your loverboy back there. Your sailor friend?"

"He ain't no loverboy. He just likes to get fucked," the boy sneered. "Hey. How you know about the raid? You have something to do with that? You a cop?"

"Maybe. You want to end up in jail with your sailor?"

"Ha! You ain't no cop. You think they got cells enough to hold every queen they collar? Shit, he'll be back on the street tomorrow morning, if not sooner. Although it'd do his ass good if he spent some time in the Toilets."

"He won't go to jail? That's good to know. Then you can give him my message."

"What message?"

"I'll pay both of you three hundred dollars if you go to the police and withdraw your accusation."

The fingers stopped drumming.

"Tell them it was a case of mistaken identity. Or that you remembered incorrectly things I said. It doesn't matter, so long as you tell them you were wrong."

"And if I say we will? Do we get any money up front? Payment in advance?"

Blair hadn't considered that. If he were dealing with the sailor, he might agree, but since this was only a flighty colored boy—"No. You don't get any money until I see that my friends and I are no longer being followed."

"If that be the case." The boy snorted. "I'd love to take your money, honey, but I don't know what the hell you're talking about."

"Don't play coy. You want me to raise my price?"

"You think I'd go to the cops? Oh, baby. You don't know the facts of life. We may play kiss and tell, but never with the law."

"Somebody told the police. Was it your boyfriend?"

"He *ain't* my boyfriend. How should I know what he did? I don't know that cracker from Moses. Oh, yeah. You watched me go up his ass. Well, that don't mean I know what goes on in his head."

"I want you to forget that night."

"Wanna forget it myself. Is that what's eating you? You're afraid somebody's found out you're a pansy? And a pansy too yellow to do anything—a circus queen into two-tone."

"Stop talking that way! You forget I have a gun pointed at you."

"And you got a pecker but you don't use that either." There was a weary sigh. "You bore me. All you big tough men with your big tough secrets bore me to tears. If it ain't love you're scared of, it's the cops. Like you're so important the cops really care. Screw every damn one of you. I'm going home." He stepped forward and his foot hit the pipe. Blair felt the object budge beneath his shoe as the boy went, "Ow!"

"Stand where you are!"

But the boy bent down into the dark.

Blair bent down and grabbed the pipe. "I said get back!" He picked up the pipe and it wasn't a pipe but a long metal rod, not nearly as thick as it had felt through his shoe. He gripped it in his left hand and tapped it against the ground. The rod was four feet long and solid.

"I hurt my foot. Shit, mister. You're scared of cops, you're scared of a little ole drag queen stubbing her toe. You're a regular Clark Gable."

"Shut up. You know what I really am. You're lying when you say you don't." Holding the heavy rod in one hand and the gun in the other, Blair was confident the boy was lying, had been lying all along. "You know who I am and you're scared."

"I'm more scared of catching cold in this wet frock."

Blair cocked the revolver. "You hear that? You know what that is?"

"Your compact."

Blair swatted the darkness with the rod and hit the white dress.

The boy flinched, suppressed a gasp, then said, "You're nuts. I don't wanna play no more." He stepped forward again.

"Get back or I'll shoot." Blair's heart was pounding. It was like a dream where the darkness itself threatened to rush you like a hundred phantoms, only Blair had a weapon in each hand and the phantoms were as fragile as papier-mâché. He swung the rod again.

"Whatta ya got in your hand?"

"What hand?" He swung again, trying to feel in his fingers the hit of the rod into a body. The rod was so heavy he felt nothing. "You scared now?"

The white dress retreated a step. The red fingernails reappeared. "No."

"Don't move or I'll shoot you." Holding the gun on the boy to keep him at bay, he swung more wildly, hit nothing, swung at the darkness above the dress, hit something hard. Feeling that, he increased his strokes, wanting to feel it again and know he could hurt the boy. The boy never cried out and he had to swing harder. The rod hit the cinder block wall with a clank he felt in his shoulders.

The dress had dropped down to cower at the base of the crates.

Blair prodded him with the rod. "Get up, boy. Get up or I'm pulling the trigger."

A radiator gurgled, then was silent.

Blair poked harder, until he had the sickening thought the rod had pierced the marshy body. He jerked the rod back. He backed away, out from behind the screen of crates, then turned and took the rod to the front of the car. The motor was still running, the headlights still on. He inspected the rod in the glare of one headlight. ·

It was veined and ribbed, a length of steel rod used to reinforce concrete. There must be construction nearby. The tip was only rusty, the rust turning bright red two inches down the rod. More red was spattered over his black hand—it took Blair a second to remember he was wearing gloves—and his coat sleeve.

He went back under the shed roof. The dark was darker than before. He kicked around with his shoe until he kicked something soft. He bent down, touched a soft heap and a hard surface. The heap felt enormous in the darkness. He stuck the gun back in his pocket and felt his other pockets for matches. His valet service left extra books of matches in all his coats. He found a book, removed a glove and struck a match. A face flared up on the floor, scowling, with one eye open, the other crushed shut. The expression changed when Blair moved the match back and forth. He moved the match down the body. There was no sign of any puncture from where he had poked the body with the rod. The right sleeve was bent in a fantastic manner, as if the arm had extra elbows. The match burned down to his fingers and flickered out, without Blair feeling anything.

He had killed the boy, it seemed. And his first response was regret that it had happened so quickly, without time to savor the act. He lit another match so he could look again. The right side of the face was collapsed and bloody. Satisfaction began to set in. He had killed a man. How many other men shared that rare experience? He passed the match to his gloved hand so he could touch the face with his bare fingers. The blood welled up like a slow, warm spring. He could almost hear the blood. He scooted back a little to keep his shoes out of the puddle on the clay.

Blair carried the steel rod out to the automobile. He proudly wrapped it in the New York *Times* he had on the front seat, then laid the bundle on the car floor. He wanted to save the weapon, even show it with the blood to Anna as proof of his strength, but he knew he had to get rid of it. He went back beneath the roof, struck more matches and checked for evidence. The colored boy lay there in his white dress. A queer had been killed and the police would treat it as perfectly natural. Blair suddenly realized it was the perfect solution. He had killed the boy; he could kill the sailor. Even if the police arrested him for espionage, they could prove nothing when the only witnesses to his loose talk were dead. Glorying in the deed, he knew it was the right thing to do, and that he could do it again. The murder had put him in touch with his true power.

When he returned to the car, he pretended to redo his fly, as if he had stopped here only to relieve himself. But there was nobody to see him. The street was utterly deserted. He climbed into the car and drove away, loving himself more deeply than he had ever imagined possible. The second kill would be even finer, because he would plot and anticipate it. He would hunt the sailor, catch him alone and kill him.

17

THE FACE looked freshly washed, but there was a gray bloom
to the skin, like mold on chocolate. The eyes were closed, the
thick pale lips slightly parted. It seemed to be two faces: angular
adolescent on the left, a plump baby on the right. The baby's face
was blue-black and shiny, where the skin had swelled up over the
caved-in bone. There were black patches of dried blood beside
the temple and right eye. The hair pulled back from the forehead
kinked in slight zigzags. Juke's face had been through so many
metamorphoses it was difficult to tell if this was another, or an
entirely different person.

"Can you identify him?"

"Oh my Gaaawd," sobbed Mrs. Bosch. She had a handkerchief
out but only clutched it in her fist while her wide eyes ran with
tears. "The poor, poor boy," she murmured. Erich had never suspected her to have so much feeling.

Fayette looked down at the enameled metal table. Jaw working
from side to side, he lifted a heavy hand and, with surprising gentleness, touched the swollen skin. Then, more bluntly, he stroked the
neck, touched the bare shoulder, touched at the body through the
sheet and, delicately again, ran his fingertips over the spot where the
genitals would be.

Erich stepped back. He was an intruder here. He could not have felt more ill at ease if he had killed the boy himself. Fayette had telephoned the Sloane House first thing this morning to say the police had asked Mrs. Bosch to come up to the city morgue and identify a body: Negro, male. Juke had not returned last night. In the cold electric light, in a tiled room like a hotel kitchen, Erich watched Fayette and Mrs. Bosch confront the death of their friend.

"Yes. It is him," said Mrs. Bosch. "Our leetle troublemaker. Who could haf done such a thing to that boy?"

The pink, piggish assistant who might be German but was probably Irish pushed his way between Fayette and the wheeled table. He tossed the sheet back over the face and rolled the table back toward the refrigerated closet. The wall was lined with identical closets and doors. A bare foot with a white sole stuck out from under the sheet. The paper tag wired to the toe fluttered like a moth.

"We'll need a statement," said the police sergeant and led the way upstairs. Mrs. Bosch clung to Fayette's arm, sobbing and going on about the poor, poor boy. Erich followed, studying the billed cap in his hand—he was in uniform this morning—as if the gold insignia pinned there might prove or disprove the Navy's involvement in this death.

"Name of the deceased?"

"Alpheus Cooper. But efryone knew him as Juuuk."

They sat around a desk in a room full of desks while the police sergeant typed it all up on a tall typewriter like a Model T car. On the desk were a neatly folded white dress, a pair of nylons and a brassiere with hemispheres of cork sewn into the cups. Mrs. Bosch did all the talking, answering the questions—the boy's arrest record, his time in her employ, the whereabouts of his family—and asking what happened. The boy had been bludgeoned to death sometime the night before. His body was found early this morning, outside a poultry butcher's a block from the Bosch house. Erich watched Fayette, trying to see how he reacted to the information. Fayette sat there like a statue, staring past the sergeant. The sergeant seemed to know nothing of the mass arrests the night before, or the exact nature of Mrs. Bosch's house. Mrs. Bosch was dressed as an innocent hausfrau this morning.

"Cooper was a transvestite, a homosexual?"

"I do not know of these things, officer." Mrs. Bosch glanced at Erich.

The sergeant explained that the boy had been found wearing the dress and "gay deceivers" now on his desk. The police assumed he had been prowling the waterfront, had propositioned a man, then was beaten to death by the man when he discovered the Negro was male. The sergeant asked what was Erich and Fayette's connection with the deceased.

"They are my friends," said Mrs. Bosch. "Here in my time of need."

"I was Juke's friend," said Fayette, angrily.

The sergeant glanced at Fayette's uniform, without noticing the slightly soiled cuffs and elbows. "I've got a boy in the service. Army Air Corps. As servicemen away from home for the first time, you boys are probably getting your first taste of a place like New York. There are certain elements you have to steer clear of. You probably have no idea the kind of sordid life you exposed yourself to by knowing this Negro."

"You going to find his killer?"

"I got to be honest with you, son. Hardly a night goes by without some homo getting himself killed. We look into each case, briefly. But there's not much we can do. And the general feeling is these fellas had it coming to them. Take my advice. This friend of yours was bad news. Forget him and be more careful in the future about the company you keep."

Erich frowned at Fayette, trying to stop the outburst he thought was coming.

Fayette breathed deeply and surveyed the busy room. He abruptly stood up. "I want to get out of here."

The sergeant said he was free to go, but he needed Mrs. Bosch a minute longer.

"Will you not wait for me, Hank? I am not wanting to go home alone."

"I'll wait for you outside," Fayette snapped. He marched furiously through the room, hands rubbing his hips in a vain search for pockets.

Erich asked for permission to leave, then went after Fayette.

He found him pacing the steps out front, in the long shadow of the police building. It was still early and the sidewalk was full of seersuckered Americans on their way to jobs in the gaudy Viennese-looking buildings that surrounded City Hall. Fayette saw Erich, came up the steps and motioned him over to a fluted granite column.

"I'm terribly sorry, Hank. I know he was your friend."

Fayette stood behind the column and looked down at Erich. "We know who did it, don't we?"

"We don't. The police are right. A boy like that might offend anyone. There's no telling who may have met and killed him last night."

The blue eyes stared coldly.

"I've thought about it," Erich admitted. "Your man had no motive for killing the boy, no reason to believe the boy was involved in this. But the chief argument against it is that the man's being watched by the FBI. He could not have killed the boy without being seen and stopped by whoever was tailing him." Erich believed everything he said, but he was so accustomed to lying to Fayette that all beliefs sounded untrue the moment they were shared with the sailor.

"Maybe he lost his tail."

"Maybe. But we don't know that yet, do we? Let me speak to Mason this morning. The FBI can tell us where your man was last night."

"No. I know in my bones he did it. Rich little bastard," Fayette angrily muttered. "It's our fault. It's my fault, for taking that crazy kid into my bed that night. He had no business getting killed." He slammed his head against the pillar. "Jesus. That crazy little nigger kid." He sounded close to tears, but his eyes were bone dry.

"Stop talking like that. We don't even know if he did it!"

"Oh, yeah? You were right about one thing, jewboy. You can't be too suspicious." He folded his arms across his chest, tightly, locking his fists in his elbows. "I trusted Mason and the rest of you to know what you were doing. But we've gone and got that kid killed by a loudmouth bum. If that bastard comes back to the house, I'll kill him with my bare hands."

"Don't even think that, Fayette. He's part of something much bigger. Don't do anything until I've reported this to Mason. We have to let the Navy handle this."

"I don't trust the Navy now."

"Then trust me. Let me learn what I can about this. You can trust me, can't you?"

"Can I?" Fayette's eyes burned through him.

"Yes," said Erich. "You can." And the words hung there not so much like a lie as a desperate, feeble wish.

Mrs. Bosch came outside, handkerchief still in her hand, mouth and eyes drawn down. She mournfully looked around before she saw them. She came over, grimacing when she attempted to smile. "Poor little Juke. So many times he deserved a good slap. But he did not deserve to die." And the tears began to flow again. She could not say another word until she had blown her nose. "Did I do all right, Meester Zeitlin? I did not say anything I should not have?"

"You were fine, Mrs. Bosch. Again, I'm sorry." Her grief seemed genuine.

"Yes. We had our outs, Juke and me. But he was all boy." She blew her nose again. "Hank, dear? Would you hail us a taxicab? I need to go home and lay down." She waited until Fayette was down at the curb before she whispered, "Do you think what happened had anything to do with *our* business, Meester Zeitlin?"

"No, Mrs. Bosch. None whatsoever."

"Good then. Because I could not live with myself if I thought our spying might have brought harm to the boy. Good day."

A taxi had pulled to the curb. Erich followed her down to the street. Hank held the door open for her and Erich was able to speak to him while Mrs. Bosch climbed into the backseat.

"I'll come to the house this afternoon, Hank. I'll tell you everything."

Fayette looked at him, lowered his eyes and got in beside Mrs. Bosch. He slammed the door, the taxi drove away and Erich knew he wouldn't tell Fayette everything, despite the murder.

Church Street and Navy Intelligence were a few blocks to the south. Erich walked, steeling himself with speculations. He could not believe a foolish worm like Rice had killed the boy. He knew the type all too well—the superfluous man, a modern Hamlet, Marcel Proust among gangsters. Erich himself was such a man. Rice was incapable of murder, but it would be impossible to convince Fayette of that. Now, in addition to protecting Fayette from Mason, Erich would have to protect Rice from Fayette. He was helpless at both tasks. He wanted to step back, let Fayette kill Rice and go to the electric chair, ending the whole vile business.

Full of messengers and the clatter of teletype machines, the corridor seemed like part of a larger, efficient machine. Erich tried to feel impersonal and efficient. Full of urgent news, he knocked on the door of their office and entered without waiting for an answer. The commander was not alone.

Sitting across from Mason, frowning over their square shoulders at Erich, were Sullivan and yet another gray-suited, elderly boy from the FBI. An interrupted sentence seemed suspended above their heads.

"Excuse me, Commander Mason. I apologize for being late, sir. I've come straight from the city morgue. There's something you should know immediately."

"Good morning, Mr. Zeitlin. Something concerning this?" Mason took a sheaf of photographs off his desk and handed them past Sullivan to Erich.

The photos were large and shiny. The first was of a chalk rectangle drawn on a patch of ground beside some crates. A square marked off one end of the rectangle, like a head. The other pictures showed the same patch of ground, the chalk lines replaced by a body in a white dress. Head and dress were black with blood. Two policemen stood in the corner of several pictures, eyes cut out, mouths grinning.

"You can't be so free with those pics, Mason."

"Erich's to be trusted," Mason assured Sullivan. "He knows as much about this as we do. Almost."

The death that had seemed brutal but clean at the morgue became horrifying in the photographs. Erich restrained his rage and coldly returned the pictures to Mason. "How did the police know to send these to us?"

"We asked for them." Mason watched like a man waiting for you to get the punch line.

Erich knew what was coming. "How did you know the boy had been killed?"

"Because Sullivan's man here—" Mason gestured at the young man sitting importantly in the other chair "—watched Rice do it."

"You arrived too late to stop it," said Erich.

The young man looked insulted. "No. I followed the suspect all night without losing him once. It was too dark for me to actually *see* the homicide, but I was close enough to hear it. A man makes quite a racket when he beats another man to death. I would have had no trouble stopping it. Of course, I couldn't intervene without revealing to the suspect he was still being followed."

"Do you see now?" said Mason, grinning happily. "Rice killed the houseboy. Which means Rice *is* a spy. He knows we're on to him and thinks he can save himself by killing the witnesses. He doesn't know about you and Sullivan in the basement or he wouldn't have lifted a finger. But now he's tipped his hand. We reported it to Whyte this morning and he agrees. We'll be able to tail Rice through hell or high water, until he leads us to the others. Yes, my little brainchild is beginning to pay off."

Erich felt sick. "But the boy. He was innocent."

"It's regrettable the colored boy had to die, but he was hardly innocent. Just your garden-variety Negro deviant. They have a high mortality rate anyway, second only to firemen."

What would Fayette do if he learned this? And thinking about Fayette, Erich recognized something else. "If Rice thinks there are only two witnesses, then won't he try to kill Fayette?"

"I'm sure of it. You might tell Hank to take care next time he sees Rice. Without giving away too much of the game to Hank, of course."

"I just spoke to Fayette. He already thinks Rice killed the boy."

"A natural paranoid response," Mason explained. "Although in this case he happens to be correct."

Erich took a deep breath. "You should know, sir, that Fayette talks about killing Rice the next time he sees him." He wanted to wake up Mason to the fact that the violence springing from his clever scheme threatened to be endless.

And Mason became more serious. "We can't let that happen."

"No," said Sullivan. "I'll instruct my men to intervene if that looks likely."

"The way *he* intervened when Rice killed the boy?" said Erich, nodding at Sullivan's man.

Sullivan glanced at Mason, blaming him for his subordinate's disrespect. When Mason said nothing, Sullivan said, "That was different, Zeitlin. We have priorities. Our chief priority here is to keep Rice alive until he leads us to others in his organization. Sometimes the only effective means of intervention is a gunshot."

Erich had to fill in the tense gaps between Sullivan's matter-of-fact sentences, as if they were code. "Do you mean . . . if it looks like Fayette might kill Rice," he said, "you'll shoot Fayette?"

"If it's absolutely necessary, yes."

"But if Rice tries to kill Fayette—?"

"We have to live with it."

Erich looked at the calm faces around the desk: Sullivan annoyed that an explanation was necessary, the younger man impatient but polite, Mason mildly curious about Erich's reaction.

"No, it's not really fair," Mason admitted philosophically. "But wartime, Erich. And all is fair in love and war."

"But we're not at war with *Fayette*. He's one of us."

"Well," went Mason. "Yes and no."

Erich exploded. "You can't let him be killed just because *you* think he's mentally defective! That's murder! You're his commanding officer. He's in your care. Would you let your own son be murdered just because he's a deviant?" Erich was so angry he grabbed at any argument, no matter how irrational.

"I told you not to let your subordinate in on this," Sullivan grumbled. "These Jewish intellectual types are all alike. They care more about splitting hairs than getting a job done."

That infuriated Erich further, made him too furious to speak.

"Let me handle this," said Mason. "I know how to talk with Erich. You and your man may go now. Again, you've done a remarkable job."

The FBI men stood up and stepped around Erich without looking at him. He stood helpless with anger, burning from Sullivan's rebuke, unable to come up with an answer until the men closed the door behind them.

"Killing a man—two men—for no clear purpose," he told Mason, "is better than doing nothing at all?"

"You're overreacting, Erich. Sit down. You saw the body at the morgue? It's natural you'd be upset right now."

Erich sat down. He wanted to stay angry, but anger confused

him. He wanted to take refuge in Mason's calm rational manner.

Mason leaned back and pulled the cord on the venetian blinds. The slats opened and there were trees and sunlight outside. The room became less sinister, more normal, even commonplace.

"You know," said Mason, settling into his chair. "There's a very good chance Hank won't be killed. By either Rice *or* our friends. That's the worse that could happen. Things don't always turn out as badly as we fear."

"Why not send Fayette away from here? Place him somewhere where Rice couldn't get to him. A ship or jail. Even a mental hospital." Erich could mention the hospital only because anything seemed preferable to death now.

"No. Sullivan needs him on the street. New York's a difficult place in which to follow someone. The job's much easier when you know what your subject is after."

"Fayette's life is at risk because Sullivan needs bait?"

"There's more than just individual lives at stake here, Erich. There's a war on, to coin a phrase. What we uncover with Rice may save thousands of lives."

"Or none at all. His spy ring could be as inept as he is."

"There's that possibility. There's also the possibility that, if Hank were still at sea, he would die anyway. Ships are torpedoed every day."

"Americans die in auto accidents every day. But that doesn't justify letting them murder each other." Erich looked down at the police photos still on the desk.

Mason looked down and saw them, then abruptly turned the sheaf of pictures white side up. "Who *are* these people to you, Erich? What makes you so concerned about this riffraff?"

"It has nothing to do with them. It's the principle involved."

"You're not in love with Hank Fayette? Just a little?"

It was said idly, a random suggestion without any note of accusation. The suddenness of it stung Erich. He refused to be flustered. "No, sir. This assignment has not awakened any hidden desires, if that's what you mean."

"Just an idea. Something for you to keep in mind."

Erich felt Mason had mentioned it only to cast doubt on his righteousness, and as a subtle piece of psychological blackmail. Side with us or we will suspect your sexuality. Erich held tight to his righteousness. "What we've done with Cooper and now with Fayette is identical to what we condemn the Nazis for doing."

Mason's eyebrows went up ever so slightly. He closed his eyes and sighed. "I'm sorry you feel that way, Erich. You leave me no recourse but to pull rank on you. Take out one of those triplicate forms for travel orders, will you?"

"Sir?"

"I thought we might reason this out together. Since you remain adamant . . . I have some documents I want hand-delivered to Washington. You'll leave by train this afternoon and remain in Washington for a week. That should give our situation enough time to resolve itself."

"Sir, I'd prefer to stay here while this is going on."

"Why? What do you hope to accomplish?"

Erich was silent. He knew of nothing he could do, except continue his role as a witness, a voyeur.

"If you stayed, I'm afraid your conscience might lead you to do something dangerous, to both our operation and your future in the Navy. You do see my point? It's either that, Erich, or I send you to the brig for insubordination. That could mean a month or more."

"That's my only alternative?"

"Yes. You know where you keep the forms. Get one out and type yourself a brief vacation. I understand Washington's lovely this time of year, almost tropical."

Erich went to the filing cabinet, found the correct form, sat down at the typewriter table and typed last name first, first name last. He went through the motions of obedience, expecting any minute to feel indignant again, full of anger over the easy manner with which Commander Mason got him out of the way. Instead, what Erich experienced was relief. It was being taken out of his hands. Erich could not, in good conscience, wash his hands of Fayette. But Mason was washing his hands for him. There was nothing to gain by standing to his principles and going to the brig. Mason already knew where Erich stood. There was nothing to do but obey. The tension of the past week, the past month in fact, suddenly gave way to a numb, soothing peace.

"You are to leave by noon, Erich. If you haven't reported to the

Office of War Information by seven tonight, you'll be arrested by anyone inspecting your papers. I'm leaving you on your own cognizance. Don't disappoint me."

Erich typed in the correct times. "I won't have time to see Fayette before I leave? I'd like to warn him at least against leaving the house, sir." It was a final moral gesture, nothing more. Erich knew the request would be denied.

"You know too much. There'll be the temptation to tell him everything. I won't give you that temptation, Erich. I'll go down there myself sometime this evening. Yes, I'd like to get a peek inside the house before this is over."

Erich whipped the form from the typewriter and presented it to Mason.

Mason was suddenly suspicious, surprised by Erich's quick obedience. Then, signing the order, he said, "I'll have one of Sullivan's men run you up to your hotel in his car. He can put you on the train. Any objection?"

"Not at all, sir." It made Erich feel better, in fact. He was not responsible. He was not his own man anymore. He gave himself up to the machine, which was what he had wanted from the Navy all along. He was free from the terrible nuisance of self, morals and loyalties.

An hour later, a bored FBI driver escorted him beneath the soaring iron trellises of Penn Station to a smoking train packed with servicemen like himself.

The house stood at noon on the other side of the noisy farmers' market. Disguised in a loud necktie and workman's cap, Blair walked among the haggling Italians and Greeks who bought produce off the trucks to sell from their own street carts and horse-drawn wagons. The hot square stank of horse urine, human sweat and rotting vegetables. Blair bore with it all, keeping an eye on the door beyond the trucks and sun umbrellas, waiting. Once, he walked around the corner to the spot where he had killed a man. That seemed like days ago. The corpse was gone, of course, and the only blood was on the aprons of paper-hatted men lugging crates full of frightened chickens into the building. Blair stood in the sun, fingered the warm weight in his coat pocket and knew he could do it again. His only bad moment today had been when he tried Anna's number. A man answered, said he knew of no such person, then gave the game away when he angrily said, "You are never to call this number again." Blair could kill anyone who stood between him and Anna, even her father.

Out in the square, he waited and watched. He burned to enter the house, but it wouldn't do to ask for the sailor, go up to his room and shoot him there. The sailor was too large to be killed any other way except with the gun. Blair had to wait until he went out. Then he could follow and catch him alone. He hoped there would be enough light this time to see what a man looked like when he was dying.

18

HE GASPED and woke up, as if he had dreamed something terrible. He remembered no dream. For a moment, he remembered nothing. It was as if he'd been knocked cold. He was naked on a sweat-soaked bed in a room where the only light was the yellow glow of a drawn window shade. A fly bounced against the glowing shade. Other beds, bunks, rooms and barracks came to mind until he recognized where and what he was. His cock was hard. Hank touched his cock, and remembered.

He quickly sat up, putting both feet on the floor. He could not stand. There was a taste of sickness, like the smell of boiled cabbage, and a feeling of anger so strong he seemed unable to move until he broke something, a window or something. He sat there for the longest time, thinking about the corpse this morning, then Juke, knowing one was the other. His mind shut off. He stood up and pulled clothes over the hot and cold of his skin.

His footsteps treaded the stairs—the house had never seemed so deserted and haunted during the day. Piano music played softly behind Mrs. Bosch's closed door. Hank walked back to the kitchen, then turned around and walked back out. Juke's absence was too present in the kitchen. He knocked on Mrs. Bosch's door.

She looked up from the arms of her chair and turned on a lamp when he entered. She seemed to have been sitting there all day. When they got back from the morgue, Mrs. Bosch asked Hank to sit with her, but he had gone upstairs to be alone with his anger, only to fall asleep. She dabbed her eyes with a fresh handkerchief and turned the radio down. There was a glass of sherry on the table beside her and a half-eaten box of chocolates. She sniffed and sadly said, "I don't know what to do about dinner, Hank."

"Did Mr. Zeitlin ever call or come by?"

She screwed up her face to remember, then shook her head.

It didn't surprise Hank. The little foreigner was as cold and two-faced as the others, acting more guilty than the others, but still one of them.

"But Dr. Mason—Commander, I mean. He rang up," said Mrs. Bosch. "I am to tell you not to leave the house tonight. Because he wants to see you. Here."

"What does that jackass want?" Hank sneered.

Mrs. Bosch looked at him funny, then raised her long nostrils and inhaled. "You do not smell so good, Hank. You will wash up and shave before our guests arrive?"

"Screw it," said Hank and he left the room. He wanted to leave the house, Mason or no Mason. But he would stay here, and not because he wanted to hear what that glad-handing bastard had to say. There was a chance the biggest little bastard of them all would return tonight. His Nazi pretty boy, his spy. His spy was dumb enough to think Hank too dumb to know who killed Juke. When he returned, Hank would be here. He wanted to kill the bastard, but knew he shouldn't. He didn't know what he would do to him.

The sun went down and Mick, Smitty and the others began to arrive, then a few johns. Hank sat with them upstairs but spoke to nobody. He slouched down in the armchair in the corner and glared at everyone between his open knees. They chattered away like a treeful of cemetary wrens at a funeral. Sash strolled over, as cool and aloof as ever, glanced nervously at the others and bent down to whisper to Hank about last night. He was terrified Hank might tell the others he had seen Sash in drag. Hank had no idea Sash had been on the boat. Sash talked with great importance about being arrested, fingerprinted and jailed before his "friend" paid his bail. As if Hank could give a fuck.

"Where's the nelly houseboy tonight? That was him with you on the boat, wasn't it? He still in jail?"

"How should I know?" They hadn't heard, but Hank refused to share Juke's death with any of these phonies. Juke's death was his, and his alone.

Hank never moved from his chair, only looked up each time a new man entered the room. Smitty teased him from across the room, asked if it was that time of month. Hank cut his eyes at him and looked away. Mrs. Bosch was in and out of the room, bringing up customers and refreshments, quacking in her usual singsong as if nothing had happened. If she didn't mention Juke, it was only because talk of death was bad for business, Hank decided. She gave him a sympathetic look during one of her rounds, then quietly ignored his brooding. The longer Hank sat, the more blank he felt. He didn't feel like he was grieving for Juke *or* burning to kill Juke's killer. Grief and anger were so tightly knotted together Hank felt neither. All he felt was hatred, and a desire to explode like a bomb, blowing himself and the house to pieces.

Mrs. Bosch returned with Mr. Charles, fat and debonair, great black bags under his eyes. With Mr. Charles tonight was a teacherly-looking gentleman with twinkling eyes and a bushy beard. There was a flurry of looks and whispers through the room when people noticed the man with the beard. Mrs. Bosch herself seemed particularly pleased with Mr. Charles's friend. Her house was beginning to attract stars.

"He's one?" Sash whispered in awe.

"He? Who he?" said Smitty.

"Don't you know anything? That's the Beard. In the movies? Woolley Monty."

"Monty Woolley," a customer corrected Sash. "Hmmm. Wait until I tell the girls."

The famous man looked over the room, smiling in his beard as he shared a joke with Mr. Charles. He stepped over to the sofa, sat down and was instantly surrounded—Sash on his left, Smitty on his right, Lou sitting at his feet and eventually in his lap. Mr. Woolley chuckled at the boys and addressed them formally, like an uncle among nephews. He showed pleasure in being wicked only in the occasional glances exchanged with Mr. Charles.

Mr. Charles remained standing, looking disappointed that his usual man, Mick, was apparently off with another customer. Hank had gone up once with Mr. Charles, then left when the man explained what was wanted: Mr. Charles liked to be whipped. That was too strange, both cruel and silly, but the idea felt less strange tonight. Hank needed to hit something hard or he was going to go crazy. He stood up and approached Mr. Charles.

"Want me to beat you?"

Mr. Charles smiled. "My dear fellow." He glanced at his famous friend, then led Hank into the corner. "I thought that wasn't your cup of tea."

"Shut up. Do you want it or don't ya?"

"I like your attitude. Yes. Let's give it another try." He made a courtly bow to his friend across the room, proudly pointed out Hank to Mr. Woolley, then followed Hank into the hall. "Do you have any ropes or straps?" he asked on the stairs. "What kind of belt do you wear? Ah, one of those webbed ones with the metal tips. Never mind. You can use my belt." Mr. Charles continued to talk once he was in Hank's room, carefully folding his clothes. "You're a big one. And you look mean. You look like a killer. It wouldn't surprise me to hear you once killed a man."

Hank almost slugged him. He opened his fist and slapped the man across the face.

"Oh!" The man was overjoyed. "Here. Take my belt. And be careful about the face. Marks, you know." He quickly finished undressing, then dropped down on his knees and clasped his hands together. Naked, he was as pink and plump as a baby. "Mercy!" he cried in a different voice. "Punish me, yes! I deserve to be punished! But please don't kill me! Anything but death!"

Hank knew it was playacting, but he felt mocked and angered by the man's fantasy. He snapped the belt across the man's back.

"Yes! And spit on me. I deserve to be spit on."

Hank's mouth was dry. He hit the man with the belt again.

"Oh, yes!"

Hank worked his arm back and forth, whipping the man's front and back. The pink skin turned red; the man's breathing grew more excited. When he jumped up to scramble on to the bed, the bud of genitals under his belly had opened out. He lay face down on the bed and covered his head with the pillow. His body was heaped on the mattress like a block of fat.

"Anything now," he called from under the pillow. "This vile, disgusting flesh."

And Hank laid into him, listening for the crack of leather against skin, the moans from beneath the pillow. The flabby back and ass were criss-crossed with red stripes. Hank swung harder, wanting the stripes to break open, as if the man were his spy and he could whip him to death. The man wasn't his spy and the belt was too wide to break the skin.

Then the moans sounded less like pain, more like fucking, and Hank felt a sudden warmth around his eyes. The man squirmed and moaned like he was fucking Hank's bed. Hank thought of Juke. He was whipping Juke, beating Juke to death. He continued to swing the belt, less furiously now, while the warmth around his eyes spilled over. He was crying.

The man groaned louder than ever, and was still.

Hank stopped swinging. He used his free hand to wipe his eyes, but the tears continued to run. Juke was dead. He was grieving for Juke. Whether Juke was friend or lover or what, it didn't matter now that the kid was gone.

The man tossed the pillow aside and rolled over, his face glowing. "I feel warm all over. Like you've peeled my body right off my soul." He lay on his back, catching his breath, and saw Hank. "My dear fellow? Are you crying? I'm the one who should be reduced to tears. You're supposed to be a cold-hearted killer."

"Go to hell," said Hank. He threw down the belt and ran from the room. He raced down the stairs to the ground floor and back to the kitchen. But the kitchen—the stove and sink where Juke had worked, the oilclothed table where they taunted each other—was not enough. He went to the pantry, which was Juke's room, opened the door and turned on the light.

The pantry was a little bedroom. Mrs. Bosch hadn't touched a thing yet. The room smelled of Juke. Hank stepped inside and sat on Juke's cot. He sat there for ten minutes and let himself cry. Seeing himself in the mirror over the little table could not stop Hank from crying, or seeing the picture of Lena Horne clipped from a magazine and taped to the mirror. Juke had looked nothing like Lena Horne last night, except that both were colored. A pair of brown and yellow knob-toed shoes gaped on the floor.

He loved Juke. It had been difficult enough just liking the boy when Juke was alive. Hank could recognize love only now when Juke was dead. Love had been bound up with the grief and anger that paralyzed Hank tonight. The scene upstairs had released enough anger to give him room to grieve for Juke. Crying released enough grief for Hank to recognize love.

He breathed Juke—sweetish odors of talcum and pomade, the harsh smell of the lye Juke used to conk his hair. Anger over his death returned, clearer now, as sharp and pointed as a knife. Hank was looking at a closed knife that lay on Juke's table. It looked like some kind of straight razor. Juke must have used it to shave his legs only yesterday. Hank picked up the pale green handle. It was a gravity knife and Hank flipped the blade out with a twist of his wrist. The blade was filmy with soap. Both the curved and straight edges were sharp. The blade ended in a point. He closed the knife and stuck it into his blouse pocket. When his spy returned tonight— But Hank no longer believed his spy would actually come here. He could believe that only when he was too paralyzed to do anything but wait.

Hank went back through the kitchen and up the stairs to the second floor. They were as ignorant as he was about such things, but Sash might know.

Sash sat alone. The man with the beard had chosen someone else.

"You ever heard of a place called El Morocco? You know where it is?"

"Of course I've heard of it," Sash said snootily. "I've even been there. It's in the East Fifties near the Third Avenue El. What's it to you?"

"None of your business." Hank checked his pockets. He had the money and the knife. He left the room without saying goodbye to Sash or the others, people he felt he'd never see again. He went down the stairs, shouldering his way past Mrs. Bosch, who came up the stairs with a customer who wasn't his spy.

"Hank," she called after him. "You going somewhere?"

"Out!" he shouted.

"You are to wait for Dr. Mason! I am not to let you leave!"

"Screw Mason!" He unlocked the front door and threw it open. He tore down the steps to the curb and darkness, his feet stamping out the shadow of a sailor cast across the cobblestones by the open door. He hurried into the pitch-black square.

"Get back in here, Hank Fayette!" shouted Mrs. Bosch from the door, her voice echoing across the square. She stood there exasperated, heaved her shoulders and slowly closed the door.

The square was so dark Hank felt he was floating, felt he stood still despite the rapid clack of his shoes breaking the silence. The streetlight up a narrow street on the far side of the square bobbed in the distance without getting closer. It was like being dead, it was so still; or being watched, but that was his memory of the giant Coca Cola boy painted on a building somewhere overhead. Blood and adrenalin spun through him while time stood still. He walked faster, trying to catch up with the hurry he was feeling. He broke into a run.

He ran up the narrow street and past the streetlight, shoe slap and breathing burning up his impatience. He stopped running when he came to a street where there were people and splashes of light. It was Fourteenth Street. Hank walked east, past men playing dominoes on upended milk crates, past knots of drinkers gathered outside bars. A drunk stumbled into his path and Hank shoved him out of his way. There was almost no traffic in the street or he might have hailed a taxicab. A black automobile motored alongside Hank for a moment and sped off—a horny fool looking for a sailor.

Several blocks across town, beyond Union Square, Hank found the station for the Third Avenue El, a cuckoo-clock house on stilts. Standing upstairs on the open platform, he had time to look at the civilians in their shirtsleeves and cotton dresses, and feel apart from them. This was the first time he had gone out into the world since he entered the house. Racing uptown, he looked out the train window at the third-floor windows outside and saw plain people in kitchens and living rooms going about their lives as if everything were sweet and fine. Hank had never hated the world the way he hated it tonight. He loved Juke. He had not loved him alive but he would love him dead. By killing his killer.

He descended the stairs to the street. He asked a fish-mouthed man at a newstand how to get to the El Morocco, then walked beneath the long, thick cage of the elevated track that covered Third Avenue. Wartime was a good time to kill a man, he decided. Shop windows were dimmed and there was little motor traffic. The cross street he turned down had no trestle overhead, but the streetlights were off because of the brownout and the street still felt like it was covered with a dark roof.

A canopy ran from a well-lit doorway to the curb. The name was printed on the canopy: El Morocco. A wide doorman in khaki stood out front, rocking on his heels. Hank walked past him to the door. The pavement beneath the canopy was zebra-striped, like the matchbook Hank had found.

"Hey, hey, bub." The doorman pressed his hand against the door, keeping Hank from opening it. "Where ya think you're going?"

"I'm looking for someone. I'll be right out." He wanted to see if his spy were here, then wait for him outside.

"Sorry, friend. No enlisted men. You won't find no friend of yours here, especially if they look half as bad as you do. You been on a tear all night? Good night, Mr. Rubirosa, Miss Johnson," he said, opening the door for a giggling couple in evening clothes, still using his large body to keep Hank from stepping around him.

Without noticing either the doorman or the sailor, the couple laughed their way to the taxicabs that lined the curb.

"See," said the doorman. "Nothing but swells. Go have a good time with your own people. You don't have the bread for a joint like this." He spoke like he'd been turning away sailors all night.

Hank pleaded with the doorman, even offered him money, but it was no good. He finally let loose with what he was thinking—"Draft-dodging lard-ass. That ain't a real uniform"—and walked away before he pulled a knife on the man. There had to be another entrance to the club, a side door or delivery entrance.

At the end of the club's white front was an alley, the iron gate there wide open. Hank glanced back at the doorman and ducked into the alley. He heard band music, muffled voices and tinkling glass coming from the narrow windows overhead. The alley ended in a loading dock and a bright steaming kitchen inside an open screen door. Men sat on the dock, peeling shellfish and smoking cigars. A dozen bottles, an inch or two of wine in each bottle, stood at their feet, and mounds of thin, pink shells, like fingernails.

"No. No handouts. Get lost," said a Mex-looking man when Hank went up to the door. "Get lost," he repeated, shooing Hank off with a short knife curved like a spoon.

"I'm looking for someone. It'll only take a minute."

When Hank tried to push past, all the men jumped to their feet, jabbering in a Spanish like no Spanish Hank had heard in Beaumont. They shook short knives and gutted lobsters at him.

He backed off, lifting his hands to show he meant *them* no harm. "I'll be right out. Honest." But there was no reasoning with people who spoke a different language.

Hank turned and went back up the alley. It didn't matter if the man was already here or not. Hank would go out front and watch for his spy from across the street. Coming or going, Hank would catch him, if it took all night. He knew in his bones his spy would come here, knew it the way you know you'll find rabbits on certain mornings when you're hunting.

Hank peered around the corner to see which way the doorman was looking. The doorman spoke to a man in a cap and painted necktie who seemed to be out of breath. They were fifty feet away, but the light was good beneath the canopy. The man took off his cap to smooth his hair. Hank recognized him. It was his spy.

The doorman nodded respectfully and pointed down the street in Hank's direction. His spy looked, but it was all shadows here and he couldn't see Hank watching him. He slipped a bill into the doorman's hand and, instead of going into the club, started toward Hank, slowly, as if uncertain where he was going. He kept patting his right coat pocket.

Hank stepped back. It was miraculous, like God sent the spy so Hank could kill him. He took the knife from his pocket and flipped it open. He let the hand with the knife hang at his side. He would wait until the man was very close before he stepped out, would walk into the man before the man knew what was happening and jam the knife under his ribs.

He threw down his cap and peeked out again. His spy had stopped thirty feet away to stare at something across the street. He resumed walking, still looking across the street. Hank ducked back and listened. There were two girls out there but they were walking in the other direction. Hank listened for the footsteps approaching him. He loosened the grip on his knife, tightened it again. He was very calm, very steady.

"Drop the knife or you're dead."

The voice came from behind him. Hank swung around, the knife flying up to slash the voice. He glimpsed the silhouette of a hat before something whizzed at his ear and there was a blinding flash inside his head. He heard no gunshot before the pavement hit his face.

Blair stopped again when he heard a bang and clatter around the corner. When silence followed, he continued walking. He glanced at the alleyway as he walked past and saw a pair of upended shoe soles being dragged into the shadows. He promptly looked away, as if he had caught a man urinating. Somebody was rolling a drunk, he decided and kept walking. He had to catch up with the sailor that Mike the doorman said had gone around the block. He hadn't tailed the sailor across town, on to the El and off again to let himself be scared off by someone else's crime. The city was going to the dogs. Blair tried to distract himself from his nervous alertness by savoring the irony of his sailor wanting to visit Blair's favorite club.

When Hank opened his eyes, the alleyway was upside down. A man hung by his feet in front of him, a stick in his hand.

"Go ahead. Beat me to death, too," he thought.

"Quiet," the figure whispered, as if Hank had said the thought aloud.

Hank felt a jagged pain and saw the empty patch of street outside the alley. He was ten feet further from the street than he remembered being. Slapping the cement with his hand, feeling for the knife, he twisted around to see his killer.

The figure dropped the stick. It bonked like wood. The figure was breathing heavily, like a man about to faint. He suddenly knelt down. "Sorry," he whispered. "Are you all right?"

Beneath the breaths, there was a familiar distance to the voice. Hank squinted at the face beneath the hat brim.

The figure whipped off the hat and fanned his face with it. Circles of light flashed on a pair of eyeglasses that looked out at the street in a panic.

"Erich?"

19

ERICH LOOKED OUT at the street, across the street, down at Fayette, then out at the street again. The man who just walked past had to be Rice. It was Erich's first glimpse of Rice: American jaw, Hollywood nose, English eyes. Everything around Erich registered with a quickness and intensity he had never experienced before. It was overpowering, like omniscience. A man had tried to knife him and Erich had knocked the man out. He had saved a man's life and the man didn't know it yet. He had disobeyed orders to obey his conscience and the solitude was breathtaking.

"Why . . . ? You're with him?" said Fayette. "You Jew." His right hand convulsed at his side, slapping the pavement. "You can't be a Nazi."

"Quiet. They're still out there."

The hand stopped slapping. "Who?"

"Sullivan's men," Erich whispered. "The FBI. We have to be very quiet. The man following Rice will go after him. There's a man following you, but he'll leave us alone so long as you don't get close to Rice."

"Who the hell's Rice?"

Then Erich saw the knife out on the pavement beside Fayette's white cap. That was what Fayette had been slapping for in the darkness. Even when he knew this was Erich, Fayette wanted to stab him. "Rice is your spy," he said angrily. "The man who killed your friend. He wants to kill you next."

"Not if I kill him first. Don't get in my way, Erich, or I'll kill you too."

"Shut up and listen! There's a man following you. If you get close enough to lay a hand on Rice, he has orders to kill you. Can't you understand that?"

Fayette stared at the street.

Only a section was visible from the alley but, among the parked cars and darkened doorways across the street, were a dozen places where a man could hide. To Erich, every deep shadow seemed to be watching them.

"You're nuts," said Fayette. "Where?"

"Somewhere out there. Believe me. I wasn't following you or Rice, so I wasn't able to spot the people following you."

"Who told you I was gonna be here? This Rice guy?"

"I'm not with Rice! I'm not with the FBI or anyone. I'm on your side, Hank."

Fayette narrowed his eyes at him and rubbed his head with the butt of his hand.

"I'm sorry I had to hit you. There was no other way to get your attention," Erich explained. "I'm disobeying orders, dammit. I'm not supposed to be here. I came straight here because there was nowhere else for me to go after I telephoned Mrs. Bosch. She said you were gone. I knew you were after Rice. I knew you knew that Rice came here because of that book of matches you found." Erich was losing his patience: it was all so insufferably complicated. "Look, Hank. I'll tell you everything once we get out of here. But we have to sit tight for a few minutes. It's damn lucky for you I was here. Or you'd be dead right now."

"Yeah? You think so?" Fayette gave his head a dog-like shake, then climbed to his feet before Erich could help or stop him. He stepped to the front of the alley, scooped up his cap and saw his knife. He snatched up the knife and looked at Erich.

The two-by-four lay at Erich's foot, but there'd be no hitting Fayette a second time when he was ready for it. Erich kicked the piece of wood aside.

Fayette saw that, studied Erich and closed the knife. He held the closed knife in his fist and turned around to look at the street.

"Get back here," said Erich. "You want them to see you?" He came up behind Fayette and grabbed him by the arm. It was like grabbing a tree.

"I wanna see if you're nuts or not." Fayette surveyed the street.

Erich hoped Fayette's eyes were better than his, because Erich saw nothing. Then a taxicab pulled away from the entrance to the El Morocco and made a U-turn. The headlights raked across the storefronts opposite the club. They flashed across the doorway where a slouched hat darted behind a corner. Even Erich saw it.

"Somebody's watching somebody," Fayette muttered. He slowly stepped back, tapping his leg with the fist that held the knife. He lifted the fist and dropped the knife into his pocket.

"We have to get you out of here," said Erich. "Back to Mrs. Bosch's."

"I'm not going back there."

"No? Somewhere else then. It's too dangerous here." Erich was afraid Rice might reappear any minute: there'd be no way of stopping Fayette. He had to get Fayette off the street. "My hotel then. You can spend the night there." Maybe a few hours off the street would be enough to cool Fayette down, along with Erich explaining everything to him.

But Fayette already seemed cool, unnervingly calm as he stood looking at the street and thinking. He seemed not to have heard a word Erich said. "Let's go," he announced and struck off, marching out of the alley and up the sidewalk.

Erich had to run to catch up with him. "What the hell are you doing, Fayette?" He thought Fayette might march across the street and confront the FBI man in the doorway. But they matched toward the club, past the doorway, and Erich pulled down the brim of his hat on the side that faced the street, although they would learn this was Petty Officer Zeitlin sooner or later.

Fayette opened the door of the last taxicab in the line of taxicabs parked along the curb. "Get in," he told Erich.

The driver said, "There's cabs ahead of me, buddy."

Fayette reached into his pocket and Erich thought he was going to pull a knife. "Here's ten bucks. Just get us outa here."

"Yes, *sir.*" And the cabbie tossed his newspaper aside and started the engine.

Erich watched as they pulled away and in the frame of the rear window saw a man run out from the doorway, look after them and raise his arm for help.

"Once around the block," Fayette ordered the driver.

"No," said Erich. "The Sloane House. Near Penn Station."

"I'm paying, mister. Once around the block. I just gotta see where he is," he told Erich. "And see if I can see who's tailing him."

Buildings and corners slowly pivoted on their right as they drove around the block. All Erich could do was think hard, willing Rice off the street. There was no sign of Rice. They approached El Morocco again and Erich spotted Sullivan himself talking to the doorman beneath the canopy, showing him something, his badge perhaps. Maybe Rice had gone around the block and into the club.

"There. See him?" he told Fayette. "You remember him visiting the house? Just drive past," he told the driver. He leaned back and drew Fayette back with his hand, so they were both away from the window when the canopy and Sullivan swung past. "Do you believe me now? They're everywhere. There's no telling how many others there are, sitting in parked cars or . . ." Erich looked in the rear window but no headlights followed them, yet.

"They're protecting him," Fayette muttered. "They're protecting him from me?"

Erich repeated the directions to the Sloane House. "I'll explain it all when we're alone." He nodded at the driver to make it clear why they couldn't talk about it yet. But Fayette did not look at all curious or confused. He sat very still, his mouth and eyebrows moving ever so slightly, a man who moved his lips while reading.

Suddenly, Erich was able to think beyond the immediate present. It wasn't at all the way he thought it would be. He was saving a man's life, yet he was angry with the man for refusing to appreciate that. He had not expected to be received like a hero, but he did expect something resembling gratitude, comprehension or trust. Fayette rode beside him, burning alone.

Erich had only gotten as far as Trenton that afternoon when his relief gave way to guilt. It was as though he'd grown so accustomed to guilt he felt guiltier feeling guiltless than he ever had when he was genuinely culpable. Culpable innocence was terrible. If only he hadn't been alone in a train full of hooting, skylarking soldiers and sailors, every one of them reminding him of Fayette, he might have made it to Washington. Or if an FBI man had accompanied him the entire trip. Freedom was the worst of it, when all authority was in your head, yours as well as theirs. His relief and calm began to feel unearned, cowardly, poisonous. It was too much like what he felt over all he had been spared in Austria solely because he was the son of a useful man. It was absurd to want to suffer, but the suffering imposed by others was preferable to the suffering imposed by your conscience, which you experienced alone. Erich stepped off the train in Philadelphia and boarded the next train bound for New York.

Because he wore a petty officer's service cap, nobody asked to see his orders. Because there were more civilians than servicemen on this train, the world felt less like an armed camp—a man could feel good following his own conscience. But conscience felt imaginary now that Erich was in the thick of it. Conscience seemed as much a luxury as the taxicab carrying them across town. Every decision only led to the next dangerous choice. He doubted he could save Fayette, or even help Fayette save himself. You can sacrifice everything without helping anyone. But Erich had committed himself. He was in this to its conclusion. He only wished he did not feel so alone in what he was doing.

They arrived at the Sloane House. Fayette stood in the lobby, studying every face that walked past. The hotel was full because of the Fourth of July weekend. There were already servicemen sleeping on the leather sofas in the lobby. The desk clerk didn't object when Erich asked if his friend could spend the night in his room. He asked for a cot, but all the cots were taken. "Your room does have a double bed," the clerk reminded him. He called Fayette over to sign the register before Erich could warn Fayette not to use his real name. Fayette already knew: he registered as "A. Cooper."

Erich's room became painfully small when Fayette entered it, like a prison cell for two men. Erich's uniform lay on the bed where he had thrown it the instant he got back from Philadelphia. He gathered the uniform up, but Fayette remained standing, as if he intended to stay only a few minutes.

"Sit down," Erich told him. "You want a cigarette? A drink? I think I have some Scotch. A birthday present from my father."

Fayette shook his head and remained standing. "So how about it? This Rice guy killed Juke and wants to kill me. Mason and them are more concerned about protecting Rice than protecting us. What gives? They're using us as bait?"

When you believe the world's against you, the connections come easily. Erich sat in the chair and told Fayette about Rice and Juke, Rice and the FBI, the uses of Rice. At first, he tried to make it as simple as possible, but Fayette kept jumping ahead, or jumping backward. He understood it all too quickly. He paced a little, then finally sat on the bed. He took it all in with a coolness that was disturbing. He showed no emotion, no surprise, not even when Erich told him Mason intended to send him to a mental hospital if he survived, because Mason assumed he was mentally defective, an imbecile.

"An idiot? Yeah. I been an idiot all right. I believed them up and down the line. No wonder they thought I was simple-minded."

But Fayette's large silences no longer seemed like evidence of stupidity or even innocence. He was like a cowboy in a Western, or a poker player, or a man with many secrets. He gave no sign of what he intended to do with the information Erich gave him. He barely acknowledged Erich as anything but a voice, never looked at him, not even when Erich insisted on his objections to this business from the very start or when he admitted his complicity. Erich seemed to mean nothing to him.

Erich finished and Fayette was silent for a long time. He sat with his shoulders pitched forward, his elbows resting on his thighs, chewing as if he had a mouthful of gum. Then he looked up at Erich, blue eyes staring through the squint that had grown permanent. "So what puts you on my side all of a sudden?"

It sounded like an accusation. "I decided it was wrong. I decided I couldn't consent to it any longer."

"But you've jumped ship for me. Why?"

Even now he didn't trust Erich, and Erich didn't know what to say except, "It was something I had to do if I wanted to live with myself."

"You don't like men, do you, Erich?"

He knew what Fayette meant. "No."

"Do you like me? Just a little?"

"Not at all." Which was true right now for any meaning one gave the question.

"You're not doing this cause you're in love with me in some way?"

"*No.* I'm doing it because of what I believe. You have nothing to do with it, Fayette. Personally, I mean."

Fayette said nothing, showed nothing. He seemed to play poker with every secret Erich shared with him, but his silence here felt like skepticism.

Erich wondered if there was something to gain by lying to Fayette and claiming he was like him. Instead, he said, "There's nothing else for me to tell you. So. What should we do?"

"I don't know about you, but I'm gonna hunt down Rice. And kill him."

"Haven't you heard me, Fayette? They'll kill *you!*"

"I don't care. So long as I kill Rice first."

It was like trying to reason with a falling rock.

"I knew I was gonna pay for it," said Fayette. "Thought I'd pay for it in prison or the electric chair, but I can pay for it on the street. Those people aren't so smart. I can outsmart them and get Rice before they get me. Be easier now that I know Rice is stalking me."

Instead of preventing murder, Erich had made murder a certainty. "Rice is a spy. And a killer. They know he's a killer. If you get out of the way, Fayette, they'll arrest Rice when they're finished with him. He'll be tried for Juke's murder as well as for espionage. Let *him* go to the electric chair. Alone."

"It's not the same thing as *me* killing him."

And Erich understood him perfectly, better than he understood his own motives. Crude emotions, Fayette's morality was as obvious as hunger.

"I ain't asking you to join me, Erich. This is my business and nobody else's. You shoulda stayed on that train to Washington."

"No. I had to do something."

Fayette looked at him, unsure what to make of that. Then, "I'm going back to Bosch's. Where Rice can find me and I can get him."

"Nobody's getting anybody tonight, Hank. Spend the night

here." He could at least keep Fayette off the street for a few more hours.

"Yeah. I could do that. Keep the G-men guessing for tonight maybe."

"Yes." But Erich assumed Sullivan's men would have no trouble tracing them to the Sloane House. "You take the bed. I'll sleep on the floor."

Fayette's poker face was replaced by an angry stare. "What's the matter? You want to save a homo's life but you're afraid to sleep in the same bed with him?"

"No, I just thought . . ." What had he thought? "Of course. It's big enough for both of us." Fayette didn't trust him. Maybe sharing the bed would prove to Fayette that Erich was to be trusted. "You should take a shower though." Erich was going to share a bed with a murderer and he was concerned that the man smelled bad? Everyday life forced its way into the damnedest places. "A shower should cool you off, make you feel better."

"You think a shower's gonna change my mind?"

"Not at all. You look terrible, Hank. You look suspicious. You can use my razor tomorrow."

Fayette stood up and looked at himself in the mirror over the dresser. "Yeah," he said and began to undress. "I stick out like a dipped sheep."

"I wonder if my shirts might fit you," Erich suggested. "I know my trousers won't, but your whites make you awfully conspicuous."

"Yeah. You're right. Have a better chance of shaking the G-men and getting Rice if I was in civvies."

Erich only intended to gain Fayette's trust, but when he heard himself helping Fayette he realized something in him *wanted* Fayette to kill Rice. "The soap and towels are by the door." He waited until Fayette had a towel around his waist and was going out the door before he looked at him again.

Erich undressed, carefully folding his clothes as if they were all that mattered to him. He turned out the light. There was a little light through the open transom over the door, but not enough to feel embarrassed. Erich hated being seen in his underwear. Not even boot camp or barracks life had accustomed him to American immodesty. It was strange to think about that now. He went to the window and pulled up the shade. As always, the city smelled as if there'd been a fire somewhere.

There was a fire escape outside the window and an impression of prison bars. Erich looked down at the street two stories below. He expected to see another slouched hat already down there, but he saw only the usual gaggles of sailors and women going in and out of the tavern where a neon Popeye in the window slugged Bluto in slow-motion jerks, again and again. If they arrested him now, Erich should be happy. He had done what he could, told Fayette all there was to tell. But Erich didn't feel finished with this yet.

He heard the door open and close behind him, then the clomp of a body on the bed. When he looked at the bed, he saw Fayette stretched out in the shadow against the wall. He lay on top of the sheets, insultingly naked, his back to Erich.

Modesty was superfluous now. Erich lay down by the edge of the bed, as far as he could get from Fayette. Fayette breathed against the wall. Despite everything, he was already asleep. Erich folded his arms across his chest and looked up. The light from the transom stretched across the ceiling. He thought about getting up to lock the door.

Erich awoke with a start. Rice had gotten into the room and was struggling with Fayette. The bed was trembling. There were half-strangled breaths.

"I'm sorry, Juke. Forgive me. Ya gotta forgive me." A voice was sobbing.

Erich found a pair of large bare shoulders shuddering beside him. He reached out and lay his hand on Fayette's shoulder.

His touch didn't seem to startle the man. Still trembling, Fayette slowly rolled over. He had one hand below his waist; he was masturbating.

"Juke, yeah. Thank you." And he threw his free arm around Erich and began to kiss him.

Erich was too startled to resist. His mouth was suddenly invaded by a tongue. The body pressed against his was large and muscular. The weight and heat of it startled Erich's mind awake. He was horrified, but his body seemed miles away, trapped in Fayette's embrace. Mind watched from far away, just as Erich had listened from far away, in a cellar. Only this was his body. He used his tongue against Fayette's, trying to get him out of his mouth without biting.

Fayette responded by pushing his tongue deeper, and ran a hand through Erich's hair. His tongue and mouth abruptly jerked back. He stared and blinked, shocked to find Erich in his arms.

Erich's mouth was full of saliva. He had to swallow before he could say, "You were having a nightmare."

Fayette breathed like a man waking up. He touched Erich's thinning hair again, trying to remember who this was. He looked as frightened as a child.

"It's all right," Erich whispered. He hugged Fayette as he would a child.

Fayette hugged back—and did not let go. His hands were all over Erich, his mouth in Erich's again.

Erich flinched, then tried to give in. It was ticklish and strange: hands beneath his undershirt and inside his shorts. He tried to get into it, tried telling himself Fayette needed this and it would close the distance between them. He kissed back, but the face was gritty instead of smooth. He ran his hand down Fayette's back, but the muscles beneath the skin were as hard as bone. There was a womanly softness just beyond the spine, but a few hairs sprouted there and Erich realized he stroked a grown man's bottom. The strangest sensation of all was having so much muscle and bone, which could break Erich's arm or neck, handle him with such passionate gentleness. Erich felt very small and pursy. With a woman, you were never conscious of your own body, only hers.

He was embarrassed knowing the hardness knocking his hip was Fayette's erection, while his own penis was balled into his testicles. It was humiliating, but humiliation felt needed, necessary. He lifted his hips when he felt a hand tug at his shorts, then he pulled off his undershirt himself. He was naked with another man. He touched another man's cock, held it a second and let go.

Hank pulled away from his mouth and Erich was relieved, as if a dentist had finally finished with him. But Hank was kissing his chest and belly—it was bizarre seeing a crude, masculine peasant kiss and nibble skin—until he was licking Erich's privates. Erich was ashamed for Hank, catching him in such an unclean act, then ashamed of himself for becoming so small, soft and ticklish. It was painfully ticklish and he had to grit his teeth. He tried thinking of the woman from the other night, but definite whiskers bit beside the interminable nibbling, and the woman had been a complete stranger. Erich *knew* Hank Fayette, who had lost a friend and would lose his life because of what Erich and others had done.

Then it stopped. All touching stopped and Erich looked down.

Hank had raised his head to gaze at Erich. "You don't want to do this," he said.

"No. But you continue. Maybe you should try the other thing you do." That frightened Erich as he said it, but it was preferable to using his mouth again—less personal, more painful and humiliating. It was humiliation that gave him what he needed. When Hank only looked at him, he tried rolling over on his stomach to show what he meant.

Hank was between Erich's legs. He held the legs down so Erich couldn't turn over. "You're not queer, are you?"

"Sorry, no. Why should that matter?"

"You don't like this, you won't like being fucked. You don't have to be queer to get it up for a guy, but . . ." He was looking at the genitals that were like a fat, wet snail. "How come you didn't stop me?"

"Maybe I thought this would pay you back a little." His emotions seemed sick when treated as reasons, but Erich continued. "Or you could pay me back for what I've done to you. Why should I have to like it?"

Hank frowned, untangled himself from Erich's legs and stood up. He stepped away from the bed, agitatedly running both hands through his hair.

Erich felt he had failed, which was a strange thing to feel when you can't do what's unnatural and immoral. "I'm sorry I interrupted you. If you want to go ahead and finish what you were doing . . ."

Hank stood six feet from the window, facing the gray light from the street, his hands on his hips. He looked like a Greek statue to Erich's nearsighted eyes, with a badly chiseled face and an erection that hung like a faucet. "I dreamed you was Juke," he said. "I was so damned happy to see him again. Then I woke up and saw it was you, and figured this was what you wanted from me all along."

"I'm sorry, Hank. I don't like men in that manner."

"You don't apologize for that. I don't *want* you to be in love with me. So how come you want to do all these things for me? Not just the fucking, but all of it."

"It's very much what I told you. Principle. And guilt. Maybe loyalty. I feel an obligation to you, Hank. I won't be able to live with myself until I discharge that obligation. In some way."

Hank nodded, believing Erich this time, understanding him. "Yeah. Like the obligation I feel with Juke."

"But you were in love with him. Weren't you?"

There was a long silence, and a look, as if after an insult. Then Hank said, "Yeah. Only I was too chickenshit to admit it until after he was dead. But that's got nothing to do with the feeling I owe him one. It just makes clearer what it is I got to do."

The personal life was so much simpler than the principled life, thought Erich, and more dangerous. "Which is to kill Rice."

"Uh huh." He walked back toward the bed and sat down beside Erich.

Erich was instantly aware that they were still naked, both of them. After sex with a woman, he wanted to get dressed as quickly as possible, but he and Hank had not had sex. Their nakedness suddenly felt right to him.

Hank leaned over and whispered, "You won't do anything to stop me, will you? You won't warn Mason or the others what I'm doing?"

"No, Hank. Because I want to help you. Actually." Erich heard himself and could not believe what he was saying. But as soon as he said it, everything became simpler. "I was their accomplice. I'll be yours now."

"You don't owe me anything else, Erich."

"No?" His declaration seemed to have come from nothing more than his need to stick with this until its conclusion. But, once said, his feelings of failure and doubt, his wish for humiliation or some kind of pain fell away. He wanted to throw himself into the fire, with Hank. "This isn't for you. This is for me."

"You're already in deep shit. This is my fight. I don't need your help."

"You need another pair of eyes. I know I couldn't kill a man"—he heard himself use the real word—"but I could at least keep you from getting killed. Until you get to Rice. I did that once tonight already."

Hank seemed more stunned by the idea than Erich was himself. "I don't know," he said, almost angrily.

"You don't trust me? You think I'm still on their side?"

"No. I trust you, Erich. I'm afraid you might only get in the way, only . . . How *did* you get the jump on me back there?"

"I was lucky," Erich confessed. And he told how he had arrived at the El Morocco, spoken to the doorman, then gone up the alley to see if anyone in the kitchen had seen a blond sailor that night. He was halfway down the alley when he saw Hank arguing with the help. He hid in a doorway. "You walked right by me when you came out. Don't you see? One man can't see everything alone."

Hank rubbed his head where the two-by-four had caught him. He almost smiled. "Okay then. It's your funeral. But if that's the way you feel—" He looked at Erich, hard eyes softening a little. "I know how I feel, and there's no arguing with what a guy feels. All right then. You're in this with me."

There was no embrace or touch between the two men. They sat on the bed, as innocently naked as two Adams, breathing together, thinking together, bonded to each other by a desire that seemed—to Erich—very pure and American.

20

ON SATURDAY morning, July 4, 1942, the world was united in war. The Russians admitted the Germans had taken Sebastopol, or what was left of it. The Afrika Korps had caught up with the British army inside Egypt, outside the town of El Alamein. The Japanese began construction of an airfield on Guadalcanal in the Solomon Islands, intending to cut the Allied supply route to New Guinea. In Washington, the Joint Chiefs of Staff debated the merits of Operation Sledgehammer, the 1942 invasion of France, against Operation Torch, the invasion of Morocco and Algeria championed by the British. There was another claim by the Polish Free Government in London, reported in the back pages of the New York *Times,* that the Nazis were randomly killing Polish Jews.

American officials looked forward to a safe Fourth of July. Fireworks were banned in most cities and traffic on the nation's highways was expected to be slow due to gasoline rationing, the tire shortage and the Government's request that defense workers forego the holiday. The sun rose in Maine, made its way down the cloudless Eastern seaboard and the telephone rang in a room at a motor lodge on Long Island.

"Mr. Thomas Blair Rice? I am a friend of your friend. We want you to take care of that sailor so you can see us again. You are intending to wait for him outside that house near the docks today?"

Blair said he was. He was too asleep to be surprised someone else knew what was happening. His sailor had vanished into thin air the night before.

"Then I must tell you he is not there today. He spent last night at the Sloane House on West Thirty-fourth Street. If you go now, you can catch him before he leaves."

"Who is this?" Blair realized the voice had a foreign accent. "Is this Anna's father?"

"Anna? Anna's father? No. But a friend. Have you spoken with Anna recently?"

"Of course not. She refuses to see me because she thinks I'm being followed."

"You will see her soon. I promise you. She sends her best. Good-bye for now. There is no time to talk." Click.

Blair was overjoyed. Anna had not abandoned him after all. He was a bit disturbed to learn the other spies knew where he was—he assumed he had shaken them along with the police—but it was good to know he was not alone. A network of spies looked after him; a vast net of eyes and ears still connected him to Anna. He dressed quickly, paid his bill and left for the city.

Anna Krull came down to the lobby of the Martha Washington Hotel. It was Saturday, a day she often spent with her father. Sometimes they rode back and forth on the Hudson River ferries on Saturdays, her father taking snapshots of Anna posed against the rail—destroyers and merchant ships directly behind her. She hadn't seen Simon in four days and missed him painfully this morning. She missed Blair, too, but Anna couldn't remember him without hating herself for letting desire separate her from a loving father.

She was dreading another anxious, purposeless day when she noticed the poster beside the desk clerk's window:

FOURTH OF JULY RALLY!
STARS! MUSIC! BONDS!
NOON AT TIMES SQUARE.

That was right around the corner from the Lyric Theater. In a crowd at a war bond rally, she could lose the man or men following her, slip into the Lyric and see her father. He worked on Saturdays now. She would be very careful. If she suspected for a minute someone was still following her, she would walk right past the theater and nobody would be the wiser.

She returned to her room and put on her makeup and her prettiest day dress.

Hank shaved and put on Erich's white dress shirt. The sleeves were too short, but he rolled them up. The tail was long enough to be tucked in only in the front and his neck was too thick for him to button the top button. Still, it made him look like a dumb, innocent civilian. He put Juke's knife in the pocket over his heart.

Erich put on a necktie, coat and hat. That way, they wouldn't look as if they were together. The FBI knew who Erich was, but Rice didn't. Hank watched Erich get ready and suffered second thoughts. It felt very different when there was another person along—less simple, less pure. It made you more conscious of what you were doing. And yet, Erich had made it clear this was going to be more complicated than Hank had thought it would be. His instincts would not be enough. He needed a cooler head and a second pair of eyes to get this done. His chief fear about Erich was not that he might betray him—not after last night—or fail him in the clutch. His chief worry was that Erich was too green to be a party to murder, too naive. He didn't know what he was getting into, and Hank felt responsible for him. He would ditch Erich at the final moment and kill his spy alone. Until then, he could use Erich as a thinking, talking bird dog.

The lobby was deserted, which made both of them uneasy. Hank followed Erich through it, keeping a good fifteen feet behind him. They could not walk together, but they would not get too far apart either. The FBI might not swoop in and arrest Erich if Hank were present, for fear of giving the game away.

Erich stepped outside first, looked around and lifted his face into the sun, as if he were only seeing what the weather was like. Then he started walking. Hank came out the door and followed. It was late morning and the street ran east to west, so everything was in full sunlight. The plan was that they walk around the city, see which faces repeated themselves from place to place, pinpoint the men following them and do what they could to lose them. Not until sunset would they race down to the Bosch house, where Rice would be watching for Hank. There was sure to be a man watching Rice, but one man would be easier to deal with than two or three, especially if that man thought Hank was being watched by someone else.

Hank caught up with Erich waiting for the light at a crosswalk. He stood beside him in the handful of pedestrians and muttered, "Whodja see?"

"Man reading a paper at the bus stop. Man in an auto parked across the street. Another man in a cap dozing on a park bench."

"There was a guy getting his shoes shined at the newsstand back there. Shoes looked kinda shiny already," said Hank.

"Too many possibilities yet," Erich admitted. Now that they were on the street, he wondered if they should have stayed in his room until sundown. But staying still only gave the FBI time to decide what to do with him. Erich had not been able to use the toilet without fearing he'd find a man in a slouched hat waiting for him there. Out on the street, all fears felt justified and there was no room to acknowledge any second thoughts. He was too deeply engaged with the details of the immediate present.

The light changed and they parted as they stepped into the street. Opposite them was Pennsylvania Station and Erich noticed a crowd of people gathering out front, men, women and a few children, some of them carrying signs. More people came out of the train station and joined them, as if they'd come into the city together. Everyone was dressed as if for a Sunday picnic, in straw hats and sun bonnets. The signs tilting over their heads were hand-lettered: "Axe the Axis," "Scrap the Japs," "Stamford Stamps Out Nazis." Erich saw a small gap-toothed boy wearing what must have been a brother's army jacket, complete with ribbons and insignias, so big on the boy it hung to his bare knees like a dress. He proudly held a sign that read "Kill All the Japs, the Rats." The group, thirty or so people, moved together along the sidewalk and Erich and Hank had to stop to let them pass.

Erich glanced at Hank and nodded toward the group. Hank understood. They joined the group, working their way through it until they walked with them on the side away from the street. Shielded by the little crowd, they could peer between the patriotic signs and see who was out there. Bystanders applauded as the group made its way uptown. Other passersby joined them and the group grew.

They came to Forty-second Street and turned east, going past the penny arcades and movie theaters, half-deserted at this hour. Red-eyed servicemen came out of the arcades to see what the noise was about. Some of them applauded. The crowd applauded them back and somebody cried, "Three cheers for our men in uniform!" Erich and Hank were surrounded by hip-hip-hoorays. Not joining in, Erich felt like a traitor, then realized that, in the eyes of these people, that's exactly what he was. He noticed Hank's similar silence and frown.

Hank was looking across the street, at the rows of movie marquees, one of them over the entrance to the theater where he'd gone when he was somebody else, someone who would've been enjoyed being hoorayed by these people. He despised them now, despised the servicemen they were cheering. It was all such a pack of lies.

Up ahead, from Times Square, there was an electric cawing, a voice echoing against the buildings and billboards overhead. The electric sign wrapped around the *Times* Building ran with "Buy Bonds . . . Buy Bonds . . . ," the words barely legible in the sunlight. Then there was a cheer like an enormous breath. Beyond the wall of people standing on the corner, the rally itself appeared.

Seventh Avenue between Forty-second Street and Broadway was an ocean of white shirts scattered with dresses, a few hats floating over it all. A stage was erected between the enlistment office and the war bonds booth that stood in the narrow triangle of Seventh and Broadway. A twenty-foot Statue of Liberty stood on the roof of the war bonds booth, dwarfing a bearded man who stood on a stage behind a fence of microphones. His voice became a dozen voices buzzing from loudspeakers scattered all around the square.

"Good afternoon, ladies and gentlemen. My name is Monty Woolley. And I am here to remind you what all of us already know. Our freedom is at stake."

There was a thunderous exhalation of cheers and applause from the crowd. The group from Penn Station came to a halt at the edge of the crowd, but Hank kept going, followed by Erich. The billboards as big as football fields hung overhead, advertisements for cigarettes, liquor and peanuts. Beyond the stage, streetcars and automobiles continued to run up and down Broadway, indifferent to the heartfelt words drumming the air.

"There are some lovely young ladies to my left, who will be only too happy to take your pledges today to buy more U.S. Bonds, your investment in Democracy. We must give until it hurts. To show you what your money buys, the Army Air Force has provided us with one of their bombs. *Sans* detonator, of course. So there's no chance of *us* being blown to smithereens. Anyone who pledges to buy twenty dollars or more in war bonds will be given a piece of chalk with which they can sign the bomb with their own personal message to Tojo. I've been assured that General Doolittle himself will personally deliver your message the next time he pays a call on our treacherous Nipponese neighbors."

The crowd grew thicker and more impassible the deeper Hank and Erich went. Twenty feet from the curb, Hank stopped, looked around and said, "God loves us. If we can make it to the other side, we'll lose all of 'em."

Blair had arrived at the Sloane House shortly after ten. He went inside and asked if a sailor was staying there. The desk clerk laughed in his face: the place was full of sailors. Blair tried describing the man, but it was no good. He went back out to his automobile and waited. Towards noon, he was fearing he had missed the sailor, or that the anonymous caller had been wrong, when a tall man dressed in white came out the front door. He wasn't a sailor, but looked a bit like Blair's sailor. He even walked like the sailor, a hurried lope that Blair had learned to recognize from a distance. The man's white shirt bound him under his arms and left an inch of his back exposed. Then Blair realized that the trousers were from a Navy uniform. He jumped out of the car and followed him from the opposite side of the street.

He followed him to Penn Station, where the sailor was swept up in a crowd of sign-carrying yokels. The man was tall enough for his blond head to stick a little above everyone else's. Blair kept touching the revolver in his coat pocket. He was not certain what he could do in broad daylight. It would be better behind the docks at night, but what if the sailor never returned to the house behind the docks? Blair would follow him, all day if necessary, and seize any chance that was given to him.

Walking on the uptown side of Forty-second Street, beneath the movie marquees, Blair heard the noise up ahead, but gave it no thought until he came around the corner and saw the mob. The entire end of Times Square was jammed with another damn war rally, fools being sold Stalin and Churchill the same way they were sold radios and coffee. Why today of all days? He stood on the corner and watched his sailor cross the street and wade into the crowd. Blair went after him, but the man was impossible to see once Blair was surrounded by people. The backs of so many hatless heads all looked the same. All the men seemed to be wearing white shirts today. Blair squeezed his way through with his hand and elbow, using the other hand to cover the gun in his pocket so nobody would feel it. He saw the stage beyond the swaying signs, men with musical instruments climbing up there. He recognized Dr. Woolley at the microphones, who had taught at Yale before he sold his soul and went to Broadway and Hollywood. It made his skin crawl to hear that sophisticated voice condescend to the masses who pressed around Blair like a bog of elbows.

"And now, without further ado, it's my pleasure to introduce a percussionist whose sounds may be a tad barbaric to the ears of an old fogey like myself, but I trust they'll be music to your ears. Ladies and gentlemen, now appearing at the Paramount Theater, Gene Krupa and his Orchestra."

When there was music, everyone turned to face it. The path of least resistance turned Blair to the left. He went up on his toes and thought he saw his sailor, but that man wore suspenders and his sailor didn't. Blair looked back toward the sidewalk, into a hundred different faces, half of them nodding to the music. With their hair combed back, all the hatless men wore long faces. They looked grim even when they were smiling. Damp hairdos lay on the women's heads like loaves of dough. Blair kept losing his breath, as if drowning.

Anna heard it underground as she approached the stairs. Crowd and music echoed in the cavernous subway, promising the confusion that would enable her to lose her followers. She hurried up the steps into the sunlight and commotion. She glanced down Forty-second Street, saw the Lyric's marquee and walked away from it, into the crowd. Anna was so much shorter than everyone else that the crowd seemed to swallow her. Approaching the stage as the piece of music came to its end, she worked her way past bellies, neckties, arms hung with jackets, Anna intended to circle around to the sidewalk and walk back to Forty-second Street, leaving her tail stranded in the crowd.

When the band finished its first piece, the drummer in sunglasses drew the microphone towards him. All the loudspeakers around the square let out an electric shriek. "We're gonna do an old favorite for you on this glorious Fourth," said the drummer. " 'Sing, Sing, Sing.' And to help us out, we got my old boss, the King of Swing hisself, *Benny Goodman!*"

The crowd went wild, hoots and hollers coming through the storm of applause as a man in a sports shirt and spectacles mounted the stage, carrying a clarinet. He smiled at the crowd, exchanged some remarks with the drummer that were not picked up by the microphone, then bowed as if to say the drummer was boss here. He stepped back and waited. Krupa began by beating on his drums, playing the bass drum like an Indian tom-tom. The crowd's noise subsided and drumbeats like heartbeats echoed in the canyon of buildings and billboards. The band came in with a blare of brass like the trumpeting of elephants, then swung into the melody.

A shudder ran from the stage out into the crowd when two sailors cleared a space beside the music where they could dance with their girls. Other people crowded forward, to hear the music better, packing the crowd even tighter. Erich and Hank could not move another step toward the uptown end of the square.

"Where to now?" Erich whispered. He had to whisper, the crowd was so silent and attentive. A bobby-soxer beside him had closed her eyes and sucked her lower lip beneath her front teeth, the better to hear another roar of elephants, more raw and raucous than the first.

"Back over to the right," said Hank, and they stepped past the girl and others who were, all of them, leaning their ears into the music. There were a few hard slaps like gunshots, and the clarinet started crying, alone for a moment, then accompanied by the drums. The drums raced like a runner's heart while the clarinet only floated, hovering sadly in the upper stories above Times Square. It was music for a dream where you run as fast as you can but can only run through weightless air in slow motion.

Lost in the music, people were easily pushed aside as Anna eased through the crowd below their shoulders. Everyone stood perfectly still, except a large straw-haired thug who shoved past Anna, knocking her chin with his elbow without a word of apology. He was followed by a shorter man in coat and tie and eyeglasses who apologized to everyone. Anna let them pass, then took her bearings off the enormous scaffolded letters of the Planter's Peanuts sign at the other end of Times Square and began to thread her way back towards the sidewalk.

Twenty feet behind her, Blair wrestled through the crowd. He hated hearing "Sing, Sing, Sing" played in this rough, nasty manner. At least when they played it at El Mo, they sweetened it, smoothed it out. He tried not to listen, but the agitated music was too much like his nerves in this can of human sardines.

Hank pushed his way around a boy and girl necking in the privacy of the crowd. There was an abrupt machine-gunning of drums up on stage, and Hank automatically turned to look. When he turned back to the direction he was going, he saw a man in a cap pushing towards him. *His spy.*

Blair saw a big man coming at him through the crowd. He glanced up the white clothes to the man's face, and saw his sailor. He froze.

They both froze; they stared at each other. They stood three feet apart, their eyes locked, their breaths held.

The drums were tom-tomming again, alone, interminably. Then a drumstick banged a cowbell three times and the entire orchestra kicked in.

And Blair spun around and charged the bodies behind him. They gave way and he fell. His hands hit the pavement and he continued charging, running through the forest of legs on all fours. Voices cursed overhead and knees knocked him as he scrambled past, until his hands left the pavement and he ran bent over.

Erich had seen Hank come to a halt ahead of him. Hank's hands hung at his side like the hands of a cowboy about to draw his gun. Before Erich understood, Hank hurled himself at someone in the crowd, someone whose gray cap flew off before they disappeared in the thicket of bodies. There was a ripple through the crowd like the wake of an invisible ship. The crowd recoiled around the thing moving through them, packing everyone tighter behind it. They pushed back when Hank pushed his way through. His size worked against him. The wrinkle through the crowd streaked ahead. It had to be Rice.

Erich hurled himself after Hank, and was jerked around by his own arm. He found Sullivan gripping his arm.

"You crazy bastard!" Sullivan's moustache was stretched above his bared teeth. "Why're you with him? You gone queer, too?"

"Dammit, Sullivan! Didn't Mason tell you that I'm to stay with Fayette and make him think we're . . ."

For a split second, Sullivan was frightened by the thought that he was in error. His grip loosened slightly.

Erich yanked his arm free and pushed Sullivan hard with both hands. He ran after Hank, plunging into the path closing behind the sailor. People hollered at both of them. When he glanced back, Erich saw Sullivan trapped among heads, shouting at somebody far away and raising one arm to point his finger at Erich.

He caught up with Hank and grabbed his belt. Hank kept going, dragging Erich.

"Get down, Hank! Bend down so Sullivan can't see us!"

"Rice is here! I seen Rice!" But Hank realized he didn't see Rice anymore, had no idea which way he had gone. He stopped and surveyed the acres of heads around him.

"Sullivan's here, too, dammit! He was right beside us back there. Get down so he can't see you."

Hank could not see Rice, so he obeyed Erich, slouching down and bending at the waist. "Damn," he whispered. "We just stood there eyeballing each other. I coulda whipped my knife out and stuck him right here, but I wasn't expecting him. Damn."

"Shhh," went Erich. A woman beside them looked at Hank funny. "We have to get away from Sullivan. He was close enough to have shot you back there."

Hank followed Erich through the crowd. Bent down like this, it was like hiding from a farmer in his cornfield. They reached the curb and moved toward the right, away from Forty-second Street and behind a clump of boys who stood on the base of a street lamp, four boys clinging to the lamp post and each other.

Blair reached the curb and turned left, toward Forty-second Street, scrambling more carefully so the people overhead would not give him away with shouts or stumbling. He did not stop until his path was blocked by a newsreel truck parked at the curb, the roof of the truck crammed with men and movie cameras recording the rally. Looking for a way around the truck, Blair realized that nobody followed him. He stood up, suddenly wondering why he had fled. He was the hunter here, not the prey. What had he been thinking? The sailor didn't even know Blair was hunting him. There had been a chilling look of anger or terror when they locked eyes in the crowd, but the sailor must have been only stunned to run into the man he had betrayed. Blair had no cause for panic. He had a gun. He should have pulled it out, pressed it to the sailor's gut and fired. With the drums banging away, nobody would have recognized a gunshot until they saw a man bleeding to death.

He stepped up on the curb and looked for the sailor, but saw no trace of the man. The shadow of the building behind him stretched a few feet out into the street, lying on the crowd like the shadow of a cloud on rough water. On the sunlit stage they were still playing the same damn song. Despite everything that had happened, the band was only at the part where a piano quietly talks to itself, drums softly hurrying alongside like a locomotive. It was eerie hearing two thousand people listening to a lone piano while the city continued to rumble around them. People filled the windows above Times Square. Blair saw them in the building behind him, faces and hands piled on the sills. He decided to go inside and upstairs, where he might be able to spot his man from above. He glanced over the building, looking for its entrance. A pretty woman crossed his line of vision, briskly walking through the crowded shadows on the sidewalk.

The woman had reminded Blair of Anna. He looked for her again and saw a petite back and familiar walk against the brightness of

Forty-second Street. Then the woman stepped into the sunlight, turned right and Blair saw the profile of Anna's pout and breasts disappear around the corner.

"Anna!" he shouted. Already moving after her, Blair glanced back at the crowd. He would not find the sailor here again. "Anna!" He broke into a run, stopped by a pack of soldiers, then hurried around them to the corner.

Erich looked for Sullivan from behind the crowded lamp post. Hank began to stare at faces on the sidewalk, looking for Rice again, hoping he had come this way. Maybe Rice had gone back into the crowd, or maybe he had gone off the other way, toward the truck with the movie cameras. Knowing his enemy was nearby, Hank lost all patience. He jumped up on the base of the street lamp, knocking the boys loose.

"Whaya think ya doin', ya moron! Go find ya own lamp post!"

"Hank!" said Erich in a panic. "Get down! They'll see you up there!"

But Hank wrapped his hands around the pole, then his legs and shinnied a few feet up it.

All heads, a waving carpet of heads, were turned away from Hank and toward the stage, except for one. But that single face beneath a slouched hat was not the face Hank was looking for. His eyes scanned over the crowd to the shaded sidewalk and the pedestrians weaving through knots of spectators. *And he saw him.* His spy zig-zagged up the street, glancing once over his shoulder so that Hank saw it was definitely Rice. He slid down the pole and jumped to the sidewalk. He pushed past the whining boys and headed up the street after Rice.

"What? You saw him?" said Erich, breathless but beside him. "But they probably saw *you* up there! They'll be coming at us right this minute!"

"Then I gotta work fast!" He dodged people on the sidewalk, wanted to dodge Erich, but the huffing petty officer kept up with him. They came to a smoke shop on the corner and went up Forty-second Street. Hank stopped and reached behind him to steer Erich closer to the wall. "There!" he said.

Erich saw Blair Rice fifty yards away, beneath a movie marquee that said, "Hope & Crosby, *The Road to Morocco.*" Rice was wiping his palms against his coat while he stared at something inside. Then he walked slowly into the foyer.

"Too crazy for you out there today?" said the woman in the box office window.

"Did a lady buy a ticket from you just now?" said Blair.

"No. Nobody's been by in the last minute except the projectionist's daughter. But she gets in for free."

"Projectionist's daughter? Do you mean Anna?" He looked around the foyer again, at the naked lightbulbs beneath the marquee, the canvas banner that promised air-cooling, at the shiny, stout woman behind the glass. He was in love with a girl whose father was only a technician, a motion picture projectionist? "I have to talk with Anna," he said.

"Then you'll have to wait for her here. Unless you want to buy a ticket."

Blair bought a ticket and went inside, asking the usher who tore the ticket in half if he knew Anna and where he might find her.

"She's gone up to the booth to see ole Kraut-puss, her father. Hey, was you at the rally? Who's that playing? That Goodman out there?"

Up the street, the entire band was at it again, playing full blast, audible even through the closed glass doors.

"I don't know," said Blair and went up the stairs without asking for directions. If Anna's father were German, maybe he was a spy after all. But there was something unseemly about a foreign agent who was working-class.

Walking along the wall, Erich and Hank quickly approached the theater. Erich kept looking back to see if they were being followed yet. Everyone else on this side of the street hurried toward the rally, where the music was frantically pounding toward some kind of conclusion. Hank stopped in front of a glassed-in poster of two men and a woman. He peered around the corner. The foyer was empty and there was only a uniformed boy inside the lobby. He crossed the foyer toward the ticket window, stopping when he recognized the woman behind the glass.

"Damn," he told Erich. "I been here before. Why'd he want to go into this place?"

Erich was too busy watching the street to answer.

"But yeah," Hank whispered. "This'll suit me. Dark movie house. Be as good as night. Okay," he told Erich. "You stay out here. I'm going inside."

"What? No. I'm going inside with you."

"Uh uh. I need you to keep a lookout," Hank lied. This was where he would drop Erich and do the killing alone. "In case Sullivan and them get here."

Part of Erich was relieved by the proposal. He wanted a man to be killed, but did not want to see it. And yet, he felt excluded by the proposal, hurt. "All right, then. But I should watch from inside the lobby. I'm too easy to spot when I stand out here."

Hank agreed. He bought two tickets and they went through the door, just as the crowd at the rally roared its approval at the end of "Sing, Sing, Sing."

"Very busy today?" Erich asked the usher.

"No, sir. Almost empty, what with the free show outside."

Erich and Hank stepped deeper into the lobby. After the fury outside, the place felt almost haunted, the noise of the rally and street muffled by the glass doors, the buzz of a movie muffled by the heavy curtains hung over the theater exits.

"Now," Hank whispered. "You stand out here away from the doors. Anyone comes in, run in after me and shout, 'Jones.' Okay? If I do this right, nobody's gonna ever know. Except you and me. I'm gonna sit down behind him, and cut his throat." Hank pulled the knife from his pocket. Closed, it was almost invisible in his fist.

Erich watched Hank disappear through the curtain into the orchestra seats. The usher was standing at the front of the lobby, pushing the door open and leaning out, trying to listen to the rally. Erich wondered what it would be like, if there would be a scream or nothing at all, only Hank coming out with blood on his hands. He began to shiver, but told himself it was only the chill of air-conditioning after the heat outside. New thoughts darted through his head. He had trusted Hank, as a real American, to know how to kill a man. But did he? There was reason to believe the man who killed the houseboy might kill Hank, too.

The movie bleated between the opening and closing of the curtain. Hank reappeared, as expressionless as a butler. "Not down here," he said. "He must be up in the balcony."

Erich followed Hank around to the stairs. "I'll stand on the landing. I can watch the doors from there and have time to come after you if anyone comes in." He calmly trotted up the flight of stairs to the landing, then suddenly grabbed Hank's sleeve. "Will you be all right?" he whispered. "What if he has a gun?"

Hank remained stone-faced. "He didn't have a gun back at the rally." Hank looked over the brass railing. There was a clear view of the glass doors and the foyer outside, but Hank couldn't believe there'd be any need to warn him. He was so impatient to kill Rice he could not imagine anyone stopping him. He patted Erich on the back and went up the last flight of stairs to the balcony lobby.

Blair stumbled into darkness. His eyes adjusted to the light and he found a low wall in front of him and, beyond the wall, rows of empty seats sloping down to the lip of the balcony. The black, white and silver image of a man singing to a woman hung in front of the balcony; a voice crooned about moonlight and hair. A ray like moonlight ran back from the screen to a tiny window on Blair's right, where the ray came together. That was the projection booth, where Anna must be. He looked for a way to get into it. The booth jutted into the balcony like a fortified pillbox. This side of the booth was flush with the aisle Blair had come down, but there was no door in the wall. He had seen no door in the balcony lobby. There was an aisle between the front of the booth and the low wall in back of the seats. Aisle and low wall ran the width of the balcony. The door to the booth must be on the other side.

A man stood at the low wall directly beneath the projector beam. He saw Blair coming, clasped his hands behind him and turned back to the movie. Blair walked one step past him, and heard voices overhead, from a window in the booth ten feet above him. He stopped to listen. He could not make out any words because of the singing on the screen, only the guttural grumping of a man, and a woman's voice—it had to be Anna's—that sounded close to tears. He glanced at the low wall, wondering if he could climb up on the parapet and look into the booth, and see who Anna really was. The man standing at the parapet was watching Blair.

"Little blowjob, friend?"

Blair drove his hand into his pocket and backed away from the man. "Get away from me. Who are you?" Blair slipped his fingers around the trigger and handle. But he could see the man's head in the movie light, bald and shiny. Not his sailor. "Get out of here," he told him. "Leave immediately or I'm calling the police."

"Sheesh," said the man and walked away, but only to go down the steps into the balcony and sit beside another figure. Blair counted four, no, five figures scattered among the seats up here. Were they all queers? He had to save Anna from this awful place.

He reached the righthand corner of the booth. At the end of a dark aisle was an exit sign, the curtain below it outlined in wiggles of light, like the curtain he had come through on the other side. In the booth wall was a recessed doorway and two steps. Blair went up to it, felt the darkness and found a doorknob. He was about to knock. Instead, he pressed his ear against the door.

"They are stupid, but they are sometimes stupidly smart. You were a fool to come here today."

"I know, Papa. But I get so lonely in that hotel."

So they *were* spies, Blair decided. He was glad to know that it was real. Ever since he entered the theater, he had been afraid it might all be some terrible joke.

Lifting his ear from the door, Blair saw a figure standing in front of the screen, looking around. Another queer? This man was taller than the first and dressed in white.

The theater suddenly lit up. The moonlit screen instantly became a bright desert. Someone laughed and Blair pressed himself against the door. That was his sailor out there.

The man was looking for Blair. Why? Maybe he knew Blair killed the nigger. Although what did these people care what happened to each other? Maybe he had come in here only to be with queers. It did not matter. Blair eased the revolver out of his pocket. He would do here what he had forgotten to do at the rally.

The sailor looked up the dark aisle and stood still a moment. He must not have seen Blair, because he resumed walking, to the left, past the front of the booth and out of Blair's view.

Blair stepped away from the door. He could do it, knowing the woman he did it for was only a few feet away.

Hank stepped past the aisle, then pressed his back against the wall. That was his spy beneath the exit sign around the corner. Hank drew a deep breath. A faint glow in front of him flickered like heat-lightning each time the movie cut to a different shot. He listened for another burst of talk from the screen before he snapped his wrist and clicked the knife open. He would swing around the corner and charge the man. It was so near, so easy, he had to picture Juke's face before he could do it.

The projector ground loudly in the booth. Simon held Anna's hands and kissed the tears off her face. "I love you and I am sorry. But you cannot stay here." His voice had softened but the frown never left his face.

Anna sniffed and nodded. "Yes, Papa. I'll go now. I won't try seeing you again for a long time, I promise."

Simon stood up and helped his daughter to her feet. "Let me go first and make certain nobody is out there," he said, and started down the short flight of steps to the door.

Erich stood on the landing for half a minute after Hank disappeared into the balcony, then another half minute, and he saw gray trousers and brown shoes run into the foyer outside. Sullivan and two other men appeared at the box office window, Sullivan flashing his wallet as he spoke. The woman answered. Sullivan and one of the men ran toward the glass doors.

Erich turned and ran up the stairs to the balcony lobby. "Jones!" he cried and ran past the first curtained doorway to the second one. He plunged through the curtain into a dark aisle, where a man stood with his back to the exit. "Jones? Hank?"

The man turned. Before he could answer, a door opened beside him.

Light poured from the door. The man glanced at the light and Erich saw Rice, the hand at his side clutching a gun.

Hank appeared in front of the movie screen, coming towards them with his fist.

Erich had to shout about the gun, but it was too late to shout. He jumped at the man's back, grabbed the wrist with the gun. He threw his other arm around the man's neck to stop him from breaking away and freeing his wrist.

Blair had been grabbed from behind. He tried twisting free. Twisting back, he saw his sailor coming towards him. He raised the gun to fire—but something held his arm.

Hank saw Rice as paralyzed as in the crowd. Juke's knife was open. Hank rushed into the man, slipping his left arm around the man's shoulders, holding him against the knife. The blade pressed against clothes and ribs, then broke through.

The gun fired at the floor.

The body in Erich's arm stiffened as if given an electric shock. The man threw his head back, his mouth opened wide for a squeak from the back of his throat. The gun dropped from his hand.

Hank saw Erich's face behind the man, saw Erich for the first time and understood they held the man together.

"Hands up! All of you! Hands up or I'll shoot!" someone shouted.

There was more light, from behind Erich now. Then a second gunshot. And despite everything Erich told himself, about Hank's life and his depending on holding Rice, Erich let go. Erich's own body collapsed beneath him. His right leg was burned out from under him.

"Release him, Fayette! Let go of him!" Sullivan stood in the open exit, the curtain ripped to the floor. His gun was pointed at them, ready to fire again.

Blair arched backwards, trying to unknot the pain in his chest that left him breathless. The weight embracing him from behind disappeared. He pushed away from the weight in front of him, only to grab at it with his right hand when he felt his legs failing him. He turned to the left. He remembered a door opening there, but had not had time to see who was behind it. Gripping the shoulder above him, Blair raised his head and saw a balding gentleman in a long white duster. Behind the man stood Anna, his Anna, her pretty face spoiled by enormous eyes and red lips pinched back in disgust.

"Is it this awful tie?" Blair wondered. He lay one hand over the

ugly necktie, and found something hard sticking out. It hurt when
he touched it, as if it were part of him. He looked back at Anna,
ashamed, but all he saw now was ceiling, then red like sunlight
through closed eyelids, then nothing.

"What did you do to him, Fayette?" Sullivan stepped over Erich,
who lay there clutching his leg, and knelt beside Rice, keeping his
gun aimed at Hank. "Don't move. One move and I'll shoot *you* in
the head."

But Hank stood perfectly still, empty hands at his side. He looked
down at the body curled around Juke's knife. Now that the deed was
done, it seemed cheap, nasty. The man needed to die, and yet he was
so pathetic in death that Hank was sorry he was the one who had
done it. He had felt the same way the first time he killed a chicken
for his aunt by wringing its neck. But you can eat a chicken.

"Buddy? You okay, buddy?" Sullivan rolled the body over. Only
when he saw the blood did he see the knife. "Dammit to hell! Look
what you've done!" He glared at Hank, his gun pointed at the
sailor's face. Then he remembered the projectionist standing in the
door. "You there! Stop rubbernecking and call an ambulance. Turn
on some house lights. And shut off that damn movie! We have a
murder here!"

Rice was dead? The carpet around Erich was wet and warm, but
he had thought it was all his blood. The old man disappeared from
the door. A pretty girl stood in his place, hand over her mouth as
if she was going to be sick, her eyes never leaving the body at her
feet. Then she was pulled into the booth and the door closed behind
her. The house lights came on. The movie continued to play in the
distance, a pale pair of ghosts exchanging wisecracks on the washed-
out screen. Above Rice, above everything from where Erich lay,
Hank stood like a cold, white angel of death, a bit of blood on his
pants leg. His eyes met Erich's.

"You're bleeding," he said, a dry sadness in his voice.

Erich nodded. He almost smiled, proud to be bleeding.

Hank stepped forward, unbuckling his belt.

"Don't move, Fayette!" Sullivan jumped up, waving his gun at
Hank. His other hand held Rice's gun, a handkerchief wrapped
around it. "Put your hands on your head."

Hank pulled his webbed belt through the belt loops. "I'm putting something around my friend's leg. So he don't bleed to death."

"Get back, Fayette. I'll kill you. I'll—"

"Go ahead," said Hank, stepping past him. "I've done what I was gonna do." And he crouched beside Erich to slip the belt around his thigh, above the wound.

Sullivan lowered his gun. He looked around, embarrassed. "FBI!" he shouted to the people on the balcony. "Everybody out! We're clearing the theater! Use the other exit!" Returning his gun to his shoulder holster, he looked back at Hank and Erich. "Yeah, let the authorities take care of you two," he muttered. "I don't want the blood of the likes of you on my conscience." Another man appeared in the doorway. "Where the hell have you been?" Sullivan hollered at him. "Clear this balcony. We don't want anybody seeing this. There's a projectionist in there. He stays. We have to talk to him. Send Brown and Cohen over here when they come in."

Erich watched Hank cinch the belt around his leg. There was pain, but he was pleased to feel pain. He knew he was getting giddy from the loss of blood. It began to feel almost tender: Hank tending his wound, the fact that they had just killed a man together. Pain was Erich's way of paying everyone back. He felt all distance disappear between himself and Hank, conscience and world, watcher and watched. Looking at the dead man beside him, Erich felt he understood everything. And then he passed out.

21

WAKING EACH MORNING in a hospital bed, in a ward full of enlisted men, Erich was thrown back to his first weeks in the Navy, in boot camp, where he always woke up one minute before reveille only to lie very still in his bunk, dreading the moment when the lights went on and the shouting began, the start of a whole new day of humiliation. He would lie alone in the winter dark, wishing he could stay still one second longer, wishing he had awakened a second sooner so he could have one more second of peace. In those long, brief seconds, Erich often wondered why he had gone to so much trouble to enlist and subject himself to so much misery.

Lying very still in the hospital, day after day, was like that anxious minute of peace before the authorities enter the barracks and shout you out of bed.

After the bone was set and his wound sewn up, the anesthetic wore off. All that remained was a leg encased to the hip in plaster and a dread of unknown consequences. The exhilaration had vanished and Erich was stunned by what he had done. His fourteen hours with Fayette now seemed like a moment of temporary insanity. He seemed to have been hypnotized by the man. Erich's feelings about it changed from day to day, from hour to hour. Sometimes he was angry with Fayette; sometimes he was grateful to him. An effort of thought was required to prevent Erich from dismissing what had happened as insane, unnecessary or wrong. Once you commit yourself, it never ends. You cannot stop thinking. The gunshot had not really broken the distance between Erich's conscience and self.

It was being in the dark about the future that filled Erich with doubts about what he had done, and being utterly alone. There was no word from Mason, no visit by the FBI or police. He was in a Navy hospital, not a prison hospital, and the doctors knew Erich only as a gunshot wound and shattered femur. The world became closed and foreign a few feet beyond his bed. Worst of all, there was no news of Hank Fayette. Hank had disappeared into an unknown as opaque as government. Watching Hank bind his leg had been the last Erich had seen of him, before he lost consciousness.

The other men in the ward were the survivors of ships torpedoed or shelled by the Germans. There were shrapnel wounds, burns and missing limbs. A simple gunshot wound was a rarity here, although Erich's wound had other complications. The man in the bed beside him, in traction with a broken back, was frequently visited by shipmates from other wards. They sat around him in bathrobes and pajamas, telling each other over and over what had happened to each of them when their ship went down. Erich ached to tell someone his story, but realized he couldn't, not yet. His story, if used properly, might be his and Hank's last, best hope. When he recognized there was something he could do, Erich's storm of doubt lifted.

On the fifth day, an orderly came to Erich with a wheelchair and said he was taking him to the porch for some fresh air. Erich asked to be wheeled instead to the hospital library. While the orderly flirted with the pretty librarian, Erich went through every newspaper from the past five days. He found it, not in the paper the day after it happened, but in today's paper. And not in the news but the obituaries. It promised more than anything Erich had hoped for. Thomas Blair Rice III, son of parents about whom there was more to say than there was about him, died on July 6. *In his home.*

"I can't tell you how disappointed I am in you, Erich."

The following afternoon Commander Mason finally came to the hospital, bringing a bottle of rum, which was confiscated at the door. He sat in a chair beside Erich's bed, in full view of the entire ward, as if he and Erich had nothing to hide from the others.

"I trusted you, Erich. Completely. And you did what you did. You spoiled it for everyone."

"Where's Hank Fayette?" said Erich.

"Hank? Oh . . ." Mason looked into his eyebrows as though trying to remember. "I think Hank's on Governor's Island. In the brig. How's your leg?"

"How come I'm not in the brig?"

"What for? Insubordination? Absent without leave? Neither of these seemed to warrant bars for a man shot in the leg."

"What about murder?"

Mason looked straight at Erich and calmly smiled. "What murder?"

"Rice."

"Rice didn't die."

"I saw him die," said Erich. And he let go with what he knew. "Thomas Blair Rice, who died in his home. Two days after he was killed."

Mason flinched, stared hard at Erich, then stood up. "Nurse!" he shouted. "Bring us a wheelchair. I'm taking this patient out on the grounds."

Erich did not smile or say a word while the orderly lifted him into the wicker-seated chair and propped his heavy leg out. Mason stood by, impatiently fingering the cap in his hands. He dismissed the orderly and wheeled his subordinate through the ward to the porch and down the ramp to the graveled path.

It was hot on the treeless lawn: the other ambulatory cases remained under the porch that ran the length of the one-story hospital. Beyond the sunburned lawn were the cranes and canted gray smokestacks of the Brooklyn Navy Yard. Beyond that was the low jagged ridge of Manhattan.

Erich rode the bumping chair, holding on to the arms with both hands. "Died in his home. Isn't that a euphemism for suicide?"

"You can't believe everything you read in the papers," Mason grumbled behind him. "We tried to keep it out of the papers. The boy's family was apparently too important for there not to be some kind of mention."

"How did you convince the police and press it was suicide? Did you actually plant the body in Rice's apartment?"

"We're not criminal masterminds, Erich. All that was required was a little paperwork, our own mortician and a closed-coffin funeral. Which was yesterday."

"What about the witnesses?"

"There was only the theater's projectionist. He had no idea who Rice was, of course, but we explained this was an espionage case and none of it could be made public. He understood perfectly. He's a veteran and a member of the American Ordnance Association. He can be trusted."

"And the girl?"

"What girl?"

"There was a girl with the projectionist."

"No. Sullivan cleared the theater thoroughly and said there was only the projectionist in the booth. His assistant had gone out to watch a rally in Times Square. Perhaps you hallucinated the girl."

Erich was certain he had seen a girl, but she had nothing to do with his case.

The wheelchair stopped and turned. Mason pulled it up beside a park bench, where he sat down, took a deep breath and pulled out his cigarettes. "I'm sorry you saw that newspaper, Erich. Damn the *Times.* I had hoped to convince you Rice *didn't* die. You did pass out at the end. So . . ." He lit his cigarette, drew on it and wearily exhaled. "You understand, we've done all this to protect you and Hank."

Erich almost laughed. "No, sir. You've done it to protect yourselves. Because you can't secretly court-martial a man for murdering a civilian. You have to try him publicly. And you're afraid of what would be made public if Hank and I testified."

Mason frowned. "Leave it to a foreigner to know more about his new land than the native. Yes. We can change murder into suicide but we can't try a murderer in private. Silly, isn't it?"

"What do you intend to do with us?"

"There are highly damaging charges against you, Erich. You're an accomplice to murder, for one. You'll sign a confession. Which we'll sit on. So long as you keep your mouth shut about what happened, that confession will remain sealed in your file with the

FBI. You'll be transferred out of New York, of course, but we're keeping you in the Navy. You'll be easier for us to watch, at least for the duration. But for the rest of your life, Erich, there'll be a confession in Washington to be used against you the minute this story becomes public."

None of it surprised Erich. He had imagined several schemes to keep him silent, including this one. "And Hank Fayette?"

"Hank will be institutionalized. As planned. He's very lucky. He assumes he'll be sent to the electric chair, almost wants to be sent there. He confessed to everything, claimed full responsibility for the murder. He even claimed you were there only to try to stop him. Is that true?"

"No." Seeing where everything stood, Erich could tell other truths. "Fayette isn't mentally defective or retarded, you know. He's just innocent. Or was."

"Yes? I've wondered that about Hank, now and then. Well, the proper cranial surgery will fix that, whatever the truth is. But you deliberately took part in the murder? What was it like? I ask out of professional curiosity."

Erich made his move. "What if I told you I won't sign anything unless you make the same arrangement with Hank?"

Mason looked mildly surprised. "Release Hank, hoping he'll remain silent out of his own self-interest? I'd say that was a very foolish impulse, Erich."

"Fayette has no more to gain than I do by telling his story."

"But Hank's not rational the way you are, Erich. This way, you have only your own silence to worry about. That way, you have Hank's to worry about, too. If we released Hank, and he talked, sometime in the near or distant future, both of you would be charged. You'd lose the secret protecting you from prosecution. You want to make yourself hostage to this man's silence for the rest of your life?"

"Yes," said Erich. "I trust Hank Fayette that much. And he'll be my hostage. For the rest of his life."

Mason leaned back and studied Erich. "Then Sullivan was right about you? That you've become . . . you and Hank are lovers?"

"No. Not that it matters, but we're not. Do two men have to be lovers to care what happens to each other?"

"Not at all. Only this is an extreme case. You're talking marriage for life."

"We're bound together for life anyway. In my conscience."

"Of course," said Mason. "Guilt. The root of so much unhappiness. People do the damnedest things out of guilt." Another sigh, then, "What if I come back in a week and see if you still want to insist on that condition?"

"It took me this long to make my stand," said Erich, "a week or a month isn't going to change me."

"No. I don't think it will." Mason tossed his cigarette down and ground it with his heel. "All right, then. I'll have to speak to both Sullivan and the rear admiral about this. If they refuse and it's not a bluff, it means humiliation for us and prison for you."

"It's not a bluff, Commander."

"No. I realize that. We also have to see what Hank's response is."

"Can I talk to Hank?"

"No. The rear admiral's given in to Sullivan on that. You are not to see each other, for fear you'll conspire against us in some way. I suspect it's just Sullivan's way of punishing you. He really does think you're boyfriends." Mason stood up, positioned himself behind the chair and began to push. "Uh, I'm sorry about your leg. That was awfully clumsy of Sullivan."

Mason wheeled Erich back to the porch, then called for an orderly to take the patient back to his bed.

"Goodbye, Erich. I'll get back to you in a day or so." Mason walked around the building to the parking lot in his usual undefeated, un-naval gait.

He did not return for three days. During that time, Erich's only doubts were about Hank. Mason had said Hank seemed to look forward to dying. Was it right to deny him that death? Erich thought it was. Hank would learn to live with the killing.

It was raining the day Commander Mason came back, and they couldn't go outside. Mason asked for a room with a table. They were given an examining room with tiled walls and a metal table. Mason turned on the light and set two pieces of paper in front of Erich.

"I think you're a fool. Sullivan thinks you're a deviate and the rear

admiral, oddly enough, thinks you're a most stubborn but principled young man. But they've agreed to your conditions. All you
have to do is sign the agreement and your confession."

The agreement was simple enough, words to the effect that any
charges for actions committed on July 3 and July 4, 1942, were
waived so long as Erich did not make those actions public. The
agreement was in triplicate, each copy already signed by Rear Admiral Whyte.

The confession, typed on a single sheet of Navy letterhead, was
equally simple and to the point. There were only the dates and the
charges: insubordination, dereliction of duties, aiding and abetting
the murder of one Thomas Blair Rice III. It was explained that all
evidence of that murder had been suppressed due to the wartime
emergency.

"A bureau lawyer drew these up," Mason explained, "so it's all
very legally illegal. The confession's vague but enough to bring you
to trial, where the details would come out. The agreement's just a
scrap of paper. Useless in court but it makes the rear admiral
happy."

"How do I know you offered Fayette the same deal?"

"I have this to show you. And this." Mason laid two more sheets
of paper on the table. One was a confession similar to Hank's,
confessing to the murder of Rice in the first or second degree. The
signature on it was as plain and legible as a name written by a child.
Erich was realizing he had never seen Hank's signature, when he
noticed the other sheet of paper, covered with the same grade school
script:

Dear Eric,
   I am writing you to show you this is me.
   *I think I should die for killing the spy. He kills Juke and I kill him
and the law kills me. An eye for an eye. It is what I owe Juke.*
   *I did not want to get you in this. I thank you for getting in. The
best way I can thank you is to stay alive. If I am dead it will be more
easy for them to kill you "by accidunt." If there are two of us know
what happened it will be more hard for them to kill us both. I will stay
alive and silent.*

Good luck and thank you. Maybe we see each other in or after the war.

Love, Henry Fayette

P.S. To prove you this is me. I am sorry about the night in your room. I did not understand. I was glad you are not the same.

Erich was disappointed to find no trace of Hank's voice in the note. But then Hank wasn't a very literate man. It was natural his writing would be stilted and not part of him. Erich had forgotten about their failed attempt at sex. So much had happened since then.

"I read it," said Mason. "I must say, he's even more paranoid than you. As if Uncle Sam could arrange an accidental murder or two. You both seem to compensate for your trust in each other by distrusting everybody else."

Erich could not answer except by asking his next question. "How do I know you won't send Hank to an asylum, despite this confession?"

"You don't. You'll have to trust the rear admiral's unimaginative streak of decency. And me. Through all of this, Erich, have I ever lied to you?"

It was Erich's turn to be surprised. "No. At least not that I know of."

"I haven't. I've treated you as an equal, used you as an audience. And it's more interesting watching an intelligent man respond to the truth than it is to lie to him."

"You just enjoy playing God," Erich said. But that accusation was also a very good reason to believe Mason was telling him the truth.

"I do. It's a fascinating experience," Mason admitted. "Will you sign?"

Erich signed, first the agreement, then the confession.

Mason signed his own name on the witness line, then put Erich's papers and Hank's confession into his briefcase. "You can keep Hank's note."

"Can I meet with Hank? For a few minutes, that's all I ask." Erich wanted to tell Hank he should not feel responsible for Juke's death, or so responsible only his own death could atone for it. If Hank had died, would Erich feel like that?

"No. The rear admiral wants Hank shipped out as quickly as possible. They're keeping him in the Navy, too. He's being sent to the Pacific. You'll be given destroyer duty in the Atlantic once your leg has healed. The rear admiral isn't conscious of it, but I believe he secretly hopes one or both of you will be killed in action before this war is over. No accidents, mind you. Just fate."

The idea was too brutal to be faked. It put to rest any suspicions awakened by their refusal to let Erich see Hank.

"Well, Erich. It's been interesting knowing you." Mason snapped the briefcase shut and locked it. "I'd love to speak to you five or ten years from now, when you have a little distance on this folly. If I don't see you in court before then."

"You won't. Unless we lose the war and the next government opens the files."

"We won't lose the war. Americans never lose," said Mason. "Although Hank's premature execution of our spy certainly won't speed things along."

And that was the final reason why they gave in to Erich and Hank. Their confidence in victory was so strong they couldn't really believe Hank and Erich had done them irreparable harm. They could afford to be decent. Now that he had won, Erich wondered if they were right to be so confident.

"Goodbye, Erich." Mason held out his hand.

Erich hesitated, then picked up Hank's note, carefully folded it and slipped it into the pocket of his robe.

Mason lowered his hand. There was no look of displeasure over Erich's refusal to shake it. "Good luck, Mr. Zeitlin. You'll need it." And Commander Mason parked his cap on the back of his head, picked up his umbrella and the briefcase full of confessions, and departed.

Erich sat alone in the examining room. Rain beat against the window. It was over. It seemed to be completely over. He imagined the war over and he and Hank, out of uniform, meeting together in the ruins and explaining themselves to each other. If they were still alive.

EPILOGUE

HANK FAYETTE RETURNED to Beaumont after the war, with an honorable discharge and a Japanese flag. People were pretending the war had been only a long interruption, that nothing had changed. Like almost everyone, Hank threw himself into the traditional life—he married Mary Ellen Johnston.

Their marriage was annulled three months later when both admitted they had changed. Mary Ellen moved back to Port Sabine, where she had done wartime work as a secretary at a shipyard. Her father found Hank a job as a carpenter. Hank's own parents were long dead and there was no reason for him to stay in Beaumont. But he stayed. He worked with a construction crew building tract homes in the worn-out farmland out toward the Sabine River refineries. He could have bought himself a home, using GI Bill money, but he preferred his rooms over the drugstore on Main Street, around the block from the bus depot. For a long time there wasn't much to his life except work and late night walks through the dead town. He sometimes walked through the colored section of town, where chickens roosted in trees in people's front yards and slow talking, stand-offish boys behind the cinderblock store tried to sell him reefers or race records. They

couldn't imagine why else a white man wanted to talk to them.
Hank wasn't sure himself.

He joined the Beaumont Baptist Church, sitting every Sunday in
the row of folding chairs behind the pews, where the men without
families sat. There he met Forrest, who lived outside of town with
his mother. Forrest introduced Hank to his special circle of friends,
men who came from as far away as Lake Charles to the parties
Forrest threw in the rec room in his basement. Everyone was very
Southern and polite, until Forrest's mother went to bed.

There were no orgies, only talk, but an orgy of indiscreet conversation. The dozen or so men were very romantic, very nervous.
Hank was paired with Forrest for a time, then, one by one, with
others. Farmer or teacher, married or bachelor, handsome or plain,
it seemed to make no difference to Hank. The others didn't know
what to make of him. He was a man with whom you could be seen
in public without fear of anybody talking. He was strong, masculine, reserved. In bed he was somebody else entirely—loud and
hellacious, violently affectionate. Forrest and his friends prided
themselves on their double lives, but Hank Fayette seemed downright schizophrenic. And it was no good falling in love with him.
He loved back much too easily, almost insincerely. When someone
ended it with him, frightened by his wildness in bed or worn out
by his silences, he never made a scene the way the others did when
they changed partners. He accepted it with a nod and looked relieved.

Over the months and years, they romantically passed Hank
around without really making him one of them. They grew accustomed to his pecularities. Forrest often brought out his 16mm projector and showed the muscle movies he ordered through the mail;
nothing dirty, just crewcutted bodybuilders posing for each other
in G-strings or gladiator costumes. The dirty stuff came in the form
of comments from the viewers. Hank always left the room when the
projector was turned on. He said he just didn't like movies. They
found that strange, considering what Hank did in bed. They also
learned not to say anything against Jews or niggers in his presence.
He went nuts, called you faggot, said faggots were the niggers of the
world and that putting down the coloreds didn't make you white.
He spoiled more than one party with his ranting. And yet, they

continued to invite him back, even after everyone had been in and out of love with him. "There's one in every crowd," they said. Hank continued to see them. They were the only game in town and he had a creeping fondness for their romance, jokes and lies.

In the other world, Hank was known as a good citizen, serious and sober, a member of his church and the volunteer fire department. It was too bad about his marriage. The contractor Hank worked for made him foreman. There was a high school kid on his crew that summer, a wiry seventeen-year-old with curly black hair and a mouth, forever razzing and teasing the foreman. Hank took a liking to the boy and invited him back to his rooms one night for a beer. Once there, Hank found himself unable to do anything except show the boy the silk flag from Japan and ask what he wanted to be when he grew up. Hank did not know how to cross over from one life to the other. The summer ended and the boy returned to school.

All too quickly, the past became past. When Hank's boss and others talked about the war now, they talked about it as a guilty pleasure, a time of adventure and horseplay that would have been better spent making money and starting families. Forrest's friends, most of whom had been in the service, talked about that time as a golden age, days in a world of available men when there were more choices than the dozen overly familiar faces in this basement rec room. Hank never talked about his war.

Not until February 1953 did Hank hear from Erich Zeitlin.

There was a telephone call one Saturday from a man who said he knew Hank in New York City during the war. Erich. He was in Galveston on business and wanted to know if he could drive up to Beaumont that afternoon and have a drink with Hank. Hank said sure. Only after he hung up did Hank feel excited by the prospect, then frightened by it. Here was a man who had helped Hank kill someone, then saved Hank for the life he was now living. What do you say to such a man?

A few hours later, a man with Erich's face sat on the faded roses of the sofa's worn upholstery, a glass of Hank's bourbon in his hand. He kept on his heavy tweed overcoat. The bald spot in his hair was still pink from the cold outside. Hank felt very old just looking at him. His own hairline had receded an inch or two up his brow and the flesh under Hank's jaw had thickened, suggesting a bandage wrapped around his head for a toothache. He was often teased at Forrest's for looking like he suffered a toothache.

After the initial greeting and pouring of drinks, he and Erich sat for the longest time without a word, studying each other.

"Well," said Erich. "We both survived after all." He spoke like a Yankee now, not an Englishman, and was trying to sound cheerful. The pinch to his eyes showed he was as uncomfortable as Hank.

"What they did to your people over there," said Hank, wanting to say something real. "Was any of your family caught in that?"

Erich was startled by the question. He stopped trying to look cheerful. He said his family had been very lucky. His immediate family were all out by the time it started. There had been an aunt and uncle they were worried about, but the pair turned up in Santo Domingo. "Still I'm sure many distant cousins, forgotten schoolmates, even personal enemies . . ." His voice trailed off and he sighed. "It does shed a different light on things."

Hank sadly nodded, wondering if he meant Juke's death, the spy's murder or something else entirely.

"They did the same thing to homosexuals, you know."

"I didn't know. It don't surprise me."

"Homosexuals, socialists, gypsies." Erich shook his head. He glanced around at the walls without pictures, shelves without books. "You still a . . . bachelor?"

"Uh huh."

"It must be difficult for you now. A small town like this."

"I get by. Got some friends. But no, it's not as simple as it used to be. What about you? Did you ever get married?"

Erich had. He was happily married, with a Jewish wife and a three-year-old son. He lived in Connecticut and worked in New York for a Dutch-American shipping line that shunted sulfur and phosphate up and down the coast and across the Atlantic. He sounded more sheepish the more he described his life. "We do a good bit of business through Galveston, Hank. Actually, this isn't the first time I've been down here."

Hank understood what he meant. "No problem. We all got other things to think about these days."

"No. I've thought about it every time I flew down here. And you were certainly easy enough to find in the phone book once I decided to look. I think I was just afraid of looking."

"You were scared of what you'd find?"

Erich weighed the question, then shook his head. "Only that you might be dead. Or that they double-crossed us and had you put away after all. But those were only vague possibilities. What really frightened me was what *you'd* see."

"You? What's wrong with you?"

"Nothing." Erich laughed. "Which is what's wrong with me. I'm a fat little businessman with an intelligent wife and a beautiful child. And an accessory to murder charge in a safe deposit box somewhere, but you forget about that. Like the Bomb, you forget about it and become very smug and content about your life. I want to have more to show for what we did. For good or ill."

He was as embarrassed over Hank seeing his life as Hank was having Erich see his. It was as though they were embarrassed over being alive.

"I don't think about it much either," Hank admitted. "Not being able to talk about it has something to do with it." But he knew it was always at the back of his mind, behind certain thoughts, beneath the surface of the world. It was so easy to have a friend killed or to kill a man yourself that all human beings seemed very pitiable, touching and terrible.

"I do think about it," Erich said. "Now and then. When I'm depressed. Sometimes I think of it as something awful. Other times, I actually think it was the one heroic act I was ever part of."

"Wasn't heroic. It was as mean and lousy as what that bastard did to Juke. The Bible's full of shit there. Blood doesn't wash away blood."

Erich was silent for a moment. "Do you think much about Juke?"

"Not really. I dream about him. Which was awful at first, because I'd wake up and remember he was dead. But then I got to knowing he was dead while I dreamed him, and it was like he was still around, which is kind of nice. I'll be sorry when I can't dream him anymore." Hank looked down and saw his glass was empty, then noticed Erich's glass was empty too. "You want some more of this?"

"Thank you, no. I should be going shortly. I'm not a very good driver even when I'm sober." Erich looked nervous and ashamed.

They had not really shared the same experience ten years ago. For Erich it had been a killing, for Hank a death. "You don't have a boyfriend or lover at the present?" Erich asked.

"No. It's not a big concern for me right now."

"But you're happy here? Content at least?"

The conversation was failing and a lie would kill it for good. Hank said, "Y'know, there's days I wish they'd gone and sent me to the bughouse. I hear people are real happy once they cut that cord or fusebox or whatever it is they dig at behind your eye. Dumb but happy. Like I once was."

In a small, unnerved voice, Erich said, "You wish I'd stayed out of it?"

"Not that. No. I thank you for saving me. I do. That's not what I meant." He thanked Erich only in the course of telling him something else. "No. It's just what I feel now and then, when I'm low."

"Then you're unhappy?"

Hank smiled. "Yes. But I'm right to be unhappy. I mean, look at me, Erich. I'm a sexual nigger in a lily-white world." Hank burst out laughing. "Hell and damnation! I'd be a perfect fool to be happy right now!"

"I'm sorry."

"Nothing to be sorry about. It's good to know you're unhappy. It's a special kind of smarts. I like being smart for a change."

But Erich looked at him as if he were crazy. He said something about a Dr. Kinsey and how Hank might be happier in a bigger city, then said he really should be leaving.

Hank walked him down to his car, feeling better about himself than he had for a long time, without knowing why. Erich turned desperately cheerful again at the curb, as if he had accomplished nothing with his visit and the past was best forgotten. Hank asked him about his leg. The leg was fine. He remembered the wound only when his muscles cramped in the cold. He had remembered it that morning when he went for a walk along the seawall after breakfast.

They shook hands beside the stout car's open door and exchanged niceties about seeing each other again. Only when Hank stood alone in the cold in his flannel shirtsleeves and watched Erich drive away on the wide, treeless street did he think of embracing Erich, despite the teenagers in the drugstore, despite the man who died between them the last time they embraced.

That night Hank dreamed about Juke again.

Hank was in an enormous dark movie theater, trying to find his way out. He opened the wrong door and found himself in the movie.

There was a bright orange floor and a forest of glittering blue curtains. He saw the theater from the screen, thousands of faces looking at him. He could not get out. A hundred sailors in dress whites marched back and forth up here. Hank was in his whites, so he joined the sailors, tried to march and sing and look like he belonged with them.

There was a bugle call and, suddenly, a staircase of red and white steps ran from the floor to the blue curtains. The hundred sailors all faced the stairs and saluted. The curtains parted at the top of the stairs. Out stepped a beautiful Negro girl in a long white gown, clouds of white feathers rolling behind her like a vapor trail. She slowly descended the stairs. She stopped, smirked and tossed her long black hair to the sailors below. It was Juke.

Hank was on the stairs beside Juke, in the spotlight where everyone could see them. Hank didn't care. He was so happy to see Juke again.

"How do we get out of here?" he asked Juke.

"Shut up, darling. This is my big number." And he sang, or rather there was a feeling of song, without music or lyrics, very sad and beautiful. Juke smiled, luxuriating in the sadness.

The song made Hank feel funny. He looked at himself and saw he was naked from the waist down. That seemed worse than being completely naked. He tried pulling the sailor blouse off, but it was part of him now, like his skin.

He and Juke grew taller, thicker. They towered over the people in the theater as the song came to its end, their faces as big as houses. Then Juke turned to Hank and said, not in a voice but with thoughts, the way people speak in dreams:

"You big bareassed fool. You ain't in love with me. You just use me when you want to talk to yourself in drag. But you're right about one thing. You're smart to be unhappy with the world. Stay unhappy. Without feeling sorry for yourself and without getting yourself killed. Stay unhappy long enough and something will happen. Hold tight, darling. You ain't alone. When you see your chance, grab it. And if you're real lucky, one day you'll have the same dreary miseries as any other cracker or shine with money."

Juke stepped past Hank and down the stairs. Hank was swallowed by the cloud of feathers, completely naked now inside the billowing bath of tickles.

And he woke up, pleased by the dream and wondering how he could keep some of it for his conscious life.

ACKNOWLEDGMENTS

ALTHOUGH A WORK of imagination, this novel was written with the help of several books of history. *Gay Diary 1933–1946* by Donald Vining and the *Gay/Lesbian Almanac* by Jonathan Ned Katz were invaluable to me, works by just two of the many fine writers now uncovering the gay and lesbian past. Also useful to me were *Naked City* by Weegee, *The Game of The Foxes* by Ladislas Farago and *Debutante* by Gioia Diliberto. All historical facts, places and names have been used fictionally.

I owe a special debt to Frank Lowe, who told me the rumor that sparked this story, then shared his own memories from the period. Thanks again, Frank. For their advice, encouragement and friendship, I thank George Coleman, my editor at Donald I. Fine, Eric Ashworth, my literary agent, Peter Bejger at Henry Holt, John Niespolo, Ed Sikov, Mary Gentile, Chad Collins and, most of all, Draper Shreeve.